SMOKING

GRAHAM JOYCE

SMOKING POPPY

Copyright © Graham Joyce 2001

All rights reserved

The right of Graham Joyce to be identified as the author
of this work has been asserted by him in accordance with
the Copyright, Designs and Patents Act 1988.

This edition first published in 2002 by
Gollancz
An imprint of the Orion Publishing Group
Orion House, 5 Upper St Martin's Lane, London wc2h 9ea

A CIP catalogue record for this book is available
from the British Library

isbn 0 575 07304 7

Typeset by Deltatype Ltd, Birkenhead, Merseyside

Printed in Great Britain by
Clays Ltd, St Ives plc

To my son, Joseph William

ACKNOWLEDGEMENTS

To my jungle guides, the real Bhun and Coconut, and to companions on Trek 1: Peter McBain, Tim Butler (hell of a swim, Tim), Yvette Giles, Neil and Graeme McFarquaher, and Clare Trotter. To Luigi Bonomi, Jason Kaufman, George Lucas for input, Sarah Rennie for Thai pointers, and Brig Eaton at Jungawunga.com for superb web design. Also to my writing students at Nottingham Trent University. Finally to Suzanne, because you keep making it better.

I

Oh that Charlie of mine, how I wanted her back.

When a baby is born the fontanelle at the top of the head yawns open. You fill the hole with shimmering, molten, free-running love, where it sets and hardens over the hole with something like bone. But for the first few weeks of a baby's life you are intoxicated by the extraordinary scent of its head. The chemical fix. A gift from the gardens of paradise. You want it all the time, and you only get it when you cradle that baby in your arms.

After the first year this perfume thins out, but it never deserts the child entirely. So you keep hugging. Every time you pick up that infant you look for an opportunity to get her hair under your nostrils so you might get a hint, a hit, once more, of the perfume of heaven. It's still there when she's six years old. And even at eleven. And though between the ages of twelve and fifteen she pushes away your fatherly embrace, she still comes to you when she's tired or hurt or unhappy. Then at seventeen it seems she's more likely to come back to you, relaxed in your company again, not afraid to take a hug. And you're still getting it. That scent. That charge. The love amalgam, fixed and hardening there from Day One. It's still there.

And it's there on the October afternoon, with the golden leaves spinning all around you when you hug her and kiss her and wave her away to her life.

Yes how I wanted her back. My Charlie. Just for two minutes. Just so I could hold her, and sniff her hair to check that she was all right. But I couldn't. I couldn't because she was rotting in a prison cell in some Far Eastern jail. And it made me want to howl like a dog.

I was struggling to assemble a flatpack chest of drawers when Sheila called to tell me that Charlie had turned up in some place called Chiang Mai. The flatpack contained one hundred and thirty-three individual parts, not counting the screws and the small tube of wood glue, and the suppliers had enclosed a Chinese diagram. There were no instructions on the diagram, just pictures, and arrows that made me think of the bowmen of Agincourt. I couldn't make sense of any of it.

'Are you there?' Sheila said.

'Of course I'm here.' I was there all right. I was holding the diagram, the wood glue, sections P and Q, and I had the telephone squeezed under my neck. I was there.

'Only you haven't said anything.'

'No, I haven't said anything.'

Then Sheila dropped silent on me and I felt so angry and confused and upset I clattered sections P and Q back in the box and threw the tube of wood glue against the wall.

'What's that?' Sheila wanted to know.

'I dropped the phone.'

'Are you coming over?'

I didn't want to. Go over, I mean. I'd spent the last three months avoiding going over. 'Yes.' I thought I detected sniffle at the other end of the line. 'Look at it this way,' I said. 'At least Charlie's not dead.'

I did go round and it was terrible. Just terrible. After we'd talked about Charlie and what might be done we had nothing to say to each other, and Sheila spent the whole time sighing heavily. I'm the wronged party and yet she's the one who sighs all the time.

I looked at my watch. I had to be at the Clipper for eight o'clock. They do a decent quiz at the Clipper, and besides I'm part of a team.

'You don't have to go,' Sheila said, getting up.

'I don't want to be here when *whasisname* comes round.' I know the swine's name but I always make out I don't, even though I don't care whether he's there or not.

'He doesn't come here, Danny. I've told you before I've never allowed him here.'

'All right,' I said, 'but I've got to go. I'll give this bloke from the Foreign Office a ring tomorrow and I'll tell you what we can

2

work out.' I brushed my lips against Sheila's rosy cheeks and she sighed again.

Chiang Mai? I was very glad when I got to the Clipper.

Halfway through the quiz they stop for a breather. This is annoying because we then have to spend twenty minutes making conversation. I have to point out that the other members of my team, even though we've been playing together for some years, are not exactly choice company. You need a team of three or four, and we got shuffled together when the thing first got launched.

Quite often we win, though we do have our rivals. Among others there's an angry-looking mob of militant college teachers who huddle by the fireside; a team of pleasant lesbians; and a beery group of engineers. All of these come close, and every Tuesday the quiz provides a diversion. Though as I say, there are these twenty-minute pauses when we have to make conversation, and Mick Williams always kicks off by asking me what sort of a day I've had.

'What sort of a day have you had then, Dan?'

'Ach, not bad,' I always say, and then I try to eavesdrop on the Pleasant Lesbians or on the Fireside Tendency; not to cheat, but to avoid getting drawn in to idle chat. In any event I'm not likely to tell him that today the Foreign Office phoned my now ex-wife at our family home to say that our daughter had been arrested in Chiang Mai for smuggling drugs and was likely to face a death sentence. I wasn't going to drop that little bombshell in the middle of the pub quiz. Apart from which, Mick Williams didn't even know I had a daughter, or a son come to that, since I'd never mentioned either.

At this point in the successfully derailed conversation, Mick Williams normally grunts, takes a sip of his Old Muckster's Jubilee Ale and moves on to Izzy, to whom he puts the same question. Slightly more talkative than I am, Izzy can be relied upon to keep the pot boiling until the quiz is ready to resume. But Mick was in an unusual mood that evening, and instead of passing on to Izzy he sucked the buttery beer froth from his upper lip and stared me down. 'Not bad? Know what Dan, you've been *not bad* for three years now. Time you were summit other.'

Izzy snorted and downed her gin 'n' tonic. I laughed off the remark, but Mick wasn't smiling.

'No,' he said. 'For three years I've asked you what sort of a day you've had, and for three years you've given me the same answer. I tell you about my day. Izzy tells us about her day. But you – you never part with anything.'

His bull-like neck was thrust forward at me across the table's empty glasses. His face was pink, and blue veins twitched on his brow. The half-grin on my lips curdled. 'You're a skinflint,' he said. 'A tightwad. A miser with information.'

I looked to Izzy for support, but she was on his side. 'Splendid fellow,' she said in that cut-glass accent of hers. 'Winkle him out, that's it.'

I felt got at. Mostly I was irritated by Izzy's last remark. A bespectacled elderly spinster with a gigantic bosom and hair fixed in a bun, Izzy was a lecturer at the university across the road from the Clipper. Nylon anorak, tweed skirt, pilled woollen stockings. How she managed to keep her career together was a mystery to Mick and I. Always half-cut when she appeared for the quiz on a Tuesday night, after several large gins she was customarily plastered by the time she left the place. I could have said something nasty about her alcoholism, but I just smiled weakly. 'Drinks anyone?'

'No,' Mick said, snatching the glasses out of my hands. 'It's Izzy's round, and besides you don't cop out of it that easily.' Izzy took the hint, and after she'd gone to the bar Mick stuck his nose right up against mine and said, 'Two lines.'

'What?' He was pressed in so close I could feel an airstream on my face, warm from his flaring nostrils.

His pudgy forefinger pointed to a spot between his eyebrows, right above the bridge of his nose. 'Two thick lines. Right here. You. Worried to death. Now let me ask you again: what sort of a day have you had?'

It was a disconcerting moment. Mick's face, crowned by wispy blond curls that should rightly grace a cherub and not someone resembling a bareknuckle boxer, was so close I could hardly focus. His lovely blue-curaçao eyes fixed on me without blinking. I could have blurted it out there and then, the whole thing, Charlie and Chiang Mai and the Foreign Office. But I wasn't even sure I liked Mick Williams, let alone wanted to disclose the most intimate details of my life. Come to think of it, I knew as little about him as he did about me, even though he was as proficient at talking as I was the contrary.

A market trader, peddling squashy, over-ripe fruit and veg on Leicester market, he was a big man, a bruiser; but his blond eyelashes, pimento face and piggy eyes belied an intelligent and lively mind. He was also my snooker partner on Thursday nights, but quite apart from that he was too blustering and noisy to be the sort of person I would want to count as a friend.

He stared at me, waiting for an answer. I thrust my hands deep into my pockets and found there a ball of screwed-up paper. 'Right,' I said, smoothing out the flatpack furniture diagram on the table. 'I've spent the whole day trying to work this one out, and if you can do it you're a better man than I am.'

Mick snatched up the diagram and studied it suspiciously. His nose twitched a couple of times as he turned the thing on its side, as if that would help. Izzy returned with the drinks. 'What the devil's that?' she wanted to know, setting the drinks down on the table.

'It's an IQ test,' Mick said.

'Instructions for sticking bits of wood together,' I told her.

'Ghastly things. Too complicated,' she said. This was a woman who taught Latin and classical Greek to children with iron rings through their noses and lips.

'Made in Thailand,' Mick observed, reading the small print at the foot of the diagram.

'That's funny,' I said.

'Why is that funny?' But I didn't have to tell them why it was funny because the quiz got underway again and there were other things to think about. Mick's nostrils twitched. Though I pretended to study the answer sheet I could see him watching me. 'I'm not falling for that,' he snorted, before question number one got fired across the Clipper's bows.

I kept my head down.

2

The following day I called the Foreign Office on the number Sheila had given me, and asked to speak to a Mr Farquar-Thompson. It wasn't very satisfactory, since I had to call from a customer's house. I was rewiring a lady's house – yes, I'm a sparks by trade – and since my cellphone bill had gone unpaid I asked for permission to use her phone. I offered to pay for the call but she refused, extracting an alternative payment by standing next to me and fingering the button at the neck of her blouse throughout the entire call.

Farquar-Thompson had to get the file. At first he didn't seem to know what I was talking about. Then when he returned he spoke about Charlotte's case with surprising authority. I was trying to get as much information as I could without letting on to the lady standing next to me. All through the call I wanted to shout, 'Where the fuck is Chiang Mai? When is the next flight?'

'We can arrange visiting rights,' Farquar-Thompson intoned, 'and we can pass on supplies.'

'Is that all?'

'She has a lawyer looking after her interests, but I have to tell you that the case looks cut and dried. She was caught in possession of a fairly large quantity of the stuff. A mule, I think is the expression. Or is it an ant? We put a lot of pressure on the Thai authorities to stamp out drug dealing, so they in turn like to come down heavily on drug traffickers, particularly Western ones.'

'What's she facing?'

'As I said to your wife, she would be unlucky to be handed a death sentence, though I have to say we can't rule it out. She may however get life, or twenty years.'

The room tilted. Maybe Farquar-Thompson heard me gulp.

'We've arranged a decent legal team, Mr Innes, and she is visited by embassy staff.'

I could imagine. 'How often?'

'As frequently as we can possibly manage. You'll let us know if you intend making the journey out there?' He was tying up the call.

'Yes, of course I'll be going out there. Thank you. Thank you for your help.'

'Not at all.'

Hands trembling, I put the receiver gently back on its cradle. The lady whose phone I'd been using informed me that, after a great deal of consideration, she wanted another double plug socket in her kitchen, just there, above the work-top, so that it would be handy for the liquidiser and the toaster.

Charlotte, whom Farquar-Thompson told me was languishing in a Thai prison, was my only daughter. She was twenty-two at the time. I also had a son three years older, but fathers are more tender towards their daughters and it was Charlie whom I doted on and whom I indulged until, just after her eighteenth birthday, I waved her away to Oxford University one bright sunny October afternoon. The whiff of autumn was on the breeze that day, mashed leaves, mushrooms, fallen damsons, and I will admit to basking in a certain pride: both her mother and I left school when we were sixteen. Her teachers also told me that getting to Oxford is quite an achievement if you haven't had the benefit of a private education or friends at the BBC.

Bright girl.

Well I don't know about any of that, and I don't know what they teach you at Oxford, but Charlie came back with gold rings inserted through nostril, bottom lip and belly-button. That was just the ones I could see. She'd also cultivated the politics of an international terrorist, which she would turn on me like a flame thrower. My sweet-natured little girl. Then it seemed that every time I opened my mouth I was confirmed as a moral idiot. Oxford somehow convinced her that she was a princess of folk-tale, handed over at birth to the family of swineherds.

You can't always bite your lip. This was the daughter whose

bottom I'd wiped, whom I'd taught to swim and to play football, whose spangly, glycerine-like tears I'd licked and for whom I'd interpreted the entire world and all its levers, pulleys and creaking mechanisms. Mick Williams would say I treated her with too much seriousness, but everything was flung back in my teeth. I'd worked extra weekends fixing double sockets in kitchens to put her through university, but that made me a capitalist lackey, whatever that is. I'd encouraged Sheila to stay home when the children were small, putting love before money, but that was me oppressing Sheila. I'd put good quality meat on the table, so I was a torturer of animals and a force-feeder of infants. In the holidays when Charlie was around, I used to look forward to coming home from a hard day's graft just to see what further kind of a shit I was.

'Hey, it don't stop you staying here and sponging off us in the holidays, does it, sweetheart?'

'There are plenty of places I could go! I don't have to come here!'

'Bugger off then!'

'He doesn't mean it,' Sheila would say. 'He's winding you up, Charlie.'

'I bloody do mean it!'

Really, I don't know who was winding up who. Some of the deadbeats she used to bring home, I wondered if it was all for my benefit; you know, *this one will kill him.*

'This is Pete.' Or, 'This is Zak.'

Pete or Zak was usually a white boy with dreadlocks and nose-stud: the rigid deadbeat uniform of a 'traveller' without the means to travel. Coming in behind him from the hallway, Charlie would sort of lob him across the lounge carpet like a smoking bomb. It would fall to Sheila to invite this new boyfriend to sit down, whereas I always wanted to say, no, please don't, we've just had the upholstery shampooed. They weren't always called Pete or Zak, but I found myself deliberately referring to them as if they were. I'd wait until Charlie and Sheila were out of the room before letting the Leicester *Mercury* dip into my lap.

'Pete or Zak, can I ask you something?'

'It's Simon. Sure.'

'You're sure I can ask you anything? It's sort of personal.'

'Go ahead.'

'Are you black, Pete?'

'Duh?'

'Only these dreadlocks, Pete. I wondered if you were, perhaps, black. You know, with the dreadlocks.'

'Uh, no. White.'

'Confusing for old farts like me. But I want you to understand that if you were black, Pete, you would be perfectly welcome. In fact sometimes I wish Charlie would bring a proper black fellow home. And I only ask so I can tell people, you know, neighbours and stuff, when they ask.'

'Right.'

Then I would go back to hiding behind the newspaper. Sometimes my cheeks would be splitting, or I'd have to stuff a handkerchief in my mouth to stop myself guffawing from behind the Leicester *Mercury*.

But somehow the arguments lost their humour or their levity, and one Easter vacation we had a stand-up knock-down blue-blazing row, and Charlie went back to university and we never heard from her again. Telephone calls went unanswered, letters were returned unopened. We know she graduated, because Sheila opened correspondence sent to her home address.

And then Farquar-Thompson from the Foreign Office. Thailand. Chiang Mai. Drugs courier. Twenty years to life. A steep curve, from naughty girl to that.

Farquar-Thompson had told Sheila that Charlie hadn't wanted them to contact us. She hadn't wanted help of any kind. That grieved me. That in the moment when she needed our help more than at any other time, she could allow a foolish quarrel to stand between us. But the Foreign Office had informed us anyway as a matter of policy. Plus, it seemed, there were legal bills to consider.

Normally I like to do a good job for people, but I rushed the wiring that day so I could get home early, just to think about things. I say *home* when I mean my cold apartment. I'd been there twelve weeks and I was still trying to make it habitable. Sheila, bless her, had come and put curtains up for me. My clothes lay around in faintly festering piles, hence the defeated effort with flatpack drawers and wardrobes.

Grabbing a bottle of malt whisky, I stepped over the half-assembled chest of drawers and went to bed, even though it was only just after four in the afternoon. I was thinking about the day Charlotte was born. I was there at the birth. I'd missed my son Phil's birth, out of cowardice I suppose. But I was there when Charlotte arrived, and I was still reeling from the blood and the mess and the gas 'n' air and the exhaustion of it all when the midwife took Sheila to get cleaned up and dumped Charlie in my arms, leaving us alone in the delivery room.

It's a singular moment. You hold in your arms this fragile new life and you hear the click, click, click of the universe expanding into empty space.

Charlie looked up at me that day, and blinked. Her eyes moved like something from a Disney animated feature, and I don't know why but I started bawling. Big fat hot tears of happiness down my face, even though a voice inside was saying *stop it you big sap, they'll be back in a minute*. That was twenty-two years ago, and I'd never once cried since that day. Now I couldn't get the memory of it out of my mind, and as I lay there in bed at four o'clock in the afternoon, I started bawling all over again. I saw Charlie's life, with the messy salt pillar of tears I'd erected at either end of it. I just wanted to hold her in my arms again, and for her to be my little girl.

3

Thursday night was snooker night, with Mick Williams, old pimento-face. Snooker is another of those games like darts or poker, designed by men to permit just enough chat to give the impression of sociability without anyone having to say anything. In fact if anyone starts talking with any degree of engagement or gravity, even if it's just about football, then the game has to stop. And well, what's the point in stopping the game to do something you could easily do if you hadn't hired a table for a few hours? You don't play snooker to *talk*.

So the only discourse in the melancholy cavern of Osborne's snooker house, with its lozenges of lime baize receding in tight formation into the gloom, was the convivial crack and chatter of crystallite balls. Until, that is, deep into the third frame and typically with myself in boss position, Mick Williams, with extraordinary delicacy, laid his cue on the immaculate green baize. 'A moment, Danny.'

'Go on then.' I motioned affably, cue butt resting by my feet, blue chalky tip held out at a soldierly angle.

'It's been eating away at me, like.'

'Oh yes?'

'Can't sit on it any longer.'

Mick Williams is always at his most infuriating in a snooker hall. In fact I don't know why I play with the bloke, because sometimes I hate him. Passionately hate him. Something riles about the way he has to hoist his lardy gut on to the baulk when stretching for a shot; or about the way when, presented with an easy pot, he'll rocket the pot-ball into the pocket with a totally unnecessary clatter and violence. Totally unnecessary that. And, after having done that very thing he'll turn with a wry smile as if to say: there you are, that's punished *you*.

But to lay down your cue on the illuminated green while your opponent is twenty-three points ahead with only five colours left on the table, *that* is unforgivable. It's cheating, no question.

'Spit it out then.'

He pirouetted round the baulk and dropped his voice to a whisper. 'In the Black Dog Saturday night. Me and a few of the lads. Having a few jars, like. Few pints. Not bad in there; not bad at all. Black Dog. It's all right.'

'Go on.' I knew exactly what was coming.

'Saturday night, type of thing. Beers going down well. Lot of laughs. Look Dan, I don't know how to put this.' He plucked a tiny piece of lint off the baize, regarding it between his thumb and forefinger with an expression of horror. 'No,' he said suddenly. 'Forget it.'

And then he picked up his cue, took a reckless shot, and unaccountably potted the yellow. Then he sank the brown. The blue was sitting over the pocket, but he seemed to miss that one deliberately. Turning from the table, he wagged a finger, almost as if it was me he was angry with. 'I shouldn't have opened my mouth. Forget it.'

'I would. If I knew what I had to forget.'

He danced round the baulk again, wiping a fat finger under his nose like it was an expensive cigar before positioning himself sideways-on to me. Squeezing his cue by the neck in his big pink fist, he hissed, 'Look. Don't kill the messenger, like. I saw Sheila in the Black Dog. And she . . .' Here he lowered his voice. 'Well, *she were with another bloke.*'

I picked up my cue and calmly turned to deal with the blue ball. If I could sink it, that would put the game beyond Mick's reach.

'You'd want a mate to tell you, Danny, wouldn't you?' he said. 'Wouldn't you want him to?'

I rolled an agonisingly slow shot the length of the table and the blue dropped into the corner pocket with a cosy cluck. I like to stay down for a second or two after the ball goes in. It's a style thing. 'I know all that,' I said. Even though he was positioned behind me I felt his jaw drop. Lining up for the pink I added, 'Sheila and I have been separated for some time.'

'For some . . .' A volley of spittle shot from between his teeth.

His face, normally flame, turned a shade of puce in the low lighting. Activity stopped at the other tables. Other players were looking at us now. 'How long?'

'About twelve weeks.'

'And you didn't tell me?'

'Well no,' I said, lining up again for the easy pink. But I didn't get a chance to sink it because Mick was buttoning on his coat. 'Where are you going? We always play the five frames.'

He'd holstered his cue and clattered it into the members' rack before I could stop him. Breaching club etiquette and leaving the balls on the table, I followed him outside. He was so angry he hadn't even stopped to pay for the frame. 'Mick!' I tried, striding out behind him. 'Mick!'

Mick wasn't having any of it. He stormed into the Lamplighter, some vinegary, sticky-floored boozer I'd never been in before, and shouted himself a pint of Jubilee Ale, pointedly failing to order one for me. His face was on fire. 'What's going on?' I asked.

'Made a donkey out of me.' He picked up his foaming beer and took it to a table, where he sat, arms folded in a rib-cracking self-hug, his angry face averted. I shouted myself a beer and joined him at the table.

'I was about to win that frame,' I said.

'You've been split up from Sheila for three months and I didn't know anything about it. And I'm your pal. I'm supposed to be your best *mate*.'

His best mate? This was complicated. I didn't realise I was his best mate, nor he mine. We'd known each other for some years, true, but then only as snooker partners and quiz makeweights. I didn't much go in for this 'best mates' thing; I didn't see the point. Your best mate as far as I'm concerned is your wife, and your children, and the family you build your life around. You stop having best mates when you're fourteen. But I had to tread carefully, because he was seriously offended.

'Well, sorry.'

'Sorry bollocks.'

We sat in unresolved conflict, punctuating the silence with occasional sipping, swallowing and Adam's-apple noises. Finally

I threw up my hands and decided to tell him what I knew – which at that stage was next to nothing.

I told him about my position with Sheila and how she was still putting up my curtains; I underscored my difficulties with flatpack assembly furniture; and finally I spilled the beans about Charlie rotting in a Chiang Mai prison.

His face became steadily pinker. He looked as though he wished he hadn't started it. 'You're making it up,' he said at one point.

I assured him I wasn't inventing any of it, and that I wished I was.

'Where the fuck is Chiang Mai?'

'Northern Thailand.'

'So why aren't you already there?'

I shrugged. We discussed what we knew about Thailand, which was very little. I was able to point out that it had once been called Siam, something that had come up in a quiz. He alluded to the sex-tourism industry of Bangkok, and then immediately regretted saying it. I'd heard that students went there to send e-mails home. We also pooled our knowledge of drugs. It was a bit limited: he'd once swallowed something called a Purple Heart when he was a teenager and I knew another sparks whose lad had witnessed things in Holland on a school trip. Finally, when we'd talked ourselves into silence, he mustered another two pints of Jubilee Ale.

'So you'll be going out there?'

'Well, I—'

'When did you last hear from Charlie?'

'Two years ago.'

That wasn't strictly true. Yes, it had been two years since I'd seen her face to face. But there had been a telephone call, about which I hadn't even told Sheila; and that for very good reasons. The call had come out of the blue, about six months earlier, when things were getting particularly bad between Sheila and I.

'Charlie? Are you all right? Why haven't you been in touch?'

'Is Mum there?'

'No.'

'Right. Dad, I'll come straight out with it. I'm in a difficult situation and I need five hundred quid.'

'What kind of difficult situation?'

'Don't ask. Please just say yes or no.'

'Are you pregnant?'

'Don't be ridiculous. Is it yes or no? I really need this favour, Dad.'

'Charlie, where the hell have you been all this time? Do you know what it's like for us?'

'Yes or no. Dad. Yes or no.'

Daughter or not, nobody has the right to behave like that. Not a word, just give me the money. 'Yes, you can have it.'

There was a sigh at the other end. 'Thanks. I'm in London. I'll give you an address. You can post me a cheque.'

I wasn't having that. 'Don't bother. The money is here for you. To collect.'

'I don't have time to do that, Dad.'

'What do you need it for?'

'Are you going to send it or what?'

'No; you're coming here to collect it. You could be here to pick it up faster than I could post it to you.'

Then she got angry. 'Always strings with you, Dad. Always strings.'

'Being a father is one long string, Charlotte.'

The line went dead. End of conversation.

Like I say, I never told Sheila about this, and I never told Mick either. I had this slimy feeling that maybe Charlie wouldn't be in a Chiang Mai prison if I'd just scribbled a cheque and posted it off. But I couldn't do that. Fact is I was burning up with anxiety and hurt and sorrow, and I'd wanted to use her need for that money as a lever to get her back into our lives.

Mick, meanwhile, in the amber light of the sticky boozer, motioned a fat hand in front of my face, bringing me out of my wistful stupor. He leaned forward another fraction and fixed on me one of those irritating gazes clearly intended to see right to the bottom of your soul. 'You'll need a bit of help,' he said. 'And I'm the man who is going to help you.'

'Eh?'

'That's right. Me.'

And at this point my heart, which I thought couldn't possibly sink any lower, went down like the *Titanic*.

4

'You came then,' said Phil.

'Yes, I came.'

Phil, my son, had this habit of stating the obvious whenever he felt uncomfortable. He often seemed uncomfortable in my presence. I'd decided that I ought to pay him a visit before flying off to Chiang Mai, to put him in the picture. We were not close, Phil and I. Not like Charlie and I were close, at least before the bust-up. I always sensed that Phil disapproved of me in matters never expressed; and he knew what I thought of his lifestyle.

He lived in a post-war semi-detached house on the outskirts of Nottingham, about an hour's drive away. Sheila and I usually saw him once or twice a year, most commonly at Christmas, when he fulfilled the religious duty of honouring one's parents by visiting us. He would always bring with him Christmas gifts of extraordinary parsimony: a packet of dates for Sheila, a plastic letter knife with fish handle for me. Last year he brought a toothbrush for Charlie and when I told him she wouldn't be around for Christmas he made a point of extracting the toothbrush from under the tree where he'd left it, so as to take it home with him.

'Shall I take your coat?'

'I'll keep it on,' I said. His house was always freezing.

We went through to the cheerless lounge where two winged armchairs were drawn up near the fireplace. Why, I don't know, because there was no fire burning in the grate. Over a dozen plastic chairs were lined up with their backs touching the walls. A pair of bilious green curtains draped the windows. Over the mantelpiece hung the room's only extravagance, a large wooden cross of polished oak. We sat. The stiff old leather of my chair creaked noisily.

'Well,' Phil said. 'Here we are.'

You couldn't fault his logic. There we were. In his freezing house, with me already wondering why I'd bothered. 'Aren't you going to offer me a drink of something?' I said rather sharply. 'It's basic hospitality you know. Basic good manners. To offer a cup of tea or something. Surely you haven't forgotten that, have you?'

'Sorry, Father,' Phil said, jumping up. Why couldn't he call me 'Dad'? 'There is tea, but no milk. Shall I go out and get some?'

'I'll take it without milk,' I said. I didn't want the damned tea, I just wanted him to behave like a decent human being. He went out to the kitchen to put the kettle on, and I followed him.

Phil was a laboratory technician. He'd had the same job since leaving university, and was currently supervising some research into samples of skin taken from people's bottoms, or so he told me. Three years older than Charlie, Phil had studied biology at Durham University, and it was while he was working with biotoxins that he'd contracted Christian Fundamentalism. I don't know how a scientist can claim to believe that every word of the Bible is true, but we had exhausted that argument years back. Phil, in his uniform of white shirt, black trousers shiny at the knee, and black patent-leather shoes, had his back to me as the kettle boiled. As I looked at him I thought of the two, Charlie on opium and Phil on fundamentalism, and God help me I wasn't certain which was the worst.

He made the tea in two mugs, and from a single teabag, squeezing the teabag against the side of my mug with a spoon. I snatched up another teabag and dropped it into the cup. 'I want to be able to taste it,' I said. He wrung his hands at this extravagance and looked away.

Back in the lounge under the louring cross I told him what had happened to his sister. He sat with his hands folded in his lap, hunched over, his ear slightly inclined: *look how I listen.* When I'd told him the details, he steepled his fingers under his nose and nodded sagaciously. I waited some moments before he said, very slowly, 'She's in an exceedingly dark place.'

'You can say that again.'

He leaned back in his chair and began to sum up what I'd

just said, like a judge at the end of a case in the Crown Court. 'There's Charlie, she's tempted into drugs by some person, she thinks it's an easy pleasure; she gets deeper and deeper into this evil scene; she travels to a distant place, and probably needing money to support her insatiable habit, she allows herself to be talked into trafficking drugs; she is caught and spends her days languishing in prison.'

'That's what I've just told you.'

He gazed at me soulfully. 'Yes.'

I looked at the oak cross over the mantelpiece and I thought about lifting it down and tapping him on the head with it. So what did I want from him? I suddenly realised why I was there. It was a desperate and futile effort to try to begin to regroup my fractured family.

'And you're going over to Thailand to see her?'

Then I heard him apologising. About how much his time was taken up with the church (of which he was an 'Elder' at age twenty-five). About how many people depended on him being there for them. About how his house was a central venue for what he called 'praising the Lord'. About how even if he could get the time off work—

'Stop,' I said. 'Stop. Of all the people on this earth who I'd find it useful to have with me on a trip through steamy Asia, you're last on the list, Sunny Jim.'

He managed to look relieved and insulted at the same time. Then he floated a finger towards the ceiling. 'Let's at least do something practical,' he said. 'Let's pray for Charlotte.'

He put his hands together, closed his eyes, lowered his head and said, 'O Lord—'

He didn't get any further because I said, 'Fuck off, Phil. This is your father you're talking to. Your *father*. Not one of those emotional cripples down the evangelist's revival. All right?'

His face flushed red. 'Look,' I said, more softly this time. 'Look, I came here to put you in the picture. I don't want anything from you. I don't want you to fly out to Asia with me. I don't want you to leave your church and come searching for your sister. I don't even want your prayers. I just thought you might want to know what's happening in your family right now.' The admonishment was creeping back into what I was saying. 'I thought you might want to know.'

'Of course I want to know,' he said. 'I do care for you all.'

'That's a relief, Phil.' But irony had a habit of bouncing off his valiant armour.

I felt tired and I felt small and I was ready to go. Phil was too far away from me to be of any help. He was camped out in the sight of the Lord, and his family, calling from the material plane, were a messy, earth-bound embarrassment. I stood up and announced that I was leaving. I offered him a handshake, this boy who used to hug me up until he was aged twelve.

'But you haven't even touched your tea!' he protested.

'No.'

'What a waste,' he opined sadly. 'What a waste.'

5

On the following Tuesday Mick Williams insisted on dropping by my apartment before the quiz. The underside of the door scraped on some unopened envelopes as he squeezed his burly frame into my tiny apartment. He carried two plastic bags stuffed with over-ripe bananas, splitting melons, pulpy avocados and misshapen kiwi fruit. He looked around, sniffing. 'Christ.'

Perhaps Mick, a chronically ingrained bachelor, had got his own life a little better organised than mine currently appeared to be. Bruiser though he was, he did enjoy the niceties; a fusspot trying to pass himself off as a slob, he made no disguise of his assessment of my living conditions. I suppose it didn't look too good. I'd laid down a carpet, and Sheila had put up those pesky curtains with a pelmet. Beyond that I hadn't got very far. In fact I hadn't even got a chair: if ever I felt the need to take the weight off my feet I lay on the bed.

Scattered around the floor were dozens and dozens of paperbacks (I'm a voracious reader of science fiction, fantasy, horror, crime or anything with a decent story: if it hasn't got a good story I can't be bothered). Those and a stack of silver foil takeaway cartons. And a fair few beer cans. And a couple of whisky bottles. And the odd empty bottle of Courvoisier. Sure, the place was a tip, but despite the fact that I hadn't got a chair to sit on, Mick seemed more concerned that I hadn't got a TV set. He was appalled.

'No TV?'

'No.'

'Get out!'

'Don't want a telly, thanks.'

'Ridiculous. I've a spare you can have. Twenty-two incher. Text. Remote. I'll bring it round. Spare video, too. Have it.'

I told him not to bother, but he persisted. I don't know what happened but my head filled up with blood. My ears reddened and my face became hot. I'm not a shouter, but I heard myself bellowing, in a voice not my own. Screaming even. 'I don't *want* a television! Don't want! No fucking vision! Tele-fucking-vision! Fuckee-telly!' It sounded odd even to my own ears, but I continued in this fashion until I noticed that Mick, rather than being alarmed or surprised by this outburst, was actually suppressing a smile. I felt completely ridiculous. 'Sorry.'

'You don't have to have one,' he said jauntily.

Then we had a long feather-smoothing conversation about what crap there was on the TV; or rather Mick detailed a comprehensive list of crap programmes. He named all the crap actors, the crap presenters and the crap game shows. After a while he made an observation about the extraordinary number of books in the room. 'Are they any good?' he asked.

There was a kind of rhythm to the conversation tempting me to say they were all crap, which I think was what he wanted. 'Some of them.'

'I can see why you're so good at general knowledge.'

That was the sort of remark that infuriated me about Mick Williams. He had a mind that needed to shoe-horn every available bit of information into this or that space. I mean how would reading science fiction in *general* help my general knowledge in *particular*? He was referring to my strength on the quiz team. I was general knowledge; he was sport, TV and pop music; and Izzy Ballentine was literature, mythology and history. That's how we got by.

Mick dumped his gift bags of unsold fruit and shuffled into the bedroom, where the flatpack chest of drawers lay in disassembly on the floor. Hunkering down, he picked up a drawer handle and began to poke about in a plastic bag full of tiny screws. Then he discarded those things and began sorting the variously sized rectangular blocks of Formica on chipboard.

Clearly he'd begun his programme of 'helping' me. I stood in the doorway watching sort of sourly, and after a couple of minutes he put everything back where he'd found it, suggesting we should get a move on if we wanted to be in good time for the quiz.

Izzy was there before us, well into her third large gin and tonic. She had a peculiar way, did Izzy, of holding her cigarettes exactly perpendicular between first and second finger, so that she would have to tilt her head to get her lips under the cigarette, sucking the smoke down before blowing it straight back up again, quite vertically like a locomotive from the steam age. This technique, presumably invented to spare her the ravages of nicotine staining, had failed. Her fingertips were a rather putrid oak colour, and the weft of her shabby garments was slightly shiny with the tiny increments of tar that only forty ciggies a day can deliver. I often speculated what her students made of her, and I wondered if Charlie had been taught by people like Izzy, but at the unsavoury Oxford University.

All brains and no sense type of people, I mean. Much as I liked Izzy, somewhere along the high road of life she'd stumbled not just off the map but also off the table on which the map lay spread.

'So I'll be bereft,' she said, funnelling smoke directly at the ceiling as I tabled the drinks. I'd been at the bar while she and Mick filled in our quiz sheet. Our team was called the Punk Rockers; I forget why. 'Abandoned, without a team while my boys go giddy in Chiang Mai.'

I shot Mick a poisonous look.

'She's got to know,' he said aggressively. A moustache of creamy beer froth rested on his upper lip. 'I haven't said anything else.'

'Anything else indeed,' said Izzy. That was how she talked. 'Anything else indeed.'

'In fact,' Mick volunteered, 'you might as well tell her the rest. Izzy here is an educated woman. She might know one or two things about it.'

'Indeed about *what?*' She could make that *what* sound like an arrow whizzing past your ear and splitting the plaster of the wall behind you.

'About why Dan and I are going to *Thighland*.'

'Thailand,' I corrected, 'and who said anything about *us* going? Who said anything about *me* going, never mind you coming with me?'

'I thought it was settled!'

'Settled?' I protested. 'When did this get settled?'

We stared at each other across the table. Mick's cheeks were flushed and his eyes were slightly moist, as they always were in an argument. Izzy meanwhile peered hard at me through her spectacles, making it plain that, whatever this might be about, she was on Mick's side. If only to break the silence I told her, 'My daughter Charlotte has been arrested for drug smuggling in Thailand. I've got to go out there.'

'Good lord! Is she some kind of dope fiend?' All tact, Izzy.

'I've no idea. It's all new to me.'

'She's innocent,' Mick said. 'We're going to prove it.'

I put my glass down in amazement. 'You don't know she's innocent!'

'That's the position we're starting from. We're going out there to prove her innocence.'

Everything with Mick was *we* this and *we* will do that. I wanted to ask him who the hell he meant by *we*. I felt like asking if he had a pet rat in his pocket.

'All the best minds were dope fiends,' Izzy said, ignoring the dispute. 'Keats, palely loitering. Coleridge in caverns measureless to man. De Quincey. Baudelaire and the *Club des Haschischins*. Wilkie Collins—'

'I'll get some in before we start,' Mick said jovially.

'Dickens towards the end. Rimbaud. Mrs Browning. And you may depend if Keats was soaked in the stuff that both the Shelleys had a snifter or two. Poe, Crabbe—'

I stopped listening. Izzy's list meant nothing to me. It became a drone in the background while I thought about Charlie lying on a feverish pallet in a stinking cell in Chiang Mai.

'Look lively,' Izzy said. 'We're about to be tossed one.'

Since quiz teams at the Clipper were technically supposed to comprise four players, we were occasionally assigned a waif or stray who wanted to take part. Amos Magnamara, landlord and quizmaster, was at that moment pointing one such in our direction. Personally I wasn't bothered, and Mick Williams reckoned we actually performed better without the support of these loose players. This one was some kind of grey-haired hippy. He wore one of those humorous goatee beards and a single, glittering earring; plus he had what looked like the leaf of a tomato plant tattooed on the back of his hand. He nodded to us and as he squatted on Mick's stool I noticed he was drenched in a sweet, exotic perfume.

Mick returned to the table, his hands easily spanning the three drinks. 'Look,' he warned the newcomer in his friendly way, 'if you've come to grant us three wishes, you can start by climbing off my fucking stool.'

Sheila answered the door wearing a cotton nightdress. I'd got her out of bed. I tried to look over her shoulder and down the hall.

'I told you,' she said, reading my mind, 'he's never been here. Are you going to stand there all night?'

The house was extraordinarily tidy. Not that surprising when you considered Sheila's claims that I was the one who habitually untidied the place. I sat down heavily in the lounge. Sheila hovered. 'Do you want something to eat? I've got a nice bit of tongue in the fridge.'

My stomach churned. 'No thanks.'

'That chap phoned again today,' Sheila said.

'Chap?'

'Farquar-Thompson. He said that when Charlie heard they'd been in touch with us, she repeated that she didn't want either of us to go out there.'

'She said WHAT?'

Sheila's eyes were brimming with anger, and her anger infuriated me in turn. 'She said she didn't want to see either of us. She asked if we'd send some toiletries and some money but that she didn't want to see us.'

I dug my fingernails into my cheeks as I felt the evening's alcohol burning off at speed. I could scarcely credit it. Here was Charlie facing a twenty-year sentence, possibly even a death sentence, in some filthy foreign dungeon. I thought right now she must be the loneliest person on the planet, and still she didn't want to see either of the two people who loved her most and without reservation.

I was trying to remember when it was that Charlie's instinct to come to me had stopped. From the time a child begins to walk at around the first year they also start to fall. And that falling keeps happening for the first few years. They trip, they stumble, they fall, they bruise, cut, bleed; and some impulse drives them, some force, eyes full of starbursting tears and lip a-quiver, back into your arms and you want it, you want to sweep 'em up and hold 'em tight and warm until it subsides: because you feel it twice, the bruise, the cut, it burns you, it sears you; they bleed you bleed; and hell, Charlie is lying there and it's *me* who's lying there in prison without a friend facing twenty years of my life rotting away.

'She can say what the hell she wants. I'm going out there to see her.'

'I'll come,' Sheila said.

'No.'

'Of course I'll bloody well come!'

'No.'

'You just try and stop me.'

'If you go, I don't.'

Her sigh was like a sheet of ice forming over a hundred unsaid things. 'You can't go alone! I'll get time off work!' Sheila was a part-time supervisor at the supermarket, where she'd met lover-boy.

'Not necessary.' I wasn't having Sheila exposed to all that. I forbade it. 'I'll ask Mick Williams to come with me.'

'Mick?' Sheila said. 'Would Mick go out with you? Do you think he would?'

Her enthusiasm for this idea dismayed me. 'He might. If I ask him.'

'I'd feel much happier if Mick went with you. You know how angry you get. He could help you.'

That made me suspicious. I suddenly wondered if I was having my strings pulled. 'You didn't tell Mick to come with me, did you?'

'Now when do I see Mick?'

'I don't know who you see,' I said nastily. I didn't know. I didn't know anything. All I knew was that I was going to have to go to some steamy Asian place to see my daughter in a squalid jail. Sheila was looking at me strangely. I needed her to squeeze me. I wanted to stay there, back in my own house, in my own bed, with Sheila holding me while I recovered the strength to know what to do. I stood up.

'You can stay, you know,' Sheila said, also standing.

'No. I've got all my things at the flat.' I hadn't punished her enough yet.

'How was the quiz tonight?' she blurted in the hallway as I picked up my coat.

'We won.' Thanks to the fragrant hippy we'd beaten off a close challenge by the Fireside Tendency.

'You keep winning, don't you?' Sheila said.

6

After work the following day I stopped off at the central library. I had a few new books to take out. I used books the way some people use alcohol, to obliterate the noise of the outside world. It was an old reflex, to stop me thinking too much about Charlie, but this time I wasn't after the familiar escapism.

'Not your usual cup of tea, Mr Innes,' Lucy observed, efficiently stamping my loans. Lucy had been efficiently stamping my books for several years. I remembered her from when she started out with a white face and hair dyed as black as a crow. All that book-stamping had at least put some colour in her cheeks; and, over the years, in her hair, which had changed from soot-black to rocketburst silver and then, after a brief flirt as a carrot-top, to henna red. Then Lucy had a year off to have a child of her own, and when she returned I don't suppose she had time to mess about with hair, so we discovered she was actually a blonde, and a very pretty one too. A single mum with no spare time on her hands, she still read every volume of fantasy and science fiction in the library. We had that in common.

'Mugging up on poetry,' I said defensively.

'What's this one? Looks very technical.'

She flicked through the pages of a book I'd found about drugs: I wanted to find out more about the stuff. I'd also picked up a couple of books by John Keats and Samuel Taylor Coleridge, because Izzy had said they were mad-for-it dope fiends. I was hoping they might have something to say, but unfortunately they were just books of poetry. I took them anyway.

'He was a dope fiend, you know, Coleridge was,' I said to Lucy, trying to sound like I knew all about the bloke.

'The postman from Porlock.'

'Pardon?' I said.

'He was whacked out of his head writing what was going to be his best poem, and then the postman came, and he never finished it.'

'Really?'

Lucy's trained fingertips leafed through the pages to point out a title. I made a mental note to look at that one later.

'I know someone who knows you.'

'Oh?' I said. I always felt slightly nervous in Lucy's proximity, and I never knew why.

She clasped her hands under her chin as if she was going to tease me about it, but when she saw me blinking stupidly, she said, 'Decker Townsend. He's in your quiz team.'

I thought for a minute. 'Hippy type?'

She laughed. 'Kind of. He's a dope fiend, too.'

'Is he?'

'Not really. Maybe a bit. He's all right is Decker. Decent type. Says you're good at general knowledge.'

Then someone else wanted their book stamping, and I passed through the turnstile musing on the fact that I'd been cheerfully co-operating in a pub quiz with a drugs bimp.

I'd made myself macaroni on toast for supper but I couldn't face it. It's awful stuff. I scraped the yellow gloop into the bin and had a beer supper instead, settling down with my library books. Farquar-Thompson had told me that an unusual feature of Charlie's offence was that she was caught trafficking opium, not heroin. I didn't understand the distinction at first, but from reading the library book I gathered that you needed the raw opium poppy juice as a base to make heroin. Since they had the laboratories for making heroin in Thailand, it didn't make any sense to be transporting the opium. A small quantity of heroin was much more valuable on the street than the raw opium.

I didn't read anything in the book that hinted why Charlie might be trafficking opium. There was plenty of other information, however, and very little of it made me feel better. I read that in 1993 governments around the world were invited to celebrate International Drug Reduction Day. China joined in the celebrations. It rounded up a hundred traffickers, put them through a show trial and brought them to a packed sports stadium where a football match was about to be staged. Before the kick-off there were dancing girls with multi-coloured silk streamers, painted dragons, kite-flying displays and martial music. Then all hundred drug traffickers were lined up and shot by firing squad. Then the football match was played.

International Drug Reduction Day celebrations, Chinese style.

This sort of thing wasn't funny. I'd brought Charlie up to be a football fan. After a few more chapters of this stuff I put the book aside, had another beer, and turned to Keats and Coleridge.

I couldn't get on with either of them.

I'm not a great one for poetry, and my eyes wouldn't stay on the words. The Keats was the worst. It was like being given a cake, which was all currants and no crust to leaven the thing. I couldn't fathom it. I was looking for something that might let me know why Charlie, a happy young woman (at least on the face of things), might want to ruin her life with drugs. Or anyone else for that matter. Well, if Keats was a dope fiend, there was nothing in his poetry that was going to help me.

The Coleridge I liked a little better. At least I could understand it. I read the one Lucy had pointed out, the one he'd written while blasted out of his brain. It was called 'Kubla Khan'. It did stop quite suddenly, so the story of the postman might be true for all I know or care. He mentioned *the milk of Paradise* and I wondered if he was talking about the drug, but there was nothing to say why you take the stuff in the first place.

My mind turned to the fragrant hippy who had washed up on our quiz team. Decker, Lucy said his name was. I don't know why but I wondered if this Decker was ever likely to have been Charlie's supplier. We lived in a small city after all: perhaps he was the one who'd got her on to the stuff in the first place.

I had another couple of beers before going to bed, though I couldn't sleep. I kept thinking about travel arrangements and about getting out of my work commitments. I also lay there thinking up one or two raw questions I'd got for this Decker.

7

Blame, you see. A sharpened knife has to blunt itself some-where. I badly needed to blame.

I'd already constructed several scenes inside my head. Decker the fragrant hippy, in the coffee bars and the pubs frequented by the young. Decker, laughing, witty, cool, effortlessly slagging off the establishment and work-a-day daddies like me, rolling up his doped cigarettes, casually passing them on in the middle of a conversation, as if it was nothing. Decker, speaking with authority about the meaningful lyrics of some rock and roll wankers from Manchester, counting out pills to his rapt audience. Christ, I even saw him waiting outside the school gates, dispensing little plastic sachets he called sherbet fountains. And always in the coffee bar, or in the audience, or at the front of the queue by the school gates, was Charlie with rapt, shining eyes. Charlie, smoking his stuff, popping his pills, drinking in his warmed-over hippie philosophies.

I knew these images were all bollocks, but I couldn't stop them playing out on the back of my retina. I'd be chasing the plaster wall on a rewiring job or installing a new junction box and I'd realise my hands were gripping the tools so tight they'd be trembling.

I was finishing off a sub-contract job I'd been getting behind on, new house, crawling under the eaves in a sloping attic, trying to haul cable through to where I was working. My face was tracked with perspiration, and there was sawdust sticking to the sweat.

I crawled out of the hole, wiping the sweat and sawdust on my sleeve. Flipping open a box of snouts I pulled one out with my teeth. I thought about Decker, and how I would knock his teeth so far down his throat he would need a surgeon with a torch to find them again. Then I would ask him what he knew about Charlie.

I thumped the stud wall and it set up a wobble which travelled all the way round the corner. Shoddy work. Bad builders. They don't think about us poor fuckers coming behind them, having to put in the fucking wires. I crawled back under the eaves.

I spent a lot of time that week thinking about Charlie. Even though she wasn't dead, I was like someone leafing through a box of old photographs after a funeral. When she was very small I used to go into her room while she slept in her cot. I could stand there for a long time just watching her sleep, the miracle of her, the sweet, holy marvel of her. Somehow when she slept her normally fine, straight hair would billow in curls as if she was flying in a place of soft, warm winds; her effortless aerial control demonstrated by her posture, one arm pointing at the top corner of the cot, the other drifting low and behind her. I had no doubt that this child was in flight, soaring through dreams bright with music, vivid with the colours and inebriated freshness exclusive to a mind only two years old.

I could stand there for half an hour watching her trajectory, wondering where it was she might land.

I suppose I wanted to be with her on those flights, inside her dreams.

I wondered now whether I had spent my time watching her too closely. Maybe it's not healthy. Children whose fathers don't give a sod about them seem to emerge without too much damage. I knew I was setting myself up as a candidate for all this blame I was ready to discharge. I was putting myself in the frame, lined up in the police identity parade with the Deckers of the world. I wanted to know how that little flying girl came to be grounded on a filthy pallet bed in some place called Chiang Mai.

'How did you get on with them?' Lucy at the library wanted to know.

It was a rainy Friday evening, and I was returning the Keats and the Coleridge and the other book. Basically they were a dead loss. There was the odd phrase which stuck in the mind, but I couldn't see what the fuss was about. I couldn't imagine spending three years at university reading this tosh. Maybe it made more sense around the time these old boilers were actually writing, and Oxford professor types keep them going because they are too lazy to read anything new.

'Rubbish,' I said. 'I'm going to try something else.'

'Are you growing a beard?' Lucy's electronic pen chirruped with satisfaction as it scanned my returns for the library computer. I felt my chin. Apathy had raised a crop of stubble, and my hair was creeping below my collar. 'Suits you,' she said. 'Makes you look less buttoned-up.'

I stalked among the shelves looking for something else to take home, wondering what she meant by 'buttoned-up'. I was also trying to remember the names of some of those other deadbeat poets Izzy had mentioned. In the meantime I picked up another book, this time about the history of the opium trade. Then I remembered the name of Baudelaire, so I asked Lucy to help me.

She was already in the act of switching off the lights, closing up for the evening. I was the last borrower. 'You *are* going at it, aren't you?' she said, in the way you might remark to someone who's drunk half a bottle of vodka before breakfast. Anyway she found and stamped me something by Baudelaire. I might have guessed he was French by his name.

'If you don't mind waiting a moment, I'll walk out with you,' she said. 'Only I hate walking across that dark car park.'

'Not at all,' I said, quite flattered to be asked to escort a young woman anywhere, even if it was only to the safety of the well-lit street. I waited while she armed the burglar alarm, flicked off the porch lights and secured the door.

'This Decker,' I said as we carefully stepped over rainwater puddles to cut across the gloomy car park. Our boots crunched the wet gravel underfoot. 'Is he a drinking pal of yours?'

'Drinking? When do I get out drinking?' She laughed. 'I've got a two-year-old daughter to think about. I should get out drinking!'

'Where is she now?'

'My mum looks after her while I work.'

'I'll baby-sit for you,' I blurted.

She stopped in her tracks and looked at me strangely. 'Why?'

'To give you a break, I mean. A night off. I've had kids of my own. Two. A pair. Boy and a girl. I know the ropes.'

'Why?'

What could I tell her? That the reason I wanted to baby-sit was because my own daughter was rotting in an Asian jail and I wanted to watch her two-year-old baby, in flight, sleeping. It wouldn't come out right. 'Just a thought.'

We started walking again. 'I'll bear it in mind,' Lucy said, and I felt foolish beyond measure. 'I'll be all right now,' she said when we reached the parade of shops. 'Thanks, Mr Innes. See you!'

I was actually walking the same way as her, but I felt compelled to mumble a goodbye, turn on my heels and step out in the opposite direction. After a few yards I drew abreast of the Shoulder of Mutton, a roustabout's pub I never use, but I had to dive inside just to get something to put the colour back in my face.

8

Izzy was completing the *Daily Telegraph* crossword while waiting for the quiz to get underway. She could crack a crossword puzzle before the tonic had stopped fizzing in her gin. She wasn't the greatest conversationalist in the world, Izzy. But then neither was I according to Mick Williams, and that night I was too busy looking round to see if Decker was going to arrive.

Decker had proved to be a useful addition to the team on the previous occasion, coming up with one or two answers that had stumped the rest of us. He also had the tact not to volunteer answers before we did; he'd wait, and if none were forthcoming, he'd offer one. I suspected him of general knowledge. Though that didn't stop my unreasonable interest in breaking his face.

The difficulty with these occasional team members was what to do with the pot. The prize money of twenty-five pounds to the winning team always went into a pot, since we didn't know what else to do with it. The pot was kept by Izzy, and she sat on it like a dragon in a cave. Mick and I had guessed that the pot kept her in juice, but we never said anything. Then when these casual players came along you had to split the winnings for tiny returns.

But Decker, hearing Izzy mention the pot, insisted that we keep his share. Whereupon Izzy had insisted that he join on a regular basis. I should add that Izzy goes skittish and stupid when any presentable young man appears. She simpers; she smiles broadly; she flutters her eyelids and she shows off her intellect, which is considerable. Really, you wouldn't think she'd bother what with the state she's in. But whenever Decker rang the bell with a correct answer she'd lean across me to grip his knee between a powerful thumb and forefinger.

Slightly nonplussed by this romantic attention, Decker had

muttered something about not liking routines, but eventually conceded to turn up the following week. That is, this week. But with the quiz about to start there was no sign of him.

Izzy dispatched the crossword in record time, laid down her pen, glared over the top of her spectacles and said, 'Where's our sweet hippy then?'

'Cow fell on him while he were drinkin' milk,' Mick said, dragging on a snout. I didn't get this joke. Then I noticed Mick had a nicotine patch on the back of his wrist.

'I thought the point of a nicotine patch was to stop you smoking?'

Mick looked at the patch as if someone else had put it there. He was about to say something but the quiz had started.

About a quarter of the way through I got a hot blast of patchouli oil or whatever it is. A small fist, red hairs bristling on putty-white skin, parked a pint of Muckster's for me, and then another one for Mick, on the table. A gin and tonic came for Izzy, followed by another pint as a voice breathed in my ear, 'Lucy sends her regards.' I turned my head to see Decker weaving back to the bar with his tin tray.

He pulled up a stool between Izzy and Mick, and the quizmaster wanted to know who wrote, 'Ode to a Nightingale'.

I should have left it. I knew there would be trouble. But I just barked out, 'Keats.'

Disgusted, Izzy threw her pen down on the table. 'My department,' she snapped nastily.

Mick looked at me as if I'd gone out of my mind. 'Literature. Izzy's department. You know the rules.'

I picked up the pen. 'Rules? What rules? There are no rules.'

Mick turned to Decker. Talking to me by pretending to explain to the new boy. 'Izzy, literature and history. Me, sport, TV and pop music. Dan is general knowledge and odd bits of science. First run, that is. We have first run in our own department, then if we don't shout, someone else can. Not rules, Dan is right. Technically. But the way we play it.'

Decker nodded thoughtfully. 'I see.'

'Keats,' Izzy spat. 'My fucking department. Now give me back that pen.'

I handed it over before the next question was put. For the rest of the round I sat on my stool, fuming. It seemed to me ridiculous that I couldn't be allowed to answer whatever question I wanted, and as for Decker, well, I couldn't exactly chin a bloke who had just brought me a pint of Old Muckster's Jubilee Ale. At the break, I excused myself and went out the back.

When I returned to the table Mick was sharing a joke with Decker. Mick's laughter was like a traction engine turning over on a cold morning. He threw his head back and rubbed his considerable belly. Where was that pointless hostility when I needed it? Meanwhile Izzy was still eyeing me like a kestrel on a nest of chicks.

'Danny,' Mick said, 'you ought to have a word with Decker about Charlie. He knows a thing or two about that stuff.'

'What stuff?'

'Mick told me about the difficulty your daughter is in,' Decker said soberly.

'Tell the whole world, Mick.'

'I thought he might know a bit about it, that's all.'

'You thought Izzy might know a bit about it. I've spent the whole week reading Ode to a Fucking Nightingale as a consequence.'

They all looked blank at that, and then the next round of the quiz started up.

We won again, and no little thanks to Decker, who could give the rest of us a run in all our specialist areas. We were getting some funny looks from the Fireside Tendency. By the time Decker had helped me get another round of double gins and double Old Muckster's, I'd realised he wasn't my man. Mick's directness had given me the opportunity to ask him if he'd ever known Charlie, whom he hadn't; and to ask him what he knew about opium, which he said was very little.

'Hardly likely,' Izzy said, blowing a head of smoke at the nicotine-coloured ceiling, 'to come clean about it if he did.'

'Whacky-baccy man, I'd say, looking at you.'

Mick was brilliant like that. Here a fellow with a

cannabis leaf silver earring, and a cannabis leaf tattooed on his hand (of course I knew it wasn't a damned tomato plant) and there was Mick tentatively suggesting that the man smoked cannabis.

Whatever he was, he wasn't the man who'd first given the filthy stuff to my daughter. The bell rang for time and the boy came round shouting at us to leave, and Mick told the boy to bollocks, as he always does.

'By the way,' Decker said as the boy hovered for the drained mugs, 'Lucy says to tell you she would like you to baby-sit if you're still willing.'

It took me by surprise. 'Sure,' I said. 'Tell her it's fine.'

'Baby-sitting?' Mick spluttered. 'You can't baby-sit. We're off to Chiang Mai Wednesday.'

It was true. It had all been settled. Of course, I wanted to go the very next day, but this was the earliest we could manage. In any event, Charlie wasn't going anywhere, was she?

'Who's going to Chiang Mai?' Izzy wanted to know.

'I told you about that,' Mick snarled. 'Last week.'

'Aincha got 'omes to go to?' the glass collector wanted to know.

'I'm sure I can't remember,' Izzy grumbled, putting on her coat. No, she wasn't talking to the glass collector.

As usual we were the last to leave. There was that reassuring slam of the door behind us and the sound of three angry bolts shooting home. Still grumbling, Izzy peeled off in one direction and Mick departed, slightly unsteady after the strong Muckster's, in another.

I walked a short distance with Decker in the direction of town. Before he too peeled away, he stopped me. 'What have you got against me, then?'

I was a bit taken aback by this directness. He struck a match for his cigarette, and the orange flare lit up his face. For a second I saw lines and shadows etched around his eyes and at the downturn of his mouth; carelines I hadn't really noticed before. He wasn't much younger than me, maybe only a year or two. He had a light scar on the side of his jaw. Then the match went out, and I suddenly got the impression I'd underestimated him altogether. Our fragrant hippy had been around the corner.

'What do you mean?'

'All that glaring and glowering at me over my shoulder. I mean, if I've done something, I'd like to know what it is.'

For a minute I felt a flash of anger. Then it passed, and I don't know why, but I decided to come clean with him. After all, I had been pretty stupid about it. 'I'm sorry, pal. Head's in a state. Nothing against you. I keep looking for someone to blame.'

'Normal,' he said. 'It's normal.'

A breeze picked up from the far end of the street. It stung my eyes.

'I've been out there. Thailand. Laos. Burma.

'Watch out,' he told me. 'Dreamland? Fuckin' dreamland.'

I stared at him, measuring his words.

'It comes back at you,' he told me. 'Like your dreams. It's whatever you want, or don't want. Drugs? They've got everything. Religion? The ground exudes spirituality. Sex? You can have three young girls worshipping your prick if that's what you want.'

He took a quiet drag on his cigarette.

'Danny, it's a cracked mirror. No, that's wrong, it's the other side of a cracked mirror, the silver-metal amalgam-side of a cracked mirror, and you can't always get back.'

I couldn't decide if he was a lunatic, or just drunk.

'Decker,' I said. 'What about the stuff?'

'Stuff?'

'Opium.'

He narrowed his eyes at me, leaning forward, creating a sense of conspiracy. 'Two theories: one, the plant evolved quite naturally. Two, it changed and developed as cultivated by human beings. Look Danny, opium is an intelligent plant. I mean a sentient, parasitic life-form, psycho-chemically generating the need for its propagation in human brains to ensure its further cultivation.'

'What?'

'Too right, what.' He put his hand on my shoulder. 'Imagine

39

you are an alien colonising the planet. First disguise yourself as a non-aggressive plant. Secondly, make yourself useful; seductive and addictive to the planet's dominant species, who will then do all the heavy spade-work, planting you, cultivating you, exporting you, taking risks for you, even fighting each other for you. Gradually you increase your control around the world. Get it? You've got time. You can wait. This is easy.'

He drew back, removing his hand, allowing me to appreciate the full import of what he'd said. I stared into his eyes. It was the most breathtaking load of cobblers I'd ever heard. 'Cack,' I said. 'You're talking cack.'

He turned my words over in his mind, squinted in savour of the rich insight they afforded, weighed them carefully. 'That reaction,' he said, 'is part of it.'

We stared at each other for a moment, and without another word he shook my hand and turned. Then he was a silhouette, with the wind flapping at his hair and at the hem of his long hippy coat. I watched him go before spinning on my heels and setting off in the opposite direction. I turned up my collar and, weaving slightly, made my way home along a street of terraced houses.

There was a breeze at my back. I heard light footsteps behind me, but when I turned there was nothing there. At some distance further on I heard what I took to be a dog trotting behind me, or maybe it was just some litter blown along the pavement. I turned again, but to an empty street. So certain was I that someone was behind me I spent a minute or two looking up and down the lamplit street, into the stiff breeze. The wind moaned softly in an unlit alley between the terraces. I spent a moment peering into the shadows there.

Decker's ramblings had me spooked.

I was not looking forward to the trip to Thailand. I don't take to the heat. In the past I've spent a few grudging holidays in Spain with Sheila and the children, always retreating like a dog to the shade. Neither am I very keen on foreign food. I have an adverse reaction to spicy concoctions. A mild curry at the local

Taj Mahal restaurant brings sweat blisters the size of commem-
orative coins to my brow: and I happen to know that a balti
chicken jalfrezi is no more an example of Indian cuisine than is
a plate of jellied eels.

Even trying to read the Frenchman Baudelaire was making
me feel slightly queasy. For some reason, even though the poems
were in English, the translators were always too lazy to translate
the titles. Ridiculous, since the titles are always easy to translate.
Les Fleurs du Mal for example means 'Evil Flowers'. *Un Voyage
à Cythere* means 'A Voyage to Cythere'. I know that much and I
don't even speak French. So why do they make a big deal of not
translating the title? It's because it's poetry, isn't it? Anything
else and you would get your title thrown in with the price of the
other translations.

Baudelaire took lots of opium as far as I could gather, and
hashish too, and what I read was much more useful than the
Keats or the Coleridge. Baudelaire talked about the similarities
and differences between opium and hashish. This was more the
sort of thing I'd been looking for. Both of them, he says, make
you weak-willed, and both make you focus your attention on
trivial and tiny details in such a way that you get fixed. But he
also said that hashish is much more disturbing and intense than
opium. This surprised me, because I thought that hashish was
the drug of choice for these hippy types. Hashish, Baudelaire
said, is a confusing fury, whereas opium is a gentle seducer.

I could see that. I could see Charlie going for the gentle
seducer. I thought of Charlie being seduced along with other
young girls fresh out of university, the dew still on 'em. When I
felt that watery prickling again behind the eyes, I had to put
down the book and uncap a bottle of whisky, evaporate the
excess fluid with the heat of the grain.

I ran myself a bath, and while it was filling I warmed some
milk on the stove for a hot chocolate drink, to try to sober up. I
thought I'd give that deadbeat Baudelaire one last chance; and
though the words wouldn't keep still on the page it was while
soaking in the tub that I read:

What sad, black isle is that? It's Cythera, so they say, a land

celebrated in song, the banal Eldorado of all the old fools.
Look, after all, it's a land of poverty.

Dozing slightly, I let the book slip into the water and had to retrieve it from under the soap suds. I fanned it out and spread it over the taps to dry, and fell to thinking about Charlie again, and what sad, black Cythera she'd got mixed up in.

9

I was expecting Lucy to return at around midnight. In the event she didn't get back until nearer one a.m., though I didn't mind in the slightest. Even so, the baby-sitting session had been something of a disappointment.

When I'd arrived at eight o'clock in the evening, Jonquil – it's not for me to make remarks on the names parents inflict on their children – was already tucked up in bed and fast asleep. I spent most of the evening flicking between the numerous channels on Lucy's TV set and not finding anything to entertain. It depressed me to think of the millions of people glued to this poor fare night after night. I started to have ridiculous thoughts about how the bright lights from the screen might be triggering signals in their brains, like opium does, to get them to tune in again and again, pointlessly and destructively.

I made four or five visits upstairs ostensibly to check on Jonquil, but really to look at her sleeping in her cot. I'm ashamed to say I thumped about a bit and let the door bang a couple of times, in the hope that she might wake, and cry, so that I might have an excuse to pick her up, comfort her, change her nappy, carry her downstairs with me. Ironic really. When Charlie and Phil were babies we used to tiptoe round them, praying that they sleep on for another half an hour so that you might get something done. Then of course the softest muffled footfall on a deep-pile carpet would resound like a pistol shot to bump them out of sleep.

'Jonquil's got a bit of a cold,' Lucy had told me. 'If she wakes up you can give her some Calpol. I've left it on the cupboard in the hall.'

Calpol, the paediatric all-purpose medicine. Baby-dope. When Charlie and Phil were babies themselves we got through gallons of the stuff whenever they were poorly and couldn't sleep. Now

43

as I looked at Jonquil, deliberately working a squeaky floor-board with my right foot, she slept on like the dead. Jonquil had a tiny green candle of dried snot under her nose. It reminded me of Charlie's perpetually streaming nose. It also brought back the time when Charlie returned from her first term at Oxford.

'Don't say anything,' Sheila had whispered to me when I came back from work that day, dumping my gear under the coats in the hall. 'She's got a stud in her nose.'

'A what?'

Sheila tapped the side of her own nose. 'A little emerald stud just here. I think it looks quite pretty. Don't say anything.'

I moved through to the sitting room, where Charlie lounged on the sofa, watching TV. 'Hi, Dad.'

I didn't say anything, but I couldn't take my eyes off the tiny green stud in her left nostril. It had me mesmerised. After a while Charlie seemed to become aware of my staring. She flashed a smile at me before turning back to the TV set. 'You OK?'

'*I'm* OK,' I said.

Maybe I shouldn't have allowed myself to stare like that. But that nose stud, to me it looked for all the world like a tiny ball of snot. There it is. You spend the first five years of your child's life wiping gunk from their noses, until they develop the compe-tence to deal with their own streaming hooters. During that five years it becomes a reflex. Then the next decade or so passes in the blink of an eye, and your snot-nosed little girl comes home from the celebrated Oxford with an emerald stud. Well, you want to scrape it off. I know how unreasonable that sounds, but for a moment that's how I felt.

'What are you staring at, Dad?'

'I don't know.'

'How's work?'

'Fine. How's yours?'

I knew she'd been studying a course called 'Post-colonial Literature'. She gave a dismissive shake of her head, the sort that suggests there's no point going into it with an electrician. 'I brought a stack of work home with me.'

'How's post-colonial literature?'

'Cool.'

Cool? We used to laugh at people who said things like *cool*. It belonged to an outmoded and faintly ridiculous generation of people who said *groovy* and *dad-io* and *far-out man!* I hadn't heard it said in a while.

Maybe it wasn't a very *cool* thing to do but I reached out and tried to flick the stud in her nose. Did I think it would fall off into my hand? It didn't.

'Ow! OW! What the HELL are you doing, Dad? Just what the hell?'

Sheila came rushing in from the kitchen.

'He tried to rip the stud out of my nose!' Charlie exaggerated, nursing her admittedly now inflamed nostril.

'What's the matter with you?' Sheila demanded of me.

'Yeah,' Charlie joined in. 'What the hell's the matter with you?'

I didn't say anything. I went and ran a bath, locking the bathroom door against the pair of them.

The sight of Jonquil, red-cheeked, cherubic and superbly snot-nosed, summoned this back to me. To my delight she eventually did wake up and I was very happy to reassure her and to give her a small dose of the trusty Calpol. A sound, sticky, red, gooey, medicated, measured dose. I felt useful and wanted. It was what I was after, and Jonquil went straight back to sleep. Oh, that Calpol.

I was still thinking about the business of Charlie's nose stud when Lucy returned, date in tow. When she introduced us, it made my thoughts about Charlie's stud shrink to insignificance. This joker had several gold rings through his ears, a couple of hoops in his nostril and one more ring weighting his lower lip. In addition to that the sides of his head were shaved and the hair on his crown was dressed like a topiary fowl in a hedge of yew.

'This is Mark,' Lucy said. 'I'll make some coffee.'

The greater-crested Mark shook my hand limply. I had to suppress a smile what with all these fireworks going off in his face. 'Nice to meet you, Mark.' Then I followed Lucy through to the kitchen and told her not to bother on my account, and that I'd be on my way. I didn't want to be a gooseberry.

'Stay for coffee,' she answered, but through gritted teeth, thrusting an empty mug into my hand. I stood there while the kettle boiled. Lucy put a spoonful of instant coffee granules into my mug, topped it with boiling water. 'Milk?'

We returned to the sitting room together. Mark, feet up, had made himself comfortable on the sofa, but, seeing me returning with a mug of coffee for myself after all, put his feet back on the floor and chewed his bottom lip. The TV was still running, and a late-night political debate droned softly in the background. Lucy launched into an account of their evening. Mark grunted every now and again in agreement but kept an eye on the TV. Every time I looked at him I had that Christmas song going round in my head: five gold rings and a partridge in a pear tree. He stole a glance at his wristwatch.

Apropos of nothing, Lucy said, 'Danny's been reading Baudelaire.'

'Baudelaire is cool,' said Mark, twiddling with one of his earrings.

'Which in particular?' I asked, merely to make conversation. After all, it was still quite fresh in my mind.

'All,' he said shiftily. Then, 'I don't have the head to remember specific titles.' This was put in such a way as to suggest anyone who could *remember* what they'd read was clearly an inferior person. I was about to challenge him when he changed the subject by snorting derisively at a well-known politician.

'Mark's a member of the local Conservative Party,' Lucy said with levitated eyebrows.

'Get out of here,' I said, thinking she was joking.

'So what are you?' Mark said with a sneer and a curled lip. 'Some kind of superannuated socialist?'

I didn't know what he meant by that but I was quite happy to take offence. 'I'm not anything; it's just that I can't imagine you bottling chutney and selling raffle tickets for the local Tory fund-raiser, that's all.'

Lucy smelled trouble so she dived in with, 'Danny told me he's going to Thailand.'

'Thailand? That's amazing.'

'Why amazing?'

'For someone like you.'

I looked at the fancy ironwork in his face and thought what I could have done with a pair of metal pliers. 'What am I like?' It must have come out like a growl.

'Look, I'm only saying it's good that someone of your generation is going out there. It's a cool place to go.'

'It is quite popular,' Lucy said in desperation. 'Really, very popular.'

'You could say that.' Mark had had enough. He drained his coffee mug and stood up. 'I'm outa here. *Really cool* to meet you,' he said, avoiding eye contact with me.

Fuck that, I thought. 'Like totally groovy to meet you, too.' Well, it might have been laid on with a trowel, but at least it got me a bit of eye contact before he left. I mean, I can also do irony.

After she'd seen Chuckles out the door Lucy said, 'Sorry about him. He seemed interesting when I met him. It wasn't until I'd brought him back here that I was thinking *help*!'

'He's got some fancy body plating.'

'There was a stud in his tongue which you didn't see.'

I couldn't imagine that. If I have even a tiny ulcer on my tongue I spend half my time scraping it against my teeth. 'Why the hell would anyone want a stud on their tongue?'

Lucy thrust out her own tongue and waggled it at me lasciviously. It was something I hadn't even considered. I felt first my neck and then my face flush in a crimson tide.

Her hand flew to her mouth. 'Sorry,' she said. 'I made you blush!'

There weren't that many years between us, but Lucy represented a generation with whom I was completely out of step. No woman of my own day would make such a casual sexual innuendo. We're more the seaside-postcard humorists. I decided it was time to leave before I made some silly mistake with Lucy.

'Thanks so much for doing this for me,' Lucy said, getting up to see me out.

'I enjoyed it. Really I did.'

She kissed me lightly on my cheek and our eyes met a moment too long. I loved the perfume she was wearing.

'You're a sweetie,' she said, holding my arm.

That's what I mean. I didn't know whether she was patronising me or telling me she wanted to fuck me. I'm just not good at these things.

'When do you leave for Thailand?'

'Two days.'

'Promise to tell me all about it when you get back?' She stood on the doorstep, waving me away.

10

'Jesus in pyjamas!' Mick said. 'You don't need to smoke a pipe of opium.'

This irritated me, because of the reference to Charlotte, but Mick had summed up my own initial impressions of Chiang Mai exactly. I don't know if it was the jet-lag but I felt like I was dreaming with my eyes open; too stupefied even to speak. I could tell it irritated Phil, too, because he winced visibly every time Mick made free with the Lord's name.

Yes, Phil was in Chiang Mai with us. After I'd visited him in his refrigerated domestic chapel, Phil telephoned to inform me that he'd had a long conversation with God, and that God had told him that he should come to Thailand.

'You don't have to do that,' I recall shouting down the telephone receiver.

'God wants me to.'

'But what about your duties to your church? To the people who need you? You're an Elder, for chrissakes!'

'This is a greater duty. God has been very clear to me in His direction. Charlie needs me there. You need me there. I'm coming with you and I won't be put off.'

Neither would he. I'd tried my damnedest to talk him out of it, but he was on a divine mission. I remember putting the phone down and sinking to my knees, practically biting the carpet and going, 'Jesus H. Christ,' over and over. By enormous 'good fortune' or by God's design there was, for Phil, still a seat to be had on the same flight. But by even greater fortune, Phil had had to sit at the back of the plane while Mick and I had seats over the wing.

In Chiang Mai the three of us drifted like perspiring wraiths through the swarming, spice-laden streets for over half an hour before uttering a word. I was pleased to see, at least, that Phil

49

infuriated Mick by clasping in his right hand at all times a black, leather-bound pocket-sized Bible. Phil had the look of a man prepared at any moment to stop on the street corner in order to give any passing native the benefit of a few pages.

But he couldn't, because like us he was overwhelmed. Stepping from the capsule of the air-conditioned hotel was like being plunged into a glinting tropical aquarium; people as ornate fish gliding by in fluid ecstasy, breasting strange tides, bumping up against the coral of the bewildering street commerce. Even the air seemed like fishtank water in need of a change. Meanwhile busted chattering neon and fizzing sodium lights played on the contours of the night as if on the scales of a Chinese dragon, and Mick's comment about opium pipes had broken our sweaty trance.

In the alleys of the night market, food I couldn't identify sizzled in the drum pans and the cartwheel-sized woks of street vendors, spicing diesel-thick air with onion and ginger. The throb of tuk-tuk motorised rickshaws almost drowned the shouts of little vixen girls waving from bars. Fairy lights blazed against a turquoise night sky and I mistook the flat orange moon for just another oriental lantern as my sleeves were tugged by tiny women in tribal headdress. The women I later learned to identify as Akha tribeswomen peddled trashy beads and silver bangles. Their lips were stained red. Some of them had teeth sharpened to points.

With two of these pygmy women hanging from his arm Mick said, 'I've seen everything now,' but in a way which made you know he knew he hadn't even started seeing.

Phil, his head swivelling slowly, his throat working oddly like someone who found it hard to swallow, was in a state of shock. Tuk-tuk drivers slewed to a halt to offer him women, boys, massages, fake Rolexes. It was all bang in your face, right up the nostril cavity.

'Vanity Fair,' Phil kept whispering, obscurely.

And in the sweltering heat, the three of us were steadily melting. Mick's T-shirt soaked around his big belly and in big oval floods under his arms. His hair was plastered to his forehead like someone who'd just been for a dip in the river.

Counter to the frantic street activity, the damp heat had us doped.

'A beer,' said Mick, 'or I'm dead.'

I hadn't spoken to him in almost three hours, not since the most recent of our many arguments. 'Yeah,' I conceded at last. 'Yeah.'

'Perhaps a refreshing cup of tea,' Phil tried, preposterously.

I can't bear to tell you about the flight from London to Bangkok except to report that it was a nightmare. Correction: there was nothing wrong with the flight, or the airline, or the service or anything of that sort. It was Mick who was the gibbering nightmare from the instant we reached Heathrow airport until the moment we touched down in Bangkok.

The short hop from Bangkok to Chiang Mai was tolerable insofar as Mick, exhausted from his antics on the long haul, fell asleep to complete the second leg of the journey in a pink-faced stupor. I was furious with myself for ever having left home with the overstuffed oaf. I also had to contend with Phil's silent disgust at Mick's behaviour. The pair of them enraged me in different ways, one no less than the other. The entire enterprise had become a circus.

It had been while Phil dithered uselessly and while Mick swayed and rubbed his sleepy face in the middle of the antiseptic arrivals hall at Chiang Mai airport that I arranged a hotel. You could command anything from an exploded mattress in a rotting cockroach farm (which Phil suggested would be acceptable) to an air-conditioned palace, and after I'd settled on a mid-range solution called the River View Lodge Mick emerged from his stupor to argue the toss about a taxi. He'd decided I was an easy target for rip-off merchants. It didn't seem to matter that I'd found a driver prepared to take us to the hotel for only a hundred Thai bhat. Mick waved him away, bustled outside and returned with another smiling cabbie.

'Grab your bags,' Mick told us. 'I've chipped him down to a hundred and fifty bhat. You've got to know how to deal with these little Chinkies.'

I didn't say anything. I wanted to, but you have to understand that Mick and I had had fourteen (I'd counted them while in the air between Bangkok and Chiang Mai) pretty fierce arguments over the past twenty-four hours, and he'd worn me into stony-faced submission. Phil was just keeping his head down.

Ignoring the cooing girls and the pimping tuk-tuk drivers, we walked from the hurly-burly of the night market and managed to find a bar that wasn't brimful of beautiful young prostitutes. Inside, grateful for the presence of giant electric fans, we hoisted our damp haunches on to sticky bar stools and ordered a couple of cold Singha beers. And a cup of tea for Phil. The rotating fans afforded scant relief, serving only to nudge the stifling air back and forth without cooling it. The full-on effect was one of being gently swabbed with a dirty bar towel.

Mick tipped back his beer in one go (I heard it hiss against the heat of his throat), and ordered two more. He gave a scholarly burp. 'At least the beer is all right,' he said. I ladled the sweat from my eyebrows by way of agreement while Phil nervously stirred his tea.

Despite the kaleidoscope of human activity going on in the street outside, my mind was on Charlie. It was frustrating to have arrived in this place without being able to dash to the prison to see her. The British Consulate in Chiang Mai had arranged with the prison authorities for me to visit the following morning at eleven o'clock. I was killing time, but I couldn't keep my mind on anything else.

Should I hug Charlie? Would they allow me to? Would they allow me to give her the things I'd brought with me? Sheila had filled a flight bag with soap, shampoo, cosmetic creams, jars of vitamin pills, magazines, books and God knows what else. 'Take this,' Sheila had said.

'Whatever for?'

'She loved this when she was a girl. Here, take it.'

It was a moth-eaten Rupert Bear.

I'd meant to add packets of cigarettes without even knowing if Charlie was a smoker. I suspected she was. Sheila in particular had disapproved of our children smoking, so I'd left it until I got to the airport for the duty-frees. It seemed ridiculous to deny an opium addict the comfort of a few snouts.

'Stop thinking about it,' Mick said, trying to track the

airstream of the fan with a lazy and contemplative swivelling of his chin.

'I can't.'

'Difficult,' Phil said, 'to not think about it. The father encounters the daughter in prison, so to speak.'

So far Mick's way of dealing with Phil and his double-talk was to ignore him completely or to make a tiny shake of his blond curls every time Phil spoke. His disappointment on discovering that there was to be a third member of the party was still advertised in his face. 'That's why you're so tetchy,' he said to me. 'Because you keep thinking about tomorrow. Try to relax. Both of you.'

The trouble had started even before we got on the plane at Heathrow. To begin with Mick wound me up by continually mis-pronouncing the word 'Thailand'. He and I were in the duty-free buying cigarettes for Charlie when he'd said, 'While we're in *Thighland* are we going to spend any time in Bangkok?'

'What? Why would we do that?'

He'd shrugged his shoulders, casual. 'Supposed to be a fun place, Bangkok.'

'How do you mean, "fun"?'

'Where they all go, like.'

'Where who goes?' I knew exactly what he meant.

He stuck a finger in his ear, pretending to shake his earhole free of wax. 'Sex tourism.'

'You mean you'd like to go there?' I remember smiling, encouraging.

'Just have a squint at what's going on, like.' And he winked at me.

I laid a carton of Marlboros back on the shelf and turned to him. 'I'm not going out there for sex tourism,' I said evenly.

'No, I didn't mean—'

'I'm going out there for one reason and one reason only, and that reason is Charlie.'

'No, you've got hold of the wrong end of the—'

'This isn't a jaunt or a holiday or your chance to get your fat leg over, I'm going because my daughter, Charlotte, is rotting in a filthy prison in a place called Chiang Mai.'

53

'Keep your hair on, Danny—'

'We're not going to look at nude women dancing round poles and sticking ping-pong balls up their fannies, so if you've got any of that in mind you go your own way as soon as we land in Bangkok, right?'

Then he started getting angry. 'Calm down, for Christ's sake! Look at the state of you! I was only saying—'

'I know what you were saying and you're not on.'

'— that there are things to look at while we're there and you don't have to walk the length and breadth of *Thighland* with a face like a bag of spanners. That's not going to help Charlie, is it?'

I stormed from the duty-free shopping zone in search of the suddenly preferred company of Phil, concluding what was the first of our many disputes over the next few hours. And here was Mick chugging beer in a Chiang Mai bar after his appalling behaviour, telling me to relax. 'Anyway,' he said, 'we've got to find somewhere to eat.'

Eating was the last thing on my mind. The heat had drained my appetite, and even if it hadn't the million and one pavement cafés and street vendors hadn't helped. Everyone in Chiang Mai and his sister and his sister's boyfriend was in the chomping business, from the classy silver-service eateries down to the fruit-laden bamboo mat in the rat-snarling gutter.

'What do you fancy?' I said. 'Dog in cashew nut sauce or monkey with mango?'

'Don't be ridiculous,' Mick said. 'It's just like the Chinese takeaway, or the curry house. Isn't it, Phil?'

Phil cleared his throat, touched his nose and refused to take sides.

Fine for Mick. In fact he was in his element. Back home he loved nothing better than Indian or Chinese food, whereas anything remotely spicy makes me sweaty and nasty. 'I'll find something back at the hotel.'

'Phhhht,' Mick went in disgust. 'Phhhht.' He knew that all the hotel offered in the way of food was a bar with complimentary crisps and peanuts in bamboo dishes.

But I knew better than to try to come between Mick and the

imperative of his bowels. He made it quite clear on the plane that, even if he were to be denied the fleshpots of Bangkok, he was going to more than compensate his belly with whatever culinary adventure might be on offer. He had the cabin crew running back and forth to the galley for the entire flight in the service of his belly. From the moment we boarded the plane he started. When we were *wai*d by one of those stunningly beautiful and self-effacing air hostesses, Mick touched her elbow and said, 'Now, don't pray to me darlin', just fetch the gin.'

The trouble with Mick is that when these women smiled back at him, he actually thought he was making a big hit. He didn't understand that it was in their culture to smile, to be compliant; he was too accustomed to the contrary and disagreeable nature of Western women.

'I'm *in* here,' he whispered to me as we took our seats on the plane. 'These girls think I'm a god.'

'It's called a *wai*,' I remember telling him.

'A what?'

'A *wai*. When they put their hands together like that.'

'A what?'

'Don't take the piss.' I should have known it was going to be like that not only for the duration of the flight but for the entire period we spent in Thailand. He would summon a hostess, put his hands together under his nose and offer a deep, fulsome *wai* and then would whisper to them confidentially, 'See that tiny little dinner you just brought me? Do you think you could find me another one?' And it would work every time. Another thing he found hilarious would be to catch my eye, and thereafter *wai* me as a prelude to breaking wind. Then he proceeded to get rip-roaring drunk.

Meanwhile in the bar the giant fan nudged the dirty warm air hither and thither. 'I'm fucking starving,' Mick roared. 'Let's eat.'

We made to pay for the beer; or at least Mick and I did. I hadn't noticed Phil dirty his hands with money since we'd arrived. I couldn't figure what denominations I'd got in front of me and I accidentally handed the barman a monster note. Mick snatched it back and paid the tab himself. 'Give me your money,' he bellowed.

'Why?'

'Because you're *in a state*.' This was his favourite phrase. He was always telling me I was in a state. 'Look at you: nearly gave that chap a ten-quid tip. No wonder the little fucker was smiling. You can't think straight. Your mind is in another place. Give me your fucking money. I'm in the chair.'

'Don't be ridiculous.'

'Hand it over! Mick's in the chair. And you, Phil.'

I don't know why but I felt very strange. The travel and the bombardment of strange and exotic smells had upset my stomach. I was tired from the journey and I almost had double vision. I couldn't keep my mind off my encounter with Charlie tomorrow. I was afraid I might burst into tears the moment I saw her. I was living on the edge of an emotional volcano, and every time I thought about her this fluid started collecting at the back of my eyes. Home suddenly seemed to me a desperately long way away.

I handed Mick my money. Wallet, cash, credit cards, everything. 'Phil?' he said.

Phil's fingers strayed to his pocket. Then he thought better of it. 'I really don't think that's going to be necessary.'

'Good,' Mick said, stuffing them all in the bulging money pouch fastened around his considerable waist. 'You pay your expenses, I'll take care of ours.' He'd got Phil's measure, anyway. 'Now let's go and eat a pot-bellied pig. Follow me, boys, and keep close. Mick's in the chair.'

II

I woke very early the next day, on account of the jet-lag. Phil had a room on his own, and the twin I shared with Mick had now cultivated a vegetable odour. I felt distinctly queasy. I wasn't sure if it was the prospect of seeing Charlie later that morning; the food I'd eaten the night before; or the lunar aspect of Mick's blubbery bottom peeping at me from the single sheet beneath which he slept. No jet-lag for this boy. I deliberately made a commotion in the shower, but Mick merely snorted and grunted in his sleep, so I dressed quickly and left him to it.

It was five-thirty a.m. and none of the hotel staff were about. I slipped out into the garden to have a smoke. I expected it to be cool at that time of the morning, but it was already sultry and the temperature seemed to be cranking up at the rate of one degree per minute. There was a haze made golden by the diffuse sunlight. The Mae Nam Ping river at the bottom of the hotel garden ran swift and strong, the colour of green tea. It would be another six hours before I could see my lovely Charlie, and the cigarette wedged between my fingers trembled at the thought.

A stone path wound between dribbling fountains, and the hotel garden was quite beautiful. There was a spirit house on a pole, white, as if made from wedding cake, carefully tended with flowers, figurines and offerings. A night-light flickered inside the spirit house. At the foot of the garden a sumptuous pagoda with a huge smiling Buddha overlooked the river. Burned out incense sticks clustered at the Buddha's feet. The seats in the pagoda were carved from teak, upholstered in leather, and a sign invited me in but warned me to remove my shoes. This I did, and for good measure I put out my cigarette, but then I saw an ashtray placed on the low table, so I lit another one, sat down, and watched the river flow.

I'd been torturing myself about Charlie, trying to identify

57

what exactly had gone wrong between us. I'd explored the usual psychological angles, whether it was a power thing, in that I hadn't wanted her to grow up; or whether it was a sexual thing in that fathers don't want their daughters to mature. I'd been through all that stuff, and though I knew better than to dismiss any of it, it just didn't ring true.

From the earliest times, Charlie used to love to hug me. She would run to the door when I came home from work, leaping into my arms. She would cuddle up to me when she was poorly, or tired, or sad or plain happy. Sometimes several times a day. Spontaneous, fondling displays of innocent affection, and among the greatest pleasures to be found in this fleeting life.

Then it suddenly foreclosed, when Charlie was about eleven. Funnily enough, Phil was happy to take a hug until much later, which, in a boy, surprised me. I thought he might shrink from it earlier. But he too in his time felt the need to retreat from these overt displays of affection. There was no particular incident prompting the withdrawal. It was just a sign that they were growing up, becoming independent, feeling the need to cut loose. Naturally I felt a pang at this. But you accept it. You wouldn't want it any other way.

I was startled by the presence of a figure at the entrance to the pagoda. She made me jump. It was a cleaning lady brandishing a sweeping brush. These Thai ladies move softly as a beam of light, sometimes seeming more spirit than flesh. She smiled and *wai*d me deeply, before leaving me alone. I think she noticed that my eyes were damp.

Oddly enough I never saw that same lady again.

Some time later Mick came down, looking for his breakfast. He was red-eyed and his hair stuck up like the comb on a good rooster. His ghastly army-surplus khaki shorts reached midway down his meaty calves, and he'd decided to give the hotel staff the benefit of viewing his gorgeous pink and bristly chest. 'Coffee,' he croaked.

'Put a shirt on, will you?'

He glanced around. 'Why?'

'Just put a shirt on. You're a disgrace.'

He shook his head as if I'd asked him to go native and wear a sarong, but he nipped back to the room, returning at length sporting a migraine-intensity Hawaii-style top. We had breakfast in the garden: English style bacon and eggs but with two tiny strips of bacon frazzled the way a spent matchstick is burnt. Mick growled, got up and lumbered to the kitchen. I don't know what he said, but shortly after another two dishes arrived, this time lightly cooked. Mick demolished both his and my second plate, and then set about the fruit placed before us.

I tried a piece of strange orange fruit, but it wasn't to my taste. Mick noticed and snorted.

'What is it?' I asked.

'You're fucking ignorant so you are,' he said, mopping up the last of my egg with a roll of bread. 'It's papaya. Tried to sell it on my stall but no one went for it.' He held a piece right under my beak. 'Don't you think it smells like a woman's hole?'

I waved the papaya away and removed myself from the table, ostensibly to light another cigarette. Mick sniffed the piece of fruit himself, evidently with satisfaction, and popped it in his mouth. Then he set about the pineapple. 'Have you tasted this? Marvellous! Beautiful! Su-bloody-perb! Have you? *Have you tasted this?*'

'Yes,' I lied. 'Very good.' I was trying to think how to break it to him that I didn't want him to come to Chiang Mai prison with me. I was going to have to tell him that I didn't want him there when I came face to face with Charlie. I kept rephrasing it tactfully in my head, when really what I wanted to say was: *leave us alone for a minute you big fat fuck.*

'"Very good"? Is that all you've got to say? Very good? Well I've got to get some more of this "very good" pineapple.' With that he made lumbering purposeful strides in the direction of the kitchen once more.

When he returned bearing a plate of freshly sliced pineapple, I stamped out my cigarette and said, 'Look Mick—'

'I've been thinking,' he said, rivulets of pineapple juice coursing over his unshaven chin, 'about when we go to the prison. I'll go so far in, but when it comes to you seeing Charlie I'll hang back, like.'

'Oh.'

'So's you can see her on your own, type of thing.'

'Oh. Fine.'

'Father and daughter isn't it? Brought together again. You don't need me there. You might *think* you do, but you don't.'

Phil, blinking and sleepy, joined us for breakfast.

'Here he is,' Mick said, apropos of absolutely nothing, 'Cardinal Cunt.'

Deng, the hotel manageress, brought a message that we should call the British Consulate in Chiang Mai. Our previous arrangement had been to meet the consular official, a gentleman called Brazier-Armstrong, at the prison. I telephoned and spoke to a Thai lady, who told me that Brazier-Armstrong had been called away on an emergency. She confirmed that the prison was expecting us and that all we had to do was to present ourselves at the reception.

In the hour before our appointment at the prison I had a bad attack of the shakes. My stomach was in a dreadful state. I cursed Mick for the things he'd forced me to eat the night before and I swallowed half a packet of Diocalm, which helped my condition not a jot. My fingers shook so badly Mick had to do up my shirt buttons.

'We're going to roast in these,' he complained.

'It's what we agreed. Stop whining.' We'd all three brought our best suits with us, wanting to make the best impression possible. I wasn't having Mick up there in his army-surplus shorts. So we wore collars and ties and heavy, dark English suits. 'Just remember,' I said, 'if it moves, *wai* it.'

Mick placed the palms of his hands together under his nose. 'I'll *wai* like a bastard.'

I had the flight bag full of supplies for Charlie. 'Cigarettes!' I shouted. 'I forgot the cigarettes!'

Mick produced two cartons. 'Here. I got these while you were making a prat of yourself at the airport.'

I was touched by Mick's consideration. 'Did you think of bringing anything for Charlie?' I asked Phil.

He was quite stung. 'Of course I did!' He fished a couple of items from his flight bag. One was a pocket Bible not unlike the one he carried about with him, the other was probably the very same toothbrush he had left over from Christmas.

Mick gave me an old-fashioned look.

We left the hotel in plenty of time. Mick spotted a bicycle rickshaw and hailed it. The cyclist, whom Mick insisted on referring to as a 'coolie', spoke no English. He seemed a little unhappy at the idea of squeezing the three of us into his rickshaw until Mick waved a banknote under his nose. We had to show him the prison on a map we'd picked up at the hotel.

Within minutes we were caked in sweat, making laboured progress across town. Chiang Mai was as extraordinary by daylight as it was by night. The old town was enclosed by a high eighteenth-century red-brick wall and a rippling moat populated here and there with turtles and frogs. Within its ramparts we were whisked through blossom-lined streets, alongside shining gold- and red-lacquered temples, and past crumbling, ancient chedis. The rickshaw dodged a line of monks in saffron robes and women bearing yoke-panniers. It was all fabulously exotic, but I wasn't seeing any of it, because I had a deep, doomy feeling in the pit of my bowels. Mick shifted his weight uncomfortably in the rickshaw seat, and mopped his brow with a large white handkerchief. Phil, nursing his own well-thumbed pocket Bible, looked pale and unwell.

The rickshaw man peddled up the Ratwithi and delivered us into the yard of the women's prison. I was surprised to find a modern building of white concrete; maybe I'd expected to see a rat-infested hole in the ground. Before the steps leading into the building was a statue of a Thai soldier bearing a dead infant in his arms. As Mick and Phil climbed out of the rickshaw I looked around. There was a compound of crashed vehicles. I could hear music coming from behind the small opaque windows of the cells. Towels and sheets were squeezed between the narrow openings of the windows, to air.

'Ready, Father?' I heard Phil say.

Mick touched my arm. 'Come on,' he said. 'This is it.'

He paid the rickshaw man and we went up the steps and into the prison building, three men in dark suits. A few dismal-looking Thais sat around on hard plastic chairs. A row of glass-panelled offices ran off to the right. The reception desk was empty. I was relieved to have some of my preconceptions defeated by the modern, sterile, municipal appearance of the place. Apart from the heat, it looked less foreboding than any British jug.

At last a Thai officer in a blue police shirt appeared. I *wai*d him and told him who I was. He motioned us to sit down with the other waiting Thais. Phil kept sticking his finger inside his collar to air his neck. After some minutes another officer came and took us into a small office with metal filing cabinets and a giant rotating fan. He seemed in a bad mood. All three of us *wai*d him, and when Mick offered a Western handshake I was appalled to see that he had, in the palm of his hand and folded the size of a postage stamp, a Thai banknote. The banknote was trousered in one deft move as the officer simultaneously motioned us to sit down.

The officer went outside.

'You fucking idiot!'

'I know what I'm doing,' Mick said.

'What?' said Phil, who'd missed the sleight of hand.

'We'll all be doing ten years in this fucking steam bath if you keep trying stunts like that.'

'Like what?' said Phil.

'You don't know what you're talking about. Took it, didn't he? Now listen to this. I've brought my life savings out here.' Mick tapped his bulging moneybelt. 'I've got it in big American dollar bills. If that's what it takes, it's yours.'

'What's going on?' Phil wanted to know.

I stared at Mick with my mouth open. Life savings? I had no idea what that might mean. But he was offering it as a bribe to these prison guards. I felt dizzy. The officer returned, clutching a sheaf of papers. Now he was all smiles. 'You wan see dotter, yeh?'

I nodded. 'Please.'

'Yeh, we got dotter yeh. But she no wan see you!'

'I understand that,' I said. 'The consulate told us she didn't

62

want to see me. But I have some things for her.' I patted my flight bag with the shampoos and the soaps and the cigarettes.

Mick was already folding another note into the palm of his hand, before the officer said brightly, 'No problem. You her fadder. You good for her see. We make her see you.'

'We're very grateful,' Mick said, offering a cigarette, careful to leave the open packet on the officer's side of his desk. 'Very grateful.'

'We look after her good,' the prison officer said. 'Me fadder, too. We no throw your dotter to the sharks!' He smiled and nodded and blew smoke. Mick and I smiled and nodded and blew smoke. Phil fingered his collar again, forcing a grimace. It was agonising. I was terrified that at any moment this was going to go wrong.

We smoked and smiled some more. Then the officer said he was going to see if she was ready for us.

'I'm not sure about this, Mick. How are you going to try to float it?'

He was dribbling sweat from every pore, and it wasn't just the heat. 'I don't fucking know! I'm winging it, Danny, I'm winging it. I'll try to get a moment to speak to this guy.'

The smiling officer returned and beckoned us to follow him along the corridor. He unlocked a cage door and we stepped into a compound where a few female Thai prisoners were lounging in cotton pyjamas. They looked away, bored by us. The odour of stagnant hormones and dead energy was suffocating. Then we were taken into a holding room.

'I'll stay out,' Mick said.

'No! Stay! And you, Phil.' It's true: suddenly I wanted them both there with me.

'She come now,' our officer said. 'Lady guard bring her.'

Charlie. I was going to see Charlie. We heard voices and the slopping sound of plastic sandals as they approached the holding room. The female officer came in first, bringing her reluctant prisoner behind her.

I didn't recognise her. Our eyes met, and we searched each other. Nothing was said. She, Mick, Phil and I and the two Thai prison officers stood in silence in the sweltering room. Phil was shaking his head.

'I don't understand,' Mick said at last.

I turned to the male officer. 'You can throw this one to the sharks,' I said. 'This isn't my daughter.'

12

She prodded my foot and I twitched again. 'Heart,' she said. 'You got problem wiv heart.'

Mick, feet up next to me, let out a little cry and his foot masseur giggled. 'This one got problem with—' And she didn't know the word, so turned to indicate an area at the side of her lower back.

'Liver,' I added helpfully. 'He's got a problem with his liver.'

'Gercha!' Mick shouted as his foot masseur gouged under his toes with the ball of her thumb. Mick was sceptical but I was impressed. I'd had a minor heart murmur for some time, and my foot masseur had gone straight to the diagnosis. As for Mick, who'd insisted on bringing a couple of bottles of beer in for the duration of the two-hour foot massage, it would have been surprising to find any liver there at all.

The massage had been Mick's idea. After the fiasco of the prison we'd spent a dreadful afternoon wringing our hands, failing to get any sense from the British Consulate and finally drinking too much beer in a tiny bar opposite the Tha Phae Gate. Phil had adjourned to the hotel early in the session, complaining of fatigue but clearly disapproving of what was obviously going to turn into ten rounds of wrestling with the demon alcohol.

'I'm not being funny,' Mick said after he'd gone, 'but Phil is a dead weight.'

'Yeah.' I could hardly disagree.

'It's like having a vulture on your shoulder.'

'Yeah.'

'How do you suppose he turned out like that, then? He doesn't even look like you. Are you sure he's yours?'

'Give it a rest, Mick.'

In my ignorance I thought 'Thai massage' was a euphemism

for knocking shop. Knowing nothing of the deep skills of a traditional Thai massage, I would only concede to the notion of foot massage in a place resembling more clinic than brothel.

We were invited to change into sports shorts and to relax into comfortable armchairs, feet resting on stools as two ladies of about our own age set about us with coconut oil. I heard myself venting deep sighs as my masseur dug into hitherto unknown joints and muscles in my feet. A giant ceiling fan rotated slowly, chopping at the air.

So in the massage shop I lay back, thinking about Mick's remark. It must cross every man's mind at some time. Whether a child is actually his, I mean, especially when they wind up as junkies or religious crackpots. Me, I haven't got a religious nerve in my body, but Phil is the full hair-shirt. He's even got a haircut like a monk's tonsure except for the bald spot in the middle. I expect he's looking forward to baldness with some relish. But no, though he's a little shorter than me, he's got my build exactly, and my eyes, and my habit of screwing up my eyebrows when I'm trying to figure something out. Much as some days I'd like to explain it away by thinking that Sheila did a wrong 'un, I can see he's mine right through to the marrow.

Meanwhile Mick reclined in his chair. He made his lips pop on his beer bottle. 'We've got to find that twat Brazier-Armstrong. He should have been there. He was *supposed* to be there.'

Brazier-Armstrong, whoever he was, was attracting a lot of blame from Mick. I must say I was pretty angry with the consul for not being there to sort out the confusion. We'd gone by tuk-tuk, a kind of motorised lawnmower with a sun canopy, directly from the prison to the consulate office at the IBM building on Huay Kaew Road. The journey was not without its trials as the tuk-tuk driver was incredibly persistent in trying to fix us up.

Tuk-tuk man: You wan girls?
Mick: No
Tuk-tuk man: You wan boy?
Mick: Fuck off.
Tuk-tuk man: Grass?

Mick: Just drive your fuckin' lawnmower.

Tuk-tuk man: You wan fat lady? I got pleny fat lady.

Mick: You want fat lip? No? Then shut it.

Then when we arrived at the offices they were closed, and there was no sign of the lady with whom I'd spoken earlier in the day.

We were simply left hanging out to dry.

The confusion at the prison was bad enough. I'd simply walked out on all of them. Then of course I couldn't get out of the compound without the guard unlocking the cage. When I returned everyone was talking at once, except the girl whom everyone had taken to be Charlie. When the Thai officials had established she wasn't my daughter she was whisked to her cell by the female guard, and we were taken back to the office we'd come from.

The prison officer couldn't figure out what the hell was going on. He summoned half a dozen colleagues, who in turn produced papers in triplicate with Charlie's name, date of birth and our home address in England. He also produced Thai court papers, none of which were in English. At one point we were surrounded by half a dozen blue shirts all shouting at once. The paperwork was in order, so why was I being difficult?

'She no your dotter, that girl?'

'That's what I'm trying to tell you.'

'So why you here?'

Then it would start all over again.

'She no your dotter?'

'For the hundredth time, no!'

'So who she, that girl?'

'Why don't you ask her?'

Mick had the bright idea of proposing that he and I interview the girl, but they weren't having any of that. Finally Phil suggested they get the consul down there at the double, to see what he could make of it. They phoned. Brazier-Armstrong wasn't available.

We established that there was no possibility of Charlie being elsewhere in Chiang Mai prison. It had occurred to me that she might go to some lengths to avoid seeing me. There were only four other *farang* women there in total: one American girl, one Australian and two Germans, all for charges relating to drugs. All four of them were brought to the compound for us to see, to ensure no collusion or place-swapping. (Thais think all *farang* look similar.) Charlie wasn't amongst them.

We shook hands with the officer who'd dealt with us, we *wai*d, and we left. We could still hear the officers shouting at each other as we quit the prison grounds. They were suffering badly from loss of face, and clearly hadn't enjoyed being made to look incompetent before three Westerners in heavy, dark suits. As we made our way down the sweltering street, Mick had ripped off his tie and waved it angrily at an approaching tuk-tuk. 'Bar,' he growled. 'Any bar.'

Meanwhile my foot masseur pulled at each of my toes in turn, making the bone crack. I looked into her eyes and she smiled at me shyly before resuming her work. 'Tomorrow morning,' I said. 'We'll go to the consulate first thing tomorrow morning.'

We'd spent the entire afternoon running the thing backwards and forwards, but were no closer to an explanation. I was crippled with agitation. If Charlie wasn't in Chiang Mai prison, then where the hell was she? As far as I knew, she might be back home in England. I was also left with the impact of Mick's revelation that he'd come along with me prepared to try and bribe the prison guards with his life savings. I kept stealing glances at the bulging moneybelt on which he permanently rested a fat pink hand. Naturally I was relieved that this desperate plan hadn't needed to be put into action, but what was I to make of the man who was prepared to do this for me?

Somewhere in there was another thought, one so dark that I kept trying to push it to the corner of my fevered imagination. It was the idea that Charlie might not be anywhere, that she might be dead. The thought was there, but prowling at a distance like a wild animal circling a camp fire, wanting to attack but held back by the light. I preferred to put my faith in the British Consul coming up with a sensible explanation, and, I admit, a bit of direction about what I might do next.

The masseur hit a nerve in my foot and I twitched violently. 'Heart,' she said to me softly and apologetically. 'Heart.'

There was nothing for it but to wait until I was able to see Brazier-Armstrong, to make some sense out of this.

'He should have been *there*!' Mick jabbed a finger emphatically at the floor. 'Brazier-fucking-Armstrong. At the fucking prison this morning. Pardon the French, my sweet darling,' he said to his masseur, putting down his bottle and *wai*-ing her deeply by way of atonement.

She tittered and shot a glance at her colleague.

Mick tapped my arm conspiratorially. 'See that? She fancies me.'

13

Mick was beginning to lose his temper, and the skull-cracking hangover we had in common wasn't helping. Restored to his Hawaiian shirt and calf-length shorts, Mick leaned across the desk at the consulate in a manner that might be described as menacing. Me, I'd given up on the woman. I badly needed an intake of icy, clear water to sluice away the ravages of the previous night's Singha beer.

'So what you're saying is,' Mick, wagging a finger at her, 'not only do you not know *where* Brazier-Armstrong is, but you have no idea of *when* he's coming back.'

Phil weighed in, too. He stood directly before the woman and, narrowing his eyes, placed his hands together as if in prayer, pointing his touching fingertips down at her. 'The father has come for the daughter. He *will* speak with the consul.' I don't know what the woman made of this, but his technique gave me the shivers.

The oriental concept of 'loss of face' is interesting. The woman at the consulate who had introduced herself as Mrs Duongsaa (and though she spoke impeccable English we never did find out whether she was an official, a secretary, or a general factotum) was losing hers fast. The traditional Thai smile with which she'd greeted us had slipped when we'd demanded she contact Brazier-Armstrong instantly. Before that she'd persuaded us to run through events, sympathised, expressed incredulity and promised she would 'look into' it and report back.

'When would that be?' I asked her.

'As soon as I have some information,' she replied.

'No. I want some action now. I want you to speak to the prison authorities immediately.'

Very sweetly she assured us that enquiries would be made,

that something had obviously gone seriously wrong, and that there were a lot of formalities to be negotiated.

'Stuff all that,' Mick had said. 'Where's Brazier-Armstrong?'

The maintenance of 'face' is conducted by smiles, sympathetic expressions, gentle indirection, and by body language signalling control and competence. When Mick asked for Brazier-Armstrong, Mrs Duongsaa looked as though he had slapped her. Now he was *in* her face, and her features had stiffened visibly.

Mr Brazier-Armstrong was away on unavoidable business. Mr Brazier-Armstrong could not be contacted. Mr Brazier-Armstrong had not been specific about when exactly he would be back in the office. That's when I'd asked *where*, exactly, the consular official was *at that moment*. Mrs Duongsaa was unable to be specific *at that moment*. Now her face was paralysed, though her eyes were moist with hatred.

I'd slumped in a chair. The more I tried to think about how we were going to make progress in this impossible situation, the more grinding was my hangover. After the foot massage of the previous evening I'd allowed Mick to talk me into getting smashed out of my head. We'd ended up in the Corner Bar on Loi Kroa, a neon-lit shed full of pretty young prostitutes. They made me laugh, and even with Mick trying to wind me up, I didn't implicate myself beyond buying a few beers. Sweet girls, all of them, and all about Charlie's age.

Mick made me snort when he suggested, 'There is no Brazier-Armstrong, is there? He doesn't exist. There's just you and this desk.'

'Ha!' went Phil.

Stung, Duongsaa was about to reply when the telephone rang, but it was Mick who snatched it up. Duongsaa got to her hind legs in protest, but Mick danced a couple of steps backwards, informing the caller, 'The British Consulate in Chiang Mai is closed while we sort out this fiasco with Chiang Mai prison. Goodbye. Who am I? I'm the British Ambassador in a purple vest, so fuck off.' He placed the receiver back on its cradle with exquisite gentility. Duongsaa was still remonstrating when Mick added, 'We're going to stay here by this phone until you get Brazier-Armstrong.'

Snatching up a cellphone Duongsaa tapped out a number. When she got a response she spoke in rapid Thai, staring at us icily throughout the conversation. Something that was said on the other end made her voice go up an octave. When she'd finished she said, 'Mr Brazier-Armstrong will come to see you at your hotel.'

'Breakthrough!' said Phil.

'When?' I demanded.

'Today if possible. Maybe tomorrow.'

'So why did you lie to us about not being able to contact him?' Mick wanted to know.

'Never mind that,' I said. 'You tell him he'd better be there.'

'You got what you want!' she said, her voice shrill. 'Now you go!'

'And if he doesn't come,' Mick said, 'we'll be back here tomorrow.'

'And I get the police.'

'You do that,' Mick said, puce in the face. 'And I'll give 'em five hundred dollars and they'll kick your fat arse all the way to Bangkok. I know how this country works.'

I steered him towards the door. 'That's enough. Let's go. I really do need a glass of water.'

'Water,' said Phil. 'Water is good.'

But there are more things in life to lose than just 'face'. I knew a man who had lost a daughter when she was only seven. She'd contracted a rare form of leukaemia and he had to watch her perish.

You have two incontrovertible wishes when you are a parent. One is that you will die before they do, because it is terrible ill luck to have to bury one of your own children. The second is that you in turn will live long enough to see them grow to a ripe age. In the years when Charlie became 'lost' to me, even though I knew she was still alive and just not speaking to me, my mind often turned to this poor man whose little girl had died.

You see, he never got over it. There is no getting over it. The world for him after that was a changed place. He once said to me it was as if somehow overnight two or three of the colours of

72

the visible spectrum had been withdrawn. The sense of loss shot through everything. Before this happened to him, he was a rather arrogant man, always treating everyone to his views on this or that subject; but, and beyond all his deserts, he was so humbled by nature through this event that he even seemed to discard his opinions.

Back at the hotel the afternoon following our shouting match in the British Consulate, Phil intuited what was in the back of my mind. 'I think it's time we asked God to help us, don't you?' he said. 'Come into my room, where it's quiet.'

I remember shaking my head at him, minimally, the way you shake your head when someone offers you a cigarette of inferior brand. I don't believe in God, you see, so I had to stop this tiny voice inside myself from doing what Phil wanted, which was praying that Charlie was still alive.

I retreated to the shaded side of the swimming pool. There I found an English-language daily newspaper called the *Bangkok Post*, and in it I read a story which left a bad taste in my mouth for the rest of the day. It was a case of drug smuggling. A mother with a baby in her arms had been arrested trying to leave Thailand. Her baby was dead. It had been dried, eviscerated and stuffed with high-grade heroin.

When some of the heat had burned off the day, I decided to visit a very old Buddhist temple we'd passed that morning. To be honest I thought it was a way of finding a few moments of quiet reflection on my own. I made all kinds of tactful remarks to Mick and Phil, that they needn't baby-sit me, that maybe they had things of their own to see, but they stuck to me like shit on a baby's blanket.

The temple was an oasis in the madness. The pagoda roof sweated and glittered like spun gold in the haze of the evening sun. Mick got his camera out to photograph the carved dragons at the entrance. He and I were about to take off our shoes to go into the shady interior – not Phil, he wasn't going to smudge himself in the proximity of heathen idols – when we were distracted by a small movement a little way off. It was an elderly

Buddhist monk in saffron robes, squatting under a bo tree. No, he wasn't meditating: he was enjoying a cigarette.

Mick snorted. 'A monk having a fag!' he said. 'That says it all!'

'Not very spiritual,' Phil agreed sniffily.

The 'all' that this scene spoke to Mick eluded me, but he approached the monk waving his camera. The monk was quite happy to be snapped. Then Mick sat down beside the monk and produced his own pack of ciggies. I took the opportunity to slip off my shoes and dart inside the temple. 'Coming inside?' I asked Phil.

He hung back. 'No, I think I'll take a stroll.'

I'd given him my permission to change out of his heavy serge trousers and his starched white shirt, but he was committed to sweating it out. 'But it will be cool inside.'

'No, I'll not come in.'

Something about the expression on Phil's face took me by surprise. His thumb stroked the leather cover of his scriptures, a nervous, smoothing tic I'd noticed before. I suddenly realised how he filtered all of this: the drugs, the prison, the prostitution, the heathen temples. We were in a trough, a hollow of deep sinfulness, treading a path of spiritual danger where even the beautiful old pagoda temple was an emblem of menace. Where I saw only a lacquered dragon, he saw a house of graven images; where I could smell only incense, he sniffed the breath of the serpent. The dragon within the temple rolled its lascivious tongue, waiting to lick him with all the poison impiety of a heathenish faith.

He waved his Bible at me in a parting gesture and hurried out of the temple grounds, as if afraid I might try to persuade him further. Letting him go, I stepped inside the temple.

It was indeed cooler within, but bright, not dark like a Western place of worship. The interior was painted red, like a lacquered box. A few tiny candle flames flickered at the foot of an immense brass Buddha, reflecting mildly on his polished breast, cheek and forehead. I sat down on the creaking, varnished teak floor.

The Buddha's huge painted eyes gazed down at me, neither

74

sympathetic nor hostile, but yet involved. Suddenly I vented a deep, distressed sigh. The sigh was so noisy and overstated that I felt embarrassed for myself; I even looked round, but the temple was otherwise empty. It was as if I'd been holding my breath since stepping off the plane. Then it happened again, involuntary as a sneeze with my body shaking slightly, and my profound sigh was absorbed into the nooks and crannies of the temple.

I'd spent the last forty-eight hours steeling myself against the gaudy carnival of life outside; the Ferris-wheel of exotica; the sensual onslaught; the terror at what I'd find in Chiang Mai prison; the disappointment and speculation that had followed. Now the simple act of walking into the temple had punctured my distress. I closed my eyes and held my head in my hands, waiting for another discharge to rip through me.

After a good while, I don't know how long, I felt a quiet presence come up from behind and settle down next to me. I didn't look up. If it was Mick I wasn't ready to talk to him yet. His sleeve brushed mine. Perhaps he saw my distress, but I was glad that for once he had the sensitivity not to say anything. It was so quiet in there that I heard his level breathing, at least until it fell into rhythm with mine, or perhaps mine with his. He sat there with me for ten minutes, and his silent presence had a calming effect. When I opened my eyes he'd gone again. I got up and walked outside.

Mick was sitting under the bo tree, bathed by the hazy light. The monk had gone. I sat down beside him, taking one of his proffered cigarettes. He was chuckling to himself. It turned out that the monk had spent several years in Birmingham, and his English had a heavy Midlands inflection. Mick had been treated to a short lecture on Buddhism, and decided I too should have some of the benefit. He started telling me about the Eightfold Path: right words, right action and the rest of it.

'That's great, Mick. You've shared a snout with a monk and now you're a Zen master.'

He was stung. 'Don't take the piss!'

'Shall we go?'

Mick scrambled to his feet and kicked off his shoes. 'Let me have a look inside the temple first.'

'But you've already been in.'

'No I haven't. I'll only be a minute.'

'Well who came in while I was in there? Was it the monk?' Mick looked at me oddly. 'No one went in.'

'Are you sure?'

'Not while I've been here. Why?'

'Nothing. You go inside.'

Mick had to be mistaken. A very distinct someone had squatted down next to me. I'd clearly felt them brush against my clothes. I'd heard them breathing. My skin flushed at the thought. I shivered, and concluded that the heat was getting to me. I felt dizzy again.

I suppose Mick had a point. About the monk, I mean. Is it feasible that you would turn up at the Nirvana gates with a lighted ciggie on the go? I was ready to return to the hotel, to take a nap. I waited until Mick had achieved enlightenment and was struggling back into his sandals. I asked him one last time, trying to make light of it, 'Are you sure that monk didn't come inside while I was in there?'

'Sure I'm sure,' he said. 'What's eating you?'

I was so disturbed by this experience I almost decided to explore it with Phil at the hotel. I tapped softly on his door. I seemed to have caught him in the act of sitting upright on a hard chair, since he returned to it as soon as he'd let me in.

'Phil?'

'Yes, Father?'

'Phil. At the temple. Today.'

'Yes, Father?'

'What would you say? About something.'

'Yes?'

'No, it's nothing really.'

'No?'

'No. Not at all.'

It was a hell of a conversation. I had to let myself out, leaving

Phil utterly nonplussed. I couldn't stand the expression on his face as he sat on his hard chair.

Much later, in my own room, I was having a dream. There was an old woman with a face carved out of wood. She was ringing a small temple bell, right in my face. The bell became the room telephone. I rolled over in bed and picked up the receiver.

'Yes,' I croaked. 'Yes. I'll be down in ten minutes.'

Mick blinked sleepily from his bed. 'What?'

'Brazier-Armstrong. He's in reception now. You go back to sleep. I can handle him.'

'No fucking way,' Mick said.

14

I found Brazier-Armstrong in the bar, perched on a high stool with his legs crossed. He was twiddling a straw in a tall glass full of some poisonous-looking green stuff. I suppose I was shocked at how young he was. I'd expected more formality, not this youth in a T-shirt and cotton trousers. Perhaps I wanted someone in a white suit and straw fedora. In fact he was in his thirties, but the long blond fringe dangling in his dewy blue eyes made him look fresh from the university debating club. He turned and caught me studying him.

'Ah!' he cried, jumping from his stool and extending a hand. 'You must be Mr Innes! So glad to catch up with you at last!' He made it sound as if I was the one being evasive. But he fixed me with smiling eyes and a huge grin, and shook me warmly by the hand as if we were old friends. As if we'd been together in the same debating team, it seemed to me. 'Let me get you a drink.'

'Juice,' I said.

I was expecting him to bring up the unpleasantness at his office, but he never mentioned it. He gave me a long, complicated explanation about how he'd been summoned to a neighbouring province to sort out a problem which, when he got there, was already solved. During this Mick slipped quietly on to the bar stool next to me. I introduced them to each other. Mick sniffed as they shook hands.

'Daniel and I were just having a drink. Do let me get you one.'

Mick looked at me and said, 'I'll have a beer, *Daniel*.'

Brazier-Armstrong chattered about the size of the area he was expected to cover. His mouth seemed to produce an excess of saliva, because every now and then he stroked his lips with a long and elegant white finger. He was a bag of nerves with a diploma from charm school. Or from public school, more like.

One of the more expensive ones. Brazier-Armstrong looked like he might be a useful number three bat on the Eton cricket pitches.

A working-class bloke takes a mild dislike to you, and you know it immediately; whereas you can be utterly despised by a middle-class person, and you will never discover the fact until much later. I can see how this has benefited the middle rank; they depend on upward mobility, ingratiating themselves and minimising social conflict. The working mob has less to gain from dissembling.

I don't know whether to conclude from this that the middle classes are dishonest or the working classes are thick, but at that moment Mick was resisting all Brazier-Armstrong's seductive smiles and gay chatter by staring at me with one eyebrow cocked at altitude. Half turning to the man he said, 'So you're the British Consul then?'

'For my sins,' Brazier-Armstrong replied with a gallant laugh, swinging slightly and a little girlishly on his bar stool.

'God help us.'

There was a silence while we absorbed the waves made by this remark. Brazier-Armstrong let his shoulders dip, and his face became serious. 'Joking apart, we might need a wee bit of God's help the way this case is turning out. At the moment I'm doing everything in my power to make sense of a very *hairy* situation. I've come here directly from the prison. I can tell you' – and here he resumed some gaiety – 'that you've got them running around like headless chickens.'

'It's not funny,' Mick said.

'Indeed not. Not funny at all. I was about to update Daniel on what we know.'

'Let's have it then,' I said.

'The girl in the prison. Her name is Claire Marchant. She was arrested on drugs trafficking charges. She was carrying what now appears to be your daughter's passport. She has admitted that she stole it.'

'When? Where?'

'This we don't know. She doesn't look unlike the passport

photograph, so she has been successful in passing herself off to the Thai authorities since her arrest.'

'When did she steal the passport? Can't you make her tell us?' Mick put in.

'We're trying to get this information. The trouble is that Marchant has got nothing to lose. Assuming she doesn't get the death penalty, she's already facing life imprisonment. I'm afraid she's not in a co-operative mood.'

'No problem,' Mick said, slamming down his beer and climbing off his stool. 'To the prison. Slip the guards a few dollars for five minutes in the cell with her. Let's go.'

Brazier-Armstrong pushed at some imaginary force between his knees. 'Slow down, gentlemen! There are ways of doing things in this country. I can understand any impatience you might be feeling—'

'No you fucking can't,' Mick said.

'— but there is a correct procedure and it will get us what we want. You've been patient up until now. Just a little longer, and we can unearth whatever there is to know. I'm going back to the prison right now to interview Marchant myself.'

'Can we come along?' I asked.

'The prison authorities said no. I already asked. I appeal to you, Daniel, to leave this to me. I can deal with the unpleasantness and the waiting around at Chiang Mai prison. Meanwhile I recommend that you both relax as far as possible and take advantage of the many pleasures Chiang Mai has to offer. Let me take the strain.' He was already up off his stool as Phil showed up. 'I will report back to you as soon as there is anything to tell you.'

He jabbed out a hand that wanted shaking again, saw Mick's face and thought better of it. Then he was gone. We watched him leave the hotel grounds to wave his finger at a passing tuk-tuk.

Mick was disgusted. 'His shit's still yellow. *Daniel.*'

'Who was that?' Phil wanted to know.

'Let's give him a chance,' I sighed.

'And another thing,' Mick said, picking up the bar tab. 'The little runt didn't pay for the drinks.'

15

Brazier-Armstrong failed to get back to me, as he'd faithfully promised he would, within the next twenty-four hours. In that period he became Mick's favourite topic of conversation. It had come as a shock to him to see the type of floppy-haired individual responsible for representing British interests abroad. As a tax-payer he speculated about how many Brazier-Armstrongs there were dotted about the globe, and at what expense; as my friend and aide in this expedition, he doubly hated him for his apparently ineffectual offices.

I couldn't get quite so steamed up about the prat. It wasn't his fault that Charlotte had come this way to be parted from her passport by a drugs runner. Even though I was half out of my mind with frustration I knew that blaming this soppy public schoolboy wasn't going to help the situation.

Phil, like me, thought we should give the man a chance to do his best. Mick on the other hand wanted to return to the consulate and kick his arse with a spiked boot. Meanwhile we flopped by the hotel pool, drank beer (or tea in Phil's case), had another foot massage (or didn't, in Phil's case), and ate a green curry (yes, he joined us for that) which made those familiar giant blisters of sweat appear on my forehead before I'd even dipped my spoon in the stuff.

So we lounged by the pool. Where Mick sported dazzling fluorescent lime-green knee-length swimming trunks, Phil lay on his sunbed in stiff white shirt, black trousers, black socks and black shoes. After half an hour of this, and wickedly taunted by Mick, he allowed himself to take off his shoes and socks, neatly stowing them under his bed.

I lay on my own sunbed trying to ignore the pair of them by opening one of the books I'd brought with me. My fantasies had turned to England, and misty, damp autumnal mornings or to the sudden, short downpours of April. I thought of walks along the foggy canal towpaths and of mud-squelching football pitches. I was homesick already.

My book was *A Season in Hell* by Rimbaud. I was still determined to get to the bottom of what these dopers were up to. Of course, given recent developments, I had no evidence that Charlie had any connection with drugs whatsoever. But I suspected otherwise, especially if she'd allowed drugs traffickers like that creature in Chiang Mai prison to get near enough to steal her passport. I was raking through these books looking for references to opium and its effects.

As for Rimbaud, well. A complete prick. I won't even waste your time telling you what this one was about. Half of it sounded like it was scribbled by a teenager giddy on his first bottle of cider. The book would still be lying on the bottom of the hotel swimming pool if Mick hadn't fished it out. So I moved on to trying to make sense of Thomas De Quincey's *Confessions of an English Opium Eater*.

I almost gave up on that, too. You plough through several pages of complete waffle before he even mentions opium. There is a lot of musing about De Quincey's childhood, and then several miserable passages about a rotten time he was having in London where he got mixed up with a prostitute called Ann. I don't see what that has to do with opium, but you keep reading it in the hope that soon he will get to the point.

Finally, after much whining about how difficult life is (this a young gentleman of the early nineteenth century – he ought to have thrown in his lot with the common people for a week), we get the thing named. One of his cronies from Oxford University suggested he use opium to treat a headache. (Oxford University – there's that place mentioned again – someone ought to take it down brick by brick.) While studying at Oxford he started to use opium on a regular basis. If he hadn't, I daresay he would have written a better book.

It was while we were sweating by the pool that we got a message from Brazier-Armstrong that made Mick apoplectic with rage. He'd been 'called away' for a few days and would report back to us the instant he returned.

'The little shite!' Mick roared. He pulled on his shirt and shorts and buckled on his moneybelt.

'Oh dear,' Phil said, 'you'd better keep him on a tight leash.'

'Where are you going?' I shouted

'You two stay here!'

I trotted after him, in wet swimming shorts and bare feet, to the front of the hotel. 'I don't want you causing trouble at the consulate. You'll make things worse.'

'I'm not going to the consulate.' He flagged a tuk-tuk from across the street.

'So where *are* you going?'

The tuk-tuk driver gave me a wide, toothless grin as Mick hoisted his bulk into the back of the three-wheeler. Mick barked at him to go and I was left standing in a cloud of filthy exhaust.

I went back to the poolside. Phil was also on his feet by now. 'I'm not certain how wise it was of you,' Phil opined, 'to bring Mick along. We've got to take steps to contain him.'

'Contain him? What do you suggest, Phil? Extra Bible classes?'

I flung myself into the pool. I was worried. On the one hand I was afraid Mick might do something stupid to spoil any possibility of assistance and co-operation we might have. Brazier-Armstrong was elusive and ineffectual, but his local knowledge and contacts were all we had. On the other hand, Mick's blundering around was making things happen. If relations got too bad I could always blame everything on him and send him home. With Phil still glowering at me from under angry knitted brows I dried myself, ordered a whisky from the bar, and buried my head in Thomas De Quincey so I could stop thinking about these things.

It wasn't easy. The De Quincey is written in a long-winded and old-fangled style, very different to today. Maybe it's the pace of today's life that makes writing so different. Perhaps in those days they had all day to say things in. Either that or we've got less things to say, but whatever the reason, old De Q was taking me round the houses before he was going to actually give anything away about this opium business.

One rainy Sunday afternoon he'd gone down from Oxford to

London and, on the advice of a student friend of his, he bought a shilling's worth of laudanum from a chemist in Oxford Street. (I don't know why Oxford keeps cropping up – this sort of thing can make you paranoid.) I had to read on a bit before I found out that laudanum is opium dissolved in alcohol, so I suppose he was getting the double effect. I remember pausing at this point to look at the glass of whisky in my hand. I'd been feeling so strange and queasy since arriving in Chiang Mai I had the crazy idea that maybe these Thailanders lace their booze with opium.

Anyway, he drank this laudanum. I've no idea why he called his book *Confessions of an English Opium Eater* when he spent his time drinking the stuff rather than eating it. I felt slightly misled. When I thought of De Quincey I imagined him hiding in cupboards or dark rooms, chewing on some resinous black chunks of opium; this information changed the picture altogether. Now I pictured him sitting in front of a fireplace topping up his glass of laudanum from a decanter. So why not call the book *Confessions of an English Opium Drinker*? Perhaps he thought it didn't sound so good.

Before discovering opium, what he used to do whenever he had a headache was to dunk his head in icy water. I can't think what good that did him, but evidently the opium was much better. Not only did it relieve his headache, it also gave him 'an abyss of divine enjoyment'. He was shown 'celestial pleasures' in the 'Paradise of Opium-Eaters'. But he also knew, even in that first rush, where it was taking him, because he added that he experienced the 'lowest depths of the inner spirit'. I take that to mean he knew, right from the beginning, that he was on a staircase down.

The book slipped from my hand as I fell into a doze. De Quincey, in his early nineteenth-century frock-coat, was leading me down a staircase, lighting the way with a candle. He was an irritating little chatterbox, and I wasn't listening to him because I was too preoccupied with what was happening at his feet. The staircase was forming beneath us as we moved down it. Sometimes we had to wait a few seconds for it to manifest and solidify, and I was nervous because the descent seemed to go on for ever. The odd thing about the dream was that I'd been brought there by De Quincey to install electrical wiring all the way down, about which he was very happy; but I kept rubbing my chin and thinking, heck, this is going to be a *big* job.

When I woke Mick was standing over me, silhouetted, the sun behind his head. I couldn't see his features, but in my befuddled state his figure looked ominous, menacing. I sat up too quickly. My head swam. 'What's cracking off?'

Mick stripped off his shirt and shorts and belly-flopped into the pool, as if he wanted to hurt the water. The huge splash was a deliberate affront to the tranquillity of the afternoon. He climbed out, jiggled his finger aggressively at the wax and water in his left ear, and flung himself on the sunbed beside me, face averted.

Phil came over to find out the latest.

'Well?' I said.

'Do you know that bar up by the Tha Phae Gate?' Mick muttered into the pillow of his sunbed.

'Yes.'

'I think we'll try that one tonight.'

That was all we could get out of him.

16

Mick was in a leery mood that evening. He showered with bellicose energy, blowing like a harpooned whale, water and foam everywhere; he shaved with minute attention, flicking his razor aggressively at the soapy water; and he triple-dosed on the after-shave lotion. He was, he announced, preparing for a skinful of ale, and when I indicated I might be content to hang around the hotel, he told me to go ahead, that I should only do what I wanted to do. 'Stay in with Cardinal Cunt,' he snorted.

In the end I thought I'd better tag along, just to act as a smoking brake on a wheel already spinning before we'd left the hotel grounds. 'I can't believe,' Phil said, 'that the pair of you are cheerfully marching off to a brothel.'

'It's a bar, not a brothel for crying out loud!' I told him.

'As far as I can see, all *bars* in this town are *brothels*!'

'Come out with us.'

He shook his head sadly. 'The father and his friend go a-whoring.'

'Don't stand there arguing with him,' Mick shouted. Then, '*Thighland* by night!' he roared to the otherwise empty hotel lobby, and we left Phil to write his postcards.

These vixen girls, they grab your hand, pinch your arse and stroke your thigh trying to reel you into the bars. The escape policy is to be jocular and friendly as you pass on by, but Mick wasn't in a pass-on-by mood. He was soon draped by gorgeous Thai whores while I sat next to him nursing a beer and disappointing their friends. Nonetheless, after standing these girls a drink he drained his own glass, and with a cry of, 'Onward, Daniel!' pitched in a reedy voice intended to mimic our dear consul, we were up and out and making progress to the next tiny, neon-lit grotto brimming with teenage sirens.

The girls didn't let him go easily. They had a good nose for a man in a storm, and in the third cavern he actually walked out with two petite prostitutes hanging from his neck. They made it twenty yards down the street, ultimately dropping off him like petals from a blown rose. It wasn't until the sixth bar and his twelfth beer, somewhere along the Kotcasan, that he began to slow down.

I was getting a bit worried about the state of his head. He was still the custodian of my money, and I suggested he give it back to me.

'Fuck off,' he said, standing two more starry-eyed virgins a drink. 'None of this is coming out of your stash.'

'That's not what I'm worried about.'

'Mick's in the chair. Enjoy yourself. Talk to one of these little ticklers.'

I guess I was being cold with the girls, but I didn't want to encourage them, or make them think I would pay to have them. I made some remark about AIDS.

'Look!' he snorted, nostrils flaring, nose-hair bristling at me. 'We're joking. We're laughing. We're singing. That's all we're doing. I've never been surrounded by so many pretty, smiling girls in my life. What I will do next, I don't know. But I'm not fucking stupid. Now get that sour, kicked-dog expression off your face, loosen up, and get off my back.' He turned his attentions to his pretty entourage.

I wasn't offended. I went to the bar and ordered myself another beer. A girl with hair like a bolt of shimmering black silk glided on to the next stool, sliding a draughtboard under my nose. 'Wanna play?' She showed me perfect teeth and a mythological Thai smile. 'What your name?'

'Daniel, evidently.'

'Daniel Evidently, pleased to meet you. Me, Air.' And she began counting out the draughts.

Air was charming. More than that. I bought her a vodka and we played two games of draughts. I said I was hot; she fanned me with a magazine. I put a ciggie in my mouth; she lit it for me and fetched me an ashtray. She contrived to make these small things look like the most fun she'd had all year. I made it very plain I wasn't looking for a girl. She said she didn't mind. '*Farang* no like me,' she said.

I said I didn't believe her, and she laughed prettily at my immense wit. There was a pool table at the back of the bar, so we played a couple of frames; but she was expert, and skinned me both times. Mick by now was happily ensconced with one dazzlingly beautiful Thai woman I hadn't noticed earlier. The others had drifted away, beaten by this spectacular competition. I asked Mick if he was ready for another beer. So entranced was he by this beauty queen that he peered at me as if through opaque glass.

'Sure. Haul in a vodka and tonic for Mae-Lin here.'

He introduced us. Mae-Lin, fragrant and graceful with lovely, delicate cheekbones gently shook my hand. I felt a little kick inside me as her fingers brushed mine. I could see why Mick was spellbound. She was bewitching. I couldn't imagine why a woman like that would have to resort to prostitution.

'Mick told me 'bout you just now.'

'He did?'

'Oh yes. He say you good man.'

She was flirting with me. Her flashing eyes were completely unambiguous. I wondered if she was inviting me to compete with my friend for her. Shockingly beautiful as she was, I wasn't prepared to do that. I made some throw-away remark, and turned to challenge Air to one last game of draughts.

Halfway through the draughts Mick asked me if I wanted to take Air to a nightclub called Blue Valentine. Mae-Lin wanted to go there. Air shrugged when I said no, that I was ready for my bed.

'She's not on the game, you know,' Mick whispered in my ear.

'You don't have to explain to me. Enjoy yourself.'

'Seriously. She told me. She knows one or two of the girls here and was on her way to this club where she's a DJ. Well, you know me. She made it clear she wasn't a prostitute, like. Why don't you come along?'

It was true, he did have something seriously in common with Mae Lin. Mick had an old set of decks, a tangle of lights and a vast collection of seven-inch vinyl discs. He did weddings and funerals ... no, not funerals, but family parties and the like. I guess this made him a DJ too, though I couldn't see why he needed to justify it to me. Anyway, I wasn't up for it. 'Honestly Mick, I'm whacked.'

He unbuckled his moneybelt, fished out a few small denomination notes, and thrust the belt into my chest. 'You're on duty, *Daniel*.'

'Fair enough.' No, he wasn't so stupid after all. 'Off you go. Enjoy yourself. I'll pay up here.'

Mick wanted to splash his boots out the back before leaving, and Mae-Lin and I chatted while she waited. Red and blue neon light skidded off her lustrous jet-black hair. She was perfect. Her exquisitely manicured hands fluttered like white birds as she adjusted the high collar of her blouse. It was an entirely unconscious movement, as if she was trying to hide something. It drew my attention to her throat, and that's when I saw a tiny scar, almost obscured by cosmetics. I looked at Mae-Lin again. She was rather taller than the average Thai woman. Then I looked at her hands.

My God, I thought. That is good. That is *very*, *very* good.

I was dumbfounded.

Mick came out of the toilets, rubbing his hands together, chipper, larky, ready to leave, and I thought I'd better find a way to tell him. Then I thought, no, if you don't know, after everything that's been said and done, then that's your look-out. As they left the bar and climbed into a tuk-tuk, I saw them squeezing up close together.

It was something in the pearly air. It was in the hallucinatory vapours that comprise the atmosphere of Chiang Mai. When you see two people falling in love you don't intervene. You don't try to break a moment of grace, not for anything.

I turned and saw Air looking at me. Oh yes, she'd seen me clock it. Mae-Lin was her friend. She clasped her hands together in a gesture of supplication which said, say nothing. It was unnecessary.

'But I need one more beer before I go,' I said.

'I get it for you,' Air said sweetly. 'You good man.'

At the hotel, I passed Phil's room. Light was bleeding under the door, so I knew he was still up. I thought about tapping on the door to let him know I was back, but I didn't bother. I thought of him sitting upright on his hard chair. I don't know what it was about the bloke but I couldn't even imagine him going to bed. I pictured him standing upright in a corner of the room all night, hands held stiffly at his sides.

A few hours later I heard Mick's key hit the lock from outside as he let himself into our room. He flicked on a side light, but I made out I was asleep. He blundered about, crashing into furniture, huffing and puffing in the bathroom, making such a commotion he was obviously trying to wake me. I pretended to sleep on.

At last he threw himself into bed and switched off the light. I heard him sighing and moaning in the dark, and his bedsprings complaining as he tossed and turned. At last I heard him sit up. 'Danny!' he hissed. 'Danny!'

I twitched slightly in my feigned slumber, popping my lips at the air the way sleeping drunks do, pretending to snooze on.

'Danny! I want to talk!'

I was trying not to snort, so I buried my head deeper into my pillow, blissful in the deepest of deep sleeps.

'Danny! I know you're awake! I need to talk, you bastard! Danny! Hey, Danny!'

17

I was wakened the next morning by a sound like a herd of pigs being driven to market. It was only Mick, snoring into his pillow. I got up and slipped quietly out of the room.

While he slept on I was enjoying a cigarette in the pagoda. Honey-coloured sunlight filtered through the haze, nestling in the folds and ripples of the swift-flowing green river, when Brazier-Armstrong showed up. Even though he wore dark glasses, I must say he looked terrible, like someone who hadn't had a wink of sleep. 'Good morning,' he said, flashing me a very unconvincing grin. He made to step inside the pagoda.

'Shoes,' I pointed out.

'Of course,' he said, slipping off his sandals. He looked around nervously, perhaps for signs of Mick.

I love that. When you get someone who obviously thinks they are superior, and you are able to pull them up on some small matter of good manners or common courtesy. It's terrific. I thought I'd lay it on a bit thicker for him. 'You should always remove your shoes before entering a temple or a shrine. Always.'

'I know.' He was very short with me.

'You can have a cigarette though.' I offered him one. 'They don't seem to mind that.'

'Not for me, thank you. Look here, Mr Innes, I really must object, in the strongest possible terms, to your colleague's behaviour.'

Yes, I was *Mr Innes* now. One little chat about shoes and Brazier-Armstrong wanted to go all formal on me. Or perhaps it wasn't the shoes. Perhaps it was about something Mick had told me in the night that had Brazier-Armstrong in such a state.

Mick hadn't given up trying to wake me. In fact he'd got out of bed and whisked the sheets off me, grabbing and twisting my big toe until I had to give up faking, and we grabbed a couple of beers from the room fridge and took them down to the pagoda, where we talked for two hours. Yes, it was mostly about Mae-Lin; but Mick also revealed what he'd been up to in the afternoon, when he'd raced off in a tuk-tuk.

He was in a lather over Mae-Lin. The way he told it to me, he was smitten from the moment she'd entered the bar. I could understand that – as I told you, her appearance was nothing less than stunning. Speaking man to man as we sat in the pagoda, with night-lights burning at the foot of the Buddha, he disclosed that he'd nursed an erection from the moment she sat down next to him, and that it hadn't subsided until her sudden revelation some hours later.

'Hadn't gone to do anything about it,' he assured me. 'To the Blue Valentine, I mean. Honestly wasn't thinking about getting my leg over. Honestly. But I felt great, I mean *really great* in her company. His company. Her company. Oh, Jesus! Look, we necked a beer or two, and when the time came round for Mae-Lin to do her short DJ spot, I found out this gal was an R 'n' B fan! The real thing! Knew the fuckin' lot, *a* to *z*, side to side, top to bottom.'

Up until that point, all Mick was having to deal with was an inflating lust, but this complication exploded his condition into the raptures of dewy-eyed love. As well as storing in his head an encyclopaedic knowledge of the history of pop music, Mick's lean-to garage outside his house was where he filed his huge collection of Stax and Motown originals. Here Mae-Lin might come dangerously close to unseating his notions of confirmed bachelorhood. And there are, as everyone knows, two turntables on a DJ's deck.

As he told it to me, Mae-Lin let him stand behind the deck at the Blue Valentine as they made their canoodling selections together for a half-empty dance floor. They came from behind the decks to dance together, smooching up close for Al Green, Marvin Gaye, Otis Redding, the works.

Then Mae-Lin cut the spot short so that they could sit together in the shadows, and hold hands, and kiss. It was accelerating out of control. The beer. The music. The smell of

Mae-Lin's hair. The seductive, heady atmosphere of a Chiang Mai evening. In the Blue Valentine, Mick encountered more promise of celestial bliss than anything to be found in the corrosive bowl of an opium pipe.

Why not? People fall in love. And if you walk away from that it's like abandoning a new-born baby on the steps of a church.

But Mick still suspected that Mae-Lin was a prostitute. She reassured him several times on that score, but Mick persisted in asking her why, if she wasn't after his money, she wanted to spend her time with a fat fuck like him. He couldn't accept her claim that she simply found him attractive, and so in exasperation – and bloody good for her too that she did – she'd spilled the beans.

'At first I couldn't grasp what she was saying,' Mick said, rubbing his chin. 'I just sat there with this shit-eating grin on my face, as if my jaw was paralysed. I wanted to stop smiling but I couldn't. She asked me if I were going to say anything, but I was clenching my teeth, smiling back at her, looking across her shoulder. I tell you I couldn't *move*, Danny.

'Listen while I tell you about my balls. They'd gone. Shot back inside my body, like. And they didn't drop again until a couple of hours later. Makes you walk with a gait. But here's the strangest thing: I seemed to be able to rise up from my seat and leave this smiling, grinning body behind me still sitting there. And I quietly walked out without a word to Mae-Lin or anybody. Then I was outside and I jumped in a tuk-tuk. I didn't even haggle over the fare.'

After that, Mick had made his way back to one of the bars we'd drunk in earlier, huddled over a beer and eyeing the girls with deep suspicion. Whatever feelings he had about putting his tongue halfway down a man's throat all evening, he was disgusted with himself over the way he'd treated Mae-Lin. He was haunted by an obscure expression on Mae-Lin's face; and by the inexplicable vision of the figure of himself reclining in the chair, grinning inanely as his corporeal self had tiptoed away across the dance floor.

'The thing is Danny, it's like a bit of me is still there, do you

93

see? I feel like a piece of me got torn off. I feel like I left my balls there.'

I hadn't actually got much in the way of wisdom on the subject to offer him. I mean, I could see why he was so distressed. You don't normally get this sort of thing happening on the fruit and veg stalls of Leicester market.

I did my best to reassure him that he hadn't got to scrub himself down with battery acid or anything like that. It was when we were talked out about Mae-Lin that I got him to tell me where he'd gone that afternoon before any of this had happened. True to his promise, he hadn't gone to the consulate, not at first at any rate. He'd returned, instead, to Chiang Mai prison.

At the prison he'd sought out the official we'd met on our first visit. More folded notes changed hands, and, Mick told me, they'd had a long conversation about opium, *farang* prisoners, and our friend Mr Brazier-Armstrong. Mick had complained, in passing, that we never got to see much of the man, that he was never available and was of little help. That was, the prison official told him, because Brazier-Armstrong was always across the border in Laos or Cambodia, lying down with little boys.

Mick wouldn't lie to me about that. It is of course possible that the prison official was himself lying through his teeth or simply relaying malicious rumours; but Mick, taking it at face value, went ahead and acted on that information. He went back to the consulate, where he spoke to Mrs Duongsaa. Brazier-Armstrong, he told Mrs Duongsaa, had twenty-four hours to set up an interview with the girl who'd stolen Charlie's passport, or he would telephone the *News Of The World* and the *Sunday Mirror* in London with information about what the consul was up to in Laos and Cambodia.

And here, this morning, why, not even eighteen hours later, was the man himself, objecting 'in the strongest possible terms' to Mick's behaviour. I wondered how many times in his career he had written those words in some piffling and effortless protest in the routine discharge of his office.

'Why?' I said. 'What has he done?'

Brazier-Armstrong swept back his long fringe, and wiped his

bespittled lips with an elegant thumb and forefinger. 'I really don't understand what he thinks there is to be gained by adopting this hectoring tone. My staff in particular feel very upset and provoked.'

'Mrs Duongsaa?'

'Duongsaa, yes. All this bullying is quite unnecessary. And, by the way, we are doing every single thing in our power to help you in your very difficult situation.'

'I'm sure you are. Where have you been? Laos?'

'No.'

'Cambodia?'

'No.' He looked me in the eye. I actually thought he was telling the truth on that occasion, but some tiny oscillation in his iris made me suspect that what Mick had reported to me was true. The heavy dew of perspiration above his upper lip could have been formed by the morning heat, but he was afraid of me. He looked at me and he *knew* that I *knew*.

I sat in that pagoda calmly smoking a cigarette and gazing out on the green-tea river. The smiling Buddha at my right hand was telling me to keep calm but I wanted to break Brazier-Armstrong's face. I was thinking not of the abused little boys, but of their parents. For all I know they might have sold their children into this vile bondage, and perhaps through rotten circumstances, but I couldn't believe that none of them had been touched by shame.

I too had been touched by shame, for my daughter. 'You've come here to tell me something.'

'I've arranged the interview you wanted. With the girl who took your daughter's passport.'

'You've arranged it. When?'

'This morning.'

'Good.' I was determined to show no emotion.

I finished my cigarette as he told me what time we should be there. He also suggested that Mick's presence might be counter-productive.

'And if I want him there?'

Brazier-Armstrong stood up to leave. As a parting shot he warned, 'You should tell your friend to stop bribing the prison guards. He might think it's all very simple. But another guard will become jealous and your friend might find himself on serious corruption charges.'

'Are you threatening us?'

He stepped out of the pagoda and shuffled into his sandals. '*I*,' he said emphatically, 'don't work like that.' Then he hastened along the garden path, red in the face and plucking the spume from his lips with one of those manicured fingers.

I called him back. 'By the way. You went to Oxford, didn't you?'

He looked puzzled. 'As a matter of fact, it was Cambridge.'

Same fucking difference.

'Why do you ask?'

'It's nothing,' I said. 'I'll see you at the prison.'

18

I doubt if Claire Marchant had been to university anywhere. On this occasion she had her hair scraped back and she was not unlike my Charlie. Same hair colour, similar in the shape of her face – I could see how she might travel about on Charlie's passport. Several weeks in prison had given her a sallow look but the only real difference was in the hooded character of her brow, and in her habit of peeping at you from beneath. It was not a shy peeping. It was suspicion. There was an incipient curl to her lip too, as if a sneer was kept in permanent reserve for some comment or verbal assault directed her way. I didn't like her much.

She wore green cotton pyjamas – reminding me of the outfits worn by ancillary workers in the hospitals at home – and plastic sandals. We met her in a stuffy holding room with no window and no fan. It gave me an impression of the sweltering heat of the cells. She sat at a small table where I was given a plastic chair.

For a moment we hunkered like chess players, and then I unpacked my bag with the soap and shampoo and all the guff. Sitting against the wall, also on plastic chairs, were Mick, Phil, Brazier-Armstrong and Mick's prison officer wallet-friend. A female warder stood by the door looking bored. She stepped over to the table and checked the gear I had laid out.

'They'll only confiscate it and take what they want,' the girl said.

'Not if I encourage them to let you keep it.'

The girl knew perfectly well what I meant. 'Can I go back to my cell afterwards?'

'We keep her 'lone last night,' the prison officer put in, with a beautiful, beaming Thai smile, 'for help her 'member few things. She 'member good now.'

I understood the women were locked up six to a cell, but that was obviously preferable to a windowless solitary confinement. 'You can have these things,' I said as if I governed the slammer. 'You can go to your old cell. But I need to know where and when you last saw my daughter.'

'Why should I help you? I've been left to rot here. He,' she said, jabbing a finger at Brazier-Armstrong, 'is fucking useless. I've got nothing to lose. I'm on twenty years, possibly even a death sentence. What do I care?'

We'd learned that drugs traffickers often travel on stolen passports, for obvious reasons. But Claire Marchant had maintained the pretence for a long time after she'd been jailed. I had a father's hunch as to why.

'Claire, don't your parents know you're in here?'

She bit a fingernail.

'You know, now we've found out your real name, we will contact them, and we'll tell them what you've done and where you are. They deserve to know.'

And this hard-bitten little girl started weeping.

I saw it all there. She'd kept it from her folks. I don't know how exactly, but so far she'd succeeded; they hadn't got a clue that their daughter was banged up in Chiang Mai prison.

I let her cry for a minute or two and then I found her a tissue. I asked the guard if I could give her a cigarette. The guard nodded, and Marchant accepted a snout. 'They don't know, do they?' She shook her head, looked up with wet eyes and blew a long funnel of smoke at the ceiling. Now she couldn't look me in the eye.

'My dad's very old,' she said. 'He's sick, bed-bound. I didn't even want to leave him to go travelling but he said I should go, said there was no point waiting around until he kicked it. I know he's only got a year or two. I thought if I pretended to be – you know – someone else, that he'd never get to hear about it.'

I thought about how long it had been since I'd heard from Charlie. 'But doesn't he expect to hear from you?'

'I've got a friend who sends e-mails every fortnight. My sister at home prints them out and reads them to him. He thinks I'm in Australia right now. My lovely old dad,' and here she started crying again, 'I don't want him to know about this. My lovely old dad.'

After that she told us everything she could. If Thailand's role in the Golden Triangle of opium cultivation had shrunk in recent years, it seemed it was still the Golden Gate. Much of the poppy growing had been pushed out of Thailand into Myanmar and Laos, where the opium was refined into heroin. Then it had to come back into Thailand again, because only Thailand had the wide-open communications and regular business and tourist access to the West.

I understood from what she said that there are two methods of transporting the drug, either by mules or by ants. The principle of dispatching mules involves large consignments, a high-risk policy with the possibility of confiscation incurring huge losses for the drugs bosses. The alternative policy was one of sending an army of ants bearing small amounts of the contraband concealed about the person, knowing that some of the ants would be caught but minimising the overall risk as dozens of other ants found their way through. Claire Marchant had been stepped on.

Like a lot of tourists in Thailand, Claire had fallen in love with the country but without the means to stay there. The easy solution had presented itself, and she'd been picked up in the town of Fang having brought a packet of drugs, hidden in her vagina, across from Myanmar. It was, she said, the only time she'd done it. A boyfriend, she claimed, had talked her into it.

But I didn't entirely believe that, because she'd stolen the passport from Charlie a couple of months before being caught, so I figure she must have known why she wanted someone else's passport. In any event, she was herself smoking the stuff long before her arrest, and so was Charlie.

'I was on a trek in the jungle, in the north. It's the safe way to get opium. The Thai authorities want you to believe they've got rid of the opium crops but up there the tribespeople still grow it. They offer it to you in every village.

'In one village, up near the border with Myanmar, we came across another trek. There were some English and American tourists. They'd been on the pipe, and a couple of them were sick. Their guides were upset, because they've been told to keep tourists away from the opium. Anyway, this girl and her boyfriend were too ill to travel, so they had to spend a second night in the village. We were overnighting it so their guides decided to press on with the original group, and we were to bring the sick pair with us later.

'I went to take a look at them. They were stretched out in a bamboo hut. I don't know how many pipes they'd had, but they were out of it. It can get you like that. You think nothing's happening so you smoke more and more and then you're a puddle on the floor. I went through their bags. I was really after the guy's passport, because my boyfriend wanted one. The guy had obviously had the sense to leave it somewhere safe before coming on the trek, 'cos his wasn't there. But I found hers.'

'That's when you stole Charlie's passport?'

She nodded. 'Next day our guides were up bright and early, but this couple were still sick. Maybe it wasn't the opium; maybe something else. But our guides were in no mood to hang around waiting for these two *farang* to recover. The guides were jumpy, I don't know why. A couple of strangers had walked into the village – not tribesmen – and I think they wanted us on our way. So we left. That's it.'

'You left them there?'

'Yes.'

'That was a dirty piece of work you did that day, wasn't it?'

'I'm sorry.'

'You're fuckin' sorry,' Mick said. 'We're all fuckin' sorry.'

The prison officer wanted to join in. 'Yeh. Solly. Velly solly.'

'You have a lot to answer for, young lady,' said Phil.

'If I get a map,' Brazier-Armstrong said, 'do you think you can tell me where the village is?'

'I'll try.'

He spoke with the prison officer who went off in search of a chart. Brazier-Armstrong read my thoughts. 'It's four or five months ago. Hardly likely she's still there.'

I said nothing. The officer came back and spread a good-sized army map across the table. Marchant placed her finger on the map, close to the border with Myanmar, halfway between Pai and Fang, in the mountainous region to the north-west of Chiang Mai. 'Here.'

The prison officer looked grave. His brow wrinkled. He said some words in Thai to Brazier-Armstrong. They seemed to be discussing the implications. At length, Brazier-Armstrong said, 'He wishes it were nearer the Golden Triangle area, where there are tourists making treks every day. But this place is lawless. Over the past six months there has been fighting between the opium gangs. Also the border is mined. Officially the Thai government wants the world to think it has the opium growing under control. In reality, they send in the army to burn a few fields, and the opium growers simply drift westwards.'

'When can we go there?' I asked him.

'You don't seem to understand, Daniel. There are no roads. It's an area of steep-sided ravines—'

'She went there,' Mick interrupted, pointing at Claire Marchant. 'So did Charlie.'

'You can trek it,' Marchant said. 'You would need guides, but it can be done.'

Claire Marchant had served her usefulness. She stood up. As the female guard was leading her out of the room, Phil got to his feet. He put a hand on Marchant's shoulder. 'Don't despair. You have reason to be in good hope.'

'What?'

Phil narrowed his eyes at her. 'The Lord is closer than you think.'

'Thank you for that,' Marchant said. 'It's comforting. I'll take that and smoke it. I'll put it in my chillum. I'll powder it and put it in my beaker. I'll snort it up my fucking nose.' She turned to her guard. 'Can you get me out of here, please?'

Mick was grinning, but I looked at Phil and felt desperately sorry for him. He was trying to do his best.

The prison officer spoke in rapid Thai. Brazier-Armstrong's face dribbled with sweat as he turned to me, saying, 'He says the situation is volatile in that region. There are Kareni refugees from across the border, KMT guerrilla forces, not to mention the opium gangs. The Thai government can't even move their army around up there. I have to say to you, in an official capacity, that if you do go it is against my recommendation. If you go, and I will put this on record, the British Consulate can be of no help to you whatsoever.'

Mick slapped his thigh. 'Well,' he said, 'that will be a *big* fucking loss to us, won't it?'

Securing the services of a guide was not as easy as we thought it would be. Several tour companies in Chiang Mai offered three- or four-day treks, but mostly to the controlled areas north of neighbouring Chiang Rai and up around the Golden Triangle. Our trek had to be open-ended. We had only a rough idea of the location of the village we were after, and we didn't know where we would want to go after arriving there. The tour companies failed to understand what we wanted: they worked hard at trying to fix us up with packaged treks in the company of German and Australian tourists looking for adventure holidays.

There was another problem. Whenever we pointed to the region we needed to get to, there was a marked reluctance to even try to find suitable guides. Eventually we were helped by a small company called Panda Travel. They knew of guides who had spent several years in the Thai army. When we offered to double the going rate, a telephone call was made. We would need two guides, we were told, should anything happen to one of them. We arranged to meet up.

The two guides came to the offices of Panda Travel. On arrival they went directly to the rear of the offices where the Thais huddled in conversation. The prospective guides chain-smoked cigarettes, turning occasionally to look at the three of us, coolly and critically, I thought.

Finally they were introduced to us as Bhun and Coconut. Both were wiry little guys who didn't smile nearly as much as everyone else in Thailand. Coconut, the younger of the two with long, lank black hair, did the talking in strangled English, hard to follow. Bhun didn't seem to speak at all, neither Thai nor English. For what was still a modest fee they agreed to cook for us and to negotiate with the hill tribes for places to stay en route. A commission settled the interests of the tour company, who provided small rucksacks and sleeping bags. We were told to leave our suitcases and most of our gear at our hotel in Chiang Mai.

Bhun and Coconut would be ready to leave early the following morning. We were to rendezvous at the office, where a truck would drive us to Ban Mae Kon, which was as far as the road would take us.

'That's it then,' said Phil. 'We've set our hands to the plough.'

'What plough?' Mick said.

I didn't know what Phil meant either, but one thing was certain. We were going into the jungle.

Since that evening was going to be our last in Chiang Mai for some time, Mick was hell-bent on enjoying himself. He showered and shaved and slapped on the cologne. 'We're going into the jungle,' he said more than once, 'we don't know what we're going to find, and we don't know when we're going to get our next beer.' Which was his way of telling me not to try to talk him out of drinking himself senseless.

Before we went out I tapped softly on Phil's door. He opened the door very quietly. He seemed distracted, and I had the impression I'd interrupted him in the act of prayer. 'Come with us,' I said.

'You know, a wild night on the town is not the solution to anything,' Phil said. Mick had been needling him again. 'We'd do better just to sit down and think hard, and I mean *really hard*, about what lies in front of us.'

'We've no idea what lies in front of us.'

'Exactly.'

He'd lost me again. 'Phil, we're going out to have a couple of beers and I'd like you to come with us. I don't care to think of you here on your own.'

He blinked at me. 'But that's what you don't understand, Father. Unlike you two, I'm not on my own.'

A sigh escaped my lips, and it sounded very much like the word *fuck*.

'All right,' Phil said, relenting. 'I'll come. But I've no intention of making a fool of myself.'

'That's good of you,' I said. 'And Mick will be relieved, too.'

As it happened Phil was rather more buoyant than I expected, and Mick was much more subdued. Like me, Mick was deeply apprehensive about what lay ahead. In the days we'd been in Chiang Mai, I'd started to get a little bit accustomed to the sweltering heat, the spicy food, the endless bartering over small exchanges. Mick, though, had never looked like he was away from home, but the jungle, without its bars and pool tables and hotels and ice-cold beers and Pepsi-colas was a different proposition.

Outside the Wat Pan Tong temple we passed an ancient Thai man squatting on the pavement. He had a sheet spread on the ground bearing odd merchandise. Mick stopped, turned, and went back. The old man was an amulet-seller. He had hundreds of amulets for sale, fashioned from metal, wood and terra-cotta. Mick fingered one of the amulets. The old man named a phenomenal price. Mick put it back again, and the old man picked out a more expensive looking thing which was actually dirt cheap.

'You're going to buy one?' Phil said.

'Shut up,' said Mick, and after a little consideration he chose one with a hole so that it could be hung round his neck, and paid for it. The old man surprised us by holding the amulet in the air, swaying dangerously and wailing loudly as he blessed the object. Mick was mesmerised, and deeply impressed.

'See that?' he said after we'd moved on a few paces. 'Made my skin flush, did that.'

'He buys a heathen fetish,' Phil said, 'in the vain hope of good fortune beyond the wicket gate.'

'Shut up,' Mick said.

I examined the amulet for myself. It was a flat lozenge of terra-cotta stamped with a crescent moon, horns up, as it were. The moon radiated lines to the edge of the amulet. 'Very good,' I said. 'You've just bought the Thai equivalent of a lucky rabbit's foot.'

'I don't know who's worse, Danny,' Mick said, quickening his step, 'you taking the piss in one ear, or him bleating in the other.' We made our way to our favourite bar with Phil walking a few paces behind, like Gollum from *Lord of the Rings*, muttering darkly about Mick's amulet.

I made a brief call to Sheila. I let Phil gloss the details for her. After that we had a few beers and even Phil consented to play a couple of rounds of pool with the bar girls, but none of us had much in the way of heart or conversation. Something was eating Mick. Looping his new amulet on to his neck chain, he was mumbling about 'right speech' and 'right action', but it was still a surprise when he told me, 'Look Dan, I've got a small account to settle, type of thing. Got to put something in order.'

He asked me if, later in the evening, I would go with him to the Blue Valentine nightclub. He wanted to apologise for his behaviour to Mae-Lin.

'Of course we can go.'

After that he cheered up. He wasn't ready to go just yet, he said. He wanted to cruise the bars, drink some beer, tease the bar girls, break a few hearts. Pretty soon he was his old self. I looked at him, with one bar girl fanning his face and another feeding him slices of fresh pineapple, and for all the trouble he was I was glad he was coming into the jungle with me.

Phil didn't think so. After a young Magdalene had humiliated him at a frame of pool he laid down his cue, and suggested an early night for us all.

'Fuck off,' Mick said through a mouthful of pineapple.

'Really,' Phil said, his face reddening. 'Tomorrow is going to be tough. We need to be focused and rested.'

'Look,' I said, 'you go back to the hotel and we'll be along later.'

'I'm afraid,' Phil said, 'that I'm going to have to insist.'

I was astounded. I looked at Mick and Mick looked at me. Then Mick got to his feet, brushing off the tiny bar girls in the process. 'Well, that's it then, if the man insists. Sorry girls, but I have to go. We've been called. Good night, sweetheart, and you my darling. Kiss kiss. One last embrace.'

I thought Mick was joking.

He was. He slumped back into his seat. 'On second thoughts I'll have another beer.'

Phil wasn't amused. Sweat boiling on his brow he looked at me severely and said, 'Dad?'

Dad! He called me dad, and not father. 'I'll be along soon, son,' I said as tenderly as I could. He had a point about being rested, but I wasn't going to be ordered around by him, church Elder or not.

Then Phil completely lost control of himself. Out of nothing he detonated. 'You two,' he roared, 'have *no earthly idea* where you are. You ignorant dogs! Look around you! We're awash – *awash!* – in a foaming tide of sin and you can't even see it. Whores! Drugs! Booze! Gluttony! Usury! Why don't you understand where you are? Does it have to be spelled out to you? This is iniquity! Depravity! This is a heathen place! This is a platform of stink and corruption and darkness and you think it's a joke. Well I'm here to tell you that you're going to get an almighty wake-up call!'

The bar girls, tittering at first, had gone quiet. Phil was purple in the face, his hair lit by the green and red neon bar lights, and he wasn't addressing just Mick and I any more, but anyone and everyone. His eyes were like pools of boiling pitch. Flecks of white spittle flew from his lips like spindrift. He'd completely lost it. For the first time in my life I felt afraid of, and for, my own son.

'I'm sorry for you,' he shouted, recovering slightly. 'Sorry, yes, *sorry* for you, for what's coming. And as for you, Father, all I can say is that for you I'll save my strongest prayers.'

It was his parting shot. He stormed from the bar and climbed into a waiting tuk-tuk. The driver revved his engine and belched a dirty and sulphurous cloud of diesel smoke as it departed.

'Fuck off in your lawnmower,' Mick shouted after him, too late.

I scratched my head and sighed. 'I don't know where I went wrong with that one, I really don't.'

'What's usury?' Mick wanted to know.

By the time we fetched up at the Blue Valentine our mood had changed, and we'd both become light, jaunty. I knew why. It was an antidote to Phil's outburst. Even though I didn't take his words seriously, his behaviour weighed heavily on me. He'd let go flocks of dark birds and now they were settling along the path before me.

So maybe it was self-consciousness, or maybe it was fear, but we were like boozed-up schoolboys, grab-arsing and noisy and laughing at anything. Somehow we'd dragged four girls from the Corner Bar with us on the promise of paying to get them into the nightclub. We were a rabble.

The Blue Valentine dance floor was busy enough that night. It was a more upmarket place than the street bars, and I could see why the girls had wanted to come with us. The dance floor was awash with bubbling, turquoise, blue and tangerine light. Someone up there was spinning Soul classics. 'Harlem Shuffle' by Bob and Earl struck up. Mick dragged the five of us on to the dance floor, where we shimmied in a tight circle. I don't dance much myself – can't be doing with it – but that night I was up for it. Wild, extravagant dancing. I also dance a lot with my face once I get started, and the girls found it hilarious if no one else in the club did. I don't know what the funky chicken is exactly, but I recall I did that, too.

I remember Charlie digging out some old records of Sheila's when she was sixteen. Otis Redding, Aretha Franklin, The Temptations. She played them at full belt, amazed that her parents had some of this stuff. She had a boyfriend at school who was into retrospectives. For about two days Sheila and I zoomed up in her estimation, and she began asking us about when we were courting (*courting*, who uses that expression nowadays? Sometimes I feel about as contemporary as Thomas De Quincey.).

But Mick was the Soul Man, and I loved to watch him dance. For such a fat bastard, he was an ace dancer. In fact he could have danced a professional off the mat. Turn down the lights, pump up the Soul music, and this slob, this lard-machine, this pink-faced blubber-bank was fluid and light and graceful on his feet. He was Nijinsky. Women who wouldn't normally look twice at him always wanted to dance with him when they saw what he could do, but he always preferred to dance alone. He would attract small crowds who would gather round and egg him on. Just as they did in the Blue Valentine that night.

A couple of times I glanced up at the female silhouette ghosting the dais behind the turntables. Mae-Lin had clocked Mick but was pretending not to have; though what with the commotion he was making on the dance floor she couldn't miss him. I saw her gazing at him when his back was turned. Once I saw them make eye contact briefly, and I could have kicked myself for having missed it, but I suddenly realised she was communicating with him through her choice of music. I thought back over the last two or three discs. 'Stand By Me', 'Respect', 'Reach Out'; the hits kept talking over the music.

But I could never have anticipated what happened next.

Mae-Lin locked down the mood and tempo by playing a slow number, and stepped down from the dais. Tall, statuesque and beautiful, bathed in rippling blue light, she gazed directly at Mick. He was across the dance floor, looking back at her. Some of the clubbers were already drifting off the dance floor as reverberating electric organ chords counted in the storming power vocals of Percy Sledge, giving it all he's got on 'When A Man Loves A Woman'.

I was mesmerised just watching them. Mick stroked his chin as he decided what to do next. Before the first few bars of the song were up he glanced over at me. I made the minimal gesture of nodding my head towards Mae-Lin. It was what he needed.

With his big bear arms hanging limply at his side he moved slowly across the dance floor. The remaining dancers parted for him, pure choreography. His face was orange and black shadow in the ultraviolet light. His brilliant white T-shirt was all I could see of his torso, and he appeared to glide towards her, like a spirit. On reaching her, he swept her up. I saw her long arms clasp about his neck, and then I felt someone tugging at my own elbow, breaking the spell of a moment, a crystallised breath of unlimited grace, an instant of weightlessness.

It was Air, one of the bar girls we had brought along with us. She was smiling. 'Hey! Me think your friend love her long time!'

'Maybe,' I said. 'Maybe.'

I don't know what happened after that, and I never did ask Mick. I don't need to know. It's not important. I left the Blue Valentine, alone. I didn't want to cramp his style or make him think he was being watched, or judged. His business.

Even though we were going to have to make an early start, I wasn't in the mood for sleeping. I got a tuk-tuk driver to take me across the Nawarat Bridge. There was a place I liked there on the riverfront, a short stretch of green grass on the embankment, a place where lovers and small groups of young people sat quietly in the haze and the relative cool of the night, right through to the small hours. The river was illumined by the lights on the bridge, and giant white moths flitted back and forth in the light. The colour of the night was oyster and sage.

After a while, Mae-Lin and Mick strolled by, hand in hand. They were deep in conversation, and Mick was fingering the new amulet at his neck. I shrank into the shadows so they wouldn't see me as they passed by. The air around them seemed to quiver. They passed into the haze leaving tiny ripples of light in their wake. I blinked. I wasn't certain if it really was them, or just an hallucination of them. The moment was so singular and beautiful I had the feeling that every pair of lovers of every time must have strolled that embankment, that it was a place out of time.

After they'd gone I sat there for an age, smoking cigarettes, watching the river, listening to it flow.

19

After three gruelling hours of it we got them to stop. Salt stung my eyes and my T-shirt was puddled around my midriff. I'd bought new training shoes in the Chiang Mai market, and they'd rubbed my toes into blisters. Mick slumped between spare clumps of parched, spiky grass and took out his water bottle. In his safari hat he looked like a game hunter from the old movies: the fat one who dies early so the plot can gather pace.

'Little.' Coconut jabbed a finger at Mick's bottle. 'Only little.'

Phil leaned against a tree, fanning himself with a wide-brimmed straw hat he'd also bought in the night market. Bhun squatted, sullenly smoking a cigarette. Our guides didn't have new training shoes. They wore cheap plastic flip-flop sandals. I'd assumed from this that the terrain wouldn't be too challenging, and I'd been horribly wrong.

We'd been driven up into the mountains in the back of a jolting *songthaew* truck stinking of diesel fuel, and where the red-soil winding road was too dusty we had the neckbands of our T-shirts hoicked up around our noses. It was a relief when the road ran out and we could get out of the choking, sweltering truck. Coconut took front position, followed by me, Phil and Mick. Bhun brought up the rear. I noticed that both our guides had a long-bladed knife, something between a commando knife and a machete, stuck in their belts. Our path continued steadily upwards, ascending towards the unblinking eye of the noonday sun.

My first impression of the land was of scrub and red soil, and it was not until we got into the tree line that I realised why the road had run out. The terrain had become pleated in a succession of high peaks and deep ravines. We had to hike up testing inclines and then down the sides of steep ravines. The path down was the most punishing, ramming the ball of the knee into the socket with piston-hard slaps, twanging the ligaments.

Coconut and Bhun didn't speak. Mick made a bid for a jocular mood, but they weren't having any of it. Then as Mick's lungs began to strain against the incline, he too became silent. The sun thrummed through a thick, soupy haze which protected us from its furnace but which made the warm air unpleasantly moist. My own T-shirt felt like an eelskin vest while Phil, incredibly, was still wearing one of his white polyester Sunday-school shirts, and it was so wet I could see through it to his white, rather pudgy body.

Now, as we slumped in the heat sipping water, and as Phil leaned his frame against the tree, I noticed a row of rat-sized red ants diverting from their path down a slender tree branch to creep across his shirt. I thought about not letting on, but when I did he hopped about like someone with a Roman candle in his pants, making that peculiar shuddering noise you equate with extreme cold. It gave the guides a laugh, anyway.

Meanwhile Mick and I sat on limestone rocks, oozing yeasty, beery sweat and recovering our breath. The two guides stubbed out their cigarettes, hauling their packs, ready to go. Mick cursed under his breath and glugged more water.

I decided to take control. 'No!' I barked. It came out a bit Germanic, but it had the desired effect.

Coconut stood over me. 'We go. Must reach number one village 'fore nightfall. We go now.'

We were told it would take us two and a half days of solid trekking to reach the village where Claire Marchant had stolen Charlie's passport. The plan was to spend nights in the hill tribe villages along the way. There was no other possibility than to trust the guides absolutely, but I felt the need to pretend to be in control of events. I heard myself falling into a ridiculous pidgin English. 'One more cigarette-time. Then go chop-chop.' I lit up another snout to show I wasn't moving. Coconut shook his head in disgust. Bhun appeared indifferent.

Mick wore his infuriating broad smile. His snooker smile. 'Where did you study guide talk?' he wanted to know. 'Was it in *The Rover* and *Wizard*?'

Even Phil, too young to remember these comics, found that amusing. Phil had this rarely demonstrated but irritating little laugh, halfway between a cough and a snigger. 'Himsay me top-banana fella!'

I was shocked. 'What's this? A sense of humour, Phil? I think I prefer it when you're a sack of misery.'

'Lighten up!' went Mick, and the bastard actually clapped Phil on the back.

When I was ready I scrambled to my feet, slung my pack on my back and looked like business. I jabbed a finger at Coconut. 'You boss-man. We go now.'

Coconut glanced over at Bhun, his lip twisted into a scowl.

'Did you see that?' I said to Mick when we were underway again.

'Yeah,' Mick chirruped. 'It was a look that said *cunt*.'

For the next part of the journey I had to endure Mick parodying my pidgin English. 'Oh! Many many big tree! Big fella him come here no-go chop-chop. Him fallee downee. Him say bye-bye! Him wannee drinkee plenty water me say no.' And stuff like that. For about two hours.

The two guides began talking across us, though Coconut, concerned about venomous snakes (he mentioned king cobras, and though we never saw one I did spot a luminous blue snake slipping quietly through the undergrowth), never took his eyes off the trail ahead. The vegetation altered and we were quickly enfolded in giant bamboo, banana stalks, royal palms and thorny liquorice. I knew the guides were discussing us, and it made me nervous. We'd placed ourselves in a dangerous position. They could easily slit our throats and take what money and documents we had with us. Up in the steaming jungle hills, no one would ever find us, or even care if they did.

Back at the hotel we'd debated whether to bring our cash and passports. I wanted to leave most of it in the hotel safe, but Mick had read in a guide book about the unreliability of hotel safes in Thailand. No, he decided, it was safest strapped to his belly, and I didn't argue. Though our guides didn't know it, Mick was carrying his life savings in dollar notes, plus my cash and traveller's cheques. I didn't have a clue how much Mick's savings amounted too, but judging by the tiny amount we were paying our guides, it was probably more than they could earn in twenty lifetimes. As for Phil, you could more easily take a strip of skin from his back than peel a note from his wallet, and I had no idea what he was carrying.

Bhun, the quiet one, shouted something up the line that made Coconut cackle with laughter. Coconut looked back at Mick and I, and then at Bhun. Seeing our discomfort, he made to pacify us. '*Sanuk*,' he said.

'*Sanuk*,' Bhun repeated, and they both laughed again. Their laughter ricocheted off the tall, thin trees about us.

'Who are you calling a *sanuk*?' Mick growled.

'Only *sanuk*,' Coconut said, moving off again. He withdrew his long blade from his belt and hacked at a creeper hanging in his way. 'Fun.'

The vegetation became a thick, dry and scrubby tangle fighting for growth between spindly grey tree trunks of astonishing height, canopy upon canopy. The trees were festooned with parched, creeping vines, sometimes so defoliated that the vines looked like trailing masses of electrical cable. Unlike the trees at home, there were no low branches, and where the trees did sprout it was with large, papery leaves of greens, russets and reds. The dusty path ahead was sprinkled with huge, crinkly desiccated leaves. The ground breathed back at us, dry and hot.

I tell you this as if I was interested, when really my thoughts were on Charlie. When walking great distances the mind turns in on itself, and after a while fails to register the terrain ahead. I suppose this seems quite dangerous. Sometimes the path up or down the side of a steep ravine went perilously close to the edge: quite possible to miss a footing and to roll maybe two hundred feet through the brush before crashing into a tree. Perhaps the mind has a third eye which takes care of this while the brain is busy with other thoughts.

I was trying to find a dividing line.

There was a time when Charlie thought I was like a young God, and that I knew the answer to everything, and that I could protect her from any external threat, and that all things came within the compass of my powers. All fathers permit this illusion, basking in it somewhat, knowing that it won't last for ever. It meant that I was a fixer. From when she was very small she was accustomed to asking me to fix broken toys, bicycles, equipment. That's what I did. That's what I was there for. I liked that. I liked being the fixer.

But then one day I was a downright idiot, a peasant. I don't know how it happened, but it seemed that overnight, maybe around the time that Charlie was twelve or thirteen, I'd gone from being the wonderful, all-powerful fixer to being a complete chump, with no transitional stage. From being the oracle of wisdom it seemed that now everything I had to say was pure tomfoolery, to be derided in that feminine way girls and women have of insulting you without it seeming – initially anyway – to bite.

And while I was walking through the jungle with my head down I was trying to remember the exact day, the first time this happened. The dividing line. Maybe that's what I was doing here: trying to be the fixer again.

'Hey! Look at that!' Mick cried

We stopped dead in our tracks. Mick pointed at the gnarled branch of a tree. The tree itself was utterly without foliage, but arrayed along one of its rotting branches, high in the sky, were seven sweet waxy white flowers, like a constellation of stars burning brilliantly against the far-inferior sun.

'Orchid,' Bhun said, nodding his head. It was the first English word he'd uttered since we'd met him.

'He fixes the stars in heaven,' Phil murmured, almost inaudibly.

'Now that's a sight worth coming here for,' Mick said.

I wouldn't have gone quite that far, and as I retorted something to that effect Bhun scrambled up the tree, his gymnasticism astounding, to pluck one of the orchids. When he dropped down again, he offered it to Mick.

Mick made as if to eat it, and the guides laughed. Then he put it behind his ear, fluttering his eyelids and making coy, suggestive faces. The guides laughed some more. '*Sanuk!*' they shouted. 'You *sanuk!*'

The tension between us eased somewhat. Mick began to point at some of the strange fruit we'd seen along the way.

'Jackfruit,' Bhun said.

'Taste good?'

Bhun didn't understand, so Mick tried again, holding his fingers to his mouth. 'Jackfruit. Him good eating?'

I was glad to get my own back. 'Him plenty-plenty good chop-chop.'

'Fuck off.'

'Bombast and Denial,' Phil said heavily. 'You're children. Both of you.'

Late in the afternoon, exhausted and weary from the trail, we reached the first village where we were to overnight. The trees thinned as we dipped into a valley, and some of the area had been cleared for agriculture. On the valley floor in a natural basin clustered no more than fifteen huts. A dog barked in the village.

'Lisu people,' Coconut said, naming the tribe.

I took my bottle from my pack and glugged on my water. Not because I was especially thirsty, but to disguise my anxiety. We pressed on, passing sloping terraces tilled for growing what I took to be maize in the red soil. Further down a brightly coloured weed garden grew on a slope, in which a hovering and luxurious mass of stately red, white and purple flowers flared in the golden light of late afternoon.

Drawing abreast of the exotic, showcase blooms I suddenly realised what I was looking at. Phil hunkered down and put his eye up close to one of the flowers. It was as if he wanted to squint back at Satan. 'There is a friend that sticketh closer than a brother,' he said.

'Poppy,' said Coconut. 'Opium poppy.'

20

The Lisu people inhabiting the village were not especially interested in us. I got the impression they'd seen plenty of gawping Westerners shuffling through on organised treks. The kids gathered to appraise us with huge, liquid eyes, but the adults got on with their domestic tasks as we slid off our backpacks outside a hut on the edge of the village. Coconut went in search of the headman. Mick drew a circle of kids around him when he started to hand out chewing gum and sweets. I must admit it hadn't occurred to me to bring little gifts for the children.

For the Lisu women tribal costume was a colourful blue and red tunic worn over trousers, and some of the older women wore tasselled turbans. The men wore blue or green baggy trousers pegged at the ankles. I thought how healthy they all looked. Certainly the kids had good, shiny skin and strong white teeth. Their faces were more rounded than the somewhat heart-shaped faces of the Thais; later I learned that these people had migrated here from Tibet.

Coconut returned with the smiling headman. Despite our exhaustion we *wai*d, and I remembered to offer him a cigarette. A deal was struck quickly and we were led to a pair of huts on stilts. Coconut was quick to point out that one hut was for us, and one was for them. The headman spoke to one of the assembled children, a boy of about seven. The lad trotted off, there was a brief squawk, and he returned holding a flapping chicken by its neck and legs. Bhun took a stainless steel dish from his backpack. Grabbing the flapping chicken he took out his long knife and beheaded the fowl, letting it bleed into the dish.

'We cook for you now,' Coconut said, rather unnecessarily.

'Would you ask the headman,' I said to Coconut, 'if he knows of an English girl – a *farang* – living in one of the villages?'

Coconut frowned. 'Look, they don't speak Thai. I don't Lisu. I can *hut*, I can *chicken*. That's about all.' He must have seen my face crash, because he added, 'Sorry.'

Dusk was settling on the village as the headman and his boy left us to it. Our hut was made of bamboo, with a neatly swept rattan floor. A raised area of rattan was obviously for sleeping on, and a couple of moth-eaten blankets were folded in the corner. The rattan bed which looked so inviting was actually as hard as a gravestone. With the twilight came giant mosquitoes, and though you couldn't see them they had a bite like a dog. We changed into long trousers and tried to cover up. Savoury smells of rice and ginger wafted from the guides' hut.

'Ugh!' The cry came from Phil, struggling out of his trousers in the corner of the hut. He'd discovered two ticks on the back of his right leg. We went over to inspect. I must admit, I winced. They were knuckle-sized and bloated after a good day's feed on Phil's blood.

'Let's have 'em off,' I said, reaching out to pinch one between thumb and forefinger.

Mick slapped my hand. 'Not like that,' he said. 'You'll leave its guts in Phil's skin.' He sucked his cigarette into a bright cone and held it to the tick until the parasite dropped off. Phil looked queasy. The cone had gone off the cigarette before he could burn the second, so he gave the cigarette to me. 'Get a cone on that.'

I looked at the end of his ciggie. It still seemed to have half a tick stuck to it. I didn't much fancy smoking tick, and I said so.

'Just pull on the sod!' Mick said. He didn't fancy it either. We could simply have lit another, but we were concerned about conserving cigarettes.

'You pull on it!'

'He's your bleedin' son!' Mick said.

I took the cigarette and pulled on it, exhaling quickly without drawing the smoke into my lungs. I held the glowing end to the tick. The damned thing didn't seem to want to drop. I had to do it again before the horrible insect would let go of Phil's leg.

Throughout this Phil watched me closely. I had some antiseptic lotion in my bag. I rubbed it gently into his leg.

After the business with the ticks we sat outside, our heads leaning together, our limbs aching. Mick sighed and I said, 'I know what you're thinking, Mick. I could murder one, too.'

No sooner were these words out of my mouth than did a small Lisu boy appear, baggy pants pegged at the ankle like an apprentice genie, clutching three bottles of Singha beer, *your wish is my command*. We almost sent him back again when the kid told us how much he wanted, but Mick laughed and paid up, feinting a kick to his arse.

The beer was warm, but it was nectar. It bubbled deliciously on the tongue. It flooded the gullet and scraped back a sheath of dust from the swollen throat, chasing out the taste of bamboo and replacing it with the savour of hops. It restored balance, equilibrium. It was like being rubbed down with silk, and, since Phil had declined a beer, I was ready to fight Mick for the third bottle.

Mick looked at me, looked at the spare brew, and he laughed. In our exhaustion a kind of nervous hysteria was making us telepathic. Bhun came out of his hut with a steaming bowl of chicken fried rice, and stopped when he saw the pair of us giggling like morons.

There was a table outside our hut, rough-hewn out of teak, and Bhun and Coconut laid out the evening meal. In addition to the chicken fried rice there was a soup, two kinds of curry dishes and a plate of vegetables with ginger and noodles. There were also three tiny condiment dishes, containing ferocious spices. Jungle fare. In about half an hour of mess cooking these boys had rustled up what would not have been out of place in a high street restaurant. Even the service was polite, formal. All that was missing was the after-dinner chocolate mint and a cab home. We invited Bhun and Coconut to join us at the table, but neither would be prevailed upon to do so.

Phil held us up by muttering a brief grace, throughout which Mick practised jiggling his eyebrows.

Just as it was getting almost too dark to see, the headman's boy arrived, struggling with a hefty plastic block and some wiry contraption. Immediately seeing what it was, I leapt to my feet. Bhun urged me to get on with my dinner, but a Boy Scout enthusiasm made me want to be useful around camp. The heavy object was a car battery; there was a length of cable with crocodile clips at either end; and a small fluorescent strip light. I had it rigged in half a minute, dangling the light from an overhead cross-beam. No electricity in the village, but with the car battery we had glorious illumination.

'And there was light,' said Phil.

'Happy now?' Mick said, wolfing his chicken fried rice.

Yes, I was happy. I returned to the table and tucked into my green curry and noodles with a new-found relish. I guess it was the first time since arriving in Thailand that I'd actually felt in control of events, even if it was just for a moment. Power source, bit of cable, and a phosphor-coated electrical discharge device (lamp, to you). And I was going ha ha ha. Bringing light to the jungle.

When we finished our meal, another lad brought bananas and papayas. The six-year-old beer vendor returned, too, hawking Singhas at vastly inflated prices, and we bought his entire stock. Mick calculated we were paying, almost to the penny, the same price we would pay in the Clipper for a pint of Old Muckster's Jubilee Ale. It seemed fair, but I don't know what it did to the village economy that night.

Phil sipped his mineral water. 'You'd be completely lost without your jug of beer, wouldn't you?' This was his way of making a huge philosophical point, and the only answer he got from either of us was a deeply satisfied belch from Mick, so loud that it startled some live thing lurking under the stilts of the hut.

As we sat drinking and smoking, more beautiful children with deliquescing black eyes appeared silently from out of the dark, drawn into the circumference of illumination cast by our car-battery light. Behind them their mothers, hovering at the edge of the table. Clearly we had become the evening's entertainment. One of the braver women tried to peddle us embroidered friendship bracelets and other trinkets. Mick bought one for each of us. He put his on: he was looking more like a fucking hippy every day. Phil strapped his on, too, but I resisted. They looked like the kind of things Charlie's boyfriends used to wear. But one of the boys insisted on tying it to my wrist.

Another boy tried to lift up my shirt. Coconut, who sat a little apart from all of this with Bhun, but who watched everything with a critical eye, said, 'They wan see you hairy man.'

Because the Thais, and the Lisu and the other hill tribes presumably, had little body hair, the children were fascinated by the appearance of these three ape-men. Both Mick and Phil being pretty hirsute, they rolled up their shirts to give them a squint at the tobacco crop. The children giggled and leapt backwards, as if it was a monstrous sight. The women too clapped their hands and cackled and spoke rapidly to one another.

I dandled one little boy on my knee, making primate noises and slapping the top of my head with the palm of my hand. More hilarity.

'Here they eat monkey,' Coconut said.

I thought about my green curry. It had left a taste in my mouth that even the beer wasn't washing away. I tried not to think about it, and did some more monkey business for the kids. An elderly woman, with a cataract or some other degeneration of her left eye, pointed at the empty beer bottles and spoke to Bhun. Our guides had a debate. 'I not know what she say, exactly,' Coconut said, 'but she wan know this what beer do to you.'

Mick and I laughed, but the fixed expressions of the Lisu women indicated that they considered it a serious question. They thought perhaps we were drunk.

'They don't drink beer?'

'The women? Never.'

The woman with the cataract then leaned across the table, proffering a waxy cube of black substance, a piece the size of my thumbnail. So this was it.

'This'd be the stuff,' Mick said, accepting and inspecting it.

The guides watched us with great interest. I felt angry. I didn't even want to touch it. 'Give it back to her,' I told Mick.

'I'm just looking.'

'Give it back to her.'

'Keep your hair on! I want to know what it looks like.'

Phil, watching this dispute closely, put in, 'It's not in the stuff, Father. It's in the *desire* for the stuff.'

I waved my hands, palms outwards, at the woman. 'No,' I said. 'Very bad.' She glanced over at the guides and I saw Coconut shake his head, very slightly.

Then two of the younger women, each with a liquorice-eyed baby slung on a hip, offered us a massage apiece, in return for the price of one of the kid's beers. That sounded like a prize way to close the evening, so Mick and I assented. The two women passed on their babies to their own mothers, one of whom was the opium dealer, and we went inside the hut.

They placed candles around the hut, creating a peaceful orange ambience. The only thing to spoil the mood was the cluster of mothers, grandmothers and children at the door, who seemed to regard the massage as a spectator sport. We shouted for Coconut to get rid of them. After a few words from him they drifted away. Only Phil remained, gloomily watching the proceedings. 'Tell me something Coconut,' I said as I lay face down on the rattan. 'Do you smoke the opium?'

'Never.'

'And Bhun?'

'Also never. I agree you. Bad thing. I glad you not buy opium.' Then he waved a hand at Phil saying, 'You make sure your friends keep they pants on. If they fuck, then you must pay lot of money to they husband.'

Phil wrung his hands nervously, and Mick vented an unnecessarily deep sigh of pleasure.

21

We were up and on our way early the next morning with no farewells to the villagers. There was a military air to the expedition in the way Coconut marshalled us along. I'd had a dreadful night, and so had the others. Mosquitoes like flying piranhas had savaged lumps out of us and the quaint rattan pallet was as comfortable as a bed of Welsh slate. It got shockingly cold in the night, too, and the two thin blankets we each had over our sleeping bags were inadequate. We spent half the night talking rather than sleeping.

Or arguing rather than talking. It started when I saw Mick swallowing a pink pill while performing his ablutions. At the hotel we'd taken it in turns to use the bathroom, so I hadn't noticed Mick's nightly rituals. Here the washing facilities comprised two drums of water outside the hut: one for washing your body, and one for sluicing your arse.

'What's that about, then?'

Mick washed down the pink pill with a swig of beer. 'Malaria.'

I hadn't thought about malaria. My doctor had consulted a list which declared Chiang Mai malaria-free. At that time I had no idea we might be venturing into the jungle.

'You telling me you haven't been taking malaria tablets?' Mick said.

I explained what my doctor had said. 'Moron!' Mick exclaimed. 'You're supposed to be an intelligent person.'

'You should have anticipated this,' Phil said helpfully. He, of course, had his own supply.

'I didn't realise what was in store for us.'

'Didn't realise? You might have made provision! Do you want someone to wipe your arse for you as well?' At which point he glanced down at water bowl number two.

'Well, I didn't.'

'These little midges could bite a cow to death, and you've got nothing to say about it?'

'All right. Just drop the subject, will you?'

Mick shook his head. He picked up his bottle of doxycycline and tapped a pill into his giant, pink hand. 'Here.'

'That's no use.' I knew you needed to take these things before you travel, and then for some weeks after.

'Take it. We'll divide up what we've got. Right, Phil?'

Phil gritted his teeth. 'I wish you'd had more forethought, Father. Though I suppose that's what we'll have to do.'

'Then you two won't have enough.'

'Take it,' Mick growled.

'Then all three of us will be at risk. Where's the sense in that?'

Mick raised his fist at me. 'Take the fucker or I swear I'll chin you.'

'Shut up, you big fucking stupid dumpling.'

Mick moved surprisingly fast for such a big man. He grabbed my face and forced the pill into my mouth, holding his hand over my jaw. Phil danced out of my way as we struggled. 'Is it gone?'

'Fnnnghhhh ohffff!'

'I said is it gone?'

'Neff! Ifff fone.'

'Is it gone?'

'I said it's gone! Get off me, you tub of lard!'

He'd almost dislocated my jaw in the process. I walked away, my blood up; and then I saw Bhun watching us silently from the other hut. Our eyes met, and he nodded minimally. I turned back to our hut. After all, I wasn't going anywhere.

Sometime in the night, after we'd forgotten about the nonsense with the pills, we were all three awake, with Mick and I smoking cigarettes. The candles had burned out and we sat in darkness. All I could see were the two coal-ends of the lighted ciggies. At least the smoke seemed to discourage the mosquitoes.

Mick had been sitting on a question for a while. I heard him exhale in the blackness before he said, 'Now then, Phil. Have you got over your little paddy?'

He was referring to Phil's outburst in the Chiang Mai bar. 'Yes, thank you,' said Phil.

'Believe in that, do you? Brimstone. Hellfire. Believe in it? Eh?'

No one could see another's face in the dark. If they could have, this conversation would not have proceeded past first base.

'Yes.'

'So you think,' Mick said, 'that Danny and me are on the side of Satan, sort of thing?'

'No. I don't give you that much credit. You don't get out of it as easy as that. It's not about choosing sides.'

Pause. Drag on cigarette. 'What's it about, then?' Coal-end fattening like a luminous red maggot in the dark 'Tell me. I'm interested.'

'No you're not. You're just trying to mock.'

'Not at all. I'm trying to learn. I mean those girls in the Chiang Mai bars. Damned, are they?'

Long pause from Phil. 'We wrestle, and not against flesh and blood, but against principalities, against powers, against the rulers of the darkness of this world: we wrestle against spiritual wickedness in high places.'

Long pause from Mick. 'Gosh,' he said. 'Don't you get tired? What with all this *wrestling*?'

After a while I said to Phil, 'What about Charlie? Where does she figure in your scheme? Did Satan lure her with opium?'

'No.'

'What did, then?'

'Jealousy.'

This baffled me. 'What was she jealous of?'

'Not her jealousy. Yours.'

'Eh?'

'Think about it. Now if you don't mind I'm going to sleep.'

I would have gone to sleep too, if I could. But that remark of Phil's: it sat there, hunkered in the darkness like another member of the party, looking back at me.

124

That was in the chill of night. Now the jungle had heated up quickly and we were slowly ascending the steep side of a ravine. We were shivering the nights and sweating the days. The blisters on my feet were rubbing again, I had a thumping headache from lack of sleep, and my mosquito bites itched like crazy. We trekked on in silence. I looked back to see Mick, brow furrowed, fingering his amulet.

I was still thinking about Phil's strange remarks in the night. Meanwhile the jungle vegetation changed dramatically as we climbed or descended the sides of a ravine or as we came closer to a river. After passing between towering, spindly trees with fluffy balls of leaves only at the very top, we crossed a stretch of jungle that was smoking and smouldering. Orange flames licked at charred, blackened logs strewn over wide expanses of silver ash. The smoke was choking. I tied a handkerchief around my mouth. Coconut told us it was controlled fire, slash and burn, but I saw little evidence of its management. After that we descended sharply, and had to wade thigh-deep across a river. Downstream was an Hmong village, where we were to make a noon halt.

The Hmong looked very different to the Lisu. They wore black tunics and indigo skirts with embroidered aprons, and masses of silver jewellery: necklaces, amulets and the like. The women tied their hair on their heads in a bun, and within seconds of our arrival they were waving small wedges of opium under our noses. When they realised we weren't interested, they wanted to sell us silver bracelets. I bought one to give to Charlie, if I ever found her.

Coconut and Bhun prepared lunch for us. It was while we were surrounded by chattering Hmong dope-and-silver dealers that Bhun touched my elbow and pointed to the river edge. 'Farang,' he said, and he nodded encouragingly.

I spun round. Sitting with her feet in the water's edge was a young European woman. Alongside her was a Thai male, also with his feet in the water. He had an automatic rifle slung over his shoulder.

No, it wasn't Charlie.

But I was astonished to see any European woman there. 'Where are you going?' I heard Phil shout over his shoulder as he battled to extricate himself from the attentions of Hmong women.

The lady at the water's edge had long, brown hair, tied in a pony-tail. She wore a tattoo on her arms – some sort of Chinese or Thai symbol I supposed. I walked right up to her, and said, 'Good afternoon.'

Both she and the armed Thai spun round to look at me. Shielding her eyes from the sun, she smiled broadly and said, in a warm Irish brogue, 'Well, what about ye?' Mary O'Connel, it turned out, was an aid worker, operating with an outfit I'd never heard of called Frontline Aid. She was helping with the refugee crisis, she said.

'What refugees?' I asked crassly 'Are there any?'

'Jesus, just a few miles over there, only about a hundred thousand of the poor fuckers, so there is.'

I didn't know anything about this, and Mick, coming to join us, admitted that neither did he. It seemed there were masses of Kareni people – yet another hill tribe – being pushed out of Myanmar and into the more tolerant Thailand. I asked why, and her armed escort slipped away to join our two guides. 'Because the Burmese are bastards,' Mary told us. 'Killing. Raping. Burning the villages. They want these mountains for themselves.'

'Why?'

'Why? To control the opium you fucking *idjit*!' she said gaily.

Of course. The poppy. Misery everywhere.

Mary was in the Hmong village to pick up supplies which had been relayed there. She was waiting for elephants to transport both her and the supplies back to what she called Camp Three, but the mahout was late. 'Are you boys having a nice holiday?'

I invited her to have some lunch with us – and not just to hear what an invitation like that sounds like in a Hmong village in the Thai jungle, but because I wanted to ply her with questions. She'd assumed we were holiday trekkers, and when I

126

explained what we were doing, it seemed to resolve something for her.

'You know, I thought it odd to see a trek coming through here. You used to get them all the time until the warjacks moved in. It's been pretty unstable round here for a while. Lot of desperate people roaming around.'

'That why your guide is tooled up?' Mick asked her.

'Wouldn't be good to be around here on your own. Easy target and all that. It's the bandits you've got to watch for. They say that if the villagers don't rip you off, and the opium gangs suss you're not from the government, and the KMT don't think you're Chinese, then all you've got to worry about is the bandits.' She laughed pleasantly.

'Where are you from?' Phil asked.

'Belfast. Home from home.'

I asked Mary if she'd heard of any *farang* girl living in the villages nearby. She hadn't. She consulted her Thai guide. He didn't answer directly, but had a long conversation with Coconut and Bhun in which they kept nodding in my direction. He knew no more than did Mary. Bhun and Coconut were giving her man a good listening to, and I didn't like the way they kept looking at us. I felt an intuitive unease about whatever it was he was saying.

After lunch Mary, Mick, Phil and I went to the water to bathe our tired feet. I learned a lot about the region from Mary, particularly about the opium crops. Opium, she told us, was a cure-all medicine for the hill tribes. It was not considered unrespectable for a person to use the opium as a comfort in old age, and many did. But the young tribespeople had been corrupted by the spectacle of Western trekkers trying a smoke for larks. It made the practice seem more desirable. The Western youths could always jet back to their lives at home, far away from the call of the poppy; but the young people here were left with the temptation in their backyard for every day of their lives. The path to addiction was very short.

The Thai authorities, under pressure from the West, had begun to burn the opium crops to deal with the heroin epidemic at source. The hill tribe addicts were therefore driven into the town where they were introduced to processed heroin rather than field opium. This in turn meant the use of shared syringes, which had spread infection among the ethnic people. The crop burning had caused a new AIDS epidemic.

'A mess, here and at home,' Phil said.

'Well, yes,' Mary answered. We all went quiet for a minute or two.

I got up and left the others chatting as I had a poke around the village. These people had nothing that would make anyone want to spend any length of time there, and I couldn't imagine Charlie wanting to stay put. Sure, she might have hung around for a while to smoke some opium, but even so the life of a subsistence farmer is limited in its attractions. Maybe they slaughter a pig every other month to represent a big day in the calendar. What Oxford-educated city girl is going to be impressed by that?

I tried to take a picture of one of the huts, but a Hmong woman came out and angrily waved me away. I'd been warned that some of the hill tribes didn't like it – that they thought you were stealing their essence – but the Lisu hadn't seemed to mind having their souls trapped inside my Olympus Trip. Suitably chastened, I returned to the river and took a shot of Phil wading in the water and of Mick and Mary chatting at the river's edge. They were talking and laughing. I was about to say something when the mahout arrived with his elephants at a trot.

There were three of the magnificent behemoth creatures. They thundered into the village, and stood with overwhelming presence, stinking and cooling like steam engines on a railway platform. We watched the cumbersome process of the loading of supplies. There was a high platform with a ladder for mounting the elephants. Mary climbed on by stepping from the platform on to the elephant's head and thence into a wooden seat roped precariously along its back. We shouted lots of encouraging and jolly remarks but I wasn't feeling jolly. The deeper we moved into the jungle and saw things like this, the lower was the lodging of my spirits.

'I've seen everything now,' Mick said, after we'd waved her away. I could tell he was sorry to see Mary go.

'It wouldn't have worked out,' Phil said to him. 'Your tattoos were different.' It was meant to be funny. I threw a small stone in the river and it landed with a tiny plop.

It was shortly after Mary's departure that Coconut dropped his bombshell.

'But you never said anything about this before!' I exploded, forgetting about that loss-of-face thing.

He wanted us to go downriver by bamboo raft. He said it would be half an hour to an hour, what with the water level being low, and then we would abandon the raft and cut inland, saving, he said, almost half a day's trekking. This I had no problem with. It was what came after that I found unacceptable. Coconut told us we would overnight in another village, and that the following morning he and Bhun would turn back, and we would be left to make the last half-day's journey alone.

I had a feeling they'd been spooked by something Mary's guide had told them, and I flipped. 'Alone! You must be crazy! How are we going to make it alone through this lot? How? Just how do you think we're going to do that!'

I was shouting at Coconut. Bhun tried to calm me by placing his hand on my forearm. 'You dadda,' he said. 'Me dadda. Me unstand you. You my fren. We no 'low go there.'

Wrenching my arm away I appealed to Coconut. 'What's he saying?'

'Bhun feel very bad. I feel very bad. But we not allowed to go there. Too dangerous for us. Them guys think we from government, maybe Bangkok, or maybe we soldiers. For *farang* not so dangerous. We can't take you.'

'Why didn't you say this earlier?'

'In Akha village we try to find you a guide. Akha man. Tomorrow take you where you want to go.'

'Looks like we're being relayed on,' Phil said, while Mick nervously fingered his amulet.

'It's not as simple as that, Phil. What if we do find Charlie? We'll need these two to bring us out again.'

'From the look of things,' Phil retorted, 'I don't see as we have much choice.'

An extremely old Hmong woman, hearing the commotion,

came out of a nearby hut. She looked about two hundred years old as she waved a wedge of opium under my nose. She wouldn't go away. I wanted to punch her in the face.

'Sorry,' Bhun said, stroking my arm again. 'Sorry.'

22

No prevailing upon Coconut and Bhun could to get them to change their minds. They were both family men – something that hadn't occurred to me before that moment – and they were not going to take the risk. Neither was in any sense a timid man, but they were not prepared to cross into the territory into which we needed to go. It was bandit country, a zone of lawlessness, and though Coconut tried to reassure me that the uncertainty for us was far less than the hazard to them, all their anxieties immediately transmitted to me. I asked the other two if we should turn back.

'You're fuckin' joking,' is all Mick said. 'We go on.'

'They make a journey. It gets darker,' Phil said with a thin smile. 'Swords, lions, dragons, darkness.' I remember shaking my head: he might as well have spoken in the Hmong language. At least I could understand Mick.

This trick of Phil's – of speaking in riddles – was getting to me. It riled me beyond reason.

The bamboo raft was one of many floating near the Hmong village. Bhun whittled some bamboo and expertly lashed a tripod together, from which he suspended our backpacks. We had to take off our shoes and tie them to the tripod, as the raft itself glided just under the surface of the water. Coconut steered from the front with a long, sturdy bamboo pole, and Bhun from the back. Though Mick, Phil and I were also entrusted with poles, we were pretty ineffective. At least the poles made us look a little more manly than we felt in the company of these all-action boys. The water journey passed quickly. I had a lot of things on my mind.

'How's your leg?' I asked Phil, genuinely concerned.

'Oh,' he said lightly, 'it's not *those* two ticks that are the problem.'

I stroked my pole through the water and thought about what he'd said. Then it occurred to me he was talking about me and Mick. I turned and stared at him. 'What exactly did you mean by that?'

'You're the one who knows everything,' he said. 'Figure it out.'

I took an aggressive step towards him and the raft wobbled. 'Keep your mind on the job,' Mick shouted.

The pea-green river ran swiftly. There were sections of white water where we had to glide the raft between smooth boulders. Bhun trained his eyes on the water, thwacking it occasionally with his pole. 'Snake,' he said.

We reached a spot where a herd of water buffalo wallowed. Here we abandoned the raft, laced up our shoes and continued our trek, but not before I had to pluck a leech off my thigh. Most of the walking was accomplished in a dismal silence, and I took my eyes off the extraordinary lush landscape. I looked back at Mick. He was suffering. His feet were badly blistered, he was sweating profusely, he was scratching his mosquito bites, and he had the shits. I wondered what sort of man would put himself through this for no obvious reason. If he'd thought this was going to be a jaunt with a bit of sex tourism thrown in, he was experiencing a severe re-education.

Meanwhile Phil, also caked in sweat, seemed to be retreating deeper and deeper into an inner world. His comments got briefer and more obscure. His remark about the *other* ticks suggested he regarded Mick and I as the burden he had to carry on this enterprise, and not the other way round. He was the still centre of his own private world. What's more he seemed to regard this as a perilous spiritual journey, when the dangers were material and very real.

I began to feel a deep sense of despondency, and I felt guilty for allowing the pair of them to come with me. It was starting to go wrong, and now I saw little prospect of finding Charlie. We were in the remote jungle on the word of a thieving, drug-smuggling girl convict, entering territory that scared even these hardened guides. I began to be haunted by terrible visions of myself dying in some forgotten and dreadful place, far from home, far from everything I loved.

Jealous? Phil had called me jealous. Was he talking about Sheila, and the affair? Or did he mean Charlie? Was he accusing me of being jealous of Charlie; or of him; or of both of them? I thrashed at some overhanging bamboo and pushed the notion aside.

It was madness, this entire trek. Preposterous. I lashed at the bamboo again, and my teeth started chattering, as if I was chilled. Sunlight dappled the rubbery leaves as a shape formed at the periphery of my vision, a shape which I took to be a bird or an animal. It was no more than a shadow, a silhouette even, but then the thing swooped down from the jungle canopy and started to close around me. It was like a heavy, damp cloak settling on my shoulders and pressing a great weight down on my lungs. I felt a rancid breath on my neck. There was corruption in the air, and a sound like a veil tearing. I tried to lash the thing away, and when my hand passed through it a moment of hideous panic followed. It was the loneliest thing I had ever experienced in my life.

'Stop! Stop!' I was hyperventilating. The others came to a halt. 'Something jumped on me. Out of the trees.'

'Nothing on you now, pal,' Mick said.

'We've got to turn back. At once.'

I started babbling nonsense until Mick put his big paw on my shoulder. 'Take a deep breath,' he said. 'Hold it in.'

'I can't do this.'

'Yes, we can. Take a breather, old pal.'

I did what he told me. Phil shuffled uncomfortably and the guides looked on.

'Is it all right?' I asked Mick at length.

'It's all right.' He had one hand on each of my shoulders and he was looking deep into my eyes.

'Is it?'

'It's all right. Take a sip of water. It's just one foot in front of the other, Danny. One foot in front of the other.'

I'd completely lost it. I felt unstitched. Nothing physical had come at me from the trees. I was jumping at shadows, shivering at an encounter my mind had constructed out of jungle light and shade. I don't know what the guides made of my outburst, but I was very close to flight; I mean literally running, fleeing, back the way we'd come. It was the oddest thing. I had this fantastic idea that I'd come upon some malignant spirit, some other-worldly force at the exact centre of my panic.

I felt, too, that it had singled me out for attention.

But then perhaps not. When I had recovered enough to dismiss the thing as a figment, it was made worse by Phil laughing – slightly hysterically – and saying, 'Yes, I had my own encounter with him earlier this morning! Ha ha! Ha!'

I stared at my son, laughing at me in the jungle. Then Coconut said, 'On. We go on.'

After that I managed to get my breath back and to resume the march, and it didn't happen again.

When we reached the Akha village, I realised that I'd seen some of this tribe before, in Chiang Mai, touting bracelets and beads to the tourists. They were different again to the Hmong and the Lisu, almost a pygmy race, and some of the women were so tiny I mistook them for children. Once again they saw an opportunity to milk us for a few bhat, pressing on us the usual rubbishy gewgaws. Their aggression in this was alarming, and as they got up close I saw that quite a few of the old women had their teeth sharpened to points, and that their lips were stained purple.

'Phil! Hey Phil!' Mick said. 'Are you thinking what I'm thinking?'

'That depends,' Phil said, trying to fend off the attentions of one tiny, dagger-mouthed matron, her lips puckered like the leather drawstring on a miser's purse, 'on what you are thinking.'

'What I'm thinking is: you wouldn't want those jaws round your wedding tackle, would you Phil?'

The next morning, as Coconut and Bhun prepared to pull out, I made one last effort to retain their services, but not even an offer to triple their payment would induce them to go a step further.

Shortly after our arrival in the Akha village they introduced us to a young Akha man – a teenager possibly – who had agreed to take us on from there. Our spirits had been lifted when the Thai-speaking young man claimed, through Coconut, to know of a *farang* woman living in a village at the distance of half a day's trek. Coconut said it corresponded with the place Claire Merchant had indicated on the map.

The boy, who spoke no English, had also babbled a great deal which Coconut had either not understood or chose not to tell us. When questioned, he hadn't actually seen the *farang* woman himself, but he'd heard of her. He said she was a 'guest' of the village. When I asked Coconut what that meant, he said he didn't know.

When the time came for Coconut and Bhun to leave, I thought they were never actually going to get away. They were clearly suffering terribly and in a manner surprising to the three of us.

'Are they going to fuck off, or what?' Mick wondered aloud.

'They've lost face,' said Phil.

I felt bitter. 'They're dumping us.'

With their packs hoisted they spoke quietly to each other, now unwilling to meet our eyes. Then, in a gesture almost ceremonial in its execution, they took their long army knives out of their belts. I heard myself swallow. But each laid his knife flat across the palms of both hands, stepped forwards and offered them to us. 'For cutting vines,' Coconut said, his eyes slightly damp. 'And trees. Take.'

It was bewildering to have to guess whether they were leaving these as weapons for which we might have need or as tokens of apology for failing to see the journey through to its end. We hesitated before taking the blades. 'When you want to come back, send word,' Coconut said. 'I will come here for you.'

'Sure,' Mick said. 'We'll call you on the telephone. Do we have your e-mail address? We'll fucking well e-mail you.'

Some of this sarcasm must have come across, because Coconut said, 'Send word: Coconut, Chiang Mai, come now. These people will pass message on, next village, next village, and I will come here.'

I think he actually wanted to believe it himself. 'Thank you, both of you,' I said, though I didn't feel it. They *wai*d us, and we made Western handshakes, and then they turned and were gone. The Akha boy, who had watched all this – rather stupidly and with his mouth hanging open – turned to us and said, 'Ha!'

I was a bit anxious that they'd made a gift of those ferocious-looking blades. I'd taken one; Mick the other. After we'd got underway, with the knives tucked into our belts, I kept my hand hovering near it, waiting for bandits to leap out from the foliage at any moment. I heard skitters and movements on the parched jungle floor that had my fingers flexing around the teak handle. The landscape, too, with its red earth and glistening green vegetation reminded me of every unpleasant Vietnam movie I'd ever seen in my life.

But nothing happened, and in a trek that went on for almost five hours we met no one except for the time when we passed through another very small Akha village, and where our boy guide sang out to everyone, apparently very proud of his lucrative responsibility for leading three ridiculous, sweating, pink-faced giants through the poppy fields.

And the poppies there were growing in gay profusion. The previous opium crops we had seen were nothing more than allotments. Here, entire slopes were devoted to the bloom. I noticed that beans or some similar vegetable were grown between the plants, confusing the crop. White, red and purple flowers were spread over the green vegetation like the laundry, hung out to dry, of a convocation of priests. I noticed that many of the flowers were blown and beginning to drop their petals. Under the bright sunlight, the flowers gleamed waxy, an hallucination of the gardens of paradise.

We walked through field after field. I wondered if it were possible to become drugged by mere proximity. Though I tried to make a mental note of the route, and the position of the sun, it was hopeless. We walked along intersecting pathways, and we followed narrow animal trails, and we walked through stretches of pink-leafed jungle where there was no trail whatsoever. I would have had no idea how to return to the Akha village even if I'd wanted to.

'Earlier I asked you how your legs were,' I said to Phil along the way. 'I'd appreciate a straight answer.'

'My legs are fine. Thanks for your concern. How's your leech bite?'

'Fine. It's fine.'

I gave up. *Thank you for your concern?* Where did this incredible formality come from? I'd never before realised how impeccable good manners were just a mask for hostility. Every time I tried to get past Phil's riddles and his double talk he shrank back into a language as exact as a cube of ice.

We heard the village before we saw it. At first we were confused, because even though there was no possibility of electrical power in this place, what we were hearing sounded like a massively amplified radio; or rather some kind of singing which was certainly not like the Thai music we'd heard in Chiang Mai. It was a male voice, swooping and reverberating and booming. I don't know if it was meant to intimidate, but it succeeded. My guts churned.

With the hills rising steeply on all sides, the boy led us into a natural basin. The slopes had been cleared of trees for farming, and a mist shrouded the remaining vegetation. Bamboo huts huddled on the valley floor, close together but in two separate clusters, and even as we approached I could see that the construction varied from those we'd seen before. The roofs were made from some giant, parched leaf, and all the huts were built on very short stilts.

From these details I'd already guessed that this was not an Akha village, and I sensed the nervousness of the boy guide as we went towards the nearest cluster of huts. I can't remember what I was feeling as we crossed those last few hundred yards. In any event, all detail of those moments prior to entering the settlement has been swamped by what followed, for it was here, in this unprepossessing village, that I was to find my daughter, Charlie.

23

Charlie Charlie Charlie. My wonder-girl, my daughter-in-flight, the little fist enfolding my heart the moment she entered my life, my beacon, the silk flag of my love for all that is good in a bad world.

I'd found her.

What happened in those eerie moments of our entry into that village is torched into my memory. The sun in the sky became over-charged with energy and everything seemed to take place under a white light of strontium intensity. That strange rising and falling music, broadcast from within the village, amplified and slowed.

First a dog started to bark at our approach. As it leapt at us our Akha boy guide slapped it down with his bamboo staff. The dog yelped and the commotion summoned a man from within the cluster of huts. Stripped to the waist, he wore a pair of baggy trousers pegged halfway down the calf muscles. He carried some sort of gardening adze. On seeing us, he stopped dead. My impression was one of seeing a man witnessing a supernatural phenomenon: Mick, Phil and I might have been ghosts.

The Akha boy stepped forward, speaking rapidly in a tongue which was not Thai, although I heard the word *farang* two or three times as the boy motioned towards us. The man pointed inside the village with his adze. At last he swung his shoulders away from us, indicating that we should follow.

We passed the shadowy entrances to a number of huts. Three or four women squatted around a patch of canvas spread on the floor outside one of the huts, preparing tumorous green vegetables. Without interrupting their work they watched us go by.

The man with the adze stepped inside a darkened hut, and, sensing something momentous, I squeezed my way in front of the boy, anxious to be next. A single candle flame burned inside, barely affording us enough light to see the figure, eyes closed, seated in the cross-legged lotus position on the bamboo pallet at the back of the hut. There was a yeasty odour in the hut. My stomach squeezed. Weird music vibrated the air. I let the backpack slip from my shoulders and kneeled beside the pallet.

'Charlotte,' I said. 'Charlotte.'

She was thin, gaunt even, but by the light of the single candle flame I didn't think she looked so terrible. Her eyes flickered open, and flared with recognition. Very softly, almost inaudibly, she said, 'Daddy?'

'Yes. It's me.'

'I knew you were coming. I just knew.'

Then I said, and I don't know why, 'I'm the postman of Porlot.'

'Daddy, it's *Porlock*. And not a postman at all.' Then she yawned, broke the lotus position to stretch out on the pallet, and closed her eyes. Her breathing changed. She seemed to have gone to sleep.

I felt Mick and Phil pressing behind me. 'Is it her?' they said. 'Is it?'

My hands were shaking. Not just trembling, but shuddering and jolting. My teeth chattered. I couldn't manage an answer. Phil tenderly linked his arm in mine, and Mick on the other side did the same. 'Easy,' Mick whispered, 'easy.'

I calmed a little, and releasing them I spread myself on the bed beside Charlotte. I held her head on my shoulder, hugging her, and the very first thing I did was to smell her hair. I knew exactly what I was after. That scent; that pure charge; the love amalgam and the herald note from Day One, sealed in under the fontanelle; the perfume of heaven. I inhaled her. I opened my nostrils to it, and I got that hit. I absolutely got it.

I lay there, still trembling but experiencing a voiding of relief and exoneration. I'd found her. I could take her home. We could all go home.

Or so it seemed.

I don't know how long I lay there, but when I'd recovered, I soon discovered that Charlie was not merely asleep. I'd been deceived by that moment when I found her sitting upright and she'd spoken to me very softly. I tried shaking her, patting her face, pinching her. I was alone in the hut with her: the others had stepped outside when they'd seen me climb on the pallet.

'Mick! Where are you, Mick?'

He quickly appeared in the doorway.

'I can't wake her, Mick!'

Mick came over and put a hand on her forehead. Then he rolled back the skin of her eyelid with his thumb. Her eyeball had almost disappeared. He sneezed, twice. 'Is she doped up?'

I didn't know how to answer. I didn't really know what doped up looked like. I glanced around. There was a bowl of water beside her, the single candle, and an earthenware jar in which three flower heads floated in fetid water – perhaps the source of the bad odour. I was looking for a long pipe and a box of matches, or even a syringe – hell, anything. But there was no sign of drugs paraphernalia of any kind.

'Help me get her up and out of here,' I said to Mick. 'Get Phil.'

'Just a second, Danny. Let's take stock of the situation.'

I looked at his big face, orange in the candlelight. He was sweating profusely.

'What do you mean, take stock? She needs attention. We get her back to Chiang Mai and on a plane to England, it's as simple as that.'

'Simple as that,' said Mick.

'Well?'

'Come outside a minute,' Mick said firmly. I was still holding Charlie's hand. 'Let go of her. She's been here for some time and she's not going anywhere just yet. Come outside.'

Reluctantly I released Charlie's hand and followed Mick. Outside the hut, it appeared that the entire village had gathered. They were huddled seven or eight yards from the door of the hut itself. They were a pretty sullen bunch. Only the man who had led us there – the one with the adze – was chattering happily, seeming to have earned some status in having been the first to encounter us.

Phil sat on the slatted porch of the hut, hunched over, fingering his pocket Bible.

'You've been in there for over an hour,' Mick said. This didn't seem right, but I took him at his word. 'While you were in there I tried this.'

Mick approached the huddle of villagers, toothless old men, other men with loose turbans and machetes in their belts, women with suckling babies. He displayed several banknotes prominently, waving them in the air. 'Bhat,' Mick said loudly. 'Dollars.' He fanned the notes like a deck of cards to advertise their bounty. 'Chiang Mai. Guide. Chiang Mai. Yes?'

The villagers gazed blankly at him. He approached one of the stronger-looking men, waving the money under his nose. 'Chiang Mai? Yes? Good?' The man retreated a yard. Another responded similarly.

Mick came back, tugging his pack of cigarettes from his breast pocket. He gave one to me. He sneezed again, and wiped snot from his nose with the ball of his thumb. I noticed his eyes looked red and sore. 'You see, I already tried to take things in hand. Thought I'd set it up while you were in there. This is the reaction I got.'

'Where's the kid? The one who got us here.'

'Gone,' Phil put in. 'Long gone.'

'They said something to him and he fucked off, pretty quick,' Mick told me. 'Now, I'm all for carrying Charlie out of here, carrying her on my back if necessary. But would you remember which way we came?'

Remember which way we came? I don't think, at that point, I could have found my way even to the edge of this thirty-hut village. But somehow the import of this still managed to escape me. I'd found my daughter, that was the material thing. Everything else was just logistics. Like Mick, I was prepared to carry her out if that was what was required.

The audience of villagers, bored now with the performance, began to drift away.

'Stretcher her out,' I said. 'We make a stretcher from bamboo, and we carry her. No problem.'

Mick shook his head and ground his cigarette into the earth.

'Why not?' I said.

'I'm thinking.'

'What's to think about? Let's do it!'

'Danny, it took us about five hours to reach here from the last Akha village. Fast trekking. Carrying a stretcher between us, you can calculate twice that long; and that assumes we know where to go.'

'We'll make it, eh Phil?'

'Listen to him, Father,' Phil said, suddenly sharp with me. 'You haven't taken in a word of what Mick is saying.'

'I've had time to have a look at this, Danny: we've got no food with us; we've got little water; we've got no map; and at the moment we've got no guide.'

'We'll retrace our steps.'

'Retrace? Danny, this is NOT AN EVENING'S STROLL DOWN TO THE PUB!'

'I know what it is! I know we—'

'Danny, shut up and listen! You never fucking listen! Never! Why don't you ever fucking listen! This is the jungle! We're in the jungle! We've got a sick woman to carry out of the jungle!'

'Keep your hair on!'

'You keep *your* fucking hair on! This needs some thought. We sit down and we think this through. There's about two hours left before it starts to get dark, so that means we ain't going anywhere tonight.'

For a moment, in a kind of delirium and in a knock of blood in the brain, I saw Mick and Phil as just further obstacles in my way to getting Charlie out of this place. If they wouldn't help me, I told myself, then I'd do it alone. I walked back inside the darkened hut, shook Charlie in frustration but to no visible effect, and then came out again. Of the villagers, only one old woman remained behind to watch us, a toothless hag with sugary black eyes. The sky tilted savagely again as I realised that Mick's logic was inescapable. I was going to have to accept an overnight stay in the village before getting Charlie away.

The old woman waddled up to me, pointing at the hut, smacking her lips. She had something in her hand for me. It was yet another wedge of the blasted opium. In my anger and impotence I slapped it out of her hand.

The old woman seemed unfazed. With a hand supporting her creaking old back, she leaned down and with spindly, leathery fingers plucked the opium out of the red dust. Then she turned back to me.

'Booooo!' she said before hobbling away. 'Boooooooooooooo!'

The three of us settled in Charlie's hut. If there was any permission to be had, I didn't know where it was coming from. I didn't much care; all I wanted to do was tend to Charlie.

I'd tried to deny it at first, but she was in pretty poor shape. The first thing I wanted to do was to wash her from head to toe. Phil helped me. She wore nothing but shorts and a rancid T-shirt, and when we stripped them off I realised she was developing one or two bed sores. Though a little emaciated, she was not starving, and apart from the chafing sores her skin was not in bad condition, so I concluded that the villagers had been looking after her. Someone had to maintain the candle, and put the flowers and water there.

Phil soaked a flannel towel and proceeded to dab her. Mick had some antiseptic cream which he gingerly massaged into her bed sores. He wasn't looking too good himself: he was sneezing and he was exhausted. *Don't fall ill on me now, Mick*, was my selfish thought. When we'd done everything we could for Charlie, I suggested to Mick that he lie down, take a breather while I looked for something to eat. I was only a little surprised when he acceded.

I tried to raise his spirits by mentioning the word beer. It had worked in the Lisu village, but I knew that here things were going to be different. Up until now, all our needs had been attended to by the presence of guides. I had a few bhat in my pocket, and I stepped outside to see what currency it might have.

The heat of the day was locked into the red earth, but the cooling air had a syrupy quality. Strange music was still emanating from the centre of the village, so I headed towards it. There was little activity going on. I sensed people inside the stilted huts as I passed by cautiously. Pots boiled outside unattended. Black pigs and scrawny chickens snuffled and scratched at the baked earth. Dogs lay quiet in the late afternoon shade.

I reached the source of the music. A dust-clogged old Hitachi radio set was placed on a rickety table in the centre of the village like a sacred totem, and it was belting out loud ethnic music. Long thick cable trailed from the back of the radio set, and between the swells in the music I could hear, from somewhere, the tick and wheeze of a tiny generator. I followed the cable to the generator, which was actually stationed inside a small and otherwise unoccupied hut. It was a pretty old Honda IKVA petrol-powered contraption, though it appeared to be ticking over effectively.

The generator was screened off from the rest of the hut, but there was a gap in the bamboo screen at the rear. Passing through the gap I was surprised to find that the rest of the hut contained numerous identical large cardboard boxes neatly stacked one upon the other. The boxes, and there must have been four dozen of them, were sealed. I ran my finger along one of the seals. There was no way of telling what was inside the boxes.

I returned to the radio set. It was broadcasting so loudly its blown speakers were fuzzing, not that anyone seemed to be taking much notice. It was from there, at one side of the cleared area, that I noticed a striking and peculiar structure.

It was a crudely constructed arch, or perhaps more accurately a pergola, though it was not erected for trailing leafy plants. Nonetheless, it was still some kind of gateway, with uprights and crossbeams, but with each of the uprights fenced off to create a clear pathway. What really drew my attention was the cluster of objects in the fenced-off areas either side of the pathway.

There were numerous carvings, crudely executed, of human figures. On closer inspection I saw that some of the carvings were no more than tree trunks, or tree branches inverted so as to resemble a pair of open legs. What made me gasp slightly were the huge, erect penises, carved naturally from the grainy wood or grafted on. There were five such 'men', all with boastful and healthy-looking bulbously erect pricks.

They had their mates, too. Laid out in the dust were several female forms. The tree artist had carefully selected suitably thigh-like tree forks, suggestively bent at the knee, carved vulvas prominently displayed. Each carving had a pleasantly rounded belly, neatly smoothed by the artisan, and an attractive navel. Some of the figures ended just above the waist; others extended to a carved head, disproportionately small, concave and crudely representational.

I leaned over to stroke one of the supine figures, but with my fingers inches from the smoothed wood I was arrested in the act by a small child pulling at my sleeve. Highly agitated, he flapped his free hand at the carvings. He was afraid, telling me not to touch. Evidently I'd just been saved from breaching tribal taboo.

The boy was still shouting at me in a distraught fashion. Unnerved, I went back to Charlie's hut without having accomplished my errand. When I got there I found Mick asleep and Charlie awake. She was sitting upright and was being fed by the old woman from whose hands I'd swatted the opium. The crone scowled at me as I entered the hut.

Phil looked at me and shrugged.

24

A long dark night lay ahead of me. On returning to the hut to find the old woman dribbling broth into Charlie's mouth, I'd naturally attempted to speak to Charlie. But this time there was no recognition; no 'Daddy' as in the first moment of our arrival; no banter about the Postman of Porlock or whatever; nothing, not a flicker of interest. She gulped the soup and failed to respond to anything I put to her. Meanwhile the old woman watched me with critical eyes, and with her lips pursed in what I took to be the suppression of a smile.

'Has she said anything to you?' I asked Phil.

'Nothing.'

But she'd been sitting upright, waiting for me when I entered the hut. Expecting me. Both Mick and Phil looked sceptical when I told them this. I began to doubt it myself. Almost as if our brief conversation had taken place in some imagined or telepathic universe. My sense of what was real and what wasn't real in this place was already becoming unthreaded.

When I gave up trying to communicate with Charlie, the old woman nodded. She shuffled forward, once again producing opium from the folds of her gown. With it this time came a small ceramic pipe and a box of matches. She jabbed her finger at Charlie.

'No,' I said firmly.

The old woman shrugged, and put the things away.

I knew that if Charlie was addicted then she was going to have a craving. But I had no way of determining whether her current condition was attributable to the opium or to some other condition. All I could do at that moment was to withdraw the drug and see what happened.

'The old woman's intentions are benign,' Phil said, reading my thoughts. 'She's obviously been the one looking after

Charlie, feeding her, tending to her. Opium is probably the only medicine available to these people.'

I knew he was right. I had to accept that this feeble old matriarch was not the pusher at the school gates.

'Pipe,' Charlie said in a whisper.

The old woman looked hard at me, as if to say, what can I do? Her face was simian, very old, and yet her skin was oddly smooth. I couldn't tell if she was prematurely old or immortally young. Except, perhaps, that her eyes gave it away. They were oddly translucent, like cellophane, as if burned out from staring at the sun. It made her seem other-worldly, shamanic.

She tried to tell me something about Charlie. She stroked her own shoulders and gestured outside the hut, maybe at the sky; she made utterly impenetrable signals. It was hopeless. She gave up, but with a cruel smile.

When we'd settled the matter of the opium, that Charlie *wasn't* going to be given any while I was there, I tried to make the old woman understand that we would want something to eat. I pointed at Mick's sleeping form; I pointed at my own yawning mouth. I made eating gestures. I then produced a few bhat from my pocket.

She reached out for the bhat, and swatted the money clean out of my hand, just as I had done earlier with her opium. She fixed her perplexing gaze on me.

The money lay on the floor between us. 'You've made your point,' I said.

She wrinkled her nose, not understanding.

'Boooo!' I said, and she seemed happier with that. She left the hut.

She returned with a large bowl of soup and noodles, and three spoons. I woke Mick, but he groaned and declined to have any, said he couldn't face it; he went back to sleep immediately. The soup was thin and greasy, but it contained some aromatic spice which reminded me of sage and onion, and of home. Phil and I supped in silence.

Later I tried to sleep but it was hopeless. My brain was firing on every cylinder, all smoke and no traction. I'd found Charlie, and yet I hadn't. I was ready to take her home and yet I couldn't. I lay on the pallet next to her, holding her foot while she slept. I don't know why I held her foot. It was a part of her that wasn't sore, but it was almost as if she'd jumped into another world, another dimension full of tormenting spirits and wild-eyed demons, and there I was holding her by the ankle, trying to drag her back into this world.

In the night she and I actually had a conversation. It went like this:

'Pipe.'

'No, Charlie. No more pipe.'

'Is that you again, Dad?'

'It's me darlin'. It's me.'

'You keep coming and going, Dad. Where's Mum?'

'I'm here for you now.'

'Why are you holding my foot?'

'To stop you from falling.'

'Is it a long way down? Oh, I think it must be.'

'I've got you, my baby.'

And with that she slept. Later in the night she got up and with painful steps made her way to a pan in the corner of the hut. I helped her like I did when she was two years old, holding her over the potty. Then she stumbled back to her bed.

Phil snored and twitched in his sleep through all of this. I tried hard to sleep myself but I lay awake, staring at the ceiling made of dried tobacco leaves the size of dinner plates. I sipped water. I got up to check on the snoring Mick. I placed my hand on his forehead: he had a raging temperature. I emptied my pack looking for aspirin in case he woke. I found the book I'd brought with me but which I'd forgotten, the Thomas De Quincey, which I'd failed to make much sense of earlier.

My mind was racing feverishly. I tried calming myself by reading a bit more by the tiny light still burning, in the useless hope that its long-winded rhythms might slow my own hurtling thoughts and send me off to sleep. I supposed that De Quincey used to sit up writing by candlelight, which couldn't have been good for his eyes. Then again, I suppose if you're a laudanum hop-head, you don't give much of a damn about the state of your vision.

But in that tiny globe of light and lying there beside Charlie, I read a very strange thing. De Quincey was talking about the druggist in Oxford Street who sold him his very first opium, and he suggested that the man, the druggist, may not have been of earthly origin. I know how crazy that must sound, and of course it *is* crazy, but I report it here because at the time of reading it both unnerved and impressed me. De Quincey said that he often went back to the same spot in Oxford Street to look for the shop, but he could find neither it nor the druggist who'd dispensed his first opium. It was almost as if, De Quincey suggested, that the druggist, having completed his mission, had absconded to another world.

It was minded of the strange things Decker had told me about this place. Perhaps it was because I was reading through the graveyard hours, and my mood was unspeakably low and confused. Or maybe it was because the night air still had a syrupy tang and I was conscious of being surrounded by acres and acres of opium poppies exhaling sweetly in the night. But I felt at that moment it was entirely possible that there might be a spirit of the opium, at large, roaming out there in the dark, looking for converts, searching out victims in the form of disciples, followers, supporters, benefactors.

I put the book aside. I suppose I'd still been reading with the aim of getting some sort of insight into what was going on in Charlie's head. I hoped it would tell me what would make an intelligent young woman want to live her life with this monkey on her back.

I could understand some of these jungle people smoking the stuff. What else was there to do round here? But Charlie had all the entertainments, distractions and accoutrements of modern life right at her fingertips. Pubs. Theatres. Concerts. The usual blizzard of consumer goods. Cinema. Television. Well, not television; sometimes the thought of watching yet another night's television has been enough to make even me want to turn to drugs. But the other things.

I thought about that for a while. Why did that list sound so distressingly inadequate? Sometimes I hate the sound of my own voice, and even the insidious whispering of my own thoughts. Theatre? Fucking hypocrite! There were two theatres in my town, and I'd never been to one of them in my life. Cinema? The last time Sheila and I went to the cinema they still had something called an intermission and a lady with ice creams on a tray. Shopping I detest, especially in the malls and the megastores. As for pubs, I could have slaked a beer, but I didn't need the fake Regency decor or the horse brasses or the brewery's shabby themed ambience. Or the quiz. God help us, there was the quiz. No, there were big questions forming about the nature and purpose of life itself. Questions that wouldn't go down well in the Clipper on a Tuesday night.

I tried to remember what I was doing with my 'leisure time' when I heard about Charlie. That was it, I was trying to assemble flatpack furniture. The tiny candle flame, the only light in the hut, wavered at the thought of the world's flatpack furniture. It was late, and I was dispirited. Drugs were beginning to have some sort of a case.

The next morning I prowled the village, looking for material with which I might improvise a stretcher. I would be put to assemble a flatpack again, but the task had been complicated by the events of the night. Mick's condition had not improved. He was running a fever, and though we'd dosed him with aspirin it was apparent we would not be going anywhere for some time. Phil and I had to help him out of the hut to the bamboo outhouse, and stand nearby as he groaned his way through a dreadful example of the squits.

'Hold him up!' I shouted at Phil.

'I am holding him up! It's your end that's falling down!'

It was true. Mick was a dead weight, and as I felt myself dropping him my natural instinct was to blame Phil. The fact is, Phil was surprisingly strong and, though I didn't tell him so, I couldn't have managed the job without him.

Mick was shivering wildly when we shouldered him back inside the hut. We laid him down on his bed and, wiping the perspiration from my brow, I turned to Phil. I looked at him and he returned a gaze of irritating soulfulness. 'What?' he said.

'Nothing.' I didn't want to say anything. When you're at

work, on a job and after lifting something heavy with another bloke, you maybe make the briefest eye contact, possibly offer a fractional nod in recognition of what you've just accomplished together, which is all I wanted from Phil. Thanks; good; done it; whatever. But no. I get this big beady-eyed spiritual gaze, like I should write a poem or a seven-verse folk song for him about us taking Mick out for a crap. He was driving me to distraction, so he was.

After Mick had drifted off to sleep, and with Charlie also out for the count, I had to do something to stop myself from going mad. Constructing a stretcher, I thought, would at least afford me a practical method of working towards finding our way out of this place. I left Phil with the sleeping casualties.

I had the long knife Coconut had given me, and I thought it might come in handy. I'd found a bit of trellis leaning against one of the huts. I didn't know who it belonged to but I took it anyway. It would form the basis of my stretcher, though I needed to fashion a pair of long handles at each end of the thing if we weren't going to shuffle our way through the jungle an inch at a time. My search took me to the far edge of the village, and it was there I realised why the place seemed so empty. Most of the villagers were out working the slopes.

And the entire slopes on that side of the village, acre upon acre, were flush with the waxy, ecclesiastical colours of the opium poppy.

The flowers were blowing. Giant petals, like radiant parachute silks, trailed across the fields. It was a beautiful morning. In the sunlit haze of the daybreak the villagers wore their vibrant ethnic dress. They crouched at the poppy heads, moving backwards through the plants, bobbing, settling at a poppy head, and retreating, like bees working the flowers for nectar. The sky flaked gold. The villagers, aware of me watching them, were not at all distracted from their work.

There were no suitable trees around for me to cut for my stretcher handles, so I retraced my steps. Back in the cleared area in the midst of the village, the totem radio sat proudly on its rickety table, though it had ceased broadcasting some time in the night when the generator had been shut down. I decided to check out the generator hut again.

As I'd feared, there was nothing inside I could use. I looked over the big, neatly stacked pile of cardboard boxes at the rear of the hut, intrigued about what might be inside them.

I checked the doorway of the hut, from where I could scan the cleared area of the village. There was no one about. If any of the villagers were lurking inside their huts it was doubtful that they could see into the shadows of the generator hut. I hesitated for a moment and then ducked back inside.

The cardboard boxes were well sealed. I had to wrestle one down to the floor before I could open it. I tried to slide my blade under the masking tape sealing the boxes, so that I could quickly reseal the box after I'd had a peep inside; but the blade was too thick and I couldn't get under the tape without gouging the cardboard. Instead I decided to slit the tape at the joint of the flaps; afterwards I could put the box underneath some of the others to disguise it.

I scored the blade along the sealed joint, and the box popped open. I heard a light scuffle outside the hut. I waited, holding my breath. It was nothing. I checked at the door again, but the clearing was deserted, silent.

I returned to the box to open the flaps. The perspiration from my brow was running into my eyes, and I had to stop to wipe my forehead with my T-shirt. Inside the open box were a number of smaller white cartons, each quite heavy. It was a tricky business extricating one of the white cartons, so tightly packed were they, but at last I managed to inch one of them out. Inside the carton were six brown bottles.

Each bottle was labelled Calpol.

I unscrewed the cap of one. It was Calpol all right. The same sticky, pink paediatric medicine used every night at home by millions of mothers to soothe their children's coughs, colds and other complaints. I thought of millions of infants in their urban homes at night, dreaming their Calpol dreams. But I couldn't understand what this massive consignment of the stuff was doing here. I pulled down another box, slit it open and took out another white carton. More Calpol.

'Find anything interesting?'

I turned round quickly.

It was a Thai male, a man about my own age. In contrast to the villagers he was dressed in Western T-shirt and camouflage shorts. He leaned casually against the frame of the door, an expression of amusement on his face, but his eyes were cold. I noticed a revolver in a leather holster on his belt.

I'd been caught red-faced and sticky-fingered, and I couldn't think of a word to say.

He came forward, extending a hand that wanted shaking. 'Hi,' he said. 'I'm Jack.'

25

The man who called himself Jack beckoned for me to follow him out of the hut. He didn't seem unduly worried that I'd been caught sniffing around the consignment of Calpol. It was of no consequence. He led me through the huts, his leather gun holster creaking slightly as we walked, towards the slopes where the villagers were harvesting the poppies.

'Let's inspect the crop, shall we?' he said. He might have been an English gentleman-farmer, holding his hands behind his back as he stepped up the slopes, hardly waiting for me to follow.

Without interrupting their work the villagers were careful to acknowledge him, not with a *wai* but with a slight bow of the head. There were smiles, there were jokes. He was clearly respected by the villagers, though it was plain he was not *of* them.

'We're hoping for a good season,' he said, his English impeccable.

The villagers were engaged in two different types of activity, each involving a specialist tool. Most were collecting resin from the poppy heads with a curious crescent-shaped tool, its curve fitting snugly around the pod so that the opium latex could be scraped on to its pan. The others, mostly women, were incising fresh pods with a three-bladed pricking tool. I felt like a visitor from the Ministry of Agriculture and Fisheries. 'Jack' noticed me observing closely.

'Ah! You like to look! Like to see what you can see? Eh?'

If this was a reference to my earlier snooping I pretended it missed me. 'Always.'

'I too. Perhaps we are similar chaps, you and I?'

I doubted it. No one I knew used the word 'chaps'. I wondered where he'd learned to speak English and to stroll around with his hands stuffed behind his back. 'I'm here about my daughter,' I said.

'I know that.' He cut me off with a wave of his hand. 'I know why you're here. I know all about it.' He stooped to pick up a lump of soil and he offered it to me. 'Can you tell if this is good for the poppy, by looking at it? It needs to be rich in alkaline.'

He held out the lump of soil for so long that I was forced to take it from him. I crumbled it between my fingers. 'I'm sure I've no idea.'

'Then come with me.'

We pushed our way between a troop of workers and I saw that Jack was leading me towards a solitary figure bent over the pods on the upper slopes. 'Why grow these beans between the poppies?' I asked, genuinely curious.

He let a finger drift skywards. 'To confuse the government spotter-planes.'

We reached the solitary worker, and a curious figure he was. Unguessably ancient with wisps of grey hair growing long from the back of his otherwise bald head, the man was not to be distracted from his work. He failed to acknowledge the presence of either of us. 'This is Khiem,' Jack said, laughing. 'He's angry with me because he says the incisions should be made in the midday heat. But I'm in a hurry to get as much done as I can today. Modern farming, what?'

Jack spoke to Khiem in a language which I didn't think was Thai. Khiem slowly raised his head to stare at me with eyes as black and shining as the carapace of a beetle; and from beneath eyebrows of such steep, horseshoe curves I thought they must have been painted on. Khiem wore the hill tribe costume but it was gloriously decked out with poppy flowers. He'd woven the flowers into his belt, on his sleeves and had cross-patterned his tunic with them. He looked to me like a figure from a fairytale. He stooped and scooped up a lump of red soil, just as Jack had done earlier.

'I asked him about the quality of the soil,' Jack said confidentially.

Khiem balled the nugget of soil between his fingers, sniffed it and then took a bite from it. He swirled it about inside his mouth like a wine connoisseur over a glass of claret. But he didn't spit it out. He appeared to swallow the soil before making some laconic remark to Jack. Then he returned to his work.

Jack looked at me obliquely. I was sure this little demonstration had some gnomic significance, but I couldn't work out what it was. 'Khiem,' he said, 'is the one who decides where to sow the crop. Which field. Which slope. He prefers these mountain hollows above the ridgelines. He says the soil is still as sweet as when he chose this spot. The people in this village think he is half man, half spirit. He's a kind of sorcerer. Khiem is the true Lord of the Poppy.'

'Even though *you* own the field, presumably.'

Though Khiem couldn't possibly have understood our conversation, he turned from his labours and fixed me with such a penetrating gaze I wished I hadn't made the remark. He jabbed a finger in my direction and spoke, animated and angry, to Jack. Some of the other workers a short distance away looked up from their labours.

'He says the crop will be good if the Lord of the Moon is allowed to do his work. He says why don't you take your daughter away from the village, so the Lord of the Moon can do his work?'

I was astonished, as much by the nature of this outburst as by the knowledge of my situation that it revealed. I was lost for words.

'Come on,' Jack said. 'Let's go.'

We walked back to the village. 'How does he know who I am? What's all this about the moon?'

'Don't be ridiculous. Everyone in the village knows who you are.'

We arrived at one of the huts at the edge of the settlement. He motioned me to sit down at the long rustic table outside. If Jack was king of the heap, the heap didn't seem to afford him many more luxuries than the rest of the villagers. Inside, however, I noticed three modern nylon backpacks. Jack went inside and unzipped one of them, returning with cigarettes and one other object. This object he placed at the far end of the long table.

It was a bottle. Not any old bottle, but an unopened bottle of Johnny Walker Scotch whisky. The amber liquid rippled with hue as it was struck by the strong sunlight. The light flared on the contours of the glass. Placed at the end of the table it was like an apparition, a mirage. I had to drag my eyes away from it.

Jack offered me a Western brand cigarette and seemed to forget about the whisky. He lit up, sat back, put his feet on the table and exhaled a thick, blue plume of tobacco smoke. 'What you going to do about your daughter?'

'I'm taking her home.'

'How will you do that?'

'I'll carry her.'

'Good luck.'

'I have my friend and my son with me.'

'Your friend is sick.'

'He'll get better. He's strong.'

'Which way you going to go?'

'Chiang Mai.'

'Sure. Which way is that?'

I made a general gesture. Something in that motion seemed to irritate Jack, because his pleasant demeanour seemed to switch in a fraction of a second. He leaned over the table and snarled, 'You don't even know what fucking country you are in!'

His eyes were frightening. Very cold. I did my best not to look intimidated. 'I'll get there.'

He smiled and leaned back, friendly again, puffing on his ciggie. 'Seriously, which country are you in?'

'Thailand?'

'Ha! Dear boy, I was right. You don't know.'

I tried to think how many times we'd crossed the river on our trek. 'We're not in Thailand?'

'Well, you might have a point. See, some of these villagers argue about where the borders actually are. You might be in Myanmar – Burma to you. Or maybe these are Shan lands, and the Shan don't respect the provisional borders. Either way, you don't know where you are.'

'Will you help me?'

'Why the fuck should I help you, dear boy?'

'Where did you learn to speak English?'

'Charterhouse, actually.'

'Where's that?'

'You haven't heard of it? What sort of an Englishman are you? A lower-class one, obviously. I'm an old Carthusian. I was there for four years.'

'Why only four years?'

'Some local trouble here. Money ran out, temporarily. Only a liquidity problem but by the time my father could pay my fees again I'd decided that I hated it anyway. Why do you keep looking at that whisky?'

'Do I?'

'It's as if you're drawn to it. As if it has a grip on your soul, so to speak.'

'I was thinking how much my friend would like a glass. He's in poor shape. Glass of whisky would help set him up.'

'Whisky is a rare commodity around here. Where *you* live, you can get the stuff in every corner shop. Rarity increases its market value, don't you think?'

'Would you mind telling me what that poppy man was saying about the moon?'

'You should ask your daughter about that.'

'I'm afraid she's too out of her head on your dope to speak to me about anything.'

'My dope? I don't think that's the case. Her condition has little to do with the small amount of opium she smokes. Most of the older people you see working in the fields smoke a little opium. They don't lie in bed all day.'

'Do you know what's the matter with my daughter?'

He shrugged and stubbed out his cigarette in the red earth. 'If you ask Khiem, he says that there's an evil spirit hanging on to her. He says it lies in the hut with her, like a fat leech, or a vampire, draining off her life force. Khiem says it sucks her life essence through a hole in her big toe.' He waved a hand through the air. 'I don't expect you to think much of Khiem's diagnosis.'

'And what do you think of it?'

Jack stood up. The leather of his holster creaked again. 'I think I've got one or two things to do. I think we'll talk some more later. Take the whisky with you. But save a glass for me, won't you?' With that he strode off through the huts, to where the harvesters were still hard at work.

After he'd gone I vented a huge sigh. I'd been practically holding my breath throughout the encounter. The man terrified me.

I picked up the bottle and carried it rather self-consciously back to Charlie's hut. I hadn't got very far in my efforts to construct a stretcher, but at least I'd been given something that might put the sparkle back in Mick's eyes. Meanwhile my head fizzed with questions about Jack the opium bandit. I knew he'd spent the last three quarters of an hour making an assessment of me, and had decided that I posed no threat. But I still had the feeling that while getting into this little kingdom of poppy cultivation had been relatively easy, getting out again was not going to prove quite so simple.

26

I was shocked, when I returned to the hut, to find Charlie up and about and nursing Mick, and not the other way round.

'Charlie!'

She looked at me, wide eyes all chromium and blue, like her mum's. She'd tied her dry, once silky hair in a girlish pony-tail, exposing her slender neck. 'Here's the old boiler,' she said lightly. After saying something provocative, like this, she had a way of touching her tongue to her lips – again a trait of her mum's. 'Didn't expect to see you in this neck of the woods.'

Not the kind of greeting I'd expected, for sure, but I didn't take it seriously. It was her way of making nothing of the spot we were in. 'Come here.' I threw my arms around her, squeezing her thin body to me. I nuzzled her neck. 'I can't tell you how relieved I am to see you on your feet!'

'Ouch! I think you cracked a rib! You're squeezing the air out of my lungs. Plus you could do with a bath, Dad. You smell like an Akha loincloth.' I stood back to look at her. Again that touch of the tongue to her lips. There was a sheen to her eyes, which made me think she'd be OK, and a smile making me believe our differences could be set aside. Maybe I'd expected a zombie who wouldn't recognise me. But she was smiling.

Or not smiling, exactly. The expression she wore was one of tolerant amusement. It was a facial cast I'd seen on her before, when one Christmas I'd had too much to drink at the Clipper and she and Sheila had helped me up the stairs to bed. It threw me. Given our situation, she looked altogether too composed. 'I didn't expect to see you out of your bed.'

'I have occasional moments of lucidity,' she said, 'when I can get about the hut on my own.' Yes, that old university-student way of talking; when I could never tell whether she was being serious or taking the piss out of her old man. I think on this occasion she was being serious. 'Then this giddiness comes over me and I fall into a swoon. Plus I can't abide strong sunlight.'

'Is it malaria?' Phil asked, hanging back in the shadows until this doubtless unnecessary display of paternal affection was over.

'I don't think so. Didn't get the flu symptoms. At first it was terrible: fever, swollen joints, skin eruptions. My skin looked like a war zone and I got bad pains in my bones. That's gone, but the fever hangs around on an intermittent basis. And I feel sort of feeble-minded. But that's normal for you, hey Dad?' She smiled again and levitated her eyebrows, inviting me into the joke.

I was about to answer when Mick groaned from his own sick-bed.

'I was just giving him some water,' Charlie said.

I remembered the whisky I'd dropped to the floor on seeing Charlie. 'Give him some of this instead.'

'I don't believe it!' Phil exclaimed, thrilled by the degree of his own disapproval. 'The stuff simply finds you! It really does! You come all the way to the jungle and it finds its way to you!'

With her eyes on Phil, Charlie answered him by unstoppering the bottle and taking a small swig for herself. Good girl, I thought: give your old man a break.

'I see you've met Jack,' she said, splashing some of the whisky into a bowl. I lifted Mick upright while Charlie tilted the bowl to his mouth. Mick glugged and smacked his lips, evidently to his satisfaction, before groaning and lying down again.

'Brought any ciggies with you? Yes? Thank Christ!'

Phil shook his head as I reached for my pack. I have to say that Phil's relationship with Charlie has never been much better than my relationship with him. Or mine with Charlie, come to that. Though they warred less. Anyway, when I suggested we might step outside the hut for a smoke she said, rather too quickly, 'No. Stay here.'

We squatted down on a square of rattan. 'How's Mum?' she asked. She was remarkably cool. She sat with her legs crossed under her, and with her hands dropped in her lap, like a stone idol. Anyone would think I'd just popped over to see her at college. In fact her manner was exactly like the times I'd visited her in her rooms at Oxford. It was as if, in the midst of all this, Charlie wanted to assert that she was in possession of some strange and secret power. Phil looked up to see how I would answer. I knew Sheila communicated with him frequently.

I decided now was not the time to tell Charlie we'd separated. 'She's longing to see you.'

Charlie tipped back her head, blowing a vertical stream of smoke at the leaf roof of the hut. Then she plucked at something in the corner of her eye.

'Darlin', we need to be going as soon as we can.' I said this as gently as possible, but she looked away and shook her head. Then she stared hard, very hard, at the earth floor. It was unnerving. For a moment I think she was away; gone from me, the hut, the village, everything. She was in another place. I'd seen that too before, when we used to visit Sheila's grandmother in the Pastures Hospital.

I called her back softly. 'Can you tell me about Jack?'

She looked at me through rinsing eyes. 'Stay on the right side of him, Dad.'

'What's the score, then?'

She started to tell us what she knew about Jack. As she spoke I was able to study the young woman who, until this very moment and in this precise place, I'd always seen as a little girl. Now, even in her illness, I had to acknowledge that she knew more about what was happening here than I could begin to guess at. All my life I'd tried to find ways to explain the hidden mechanics and the invisible rules of a complicated world, and now the position was reversed.

Plus she was altered. Her hair had been bleached by the sun so that although her pony-tail fell lank across the back of her neck it sported the kind of highlights that might have been fashionable in England. The blueness of her eyes was exaggerated by the caramel colour of her rather dry skin, and what I took to be residual lipstick I quickly realised was the same stains of berry juice I'd seen on the natives. Plus there was a strike-line, a vertical crease above the ridge of her nose, not a scar but a fold formed by the knitting of her brows. I hadn't seen that before.

She took another swig of whisky and dragged hard on her

cigarette, whore-tough to my eyes, but I was beyond disapproval of those things. 'Jack,' she said, 'controls the opium around here.'

The Thai authorities, she told me, had changed their policies on hill tribe opium-growing. After torching crops and condemning huge numbers of tribespeople to heroin addiction and AIDS, they had relaxed the rules on cultivation of the poppy for personal use. The opium gangs – under the leadership of men like Jack – had purchased land around the villages which they rented back to the villagers for the cultivation of opium. Jack and his men were always one jump ahead of the government, though Charlie told me the authorities were happy for it to stay that way, so significant was the opium dollar to the Thai economy. The opium dollar moved to Myanmar, it moved to Laos, it moved back to Thailand. It was always there; it just didn't stay still.

The villagers respected Jack. He got them top prices for their raw opium and he never cheated them. He brought them gifts. He paid for the children to stay in Chiang Mai, to go to school. He was a great believer in educating the people. He'd worked hard to earn the unswerving loyalty of the villagers.

He also controlled a company, she'd been told, of about a hundred and fifty men, possibly more. In that terrain it represented an unassailable force protecting his crops. He'd managed over recent months to prevent tourist interests from bringing in trekkers or adventurers into the area.

'You were only allowed in because Jack wanted you to come,' she said.

'Why?'

'I don't know.' She wagged a finger at me. 'Stay on his right side. He's a killer, that one.'

I think I'd guessed most of this from my first encounter with Jack. The only thing I couldn't possibly know was why he'd let Mick, Phil and I into his domain, and whether he intended to allow us out.

I spent the rest of the morning talking with Charlie about small things, about home, the neighbourhood, family. There was a toughness about her, a coolness which rankled. As if she was somehow aloof from these things, superior, as if she knew things we didn't. That sense of unspecified power I'd recognised earlier. I was sure it was just an affectation. Her manner still suggested we'd dropped by for a surprise visit, not struggled through the jungle to rescue her. Then by way of contrast she would display a tender aspect. She did everything she could to make Mick comfortable, finding him a better pillow, mopping his brow with a damp cloth. As for Phil, she kissed him and pinched his cheeks as if he were a boy of ten, and showed a deep interest in his tedious Christian life at home.

'Any girlfriends on the scene?' she asked him.

'No,' he said. Then, 'Maybe. Well, there is one I've got my eye on.' He blushed the colour of the rosy earth.

How easy it was for Charlie to get that titbit of information from him. He'd sooner part with his money than tell me such a thing. It made me recall how Charlie had always been – even though Phil was her elder, and male and all that nonsense – the bright star in the family firmament, and that he had had to love her from the shade. He coughed, flapping away the cigarette smoke but really waving away our interest in his love life, and stepped outside, leaving Charlie and I, and Mick sleeping.

'What did you mean when I arrived?' I said. 'When you said you'd been expecting me?'

She looked puzzled. I explained how she'd been sitting upright when I first came into the hut.

'I don't remember that,' she said.

I explained it again, and told her how we'd had a brief exchange about the postman of Porlot. Or Porlock. That crease above the ridge of her nose only deepened as she knitted her brows. I changed the subject, telling her how I'd visited Phil before coming out here. I tried to make her laugh by mocking his lifestyle. Outside the village radio started up again, blaring out weird music, deep, resounding masculine voices moving up and down the scales. It had obviously been designed to be heard in the fields while people were working. It made me think of radio ga-ga blaring out in the factories and sweatshops of England while the workers toiled.

'You're too hard on Phil,' Charlie said.

'Nonsense.'

'Yes you are. Can't you see how he's suffering while he's here? How hard it is for him?'

I made some dismissive remark, suggesting it wasn't exactly easy for any of us.

'But the point,' she said, rather sharply, 'is that *you* were always too hard on *him*.' I must have looked stung by this, because she softened. 'Can I use your leg as a cushion?'

'Sure.'

She lay with her head on my thighs, chain-smoking my cigarettes. 'Phil is sensitive. He has big needs.' Don't we all have big needs? I thought, but I didn't argue. 'You know, Dad, there are a lot of things you're unaware of.'

'I daresay.'

But you make out you know everything and that you're always right. You always do. Why do you do that?'

If this really was something I had a particular habit of doing, it was news to me. 'Maybe it's something men do to protect themselves. Maybe it was to protect you and Phil and your mother.'

'Protect from what?'

'I don't know.'

'Right. You don't know. There are lots of things you know nothing about.'

'Such as?'

'Other worlds. All around us. Busy worlds going on, unseen. You've walked right into a world of spirits, did you know that?'

What the hell was I supposed to say to that? When she was a teenager I used to say *stop talking tosh*, but right then she was too brittle to brook any argument. I put it down to the opium smoke billowing about in her brain. Though I did ask, 'What's this about the moon? Why can't the moon work while you are here?'

'The moon will eat itself.'

'What?'

Instead of answering me properly, she started to sing, and in a sweet, strong, melodious voice that took me by surprise. It was some kind of folk song, and Charlie's voice was so good it easily beat back the sound of the radio in he village.

And like a lovesick lenanshee
She hath my heart in thrall
Nor life I owe, nor liberty,
For love is Lord of all.

'I didn't know you could sing,' I said, when she'd finished. 'How come you never sang for me?'

'I was in a folk band when I was at college,' she said. She squinted at me from her cushion of my thigh. 'I thought you'd make fun of me.'

That hurt. It went clean past my ribs and deep into my heart like the trimmest stiletto. 'Why say that?'

She dismissed the question with an airy wave of her hand. Then she closed her eyes, massaging her temples with her long brown fingers. She had lovely elegant fingers, did Charlie, and I noticed with some sadness how dirty were her fingernails. After a moment she complained of feeling tired, climbed on her pallet and instantly fell into a deep, deep sleep. I sat on the rattan mat, staring at her, and as I did so, the music blasting from the radio stopped abruptly.

Mick snored on. I was in a shocking state of frustration. All I could do was stare uselessly at the two sleeping bodies in the hut, and having come so far I felt like a ship suddenly becalmed. On the other hand I was uplifted by the discovery that Charlie's condition was nowhere near as bad as I'd first suspected.

I went out again, to gather material for my stretcher. Phil sat under the shade of a bo tree, like a monk, reading his wretched pocket Bible. 'Why don't you put that away and do something useful?' I barked.

He stared at me for an inordinate period. 'Like what?'

I turned on my heels. When I reached the centre of the village I found Jack, Khiem and a couple of men standing around the silenced totem radio. These other two men were racially different to the villagers. One even had a beard. He was the first

166

oriental I'd seen with facial hair since arriving in Thailand. The two were decked, like Khiem, with dozens of poppy flowers, though I didn't get the impression they were hippies because each carried a sawn-off shotgun.

Khiem, the Lord of the Poppy, pointed a finger at me as I approached and spoke a few words to the group. The bearded Thai looked at me with contempt. The other flashed me a beautiful, dangerous smile. 'Khiem says you bring more bad spirits to the village,' Jack called out cheerfully. 'This is the second time the generator has broken down since you arrived here.'

'What's the fault with it?'

'I don't know. I'm not a grease monkey,' Jack sneered. 'But I went to a lot of trouble getting that machine here on the back of a bad-tempered elephant. Now it falls apart every few minutes.'

I saw a way to ingratiate myself with Jack. 'Got some tools?'

'Tools? You know about generators?'

'I can take a look.'

Jack slapped his knee and sent the bearded Thai away, presumably to find me some kit. Khiem looked startled. He whispered in Jack's ear. 'He wants to know what you're going to do,' Jack said.

'Tell him I'm going to wrestle with the Lord of the Generator.'

27

The Honda IKVA generator was a decent bit of kit, but in poor repair. Even at first glance it looked clogged with red dust, and I hoped that the solution would be a simple one. As I've mentioned, I'm a sparks and not a mechanic, though the principle of a generator is not all that different from a motor car engine. I'd encountered a few temperamental generators whenever contracted for on-site work where they were required to drive power tools.

First thing I did was to check that the fault wasn't something completely daft, like no petrol, but there was plenty of fuel in the tank. I traced the hi-T leads back to the piston and checked out a couple of other bits of wiring. I hoped it wasn't going to be a complicated problem with the armature, in which case I'd probably be fucked. It was while I was peering through the casing at the armature that I sensed someone watching me from the doorway.

It was Khiem, our wild poppy man. His eyes were bulging and the veins on his forehead stood out like a pair of chicken's claws gripping his skull. I could do no more while waiting for tools with which to unbolt the casing of the machine, so I made what I thought of as a few mystical passes across the generator. Khiem's eyes widened still further. Then I whistled a bit at the hi-T leads and made an eerie but theatrical raising-up gesture.

I soon tired of this tomfoolery, so I whisked the canvas from under the machine and draped it over the doorway: *if I can't see your magic, you can't see mine*. I didn't care if he was offended.

Khiem was hardly discouraged. Through the cracks in the bamboo I could see his figure outlined on the porch. Though I could see him, he couldn't see me inside the darkness of the hut. He was stooped slightly, his posture suggesting he was listening hard. I noiselessly moved to within inches of where he was standing, and put my mouth to the bamboo. Since the days when Charlie and Phil were very small, I've been able to produce a very passable imitation of Daffy Duck, and I did one now, very loud.

Khiem fell off the porch in surprise.

I mean the sound somehow seemed to blow him off the porch, and to see Khiem rolling around in the dust made me laugh so hard I had to bite my hand. I grabbed the canvas at the door and ran outside, flapping it wildly, moaning and clutching my hair as if it was on fire. Then I 'pulled myself together', spat into my hands as if I meant business, and ventured back inside the hut with my fists raised.

I re-hung the canvas at the door and peeked through the cracks in the bamboo. Khiem's head swayed back and forth, like a punter at the ringside of a bout of Thai kickboxing. The expression on his face was so fraught I was taken over again with a fit of silent laughter. My ribs were cracking. I sank to the floor and had to squeeze my sides to stop any noise coming out of me.

I couldn't remember when I'd last laughed so hard. It was like being taken over by a spirit, and the more I thought about it – stuck in the jungle with a sick friend and a doped-up daughter and trying to mend a generator while a village witchdoctor listened outside – the more I fell prey to this fit of hysterics.

Someone lifted the canvas at the door to find me lying on the floor clutching my ribs. It was the bearded Thai, one of Jack's henchmen. He'd brought me some tools. Khiem stood behind him, observing. I had to pretend that I was holding myself in pain. The bearded Thai scowled and tossed a bag of tools on the floor.

It was a gaily patterned handcrafted villager's bag, and inside was a collection of the very tools I'd seen the opium harvesters use in the fields. Two crescent blades, a standard knife, and a three-bladed incisor for pricking the poppy seedheads. I sobered up. 'What's this? I can't use these!'

The bearded Thai simply sneered, and turned about-face. I followed him out, protesting, looking for Jack to complain to. Jack was nowhere about.

With Khiem watching, I went back into the hut. The smile had been wiped off my face, but I still had plenty of ideas. The penknife I carried in my shorts pocket – sometimes I felt like a fucking Boy Scout – had a small screwdriver blade. I thought I might be able to improvise.

But I didn't need to. No sooner had I begun to dust down the machine with a bit of cloth than did the cap fall off the spark plug and into my hand. It had simply worked loose. I replaced the cap, whipped the starter cord and the generator coughed into life. I quickly stalled it again. Not wanting Khiem, or anyone else, to think I'd had too easy a victory over the spirits of the generator, I sat and smoked a cigarette, waiting until I was good and ready. I expect these Oxford professors do the same: make out it has taken them years to write something about Keats or Thomas De Quincey, something that they'd dreamed up while smoking a fag.

Before I started the generator I had another poke around the hut. The cartons of Calpol were still there, but there was little else besides a short coil of electrical cable and some engine oil. At last I tugged the starter cord and the engine sputtered into life. The dreadful broadcast swelled from the radio, filling the air again. I made sure the engine was ticking over nicely, and went outside.

Khiem regarded me strangely. I didn't know what else to do, so I walked over to the radio, snapped it off, thought better about it, and snapped it on again. After a few moments Jack and his henchmen appeared. Jack looked very pleased with me; the bearded one less so. 'Hey! You did it!'

'It was nothing. Here, take these back.' I offered him the 'tools' I'd been given. 'They weren't much help.'

Jack wrinkled his nose at the farmer's bag, and said something derisory to his bearded henchman. The beardie shrugged and obviously made some excuse. 'Good chap. Jack always pays, right? I paid you already with that whisky, didn't I? What's your name again?'

'Dan.'

'Jack always pays, right Dan?'

'Right.'

He gave me a cigarette. Beardie's face was expressionless, inscrutable as they say, but his eyes betrayed him, and he was staring at me in a way which made me feel quite nervous. I heard myself babbling. 'That's a useful generator. You could power a lot more than a radio—'

'I know that,' Jack said, cutting me off. I could see he was a man who didn't like to be told things.

'All you need is some cable and a few more bulbs and you could light the whole village.'

'I know that, too.' He sniffed. 'That's why I had the damned thing brought here. But tell me what I need. Tell me.'

I made a quick estimate of the length of cable and enough fluorescent bulbs to make one for each hut and a few spares.

I was doing my best to sound like a lackey rather than a coloniser. Jack squinted at me, puffing thoughtfully on his cigarette. 'I get them brought in by elephant and you fix it for me, Dan? Yes?'

I didn't know how long he expected me to stay, but I heard myself saying, 'Sure. It's easy enough.' If Jack really did pay his debts I'd illuminate his elephant's dick for him. I suddenly had trade. I had currency. 'All you'd need is a socket and you could run a television off that generator.'

Television? Was this me talking? Sure, I will bring you game shows and garden makeovers; teenage soap operas and costume dramas; veterinary practices and lottery draws; award ceremonies and soft porn. I will bring you the the jewels of the Western living room. The whole fucking crash.

Naw, I almost said, forget TV and stick with hard drugs. I wondered if Khiem could read my mind, because he was grinning at me like an idiot. Then he whispered something to Jack, and Jack said, 'He says he doesn't like the methods you use, but he respects your victory over the Lord of the Generator.'

Khiem grinned at me again with his toothless, red-stained mouth. This occasion was the first time I saw him smile. I decided I liked Khiem.

When I returned to our hut, Mick was sitting upright and the old woman – the wizened old dope dealer – was spooning soup into his mouth. Charlie was asleep again, and Phil too was sleeping off the heat. Was I the only one around here who could stay on his feet? The woman chattered away, giggling as she fed him. Mick blinked at her dumbly. 'Who's this?' he asked me feebly. 'Widow Twanky?'

'Feeling better?'

He scratched the back of his neck. 'I feel like I've been shagged by all the sailors of the HMS *Sheffield*.'

Yes, he was feeling better. The old woman didn't let our conversation get in the way of her chatter. Her eyes twinkled and she seemed to find something terribly amusing in everything we did or said. 'Been on your pipe, duckie?' I asked her over-loudly.

'Boo!' she said, and laughed heartily as she rammed the soup spoon in Mick's mouth. Then she jumped off her stool and started to fish about under the folds of her skirt.

'Hello,' said Mick. 'This gets worse.'

The old woman produced two small green packets, one of which she handed to me. It was a folded leaf, like a palm leaf. She mimed the act of chewing, striding around the hut, ruminating, indicating that we shouldn't swallow, but chew.

'More drugs?' I said.

She thrust the second packet into Mick's mouth and mimed chewing again. Mick looked at me doubtfully and said, through a mouthful of greenery, 'I'm wondering where she's been keeping it, that's all.'

Maybe she intuited Mick's remark. She giggled again, hitched up her skirts and danced a little jig about the place. She must have been ninety years old, but she was a live wire. I put my own leaf aside and picked up the whisky bottle instead. I was about to take a swig and she stopped dancing and became agitated, ranting, waving her hands in disgust at the whisky bottle. '*Mai! Mai!*' she shouted, seeming particularly cross that I'd preferred the whisky to her packet of leaves. She waddled out of the hut, still cussing me.

'Well,' Mick said, chewing, 'you've upset her, all right.'

'You don't know what she's putting in your trap, do you?'

'She comes here to feed me. Not going to do me any harm, is she?'

I supposed he was right, but I didn't say so.

Mick wanted to know the latest. I told him about Jack, and about Charlie, and about the generator, and about my plan to construct a stretcher. But he admitted he felt as weak as a kitten. I failed to disclose the fact that we didn't know exactly where we were, or that we were unlikely to get help from either Jack or the villagers.

Something dark red or purple from the leaf was bubbling on Mick's saliva, but I didn't tell him about that either. Then Mick said, 'Who were the other people?'

'What other people?'

'In the hut. Who were they?'

With Mick resting, and with Charlie sleeping, I had very little to occupy my time. I was less worried about Mick, who, with a constitution as strong as a farmyard horse, was on the mend. Charlie, however, seemed capable of sleeping eighteen hours out of a twenty-four-hour day. Though it had been a huge relief to talk with her, I reckoned we were still going to have to carry her out of the jungle, and the way things were going the prospect of doing that might be a few days off. Mick could barely make it unaided to the little bamboo outhouse.

I was also worried about having upset the old lady who, so far, was the sole person in the village helping us, and for no apparent reward. She'd obviously tended to Charlie for some time, and now she'd taken it upon herself to minister to Mick with her herbs and potions and chewing packets.

When I left Mick, his lips were stained red with the juice of whatever was in the packet she gave him, though he claimed it was acting on him like a tonic. He recommended it passionately, but one glance at his crimson-lipped mouthing was enough to make me stick with the whisky. I suppose my preference for a distilled grain was hardly less primitive, but the Scotch settled my stomach and steadied my nerves.

My suspicion of her came down to the idea that she was stoking Charlie with opium, and that that was contributing to her weakness. Meanwhile Mick was still riding a high temperature, which explained his feverish remarks. He wanted to know about the people he claimed had been trooping through the hut. He complained that one time he opened his eyes and thought there must have been a party going on, so many people were there milling around in the dark. I told him he'd been feverish, and slightly delirious; he'd been seeing pink elephants.

I decided to put things right with the old woman. Since most of the villagers were working in the poppy fields, she was easy to find. Squatting outside her hut, which was adjacent to the one housing the generator, she was smoking.

When I say she was smoking, she was puffing away on a length of bamboo almost as tall as she was, and the diameter of your average domestic rainwater drainpipe. Blue clouds of smoke wafted around her as she puffed contentedly.

'Opium?' I gestured at the pipe.

'Tabac,' she said. 'Tabac.'

I squatted next to her, tapping myself on the chest. 'Me Danny. Danny.'

She got the idea, and told me her name was Nabao, though she never did seem happy with my pronunciation. Laying her stove-pipe aside she led me into her hut.

Inside it was wonderfully orderly and the dirt floor was neatly swept. Some bits of furniture – stools, small tables – were rustic and improvised but there were incongruous objects like a modern chest of drawers – flatpack, possibly – and a wardrobe. The strangest article was a plastic Fred Flintstone clock; it hung on the wall telling the correct time from inside the transparent plastic sleeve in which it was first purchased.

Nabao took a cloth bracelet from the table and tied it to my left wrist. Chattering constantly she attached a small metal disc to the bracelet. She squeezed the bracelet and made sure the disc couldn't come adrift. I got the impression it was some sort of lucky charm.

Under a table I spotted a small fluorescent strip-light wired to a car battery. Since it was still connected I assumed the car battery was drained. I tapped the battery. 'No good?'

Nabao rubbed her fingers together to indicate the cost of

replacing or recharging the battery. It occurred to me to give her the money to get someone to replace it, but then I had a better idea. The cable from the generator to the radio ran behind her hut. There was that bit of spare wire I'd seen beside the cartons of Calpol. It would only take me a few minutes to take a spur off the main cable and she wouldn't need a car battery.

Twenty minutes later we had illumination. I had to shut down the generator for a couple of minutes, but when I started it up again and came back to her hut, Nabao was shrieking and spinning and dancing like a teenager. She squeezed my arm and chucked my cheek and slapped her knees. I wished all my customers at home could show half the gratitude for a bit of light.

It was the best thing I ever did in that village. It was also a big mistake.

28

You will have noticed that I have failed to report certain details concerning the attributes and customs of the hill tribe with whom we spent those days. The omission is deliberate. Over the short period in which I lived in that remote village I came to respect its small population and to view its activities from a different perspective. Even now I fear for the survival of the village, and I want to give nothing away which might act as a clue to its precise location and identity.

For this reason I have said little about the traditional costume worn by the villagers, or I have planted one or two misleading details. About the construction of the houses I may have lied. One or two names might be unreliable. These people live hand to mouth, raising the poppy out of the dust by the labour of their bent backs; I don't want to be the one who tipped off the Thai government forces who come to torch their crops.

It was from Jack that I learned quite a bit about opium growing in the region. The Americans in Vietnam, through the good offices of the CIA, built links with the minority tribes in the border regions of Thailand and Laos, particularly with Hmong guerrillas. Soon the CIA had an army of three hundred thousand mountain-conditioned guerrillas trained to battle the Lao communist forces. In the mid-sixties, to help the Hmong and to encourage loyalty, the CIA made available the services of its own airline, Air America, to ferry Hmong opium to transit points for distribution further afield.

Most of this opium was processed into what Jack called top-grade Number Four heroin and shipped to Saigon. From there it was transported by corrupt officers of the South Vietnamese government to the USA, creating the heroin epidemic of the 1970s.

The opium bandits currently operating out of these hills had prospered directly out of that wartime activity. If I was looking to lay blame for Charlie's plight I could always find a place for the CIA high on my list.

But of the hill tribe with whom we stayed, what shall I say? That in the cultivation of the poppy their prowess and knowledge rivals even the Hmong. That they match the Akha or the Yao in silversmithing, or that their embroidery skills outstrip the Kareni. That some of the women file their teeth to sharp points, and that polygamy is permitted. That they divide into sub-groups, like the Lahu. And that they originate as a people from Tibet, as do the Lisu.

And that they believe in spirits.

I tried to take a photograph of Nabao next to her new electric light, but even in her happy state, almost delirious with gratitude, she resisted most strongly. She turned her back, she waved me away. I was sorry to let the moment pass, but I had to respect her wishes.

Another time I tried to take some pictures of the villagers working the poppy fields. They became extremely agitated. At first I thought it was because they didn't want incriminating photographs of themselves to fall into the hands of the police, but I learned that their fear of the camera was of a much more spiritual cast. They were perfectly happy to let me take a few snaps of the poppies in flower, or of the village huts; which I did, and which I still have.

My early notion, that the tribesfolk feared that their soul was being stolen along with their image, was inaccurate. It was a fear of who or what might want to get in the shot along with them. They did not want their image, Jack explained to me, to be trapped in the presence of any spirit which might have been passing at the moment the snap was taken. They feared that the spirit would not be able to leave them. They feared that the spirit would not *want* to leave them.

Images were living things. Images of themselves, photographs included, were living versions of themselves, at large in the spirit world.

In the middle of my dismissal of the primitive mentality the thought hit me that I had no photographs of myself and Charlie

177

at Oxford: neither at the university nor in the town. I'd always dodged the camera's eye.

Pleased with myself over the electrification of Nabao's existence, I returned to our hut. Mick and Charlie were getting along like a house on fire. Charlie was sponging him down with a wet cloth. She had some jungle ointment which she'd put on his mosquito bites. They were laughing together when I entered the hut. 'All those awful things you told me about Charlie,' Mick said. 'And none of them are true!'

This was meant as a joke. No, a half-joke. Or a jibe within a half-joke. Heck, I don't know, but it rankled. But seeing her laugh made me feel good. I like to see people laugh. I like to see the laugh take over them, like a spirit that gets in them and pulls them out of shape.

'I told Mick that anyone,' Charlie said, 'who would come through the jungle with my dad must be some kind of fucking saint.'

I don't like that. Women swearing. Never have liked it. Back home I don't even swear in front of Sheila.

'It was hell,' Mick said, 'but if we can get out again, we'll be laughing. Won't we, Phil?'

'I expect so,' Phil said lugubriously. He looked hard at Charlie. 'Though I have a strange feeling that it's all going to be down to my sister.'

Charlie clouded over, running a hand through her hair. That mysterious power I'd identified in her darkened for a few moments.

'You do *want* to go home, don't you Charlie?' I asked.

She hugged her knees and began rocking back and forth, pointedly failing to answer, so I put the question again. She closed her eyes, but hot tears squeezed out between them. She nodded her head, yes. I had the sudden notion that Charlie might be a prisoner here. 'Is it Jack? Is it the villagers? Won't they let you go?'

'It's not Jack or the villagers,' Charlie cried. Without warning she collapsed on to her pallet, convulsed by huge, gulping sobs that made it difficult to hear what she was saying. 'It's me!' I thought I heard her say, 'It's what I've done!'

I tried to comfort her, but I was of no help. Phil stood next to me, breathing stertorously, ineffectually biting a knuckle. Mick got out of his bed and came over, himself wobbly on his feet. 'Steady on,' he said. 'Steady on, little Charlie.'

We watched helplessly, all three of us shocked by the measure of her distress. When her sobs began to subside she fumbled under her mattress and produced a pipe and other paraphernalia. She looked me in the eye. Her body language defied me to challenge her, and I knew we were in for big trouble.

'That's not going to solve our problems,' Phil said. 'Is it?'

I looked at Mick. He shook his head, *leave things be*. I watched her shave a bit of opium from a small block, heat it on a pin and then drop it into the brass bowl of her slender pipe. She puffed away on the thing, looking at me unashamedly. Her face had hardened. Her hair had fallen over one eye and she gazed at me balefully from behind the stray lock.

But the opium calmed her. It softened her features and restored a tender expression to her face. Contrary to my expectations – that she would go into a trance of some kind – she became rational and lucid. I realised this was the condition in which I'd first encountered her awake. But it was like a bad dream for me to see this. For a moment I felt that this couldn't be Charlie, and that in the orange candlelight of the darkened hut this was some demon impersonating her.

'I did something,' she said. 'I did something stupid. I didn't know what I was doing at the time. But now I have to pay for it.

'When I first came here this village was on the trekking route. I was with an American boy called Ben. Nabao sold us some opium. The other trekkers weren't interested but Ben and I were up for it. We smoked, but it didn't seem to have much effect, so we had several pipes. Next thing we were giggling like idiots. We went outside looking for water. My legs had turned to rubber. We kept falling over, and crawling on our hands and knees, still giggling.

'Then suddenly the villagers came running out of their huts. They were pointing at the sky and shouting. We couldn't figure out what was happening. The villagers had gathered every saucepan and cooking bowl and tin pan they could lay their hands on and they started bashing them with sticks, making a huge commotion. It was terrifying. My hair was standing on end.

'We finally realised what was happening. There was an eclipse of the moon. A quarter-eclipse. They were bashing their pots and pans and shouting at the moon.

'Ben and I were staggering about in amazement, laughing again and hanging on to each other. Then Ben stumbled sideways and he grabbed me as he fell. We crashed into the spirit gate in the middle of the village.'

'What's the spirit gate?' Mick wanted to know.

'I've been to look at it,' Phil said. 'Demons carved in wood.'

'I'll explain later,' I told Mick, cutting Phil off.

'The gate got pushed over,' Charlie continued. 'Ben clambered to his feet, holding on to one of those carved penises. He still thought it was hilarious, but the villagers were completely silent. Stunned. They stood over us with bulging eyes. I knew we'd done something terrible. I tried to get Ben to put down the carving. Then one of the villagers started banging his cooking pot, you know, aggressively, right under our faces. The rest joined in. The din was awful. It went on and on. They screamed at us, banging these pots in our ears. I thought I was going to die. I remember vomiting and vomiting, and then I passed out.

'When I came round I was in this hut. So was Ben. Someone had put a ring of burning candles around us. Then I fell asleep again, and when I awoke the candles had burned out and Ben was gone. He'd taken his pack and he'd left me.'

Charlie's voice had become a monotone. She stared moodily at the floor. Mick suggested this must have been the time when Claire Marchant had arrived and stolen her passport.

'Yes, my passport was taken. I remember someone coming in the hut and going through our things, but I couldn't do anything. Nabao looked after me, as she has done ever since.'

'Didn't you ever try to leave?' Phil asked.

'Many times, Phil. In the following weeks there were occasional treks coming through. I packed my bag and got ready to leave with them. But I was never able to, because I can't go outside the door.'

'Don't worry,' I said. 'As soon as Mick is well enough, we're out of here. We'll hire some of the villagers to take us to Chiang Mai.'

'I said I can't go out of the door, Dad.'

'We'll pay them a king's ransom and—'

'Listen to me, Dad! Listen! You never listen!'

'I think I see,' Phil said.

'See what?'

Suddenly Phil turned his volatile anger on me. 'She's told you she can't go outside the door! It's as simple and as complicated as she's told you! Can't you understand that?'

Understand it? No, I couldn't understand it. Somehow I'd got it into my head that Jack or the villagers had some particular reason for keeping her there. I didn't understand that her fear of the daylight was greater than her fear of spending the rest of her life in that miserable hut. 'So what exactly are you saying, Charlie?'

She sighed, lit a cigarette, blew the smoke in a steady stream through her nostrils. 'Someone put a hex on me for what we did.'

I wanted to laugh. 'A hex?'

'A spell. A charm. A curse. A malediction. How many ways do you need it making plain?'

'Sorcery,' said Phil softly. He'd become a tiny compressed ball of excitement and loathing. 'Sorcery.'

'Shut up, Phil,' I barked. 'There is no fucking sorcery.'

Mick had to come between us. 'Right, let's everyone calm down,' he said, meaning me and Phil. Charlie was perfectly calm. She was hugging her knees again. 'This is going to need thinking through.'

I'd heard of something like this. Fear of the open space. Panic. Fear of the wilderness – I'd been there myself a few days ago, had I not? Agoraphobia. But I hadn't come this far to find that the obstacle in my way to getting Charlie home was psychological. Psychology belonged to a world of credit-card payments and microwave ovens and people with too much time on their hands. It didn't have a place in the jungle, and I said that, too.

'You're out of your depth here, Father,' Phil said spitefully. He was enjoying my bewilderment. 'Way out of your depth.'

'Look, what would happen if we tried to carry you out?' Mick wanted to know.

Charlie blinked, and stared at him for an unreasonable length of time. 'The villagers did that to me one time. It made things even worse. Please don't ever try it.'

'Just asking, like,' Mick said. 'Just asking.'

We were deadlocked. Of all the difficulties I'd anticipated, this had been the last. Reduced to silence, we were at last disturbed by a commotion at the door as Nabao waddled in with a huge pan full of noodle soup. Chattering and giggling, she made a great fuss of me. Charlie and Nabao exchanged a few words. 'I don't know what you've done,' Charlie said, making a bid to leaven the awful mood, 'but she says you're her boyfriend.'

Nabao patted my cheeks and performed a little dance as she went out again.

In grim fellowship we ate. The soup tasted of curry and ginger. I tried to get to the bottom of Charlie's condition. All she could tell me was that as soon as she tried to cross the threshold she experienced hideous panic attacks, induced because she felt something tearing at her. She was in danger of being swallowed or sucked in by something voracious waiting outside the door. It tried to shake her from the hut to its jaws, she said, into which she might fall and never stop falling.

She knew she was being punished, she said, for damaging the spirit gate.

Phil was right in that I was way out of my depth. I looked at Mick and, for the second time that day, he just shook his head at me. I was trying to think of what to say or do when the village radio snapped off again. I remember going, 'Oh!'

My urge to fix the damned radio was only an expression of my desperate need to do something practical, a flight from the real problem in hand. I got to my feet and hunted through my pack for a bottle-opener, thinking I might be able to hammer it into some useful shape. As I did so, Charlie stashed her opium paraphernalia under her mattress, and I saw a blade flash there, a blade not unlike the one Coconut had given to me. I continued to rummage through my pack. 'Do you have much need for that knife?' I asked, trying to sound casual.

'Oh, some guy was pestering me,' she said, whore-tough again, in control once more. 'I can look after myself.'

'Right.' I shot a glance at Mick. 'I'll be back in a minute.'

The village was busy with activity. Dusk was falling, and having returned from the fields families sat cross-legged around steaming pans, cooking, whittling bamboo, smoking giant, fat tobacco pipes. I noted with some satisfaction that a few nods and smiles were beginning to come my way.

The generator was important to me. If I could keep the generator running, and if I could get my hands on some more cable to light a few huts, I might be able to win the help we needed. Now I knew Jack and his cronies weren't actually keeping Charlie here against her will, I needed to ingratiate myself until Mick was fit enough to get moving.

Inside the generator hut I checked the plug cap on the motor, thinking maybe the vibration was working it loose, but this time the fault lay somewhere else. In the end, I didn't even need to unscrew the cover plate, since it was merely resting loose over the machinery. A quick check revealed that the cable to the piston was shitted up and was breaking the circuit. I don't know how it got so messy – there were leaves and twigs and all sorts in there – but I cleaned it off and whipped the generator into life again. I heard a small cheer from some of the villagers. The Lord of the Generator rubbed his oily hands together in a purely involuntary gesture.

I got a bit of petrol on my rag and I gave all the visible working parts a thorough clean before I replaced the cover plate. I knew if I had the right tools to strip it down completely I could have got that baby to sing. I was going to have to present Jack with an inventory of things to bring me along with that roll of cable.

When I stepped outside there was a fracas going on next to

Nabao's hut. Jack's bearded henchman was being roundly scolded by Nabao – I could deduce that much. A few villagers looked on silently. The bearded henchman had a fluorescent tube in his hand, which I quickly realised he'd taken from Nabao's hut. My length of cable lay discarded like a dead snake in the dust. Nabao must have said something impressive, because the bearded man stepped over to her and threatened her with a backhand slap. She knew this was no idle threat, for she skittered away, retreating into her hut.

Jack turned up, demanding to know what was going on. The bearded man barked a few words and carried away the striplight. Jack stepped over to me. 'Why did you give this woman the light?'

'It was already hers. I just connected the cable.'

'Don't interfere with things here. You don't—'

'I wasn't interfering—'

'Don't talk while I'm talking! Understand me? You don't talk while I'm talking, or I'll take your damned head off!' His anger was absurdly disproportionate to my offence, and his eyes were like splinters of dirty ice. I nodded. 'You fix the generator again?'

'Yes.'

'Fix it good this time?'

'Yes.'

'That generator fucks up again, you're in big trouble, you hear me? Big trouble.'

'I need some tools. I haven't got anything to work with.'

'Fuck that. Work with your hands. And if you want to wire a hut, you wire *my* hut. Do it now.'

I pointed at the short length of cable running to Nabao's hut. 'That's all I have, apart from what goes to the radio. It won't reach your hut.'

Two deep, vertical creases appeared in Jack's brow. He stepped over to me. He was a head shorter than me, and I could feel his breath on my neck. 'Look, I've got lots of damned shit to deal with right now. Keep away from old ladies and *keep that fucking generator going.*' He spun on his heels, leaving me standing under the sullen gaze of the villagers. I saw Nabao peeping at me from inside her hut. Crestfallen, she wouldn't meet my eyes.

I made my way back to our hut. Inside, Mick, Phil and Charlie wanted to know what the shouting was about. Before I'd finished telling them, I saw Jack's bullying henchman – the bearded one – heading towards us. 'Here comes trouble,' I said.

From the threshold he jabbed a finger in my direction. 'Jack want you NOW!' he shrieked. 'You come quick NOW!' Then he turned his back and marched away.

Outside a nearby hut two villagers were slaughtering a pig. They seemed to be making an unnecessarily drawn-out job of it. The high-pitched squeals of the pig were distressing and unnerving, occasionally striking a human note.

I drew a deep breath, and followed.

29

Jack was seated before a low-burning fire outside one of the huts, gnawing a chicken bone. His back was illuminated by a strip-and-battery light, so his face was in shadow. One of his other henchmen was cleaning a dismantled bolt-action rifle, and the bearded one who'd summoned me there – old laughing boy – slumped down heavily beside Jack to resume an identical activity.

Jack pointed to the earth across the fire. 'Sit.'

I did as I was told.

'So, you're going to wire up this place for me eh, Danny?'

'I will if you get me the gear.'

He tossed his chicken bone on the fire and wiped the grease from his hand on his shorts. 'You want a cigarette? Here.' He flung a packet of Marlboros at me. 'Look, Danny, I've got no fight with you, eh? I've got other stuff on my mind right now. Big stuff. Just don't make a nuisance of yourself. Your daughter has been in my way for some time. I only let you in here because I thought you might take her from under my feet.'

'That's what I'd hoped.'

While the second of Jack's sidekicks was absorbed in oiling the bolt action of his rifle, I noticed that the bearded one only pretended to be doing the same. He was a bad actor. He was watching me closely. I had a question buzzing around in my brain. I wanted to know what had happened to Ben, Charlie's trekking companion.

Perhaps Jack saw a shadow come over my face because he asked me, 'Have I treated your daughter badly in this time?'

'No.'

'No. I've got a daughter of my own. Nearly the same age. I'm not a bad man, Danny.'

'No.'

'Yes, you think I'm a bad man.'

'No.'

'Don't fucking argue with me!' he yelled. His anger rocked on a hair switch. 'If I tell you that you think I'm a bad man, then that's what you think! You know what I'm called in your newspapers? Drugs warlord – that's a good one. *Warfuckinglord.*' He said something in Thai, and his two lieutenants laughed. 'Fucking warlord, living like this. If I'm a warlord where's my fucking Mercedes-Benz, Danny? Where's my fucking Mercedes-Benz? Eh?'

'I don't see one.'

'No. You don't see no Mercedes-fucking-Benz. What car do you drive, Danny?'

'An old Vauxhall Cavalier. The cigarette lighter is broken and a spring pokes through the driver's seat.'

He nodded sagely, squinting in appreciation of these details. Then his anger appeared to pass and a smile came over his face. 'Actually I've got *three* Mercedes, parked in a garage, over in Fang.' He laughed loudly, and repeated in Thai. The other two joined in the cackling. The first henchman held up three fingers for me to confirm the boast. 'Yeah, I'm just a slant-eyed farmer with three Mercs.' He stopped laughing suddenly. The switch from mirthful joker to volatile interrogator was terrifying. 'You a good father, Danny?'

'I try to be.'

'Me too. I try to be. Try very hard. I'm just a farmer, doing the best by my children. My daughter is in Chiang Mai, in school. The *best* school. I'm going to send her to university in *your* country. How about that? I'm sending her where I was going before I got brought back from Charterhouse. She's going to Oxford University.'

'No,' I said firmly. 'Don't send her to Oxford.'

He stiffened. Both of the henchmen sensed something, and suddenly looked uncomfortable. He squinted at me. 'Why not Oxford? Why do you say that?'

I paused for a long time, before launching into it. I mean, I was able to clue him in about Oxford, full bib and tucker. Now Jack was looking at me as though I was a man who held some cards. The bearded one obviously couldn't fully understand me, because he kept looking up to study Jack's face while I was talking, whereas the other one morosely oiled his gun. Something in the fire flared briefly.

I told Jack how Charlie and I had a terrific relationship before she went to Oxford. I let him know she was a sweet and loving girl. I tipped him off about drugs and body-piercing and tattooing and whoring and general timewasting, which is the general lot at Oxford University, particularly among the professors. I really laid it on with a trowel. 'I speak as a father,' I said passionately. 'The kind of father who would come through the jungle to win my daughter back, if I had to.'

He was simultaneously annoyed and wrong-footed. He stroked his chin. 'Maybe things have changed since I was in England.'

'Probably.' I was able to tell him about Thomas De Quincey and a few other deadbeats – making them sound present-day – and about how Oxford University has always been a hell-hole and a jumping-off point for layabouts and people of low instinct. The way I told it by the time I'd finished you'd think it harsh for a serial killer to serve twelve months at Oxford University.

He reached round behind him and produced another bottle of whisky, splashing a measure each into two rice bowls, one of which he brought round to me. There was none, I noticed, for his men. He squatted next to me, but before handing me the bowl he looked hard in my eyes. 'Are you shitting me?'

I looked at him without blinking. 'My Charlie graduated at Oxford, that's the truth. Look at her now, laid up there, drugged to the gills, unable to leave the hut. I sent them a virgin and that's what came back.'

He nodded glumly. 'What about Cambridge?'

I was able to put him right there, too. When I told him about the Cambridge University paedophiles he slammed down his rice bowl. I told him if he didn't believe me he could check the record of our man in Chiang Mai. 'Bloody fucking bastards!' he said. 'Land of hope and glory. Your country has gone down, dear boy! Down down down.'

'That's right.'

He poured more whisky and snarled, 'So where the damned hell am I supposed to send my daughter for a decent education?'

This question stumped me. The only place I really knew about in any detail was Oxford, since that's where Charlie went; and Durham, and I didn't think much of what that had done for Phil's dress sense. I racked my brains to think of somewhere. One of the sparks I'd met while doing some on-site contracting had a son studying at Nottingham, so out of ignorance I suggested that as a very fine place.

'Nottingham, you say?'

'Well, unlike Oxford and Cambridge they don't drug your children and fuck 'em up the arse, so far as I can tell.'

'Damn!' Jack said. He sat back and savoured his whisky. 'Nottingham. *Nottingham.*' He was trying out the word, savouring it on his lips. Then he sat up again. 'Hey! Isn't that the place of Robin Hood? That's me. I'm the Robin Hood of Northern Thailand!'

'So we are still in Thailand, then?'

'Some would say so.'

The smile on his face caught the light from the fire. The notion pleased him greatly: Jack did indeed see himself as a Thai Robin Hood. I learned a lot from him that night. He dismissed his two henchmen, even though the bearded one, whose name was Khao, made a weak protest before leaving us alone.

After draping himself in the Lincoln green of Robin Hood's men, Jack was in a talkative mood, and I made sure I gave him a damn good listening to. Jack claimed that his uncle was Khun Sa, an infamous opium warlord of the seventies and eighties, and that he himself had trained under Khun Sa's Muang Thai Army. Though the MTA had surrendered in 1996, Jack claimed that about seven thousand MTA were still active along the border area. I have no way of verifying any of this, and I didn't think it wise to ask questions about what numbers of men were under Jack's control.

He was determined, he told me, to give the local farmers good pay for their crops – a lesson in loyalty he'd learned from Khun Sa. Sixty dollars per kilo for the raw opium. He wanted to bring more in the way of power – electrification and the appurtenances of civilisation – to the villages but transport was a huge problem wedded to the fact that he had to move his poppy-growing location season by season.

It was when I asked him about the Calpol in the generator hut that I got an insight into who or what I was dealing with. The hill tribe with whom we were staying were particularly susceptible to opium. They had little medicine to speak of, and poor herb craft. Consequently their babies and children developed the opium habit from an early age. Jack had cut some deal which involved a large consignment of Calpol from Europe. It had been his plan to distribute it to the hill tribes. When he told me that, I realised he was a dreamer and a megalomaniac of the kind it was impossible to totally dislike.

Then he learned that he'd been palmed off with a recalled batch in which the ingredients of the Calpol were separating, resulting in dangerously unreliable doses for children. He was left with the consignment. This he shrugged off as one of the small setbacks associated with his business, and it didn't matter, he said, because the man who had betrayed him wouldn't do so again.

Here was a man who would go to extraordinary lengths to import infant medicine into the jungle but who wouldn't think twice about killing a treacherous supplier.

What with his failure over the Calpol, his faulty generator and his lack of cable, I didn't like to point out that his programme for civilising the jungle was so far modest at best. But I asked if I might take a bottle of Calpol for Mick. For some reason he thought this was hilarious, and invited me to take as much of the stuff as I wanted.

He also disclosed that he converted most of his opium to morphine before taking it away. 'I must say,' I offered in an unguarded moment, 'it's not how I imagined a drugs factory.'

'Oh? How did you envisage us?'

I thought about it. 'A laboratory. I thought you'd need a laboratory.'

'You're not educated, Danny. You know that? You think we're slant-eye little savages – yes you do, don't fucking argue with me – but you're the one who is ignorant.' He stood up, grabbed a pot and half filled it with water from a plastic container. Then he went inside his hut and came out with a mass of brown substance in his hands. I'd no idea what a quantity of opium like that would have weighed, or of its street value. He dumped it in the pan, and settled the pan on the fire without a word.

We talked some more. He treated me to his opinions about the hypocrisy of the West. He said that if he worked for the tobacco or the alcohol industry he'd be responsible for vastly more deaths than opium or heroin had ever caused, and he would be called an executive instead of a warlord.

The water in the opium pot came to the boil. He picked up a bulging paper sack, split it open and poured white powder into the pot. 'Ordinary lime fertiliser,' he said. He went on to talk a lot about the conspiracy of the tobacco industry's vigorous efforts to addict people to a known carcinogenic drug, and the collusion of all governments.

Still talking, he drained the contents of the first pot on to a flannel cloth. The solution was a pile of grey mush, and he tossed this into a second pan, setting that back on the fire. And did I know the statistics for death or injury caused through alcohol? he asked me. From violence, illness, reckless motoring? The figures for social problems?

Next he took a plastic container, and poured a liquid into the pan. 'Ordinary concentrated ammonia,' he said. He pointed out that it had suited the economies of the West to export opium to the orient in the past, to fix the balance of payments. He asked me if I knew what was meant by *karma*.

After draining off this latest solution on to another flannel cloth, he showed me the results: a small quantity of chunky grey particles. 'Morphine,' he said. 'Ninety per cent less in weight than the opium you saw me start with. Better for smuggling. Stronger high. You wanted to see my laboratory. That was it. That's a jungle laboratory. Keep your eyes and ears open and your mouth shut and you might learn something around here.'

Demonstration over, he brought up again the idea of my wiring the village for light. Then he said, 'I'm going away tomorrow. I'm leaving my man Khao in charge. Don't fuck with him. Do what he says.' I looked up and saw the glowing end of a cigarette from the hut. Khao hadn't taken his eyes off me since he'd been sent inside.

We talked a little more, about being a father. I asked Jack if he knew about Charlie's unwillingness to leave her hut.

'You've got a big problem there.'

'What can I do?'

He stood up and brushed the dust from the seat of his cut-off shorts. I guess he'd had enough conversation. 'You know Khiem?'

'The soil-taster?'

'Yes, him. She's got bad spirits in her head. Khiem is the only one who can help you.'

I left Jack, and when I returned to our hut Charlie was asleep again. Mick was up and looking better. I recounted some of my conversation with Jack. He'd told me to tell them that Mick was Little John and Phil was Friar Tuck. I don't know who I was in this scenario.

'How is she?' I asked, indicating Charlie.

'She just flakes out,' Phil said.

'Out like a light,' Mick added.

I felt very tired. 'I don't know where the fuck I've brought you two blokes.'

Mick must have caught the note of despair in my voice because he reached for the whisky bottle. 'Let's have a drop of the demon alcohol,' he said. 'You'll feel much improved.'

'No he won't,' said Phil.

'Yes he will,' said Mick. 'The one spirit keeps the other spirits away.'

30

It was good to have Mick up and about the following morning. He said he still felt frail, but he wanted to stretch his legs so I agreed to show him the villagers harvesting opium in the fields. After he'd had a coldwater shave we men sat outside the hut, discussing the Charlie problem and breakfasting on jackfruit and papaya left by Nabao. I suggested we might have to dope Charlie so deeply that we would be two days out of the village before she recovered. Phil reminded me that Charlie had said the villagers tried something similar; she'd told him that her panic on waking was so great that she'd immediately retreated into a coma lasting three days.

'You don't have to hit every problem with a sledgehammer,' said Phil, diligently carving segments of papaya.

His precision, his parsimony with the fruit, made me want to give him a fat lip. It was still early morning and already I was dribbling with sweat, and at that moment I hated the boy. I wanted to kick him. 'Is that what I do?'

He popped a perfect cube of papaya into his mouth, nodded and chewed. 'When someone has fallen into the Slough, what they need is a helpful arm, not a boot up the rear.'

The Slough? What was he talking about? My mind went winging back over twenty years and I flashed on a picture book I used to read to Phil at bedtime. A sweet little boy in oversize pyjamas, he would cling tight to my arm as I read to him, as if we shared a turbulent physical journey through the picture-book landscape. The book was a children's version of *Pilgrim's Progress*. I'd chosen it for the illustrations. The Slough of Despond. Vanity Fair. Doubting Castle.

So this was what Phil was jabbering about all the time! Phil hadn't come out here to help me or to help Charlie. He'd come on a spiritual quest, to brace himself against hardship and temptation. He was on a hair-shirt holiday, for nothing other than his own selfish salvation. *Pilgrim's Progress* and those gaudy illustrations flung back in my face, after all these years, like a pot of paint.

While chewing on sour jackfruit and wiping beads of sweat from the bridge of my nose, I suddenly remembered Rupert Bear lying squashed at the bottom of my rucksack. I went to get my pack, as much to get away from Phil's carefully cubed fruit as anything else. It had been Sheila's idea that I bring Rupert Bear. I'd wanted to tell her not to be so stupid, but some deeper wisdom inside me allowed him to be packed along with my other things, and I'd transferred him to the rucksack when we'd left Chiang Mai.

Chiang Mai! How that exotic and mysterious town with its pearly-green river and morning mists seemed like a vision of home, a second home. I wished I was there, with iced drinks and foot massages and proximity to an airport. With my thoughts on the comforts of Chiang Mai, I emptied my rucksack and dug out Rupert Bear.

Rupert Bear was, but for a few months, as old as was Charlie. Out of all the soft toys you can give a child, and for no rational reason, one gets elected as favourite. More than a favourite, it's a comfort, a companion and a condolence. It's a friend to sleep with, something to stroke, and what's more, it speaks. It articulates many concerns. Parents can learn a lot from asking it direct questions, or by listening to its demands. Over the years Rupert Bear was misplaced many times. The resulting hunt was anxious and fraught. One sneaky effort by me to buy an exact replica to replace the loss caused more problems than ever. It obviously didn't *smell* right; that is to say it didn't smell faintly of curdled breast milk, perspiration, posset, soap, vomit, dribbled juice, spilled Calpol, the breath of bedtime stories, whispers, strung-out kisses, fevers, dreams, nightmares ... the complete harness, the smoking night potion that mutates it from the rank of just another soft toy to a creature of feather and fur and bone and essence. The things that make its spirit familiar, the things that make it a talisman. Sheila had had the instincts to push on me the thing idle maturity would have rejected.

'What the fuck are you going to do with that?' Mick laughed.

'I'm going to give him back to Charlie,' I said.

Rupert Bear had faded and was a bit threadbare at arse and ear, but considering he was over twenty years old, he was wearing well enough. I went inside and at first I put Rupert Bear under Charlie's nose as she slept. I might have left him there, but I decided instead to stick him in the wall above her head. It was easy to part the bamboo and to shove him in the gap, so that he could preside over her opium dreams.

There was always something strange about the world of Rupert Bear. Stranger than Rimbaud and Coleridge and De Quincey and all of those fellows, I mean.

Later, while Mick, Phil and I sat outside our hut, we saw Khao – Jack's bearded henchman – filing through the village with four other men. They were men I hadn't seen before, all wearing army fatigues. As he passed by Khao scowled. Mick being Mick, he scowled right back. They locked eyes as Khao and the new men trooped past our hut.

'An ugly one,' Mick said after they'd gone.

'He's bad news.'

'What's he done to you?'

'Nothing,' I said. 'Yet.'

I took Mick and Phil up to the opium fields. I cannot describe how outlandish and beautiful was the appearance of these fields in the diffuse early morning sunlight. It has become mixed up in my mind with images of a radiant Eden. I decided to introduce them both to the fairy-tale figure of Khiem.

Khiem was decked in his red, white and purple petals, and today he wore a floppy felt hat, also pinned with poppy flowers. Mick approached the old man with a wide mouth and enough respect to float a sailboat. He *wai*d ridiculously deeply, and even though the hill tribes tended to shake hands rather than *wai* like the Thais, Khiem returned the honour. I told him Mick's name and the old man repeated it two or three times.

The amulet hanging around Mick's throat caught his attention. He moved in to inspect it, indicating his approval with soft, cooing noises. Mick made to take the thing off so that

Khiem might examine it, but Khiem stopped him with the flat of his hand, gesturing that Mick should keep it on. He glanced from the amulet to Mick with bulging eyes, and then back at the amulet. Something in the figure of the crescent moon impressed him deeply.

'Moon!' Khiem said.

'Moon!' Mick said.

'Mooon!' Khiem said.

'Moooooooooon!' Mick said. 'Mooooooooooon.'

'Stop it!' Phil said. This tomfoolery around the tribal medicine man seemed to unnerve him.

I glanced skywards and said, '"Then they called Superstition and asked him to look at the prisoner".' It was a line I remembered from *Pilgrim's Progress*. Mick didn't seem to hear, but Phil turned and stared at me. I'd been right. I've no idea what I meant by saying it, and I couldn't even remember the context, but I'd got the little bastard's measure. Let's see how he likes it, I thought.

Khiem seemed favourably disposed towards Mick. We left the old man to his work and moved through the poppy fields. Mick got among the labouring villagers, relieving them of their tools, making a great show of taking over their work. This amused them greatly. They giggled at his efforts, and scolded him if he incised the pods too deeply, or butterfingered some of the crystallised latex to the ground. Meanwhile Phil hung back at a distance, wincing slightly.

It fascinated me, the difference between the two of them. That Mick could do this, where Phil (and I, it has to be added) would hang back; where one man would dive into any given pool, while another would always be subject to a checking or restraining instinct. Within ten minutes it seemed that everyone in the field was laughing and repeating his name. '*Amick. Amicka.*'

'You do realise this makes you complicit,' Phil said.

'You what?'

'You've joined in the harvesting. That will go to make morphine and heroin and it will end up being sold outside the school gates at home.'

Mick looked at me, as if he might detect through me whether Phil was being serious. 'Bollocks.'

I also showed them the generator, which was ticking over nicely. The hideous masculine groaning on the radio had been replaced by some tinny female vocals only marginally more acceptable. We grabbed a couple of bottles of the unwanted Calpol to take back with us.

The village was quiet as we approached the hut. This business with Phil had me pretty agitated At last it erupted. 'Look Phil,' I demanded, 'what's all this about *jealousy*?'

Phil didn't even break stride to answer, loudly, 'The fathers have eaten sour grapes and the children's teeth are set on edge.'

I was as tired of Phil speaking in Bible quotes as I was of hearing guff from *Pilgrim's Progress*. I rounded on him angrily, grabbing his shirt collar. My eyeball was an inch away from his. 'Talk straight for just once in your life.'

'Get your hands off me.'

'You two knock it off,' Mick said.

'Not until he meets a straight question with a straight answer.'

We scuffled a bit, turning an undignified half-circle in the dust while Phil tried to break my grip. I wanted him to take a swing at me. I've never hit him in my life but with the stress I felt at that moment I could easily have knocked his brains out.

'Right, that's enough!' Mick said, coming between us. 'I said stop or I'll bang both your bloody silly heads together!'

I let go of Phil's collar. He was red in the face.

'Fucking ridiculous,' Mick said. 'The pair of you.' But I knew he meant mostly me.

We crossed the village and approached the hut in sullen silence, but as we drew near to the porch something made Mick stop dead. He put a hand on my arm and Phil, too, drew up short behind me. Through the open door we could see one of Khao's bandits standing over Charlie's bed. The man's elbow jiggled at his side. He was masturbating over her as she slept on unaware.

Mick dashed inside and surprised him. He did something I've never seen before or since. With one hand Mick grabbed the man by the face, squeezing his fingers around cheeks, jaw and nostrils, lifting him clean in the air. The man's semi-erect dick hung from his open trousers as Mick carried him out of the hut, toes trailing the earth before he was thrown twelve feet across the dusty ground.

The man was so shocked he lay in the dust for some moments capturing his breath.

'A good wank?' Mick said.

The bandit hauled himself to his feet and started screaming. He zipped up his trousers, releasing a volley of abuse and threats. We didn't need to know what any of it meant as he adopted the posture of a Thai boxer, punctuating his high-pitched curses with a number of swift jabs and kicks at the thin air. But Mick had clearly terrified him, because none of his thrusts landed within six feet of where Mick stood. Moments later this ineffectual whirlwind was joined by Khao and another bandit, both of whom instantly drew pistols.

One of the pistols was levelled at Mick but Khao, snarling, brandishing his gun, marched directly past me and into the hut where Charlie was sleeping. I followed him, three paces behind. Inside the hut he walked directly up to Charlie, pushed the barrel of the pistol into the side of her head and cocked the trigger.

I had never before been faced down with a gun. It's an instructive moment. For that period of time you are utterly in the power of the person wielding the gun, and you are afraid to move half an inch to right or left should your minimal movements provoke some action. I remember, though, that it seemed important to appear unafraid, and this I think I did. Though I felt fear. I felt it in my liver.

Gouging the gun into the side of Charlie's head, Khao shrieked at me, his face contorted, rubberised. He was totally out of control. Charlie was awake, wide-eyed, shrinking from the pistol bruising her temple, her terrified gaze flickering from Khao to me.

Khao screamed a question at me, a question I didn't understand. I couldn't guess whether the correct answer was yes or no. He had gone directly to the point of my greatest weakness. He hadn't levelled his gun at me, but at Charlie, and yet the action was directed at me. Khao knew that if he threatened Charlie, he threatened everything I was there for. I had no place or purpose there without her. He understood that if it came to a choice I would always say take me instead of Charlie. He had instinctively touched my deepest wound, the way only a killer of his nature can. And I could only stand there, motionless in that stifling hut, feeling a fat, oily globe of sweat run from my brow, down the bridge of my nose and into the corner of my mouth.

Nabao appeared from nowhere, flinging herself at Khao's feet, wailing softly, rocking, imploring him. It did enough to unsettle the gunman, and a couple of minutes later Khiem and three villagers from the fields were on the scene, standing at the door, everyone shouting at once while Nabao rocked gently back and forth on Khao's feet. I sensed that Khiem possessed a strange authority over the bandit. With Khiem standing at the threshold, a noisy argument broke out between them, and with that I felt the dangerous moment had passed.

Khao spat in my direction and re-holstered his pistol. The shouting and back talk went on for some time until Khao and his men walked away; but not before Khao had pointed his finger, first at Mick, then at me. After they'd gone Khiem waved his arms, palms downwards, and then turned with the others back towards the fields.

Nabao, who had intervened at the crucial moment, remained behind, rocking Charlie like she was her baby, clucking and shaking her head.

We had to tell Charlie what had caused the fracas. She said it happened often; that in a state of half-sleep she would sense intruders but was too sluggish to wake to see who it was.

'You're lucky,' I said, still shaking, 'that they haven't raped you.'

'They have,' she said coldly. 'Until Jack put a stop to it.'

I could only look at her. And as I did so I was aware that Mick and Phil's eyes were not on Charlie, but on me. Charlie had just said this terrible thing and the pair of them were staring not at her, but at me.

I was a husk. I was a sack of skin barely kept upright by bone. Even the breath that might make me speak evaporated in my throat, until I heard my tiny voice say, 'The one with the beard?'

'Him. And the other one.'

I wanted to know more, but there are some things a father can't ask his daughter. Phil said to me, 'We have to put this behind us.'

'Are you all right, Danny?' Mick added.

'Yes,' I said. 'I'm all right.'

'No he's not all right,' Phil said darkly. 'I know him and he's not all right. He'll try to do something stupid.'

'I said I'm all right.'

'Argue it out between you, boys,' Charlie said. 'I'm the one who was raped.'

The incident left Mick with a strange, undischarged energy. 'Fix up,' he said, clapping his hands together. 'We're going to fix up round here. This hut's a fucking shambles. Phil, get a broom off Nabao. I want this place swept out. Danny, that filthy fuckin' sheet Charlie's lying on: get off your arse and wash it or burn it, one thing or the other. As for you Charlie, I'm going to wash your hair.'

'No you're not,' Charlie said.

'We'll see about that,' Mick said. He went out and returned dragging the water drum inside the hut. He squeezed half a bottle of shampoo into the palm of his hand. 'Get over here. Mick's in the chair, and we're fixing up!'

Charlie meekly submitted. As did Phil and I. While Mick had Charlie stooped over the water drum, Phil swept and tidied the hut. I took Charlie's bedding outside and I burned it. In future she would have to lie on one of my shirts.

Mick thoroughly soaped Charlie's hair and rinsed it and combed it free of knots and lugs. Throughout all of this he looked furious. I knew why he was doing it. He was carrying my anger. He had to do *something* with it.

Later we were utterly exhausted from these exertions. Charlie, smelling of shampoo, squatted at the threshold of the hut while we three sat just outside, trying to breathe, trying to extract some air from the oppressive heat. We were all sweating externally and quivering inside after the events of the morning.

Charlie noticed the broken leather strap around Mick's neck. It had obviously been snapped off in the struggle, and Mick had lost his amulet. He was dismayed. Phil and I had a good hunt for the thing, but we couldn't find it.

'Your lucky rabbit's foot,' I said, trying to force an ounce of humour out of myself, but Mick was too upset to be teased.

After a while some village children came up to us. Mick let them stroke his hairy chest, which made them giggle. Within a moment there were three wide-eyed kids sitting on his knee and he was teaching them counting games and nursery songs, as if what had happened an hour earlier was a dream.

As I sat by the doorway talking to Charlie, one little girl made a garland from poppy petals and placed it around Mick's neck.

'I'll make you a garland, Dad,' Charlie said. 'But you'll have to bring me the flowers.'

I looked at her. She was utterly composed. How could she be, after what she'd been through? Yet she sat there with her hands in her lap, once again like a temple idol, looking back at me. It was then that I identified that elusive power I had seen in her. It was the awesome power of youth. It sat on her shoulders like a brilliant, silver carapace, barely chipped by her experiences. It gave no quarter. It forgave nothing and it surrendered to nobody. It could face any wild thing except its own inevitable foreclosure. I knew then that I had no answer for its terrible force.

'What?' Charlie said.

'Nothing,' I said. I pointed at Mick instead. 'Look. He's so good with them.'

'Why didn't he ever have children?'

I shrugged. It was not something we'd discussed.

'The villagers say that a man without children is damned to a life of tears.'

'Damned to a life of tears if you have 'em, too,' I shot back, rather too quickly.

I reached across the threshold, held her hand and gave her a thin smile. She was beyond all recrimination; really that's how I felt.

I looked again at Mick sitting in the dust, barechested and wearing his knee-length shorts, playing happily with the kiddies. He clapped his hands and sang for these mites with eyes like molasses, and he was anointed by a ray of golden light. His blond hair flared in the sunlight; his blue eyes by contrast seemed pellucid, cloudless. I experienced a sweet moment of dizziness, as if something strange was happening; he and the children were suspended an inch or two from the ground as they played, and tilted at forty-five degrees to the earth. I heard the tinkle of temple windchimes.

Charlie heard me gasp. 'What are you staring at?'

'It's Mick. For a moment he looked like something from a picture book. It was like a vision of heaven.'

'I saw it too,' Phil said, coming up behind me and murmuring in my ear. 'It was a moment of blessing.' For once Phil was absolutely correct. I couldn't argue. In our suffering and in the midst of our predicament we had been given a divine instant. 'This balances what happened earlier. There's an exact symmetry in our day. You know, this is all being watched by a higher power.'

Charlie squinted from one to the other of us. 'Have you two been on the pipe?'

'Do you know something, Dad,' Charlie said to me that evening, when the four of us were snuggling down to sleep, the air temperature dropping fast. 'I had such a vivid dream. I had a dream about Rupert Bear.'

Mick winked at me to say nothing. 'What's this about Rupert Bear?' he said.

'Oh,' Charlie said fondly. 'He's this ragged old toy I had when I was a kid. In the dream he was telling me it was going to be all right. Do you remember him, Phil?'

Rupert was still there, stuck in the wall above her bed, but she obviously hadn't seen him. Or rather maybe she had seen him but without registering the fact, and had thus gone on to dream about him. I'm quite prepared to believe that, anyway.

'Rupert. Scary,' Phil said.

'Red with blue trousers,' I offered. 'Rupert Bear was.'

'No! Yellow trousers with black check.'

It didn't matter what the subject – she was quick to contradict me on the smallest details. 'Was he? It was so long ago.'

I pretended to think about Rupert Bear so that the others wouldn't know I was churning the earlier events of the day: my scuffle with Phil; the thought of Charlie's rapists.

About Phil: I lied when I said I'd never hit him. I did, once. When he was about twelve years old. He'd taken one of my books and chopped the pages out so as to make a hiding compartment. I'd confronted him; he'd lied; I'd hit him, too hard.

Oh.

I told him that day that I'd hit him for lying. But I in turn was lying about that. I'd hit him because I'd just had a furious row with Sheila. Too hard: I hit him too hard. I remember the shock of pain and betrayal on his face. I saw some shadow creep out of him and turn its back on me that day. He never looked at me the same way after that. Over the years which followed I felt so bad about it that I think I denied to myself that it ever happened. This day's scuffle had brought the scene back to me.

It also made me angry once more as I thought about Charlie's rapists. It was a cold anger, one I'd never quite experienced before. Anger with ice at the heart of it. Anger that breathed out of you like ectoplasm, marshalling itself into a spirit or form external to your body. Phil was correct: I was determined to do something about them. I just didn't know what. But my blood was knocking in my brain.

And why did these two things seem connected, these two violations? The rape and my hitting Phil a long time ago. Apart from the fact that they'd been brought to mind by today's events, I mean.

It was a cold night again. Before settling, Mick made a silent gesture and lifted his pillow to show me his knife underneath. I lifted the corner of my sleeping bag to show him I'd had exactly the same thought. We were certain that Khao and his men, or just one of them, might be out to pay us a visit in the night.

The thinness of the bamboo walls left me feeling very exposed. Every click or movement or stirring breeze outside had me on the alert, straining to identify every sound. Some animal was prowling out there for an hour. I heard it padding round, wheezing, sniffing at the hut. There was a strong moon, doing its work on the opium that had already seeped through the poppy heads; I hoped the brightness of the moon might keep intruders away. I was wide awake. Swords of moonlight sliced at me through the bamboo slats of the hut as I seethed about Charlie's rapists. I lay in the dark with my fingers twitching on the handle of Coconut's wide-bladed knife.

31

Sure enough, in the night, the attack came, and I was glad it did. I was in a volatile state, and something had to happen. I was boiling inside, but I'd had to shut down my feelings so hard I felt like I was moving around an ocean bed in a bathysphere. When the time came, when I heard the creak of a footstep on the porch, I was ready to break out, to come up for air, and then screaming.

I'd seen a television programme about the partners of rape victims. All uselessly angry, living with a rage that had nowhere to go. The interviewer was giving them a hard time: after all, she was saying, you aren't the ones who have been violated, think of your wives for a change instead of yourselves. True enough, I thought at the time, but what does she know about being a man? I know this: if someone violates a loved one, then the rage to strike back is terrifying and holy. I don't understand religion. But I think that if there was a God, this is one thing He would forgive; more than that, He may not forgive the man who stood apart.

I knew someone had come because I heard the animal foraging beneath the hut go skittering. I felt myself glide to my feet; almost as if my spirit left my recumbent, physical form dozing on the rattan pallet. I made no noise, though I saw Mick's eyes flicker open. He too had been unable to sleep. I put my finger to my lips, to warn him, and he too produced his blade.

I could have been a wraith, a figure of dream, banded by moonlight coming through the bamboo slats, moonlight that flashed on the blade I held loosely at my flank. I felt a peculiar calm. I peered through a gap in the bamboo and I saw him set foot on the step up to the porch, and he was drenched in moonlight. It was the man Mick had flung into the dust. He carried some object I couldn't determine, either knife or gun.

Phil sat up, rubbing his eyes, and I silenced him with a gesture. The man on the porch hesitated, straining to listen. It was then I realised the object in his hand was a petrol can. He began sprinkling fuel on the hut. The bastard had come to burn us.

I kicked away the bamboo door, stepped out on to the porch and brought the long knife down on his arm in a sweeping arc from high above my head. There was a brief communion of blade and moon, like fizzing sodium light, before a blow to my own head knocked me clean off the porch, and into a syrupy, all-encompassing blackness.

I woke later in the night, back on my pallet bed, and with a raging headache. The other three were awake, and a single candle was burning. They were sitting up, whispering, but they shut up when they saw that I had come round. They all looked at me strangely.

'What happened?' I asked.

'Go back to sleep, Danny,' Mick said in a hoarse whisper. 'You've been having a bad dream.'

Bad dream? I felt the side of my head. A bruise was already forming around my eye.

'A nightmare,' Charlie said. 'We had to sit on you.'

'And I had to slap you,' Mick said. 'Here, drink this.' He tilted a bowl of whisky at my lips.

Phil said nothing. His face was white like the moon.

'Go back to sleep,' said Charlotte.

I groaned. I went back to sleep.

When I woke again it was to the grey light of pre-dawn. The other three were still awake, and they were arguing. Charlie had a broom and was sweeping the floor in a vigorous, agitated fashion. Phil saw me open my eyes, and he quietened the others. My head still hurt.

'What's wrong?' I asked.

No one would say anything.

I rose and went over to a bowl of water, splashing some of it on the back of my neck. Then I went to my pallet, and lifted up the corner of the sleeping bag. Coconut's blade was there, as it was when we'd settled down the previous night. I took it out and inspected the blade. There was nothing to suggest it had been moved by me or anyone else. I felt nauseated by the pain in my head. I looked at Mick. 'No dream, pal.'

'Tell him!' Charlie said.

'Not necessary!' Phil hissed.

'Tell me what?'

'If one of you two won't tell him, then I will,' Charlie said. She got to her feet, and in that moment it seemed that Charlie was the strongest one of all of us.

'Tell me what!' I shouted.

There was a stand-off, then Mick also dragged himself to his feet. Phil made a noise, a release of air. Mick beckoned me outside, and I followed while the other two remained in the hut.

Outside it was still chilly, but I felt the temperature rising, even though the sun hadn't come up yet. It was as if the sun was a vast machine, and I could hear the faint and distant rumble of it before it appeared in the sky. The entire village was sleeping. As we stepped down from the porch, Mick turned to me and nervously placed his fingertips first on my shoulder then on my breastbone. 'Don't panic, Danny.'

'I'm not about to.'

Mick turned, staring somewhere above the neighbouring huts. 'He's under there.'

At first I didn't know what he meant by *under there*. His eyes were fixed on the distance. Then he made a minimal gesture which made me realise he was referring to the cavity under the stilts of the hut. I ducked down to look, but I couldn't see anything in the shadows beneath the stilts, and I said so.

'Covered over, Danny. We covered him over with crap.'

I got down again. I had to crawl a little way inside. It didn't smell too good under the hut. It reeked of garbage and pigshit. I could also smell petrol. I moved aside some debris, some pieces of bamboo and some torn strips of polythene and I saw a boot. I touched it. The boot was attached to a leg. I crawled back out.

'Christ,' I said. 'Christ. I killed him.'

Phil had joined us now. 'Not you, Dad,' he said. 'Not you—'

Mick spoke rapidly, hoarsely. 'He was going to do for you, Danny. Really he was. He'd kicked you in the head. You were down. He was going to do for you, mate!'

I looked back at the entrance to the hut. Charlie was watching from the shadows. She nodded at me. She was very clear about what had to be done. 'You can't leave him there. He'll be found.'

Mick and Phil were in such a fragile state they were relieved to be directed. I made Phil get the trellis I'd been planning to use as a stretcher for Charlie. I told Mick to crawl under the porch with me and together we dragged the body out by the feet. We also retrieved the petrol can. Mick mentioned a knife and I had to go back under to find it. While looking for the knife I found a discarded backpack.

Christ, Mick! I thought when I saw the body gashed at the neck. I figured Mick had caught him with a blow of such might it had half severed his head from his body. The man's army fatigues were caked in blood. 'Strip down to your underpants,' I said. 'We've got to move quickly before the villagers awake.'

Mick and Phil understood. After they'd stripped off we rolled the body on to the trellis. Phil and I took the front corners of the trellis and Mick took the back end. With the weight distributed that way the corpse wasn't so heavy, and we hurried from the village along the very path by which we'd first arrived.

The crimson sun, like a dragon's eye, came peeping up over the jungle hillside as we shuffled along the path, sweating, shivering, slipping. Three English men in underpants and training shoes.

I wanted to get us far enough away to avoid the body being found by villagers or dug up by scavenging dogs; on the other hand, we had to get back before the villagers were up and about their business. Half jogging, half shuffling, we hurried along the leaf-strewn path without speaking, our breath coming short. But the scrubby jungle was too open, and I couldn't find the cover I was looking for.

It occurred to me that Mick and Phil were in shock. They

behaved like silent automatons, responding immediately to everything I said.

About a third of a mile away from the village I stopped them. We were all panting heavily. I'd spotted a small cavity in the ground, beside a bush and broken red-clay boulders, about twenty yards off the path. We put down the trellis and I jogged over to check it out. It wasn't the cover I wanted but it would have to do. We carried the corpse across the scrub and tipped it into the cavity, along with the fuel can and the knife. Then we rolled a few boulders over the body, but were unable to bury it completely.

'Let's get back,' Mick panted.

'Wait,' I said. I insisted that we lay the trellis over the cavity, and cover it with leaves, sticks and broken stones, so that even if anyone were to walk across it they might not sense the trellis beneath their feet. This we did with trembling hands.

'Let's go,' I said, at last.

We jogged back along the path, hopelessly out of breath. By now we were streaked with sweat and blood from the corpse. The sun was climbing higher in the sky and the day was heating up at an alarming rate. As we ran along the path all I could hear was our own heavy breathing, the three of us blowing and gasping, the sound of our panting rising like a mist above the vegetation, like stifled cries to God. As we approached the village I slowed the others down. I was afraid that everyone could hear our dreadful wheezing and hyperventilating.

Villagers were moving about the village by the time we got back. Cocks were crowing, and a dog was barking. We hid behind a bush and dashed in one at a time, making for the out-house. There we stripped off our underpants, and splashed and soaped each other in a hyperventilating and hysterical frenzy, teeth chattering, murmuring, moaning, scrubbing off every trace of blood.

We went into the hut. Charlie sat cross-legged, eyeing our naked bodies like a baleful Buddha. She was calm. At that moment she was holding it together for all of us. 'Lucky,' she said. 'Khao was here a few minutes ago. I lied and said you'd gone over to the poppy fields.'

'Right,' I said, trying to recover my breath. 'Right. We get dressed. We go to the poppy fields. From now on everything is normal. Got that?'

'Normal,' said Mick.

Phil looked sick, strange. 'Got that, Phil?'

'Normal,' said Phil.

Before going to the poppy fields, I made a small fire and burned the three bloodied pairs of underpants.

32

Nobody said a damned thing. Not to us anyway. We had no way of knowing if the boy was even missed.

I say 'boy' as if I knew the age of the dead man. I guessed he was about Charlie's age, though it is often difficult to tell with Thai men. What did it matter? Somewhere he'd had a mother and a father, and if we were going to get through this I knew I'd have to stop thinking about things like that. But the stress of going about and doing things 'normally' was excruciating. The four of us were the most dreadful bundle of exposed nerves, and if one sneezed, the others shivered.

Oddly, there was no recrimination from any quarter. There was not even discussion between us. It was too important to pretend to be preoccupied with other things, in an act of wilful denial. Charlie, who had been very clear that the dead man was one of her rapists, merely retreated to her pipe. Mick was sullen, jumpy. Phil suffered the worst: he spent a lot of time in the corner of the hut, on his knees in silent prayer.

We sensed we couldn't possibly get away with it. We'd reached the lowest point.

Can I tell you that I felt in any way satisfied that we'd killed my daughter's rapist? I can't say that it changed a single thing. The rage in me hadn't gone away. The event was always going be a wound in Charlie's life, and it still smouldered in my brain. I had not an ounce of sympathy for the heap of meat we'd buried under the trellis, but our actions had done nothing to restore equilibrium to my mind. Revenge had not delivered the promised sweets, and all that had altered was that our predicament had become even more perilous.

We took turns in sleeping, submitting to the exhaustion of a night without rest and the strain of the last few hours. Though we agreed we should only do so in turn, and for a short period, lest anyone should speculate on the cause of our collective fatigue. I dozed so fitfully that my fears and anxieties got mixed up with my dreams.

Mick woke me. He was worried about Phil, whom he said had gone to walk in the poppy fields. Mick looked grave. 'I hope he can handle it,' he said.

'He's got to,' I replied. 'He's got to.'

Charlie was deep in one of her slumbers. I let Mick take a nap, and I sat outside the hut, waiting for Phil to come back. I dug out of my pack the copy of Thomas De Quincey. Not that I had the head for books in that state, of course, but I wanted anyone watching to think that I was relaxed enough to be able to read. I sat outside the hut in a kind of trance, remembering to occasionally turn the page for the benefit of any observers.

By the time Phil returned, he looked utterly wretched; tortured and tormented. I saw straight through him to the small boy within. I followed him inside the hut. 'Can I hug you?' I asked.

'Why?'

'Because I need to.'

He looked at me with evident distaste. 'It's a bit late for that, isn't it? Yesterday you wanted to smash my face.'

'Please.'

I stepped forward and put my arms around him. He allowed me near him, but it was deeply unsatisfactory. He turned his shoulder to my chest and stood sideways to me. I was making him squirm so I let him go. 'You get some sleep now,' I said. 'Sleep is good. It knits the soul.' It was probably something I'd read in Thomas De Quincey.

'The soul!' he spat, as if I had no right to talk about these things. 'The soul!' Then he started laughing. Cackling. He threw back his head and laughed manically, but then stopped abruptly, and the fact that he stopped cackling so suddenly was more disturbing than his laughter. But he was so profoundly tired he lay down on the pallet and he let me cover him with a thin blanket.

In the quiet moments which followed, and with the other three sleeping, I took a good hard squint at the hut, trying to see what it was that might stop Charlie from going outside. What forces might bar her way, even if only in her fevered imagination. Was there a giant serpent coiled around the hut? Or prison bars of smoky green light obstructing the door? I tried to visualise these things, superimposing images where I couldn't see them.

I laid my head next to Charlie's, trying to feel my way into her dreams, her nightmares, trying to get on that flight with her all over again. I wanted to fight it for her from the inside. But there was nothing. I thought about the moment I first entered the hut and found her sitting upright. I wondered now if it had only been a spirit I had seen. It seemed possible to me that a mind in an extreme state of distress could see anything.

I imagined her spirit sitting upright again, legs crossed under her, leaving her sleeping body. I imagined her trying to tell me what she saw. At that moment, Charlie opened her eyes – her real eyes, in her real body – and appeared to stare aghast at the open door. I swung round and in that moment I had a notion of the hut tilting ninety degrees, so that we might all fall out of the doorway, and go on falling, falling into the throat of the world, parallel to the surface of the earth, hitting trees and other objects but never stopping in our descent as we plummeted further and further into twilight. I grabbed at the floor to steady myself and the hut righted. When I looked back at Charlie her eyes were shut, after all, and she slept on.

Later when Charlie woke, she spotted Rupert Bear looking down at her from the bamboo wall. She gasped. She took him down from the wall and hugged him. Then she went strangely quiet, and asked me why I'd brought him. She didn't let go of Rupert for a long time.

I was glad. It meant she was holding on to the old days.

Some time later, when Rupert had finally tumbled free of her grasp, I picked him up and made to lodge him back in the bamboo wall. It was then that I made a significant discovery. Looking for somewhere better to locate Rupert I noticed a rough star-wheel of bamboo above Charlie's sleeping head, at the point where the upright bamboo canes met the giant tobacco-leaf roof. A big dry leaf had been stuffed behind the bamboo there and I thought I could see some small object lodged behind.

'What is it?' Charlie said.

I had to get Mick to help me. We dragged a spindly, low table across the floor, and I climbed on it. A little unsteady, I reached up and pulled a folded piece of paper from behind the dry leathery leaf. I got down from the table and unfolded the paper. Mick moved in closer to take a look.

We were both shocked into silence. As we stood gazing at the paper, I heard Mick's breathing go shallow. My hand holding the thing started to tremble, not with fear, but with renewed anger. Mick grabbed at the paper, trying to relieve me of it, but I wouldn't let him take it.

In the middle of the sheet of paper had been glued a Polaroid snapshot of Charlie. In the snapshot she was wearing a swimsuit and was washing her hair in a river. She was bending over, smiling at the photographer who'd presumably caught her unawares. It was a happy and spontaneous photograph, taken in the fresh golden light of early morning.

Around the photograph, and on the backing paper, several winged demonic figures had been added with thick black lines of charcoal. The figures had bulging eyes and ferocious teeth. The cartoon style in which they had been sketched would have been ridiculous if it were not for the fact that all of these airborne figures had massive, erect penises extending from the paper and on to the photograph, so that the image of Charlie was being assaulted: between her legs, at her anus, at her mouth, at her ears and at her eyes.

I ground my teeth together in an action purely involuntary.

'Can I see?' said Charlie.

'Let's stop and think clearly about this,' Mick said. But thinking clearly about it was the last thing either of us could do. At last I let him take it from me, and he held the thing at arm's length, as if something vile and unholy might leap from the paper and crawl up his shoulders. His other hand massaged his own, leathery neck, slowly and ineffectively. Mick, the steady rock, was shaken. I could see him thinking *how much more of this?* 'Let's stop and get a grip,' he said.

Charlie stepped up quickly behind him and snatched the thing from his hand. She nodded briefly, as if understanding. 'Right,' she said, very quietly. 'Right.'

We immediately started looking for more of the same, as if we'd found a scorpion nestling in the bamboo. And we discovered two similar papers secreted in the walls. Different shots of Charlie glued to backing paper, but overdrawn with obscene figures.

'But who would do this?' Mick said. 'Out of the villagers, who would do this?'

I knew what he meant. The uncovering of these dirty objects could make our situation much worse, depending on who was behind it. I started counting. High among the suspects had to be Khiem, village medicine man and sorcerer. But somehow I didn't see his hand in this, and for once in my life I decided to trust my instincts. Either way, if I were to brandish the hideous articles in his face, I could study his reaction. 'Khiem?' I said.

'No,' Charlie said. 'It's Khao; the one with the beard. His father is a sorcerer in another village, where he left in disgrace. He would like to be a sorcerer here, for which reason Khiem is his enemy, I know that. These people live and breathe spirits. They don't simply believe in them; they live and work and play side by side with spirits every moment of their lives. They entertain the spirits. They invite the spirits into their lives.'

'Just as you have done, Charlie,' said Phil drawing up behind her. 'Just as we all have done.'

I decided to show Khiem because if Charlie was right and he was innocent, then I thought he would want to help me. There was another reason: I had to go out and look for any signs of the villagers regarding us differently. I figured if they knew what had happened, Jack would too.

I left for the poppy fields with the ugly spirit papers folded inside my money pouch. Mick and Phil stayed behind with Charlie. Meanwhile the village radio shrieked out high-pitched

Thai pop tunes. What had previously been an acoustic irritant was now a torment to the nerves.

Khiem, as was his usual habit, was working the poppies a little way off from the rest of the villagers. He was incising. Seeing me striding towards him he straightened his back.

'Khiem,' I said on reaching him. He didn't even blink, regarding me steadily. I opened a packet of cigarettes and offered one. He accepted, all the while eyeing me suspiciously. He saw that my hands were shaking. I lit him, and together we puffed away at our cigarettes without taking our eyes off each other. Then I squatted down between the tall poppies and gestured that he might do the same, which he did.

I must have been stupid to think I could outguess a man like Khiem. These people were masters of deportment and control. My Western face must have been bubbling with the signatures and tokens of murder.

But I unzipped my money pouch and rolled out the papers, studying his reaction carefully. His body went rigid and the veins stood out on his bald head like insulated cable. He let out a deep moan, and then began clicking his tongue rapidly. He let his hands fall to the earth. It was obvious to me that he'd never seen the things before; but on the other hand he seemed to know something of their significance.

He asked me some questions, which I couldn't fathom. I made a steeple of my fingers to try to indicate that I'd found the papers in the hut. He jabbed a finger in that direction and I nodded. He understood. I noticed he was very careful not to touch the papers with his hands, as if they might contaminate him. He indicated that I should put them back in my pouch. Then he gathered up his tool-kit and motioned that we should return to the village.

Khiem evidently wanted to inspect the hut for himself, though he wouldn't cross the threshold from the outside just as Charlie refused to cross it from within. Khiem peered inside. I pointed out the three spots in which we'd found the obscenities and he crouched at the door, as if listening hard for something. Without warning, he skipped away like a startled hare. I was about to ask the others what they made of it, but Mick was pointing over my shoulder.

We had other things to think about. Jack was back in the village and he'd arrived with five new men, all armed to the teeth and each fantastically decked with poppy flowers. One of the bandits was wearing a headband interwoven with red and white petals. Khao appeared to greet this group. There was a brief conversation, after which Jack turned and made his way over, looking none too pleased. My heart tightened like a fist in my chest as Khao and the new men dispersed amongst the village huts.

Jack called me aside. He was carrying what looked like a bullwhip; or maybe it was an elephant whip. His face was set like a ceramic mask. 'Something happened yesterday.'

My intestines squeezed. I felt he knew. I don't know why; I just felt he knew. I quickly chose to admit to everything that had happened during daylight hours. 'You're a father, Jack. You know that a father has to defend his daughter against brutal men. We threw the man from our hut.'

He looked wrongfooted. 'That's not how I heard things.'

'Whatever you heard, Jack, that's exactly how it was. I don't lie to you.'

'You don't lie to me, eh?'

'No.' My tongue stuck to the roof of my mouth. My guts squeezed again.

He stared hard at me for a long time. 'You know I decided to check on that. I took the trouble to have your story checked while I was away. The British Consul in Chiang Mai.' Brazier-Armstrong. I had no idea what he might have found out. 'Seems you were telling me the truth about this Cambridge man.'

I didn't blink. 'And I'm telling you the truth about what happened here.'

Jack walked up and put his face very close to mine. I could smell what he'd had for lunch. I was sweating in the afternoon heat, but I fought the temptation to wipe my brow. 'Have you seen him?'

'Who?'

He glared over my shoulder at the hut. I'd seen past the

construction of his question, and he knew it. 'The man you had a problem with.'

'No.' The simple lie clunked in my mouth. Jack looked into my eyes. One of the village dogs chose that moment to dive under our hut, scuffling about under there. I tried hard to think whether we might have left anything for the dog to bring out, a shoe, a belt, a headband, a knife.

'He's missing.'

'Oh?'

'He went missing after Little John there humiliated him.'

'I see. He must be afraid that you will punish him for what he did to my daughter.'

Jack pulled his face back from mine. 'He will have to return and then we'll get to the bottom of what happened.'

'I don't know why you keep such men, Jack.' I knew I was chancing it, but I was appealing to his Robin Hood aspect.

Jack snorted. 'He's my nephew. He's a complete fool, but he's only here on sufferance, and I'm obliged to protect him.'

'I understand,' I said, though I didn't. The salt from my sweat prickled my eyes. The dog came out from under the hut with what appeared to be a smudge of dried or clotted blood on its nose.

Jack bent down to pat the dog. 'He found a rat under there.'

'Yes,' I said. 'A rat.'

Jack turned sharply to look at me again. The air around me seemed to ping with imminent fracture. 'I've got my own troubles right now. I don't need trouble from you. Keep Little John on a leash or I won't be responsible.' I looked at the hut, from where Mick was watching us. Just as I was about to reply the radio stopped dead. Jack let out a Thai expletive.

'I'll go and fix it at once,' I said.

Jack stormed away, and as he did so he cracked his whip on the dry earth. I knew his anger was not entirely about us. Something much more serious was going on in his private kingdom, and we were merely caught up in events.

I hurried over to the generator, relieved beyond measure to be clear of the interrogation of Jack's eyes. He didn't know. He suspected, but he didn't know.

As for the generator, it seemed bad luck to have imported such a temperamental machine into the jungle, when ninety-nine in a hundred of these motors would tick along happily for years. I lifted off the cover plate to check where I'd been before. It was when I ran my fingers along the plug lead that I realised the problem was not mechanical after all.

The insulation around the lead had peeled away and the circuit was shorting out. There was no way I could have missed this the day before. Somebody had been in there and had deliberately stripped it with a knife. I thought back to the previous faults and saw how they had each been 'assisted': the missing cap, the leafy gunk, the stripped wire. All disguised sabotage.

I chopped out the exposed bit of cable and simply shortened the lead. The generator started up again and ticked over nicely. I kept the bit of vandalised cable and put it in my pocket. As I emerged from the hut Nabao was standing in the shadows of her doorway. She stroked her chin very slowly with her hand, and then repeated the gesture before dissolving into the darkness of her hut.

A signal.

When I got back to our hut, Khiem was busy outside it. He had three clay pots, each of which was smoking with some kind of jungle incense. He wanted Mick, Phil and I to take the three pots inside. He directed us to position the smoking jars under the places where we'd found the photographs.

'Jack doesn't know,' I whispered to Mick as we carried the pots inside. 'And that fucker with the beard: he's sabotaging the generator.'

'How do you know?'

'Nabao told me.'

'We've got to get out of this place before that body gets turned up,' Mick said, fingering the spot where his amulet would have been and wafting incense from under his nose.

'We've arrived in hell,' said Phil. 'Have you noticed how red the earth is here? How red it is. It's not easy to get out of hell. No, not easy at all. Did any of you know that?'

33

Jack's face was impassive as he surveyed the obscenities, but his eyes dripped venom. The defaced photographs were spread out on the table, cluttering a jungle map he'd been studying when Khiem led me into his hut.

After he'd finished lighting incense and candles around the hut Khiem had persuaded me to take the matter to Jack. The old man had accomplished strange rituals, walking backwards around the hut and placing near the door a 'spirit-house', a miniature version of a village hut in which he placed tiny bamboo figures of birds and fish and animals. Then he'd persuaded me what to do by the simple expedient of gently taking my hand and whispering Jack's name over and over.

At first I resisted. For obvious reasons I wanted as little contact with Jack as possible. But then it seemed that by pushing my problems under his nose I might appear less likely to be involved in his nephew's disappearance.

By their actions I suspected that Jack's cohort was busy with jungle business, converting raw opium into morphine for transportation. It was Charlie who had told me that the secondary translation of morphine into heroin was a much more sophisticated operation, requiring serious scientific equipment at labs across the border in Myanmar or Laos, or even near Chiang Mai. I figured Jack was getting ready to transport a major haul and that I'd disturbed him in the planning of his route.

He was transfixed by the ugly spirit photographs.

'There's another thing I have to tell you,' I said, anxious to break his unnerving silence. I laid before him the example of stripped wiring I'd brought from the generator. 'There's nothing wrong with the generator engine. One of your men is sabotaging it.'

Jack turned his head away from me and stared fiercely at the bamboo wall. Nothing was said, but I felt afraid. His lean body was utterly rigid, but he leaked an odour like iron and smoke.

'Three times I fixed it and each time the engine had been tampered with. At first I thought—'

He cut me short. 'Return to your hut. Stay there. Go.'

My hands trembling, I did as I was told. Khiem remained behind.

Mick sat outside the hut, playing with a couple of children. He'd had them hunting for his amulet without success, and now he was teaching them how to play fivestones. This time there was no golden light. I could see black lines of care striping his brow. I knew he would have calculated the danger to himself, and the real possibility that Phil might sacrifice him to spare the rest of us.

After all, there was no love lost between them. It was without doubt that in Phil's eyes Mick had committed the ultimate unforgivable act. Unforgivable before man and God. If the body was uncovered then Phil might conclude that Mick could be made to pay the penalty. The finger would be pointed. I knew Mick would have figured this out already.

A dozen candles flickered on the porch, and the pungent smell of incense from inside thickened the air. Mick scrambled to his feet, wanting to know what had happened. I told him all there was to tell and then I went inside to see Charlie. In the shadows of the hut a dozen more star-like candles burned. After a brief, pig-like snort, Charlie snoozed on. Phil squatted at the foot of the bed, reading, by the dim light, from his pocket Bible. I squatted with him, and I soon found myself stroking Charlie's foot just as before. I sat watching her as I did when she was an infant, looking for that cherubic beauty in her night-time flight across clouds seeded with gold and velvet dark. Now I had no idea what resinous nightmares she crossed in her sleep. But I sat and watched all the same.

'Didn't I love you enough, Phil? You and Charlie? Is that why things worked out like this? Or did I love you too much? I'm not a psychiatrist. Not a shrink.'

Phil shook his head. 'Will you say a prayer with me?'

'I will not. I've told you before: she's on her pipe, you are on yours.'

'Then,' he said, 'will you say a prayer *for* me?'

I gazed at him with an uncomprehending expression.

'You know what Mercy said, Dad? Mercy said: "I was a-dreaming that I sat all alone in a solitary place and was bemoaning the hardness of my heart."' With that he got up and took himself outside, leaving me with Charlie.

The sigh which issued from me at that point was very nearly a howl. My son and I were reduced to trading in obscure quotations, and it was a game in which I was always going to lose. I felt Phil had confined himself to a cage, on some unreachable summit, just as Charlie had done.

'I'm your dad,' I whispered to Charlie, still stroking her foot, 'come to get you. But I can't get to you, can I? I can't go where you are. Either of you. I don't know the way in, Charlie, but if I did, you know I would come after you. You know I would. I'd go barefoot over hot coals for you.'

When my jaws ached from this one-way talk I went and sat outside with Mick, discussing our chances. I asked him where Phil was, but he didn't know. I was hopeful that, after what I'd revealed to Jack, the opium bandit might decide to help us. We were silent for a while, and then Mick started talking about the new and exotic fruits he'd discovered since he'd been here; fruit he'd never seen before, and how he was going to import some for his market stall. Maybe he was faking it to lift our desperate spirits, but he seemed to have no doubt we would get out of this. He was going to be the first in Leicester market to import star-shaped fruit. Actually, I'd seen star-shaped fruit on Leicester market, but he was still talking like this when the attack came from nowhere.

Crack! Jack's elephant whip snapped at the red earth an inch from my fingers. Dust rose in the air like gunsmoke. 'You! Get inside that hut! I've had enough trouble from you people!' The whip cracked again, as Mick and I scrambled to our feet. The bearded Khao stood behind Jack with a loutish curl to his lip. He was enjoying this.

'Steady on!' Mick tried. A mistake. Jack cracked the whip and it whistled as it curled round Mick's bare leg, somewhere between ankle and calf. Mick winced and swore, struggling to keep his balance. When the whip unravelled he took a step forward, but Jack had his pistol levelled at Mick's head.

'Where's that boy? Tell me where he is, fat man! You know where he is!'

Mick was incredibly calm. 'What boy? The one I threw from the hut?'

Then Khao spoke loudly in Thai. Something gloating. Jack turned to him, and I said, 'Yes, he's the one who sabotaged the generator.'

Jack looked at Khao, and then at me, and then back at Khao. The heat of the afternoon and the air about me seemed to clot as I sensed events teetering on a mighty fulcrum. I had the thrilling sensation of almost hearing Jack's brain turn in rapid motion, and as he regarded Khao steadily I saw something in his eyes, as if a piece of a puzzle quite outside my range of vision had suddenly snapped into place for him. He still had the pistol levelled at Mick's head. He lowered it. 'Get inside. Stay there.'

'Do what he says, Mick. Get in the hut.'

Mick was impulsive, but not stupid. He retreated inside, like a dog to kennel.

'You too!' Jack screamed. 'And listen to this: if that fucking generator stops one more time you're a dead man! You hear me? You're dead meat.' With that he stormed away, leaving Khao to sneer at me. Khao formed his fingers into a play pistol, aimed it at me, and pulled the trigger. He smirked again before walking away.

Inside the hut Mick was nursing an angry red weal on his calf muscle. Charlie woke up. 'What's going on? Where's Phil?'

It was a long afternoon. I tried to keep my mind off the sound of the radio belting out from its lonely table in the centre of the village. There were long pauses between the high-pitched strains that made my heart quicken, but thankfully each pause was followed by another tinny, echoing piece. I was frantic about where Phil had got to.

I feared more than ever that Phil might compromise us.

Charlie, Phil and I were family: Mick was not. I was still terribly afraid that Phil, quite in desperation, might betray Mick in order to save our skins. The seriousness with which Phil took his own faith, and the gravity of Mick's crime, made this a real possibility.

Would that be how it would work out? That we had gone into the jungle and had to surrender Mick in order to bring Charlie home? Never more desperately had I wished to know the true measure of my son's character.

I returned to my copy of Thomas De Quincey, obstinately trying to stop my mind from turning on the complications of the last twenty-four hours and to distract myself from the hideous shadow that had fallen over the sunlit village. The words on the page seemed to skim past my eyes and I'd given up on the idea of learning a single thing from this book. But at least it helped me to fight against the doom-laden thoughts oppressing me.

I'd finished reading the *Confessions*, and I'd got on to the unfinished sequel, which was published in the same volume. This part was called *Suspiria de Profundis*. I have no idea what that means, but there in black and white was the clearest bit of writing in the entire sorry mess of his book. At that moment, in the middle of all my troubles, a passage stood out as if illuminated. De Quincey was talking about something called 'The Dark Interpreter'. He said that the Dark Interpreter was a part of every man and woman's nature. It exists, to use his exact words, 'in the dark places of the human spirit – in grief, in fear, in vindictive wrath'. More than that, it was a being, and this being comes to stand next to you at certain times in your life.

De Quincey met the Dark Interpreter when he was helplessly watching his own child crying in pain over some childhood illness. The next day, he noted that his child had made a spurt in its powers of observation and behaviour. In other words, it had learned through suffering, and De Quincey himself had learned through his suffering. The *dark* had been *interpreted*.

Thinking about Charlie, I understood this perfectly now. But I had the strangest notion that the Dark Interpreter had been stalking me here all the way from England, and at times I'd been dimly aware of his presence. In the gazebo in Chiang Mai.

Or in the Buddhist temple where I'd had the odd sensation of someone beside me as I'd squatted with my eyes closed. In the night when I attacked our assailant and blacked out. Or here in this village, right now, while we were waiting to be found out for what we'd done.

The Dark Interpreter was a guide – a terrifying one – to help us make sense of all this suffering and rage. It was the opium, De Quincey said, that in his case woke the being. I put the book face down at the page where I'd been reading these things. Charlie chose that moment to raise her eyes, and as our eyes met I once again felt at my side this extraordinary presence, and I was so flooded with ruined love for Charlie and Phil that I started to blub.

Charlie cradled me like a mother. 'There,' she said. 'There.'

At some point late in the afternoon a very subdued Nabao brought us a pan of noodles. Her sprightly attitude was absent as she laid the dish on the table. I got the impression that she was still loyal and brave enough to do this, but that she wanted to be quick about it. Nothing in her attitude suggested to me that she knew anything.

Phil returned in a highly agitated state. He'd been walking to and fro in the poppy fields. 'Did anyone feel the jolt?' he said.

We all turned.

He smiled thinly. 'When we landed. I felt it. We'd been falling for some time, though of course it doesn't feel like it. When you've been falling for a long time, I mean. It feels normal. Like every day is the same, perfectly ordinary. You stop feeling the air rushing past you. But then there's the jolt. I felt it. That sudden jolt, and I knew we'd landed. We're on the lowest platform, aren't we? The one reserved for people like us. This is the lowest platform of hell.'

'Phil,' Charlie whispered.

I'd had that falling feeling too, but not in the way he meant.

'We've got to tell someone.' Phil said this emphatically. 'That would be the correct thing to do.'

'No,' Charlie said firmly. Then she went over to Phil and took his hand. 'That is the worst of all possible scenarios.'

'We've got to tough it out, Phil.' I said. 'The four of us. Tough it out.'

'I've been up in the fields, talking with God. I've been asking Him if we should tell somebody about what happened.'

'And what did He reply?' Charlie asked.

'He told me,' Phil said, 'to start by telling Rupert Bear.'

With the dusk came Jack. It was a terrifying time. Phil was obviously disintegrating under the strain, and I was afraid his urge to confess might present itself at any moment. We'd had to endure the spectacle of watching Phil, hunkered in the corner of the hut, whispering a long confession into the ragged ears of Rupert Bear. I didn't hear what he was saying, but when I saw Jack coming I hissed at Charlie that she should keep Phil back, talk to him, calm him.

We watched from inside the hut as Jack approached and placed a half-bottle of Johnny Walker Red Label on the porch. This time he had Khiem, the old sorcerer, with him. 'Be careful,' Charlie breathed.

Mick and I went out on to the porch. Jack didn't have his whip, and his gun was holstered. Jack and Khiem squatted, then Jack picked up the bottle, unscrewed the cap and handed it to Mick. 'How is your leg?'

'Sore.'

'Here, drink.'

Mick and I exchanged a glance. Jack looked at me and said, 'I posted a man in the generator hut, hiding behind the boxes of Calpol. Someone came in to tamper with the generator. We've got him.'

'Was it Khao?' I blurted. I felt simultaneously sick and relieved.

Jack squinted at me. 'Not your business who it is, dear boy. My business. OK? I now know for certain it was the same person who put the pictures in your hut. Jack has solved at least one of your problems. My only problem now concerns my missing nephew. Can you help me on that?'

'I don't see how.'

'Have you seen him?'

I gulped on the whisky. 'No.' I didn't like this whisky-bearing, polite Jack any more than the whip-cracking version.

He tilted his chin at Mick. 'You?'

'No.' Mick wiped his mouth.

Again he was looking at us for too long. At that moment I despised the itching pores of my skin for dribbling sweat. Quite suddenly he said, 'Khiem here wants to help you.'

Khiem nodded fractionally at the mention of his name.

'Khiem says he doesn't like this hut,' Jack continued. 'Full of bad spirits. He says Charlie invited them in. The only way is to burn the hut to the ground.'

I instantly flashed on an image of our assailant in the moonlight, coming to burn us. Was Jack playing with me? Had he approved of his nephew's actions?

He seemed to study my response. 'But we can't do that,' he continued, 'because your daughter won't come out. So he's going to help her. Two days from now is a full moon. A good night to frighten the spirits away.'

'Moon!' said Khiem, floating a finger skyward.

'Khiem says your daughter has to pass through the spirit gate on that night to make her peace with the Lord of the Moon.'

I shook my head. 'But as you say, the problem lies in getting Charlie to come out of the hut at all.'

At this point Phil wandered out of the hut rubbing his hands, sweating, agitated. Jack spoke to Khiem. He addressed me directly while Jack translated; but as he did so Jack kept his eyes trained on Phil. 'He says you are her father. Only you know the way to speak to her. Family thing.

'He says the villagers will help, and he will do everything he can. He will summon good spirits to chase the bad spirits away. But the solution is in your hands. He has a lot of preparation to do before then and she must be ready in two nights to pass through the spirit gate or the moment will be lost. He says Charlie has gone into the belly of her own fear. Khiem says you must make her come out, the way she came out of her mother's belly.'

Throughout this speech Jack's gaze hadn't shifted from Phil.

I looked at Khiem and he nodded at me again. Satisfied with

that, the old man got to his feet and hobbled off. Jack too got up. 'Now I have to send men out into the jungle to look for my nephew. What's the matter with your son?' he said.

'Bad guts,' I said with a half-smile. 'Jungle belly.'

Jack turned quickly and walked away. I looked beyond the perspiring Phil and into the hut. Charlie was standing in the doorway. She'd heard everything that was said.

Khiem came back later to renew the candles and the incense. Still he refused to enter the hut. He performed unknowable rituals and fiddled about with the spirit house he'd constructed outside, blowing smoke through its door and hanging tiny bells under its roof.

'But we've got to do *something*, Charlie,' I said later, when we were all in our sleeping bags. The candlelight cast shadows along her face as she grimaced at me, and I realised how far she'd come from being a girl. In a certain light she looked old, care-worn, broken.

'Looks like it's going to be up to you my girl,' Mick put in.

Outside, somewhere in the village, another pig was being slaughtered. Its high-pitched squeal was almost human.

'I want to do it, really I do,' Charlie said. 'I want to do it for all of us. But I can't.'

'You can if you pray for help,' Phil insisted. 'Each prayer is a step on the way to the open air.'

Charlie shook her head, and I asked her what she thought about the photographs. I suggested it was not the mistake made on the night of the eclipse that was keeping her here, but Khao's crude sorcery. I asked her if she thought Khiem might be able to answer the spirits for her. Hell, it was all mumbo-jumbo, but it was where she was at.

'You seem pretty sure that Khao is out of the way now,' Charlie said.

'I have a feeling,' I answered, 'that he's one bad spirit who won't bother you any more.' I was confident that rapist number two was about to get his payback.

Phil was disgusted by this talk. 'Only one spirit can help us, and that's the Holy Spirit of the Lord. I don't like this talk of trafficking in demons.'

I discussed with Charlie everything Khiem had said through Jack; the stuff about making peace with the Lord of the Moon. Good spirits and bad spirits. We talked about what it might mean, and how, looked at a certain way, you could make sense of it. Behind this talk the squealing pig seemed to be taking an awful long time to die.

'He's giving you a chance to put things right,' Mick said. 'To make amends for that business during the eclipse.'

'I *know* that!' Charlie said testily. 'Don't you think I don't understand?'

'The only way to make amends is through the Lord,' Phil added angrily.

'But what he's saying is . . . what he's offering is . . .' Mick was having trouble getting his point across. 'The thing is . . . Christ! How long are they going to take to kill that pig?'

We stopped talking, and the four of us lay back in our sleeping bags. The high-pitched squeals got more intermittent, but no less piercing. No one said it, but I think all of us realised it at the very same moment.

No pig.

34

I winced when the first puncture was made in my arm, and Khiem smiled broadly. He was starting to smile at me a lot, and this made me slightly nervous. The incisor made three holes in my biceps skin, and the three holes bubbled with tiny beads of blood mixed with blue jungle-plant dye. He moved the instrument down carefully, measuring the distance with an accurate eye, and plunged the incisor into my arm again. Khiem had arrived outside our hut shortly after sun-up, clapping his hands, whistling and calling us out.

Mick, no stranger to the tattoo parlours of the English Midlands, said, 'Even I felt that one.'

'Wizards that peep and that mutter,' Phil said. 'Sorcerers that—'

'Don't you ever give it a rest?' I was smarting, and Phil's increasingly obscure remarks only set my teeth on edge.

'Leave him,' Mick said. 'Leave him alone.'

Phil, regarding the whole thing as barbaric, slipped away. I was still panicky that he would do something stupid, but this tattooing had given me something else to think about. And we all needed something else to think about.

I was second up. Charlie had been first. Her arm was swollen with the new tattoo, her fingers twitching over it, though Khiem had slapped her hand, told her not to touch it. Nabao stoked a pipe for her, to which I turned a blind eye. The idea, and this was directed by Khiem, was for me to take an identical tattoo. I'd been made to understand that this would draw some of the bad spirits out of Charlie and on to me.

Right.

Jack seemed to have appointed a new lieutenant, one who went by the name of Phoo. One of the new poppy-spangled bandits, he wore an impressive bullet belt round his waist. Phoo spoke English, after an extraordinary fashion. I don't know why he was there at the tattooing exactly, other than that he seemed fascinated both by us and Khiem's enterprise.

'He fuck-good medicine, Khiem, yep,' said Phoo enthusiastically. He had a beautiful, toothless, wide-mouthed smile and spectacular wrinkles around his eyes. Aged somewhere between twenty-five and sixty-five, Phoo was a chatterbox, very different from his predecessor in Jack's private army. It occurred to me that killers come in many different shapes and sizes. 'Khiem cure me snake-bite onetime. Fuck-good. Me dead. Oooooo! Him cure me jungle-medicine, fuck-good, tee-hee-hee! He cure Charlie fuck-good.'

Phoo had 'explained' Khiem's desire for Charlie and I to take this tattoo. 'Him say you father carry spirit for she. You carry spirit for she? Oooooo! Take mark. Tee-hee-hee! Him say you take tattoo hep you find way to she world.' Phoo was an enthusiastic translator, nodding vigorously, smiling radiantly.

I'd never had a tattoo. Most of the blokes I knew, like Mick, had taken them on while teenagers and now felt pretty sheepish about it. I know it's in vogue: Charlie already had one on her shoulder. These university-educated middle-class kids sporting Celtic knots and fortune-cookie Chinese mottoes. Soppy Oxford brats frantic to look like they've been round the corner, taken a scratch. I thought it was a brainless thing when I was a youth, and now I just find it depressing. But Khiem's intentions were serious, and I had to go along with it.

'At least,' I said to Charlie when she was preparing to take hers, 'you'll have earned this one.'

'What's that supposed to mean?' she said sharply.

'You kids. You're desperate. You wear tattoos as a badge of experience. Only you don't have any experience.'

Charlie looked hard at me with those chromium and blue eyes. 'You don't give an inch, do you, Dad? Why is it so important for you to keep us knee-high? Huh? Why?'

I failed to answer, and I must say I was a little shocked when Khiem produced from his tool-kit his poppy-head incisor as his tattooing implement. He laid it out before us and mushed up some jungle plant to make an indigo-coloured dye. A lot of ritual went with it. Still more pots of incense were lighted: the stuff was beginning to give me a headache. Khiem held his poppy incisor up to the sun and with half-closed eyes muttered an incantation.

I looked at Mick and was about to say something when Phoo stopped me with a gesture. The smile had gone from his face. 'Don't say him fuck. Don't say him joke. No for any part you. Onetime chance you say free to him go.'

I didn't understand this, but I felt suitably reprimanded.

So Charlie had gone first, sitting inside the door. Just as she refused to come out, Khiem was adamant about not going in, so it was performed on the threshold. Khiem produced another jungle herb from his bag, crushing it to rub it on her skin. Some kind of anaesthetic, it didn't stop Charlie from wincing when the first, aggressive, deep puncture was made.

'You OK?'

'Do you see me crying?'

'Hey!' I said. I was getting fed up with this. 'What made you such a bloody hard case?'

'Don't worry, Dad. You've got it coming.'

And it did hurt. Of course it hurt; progressively less with each triple puncture, though I noticed that Khiem scraped up some other dark substance from among his gear before dipping the poppy incisor into the dye. I suspected it was opium, and that this was dulling the pain in my arm with each successive puncture, in which case I was slightly compromised.

Knee-high? Is that what I did? Try to keep them knee-high? Charlie's words made me think again about the day I hit Phil. Not a slap or a prod or a push, but a stiff punch to the side of his jaw with a closed fist, and so hard that it knocked him off his feet. And not because he'd chopped up some book, either, but because I'd had a furious row with Sheila.

Sheila had said how the kids were taking up less of her time and how she wanted to go out to work, and though I'm ashamed to say this now, I said no. No, no, no. Charlie at that time was into everything, dance classes, drama groups, sleep-overs with friends, and she seemed to need us less and less. Phil too. He was twelve and had just discovered masturbating. I

232

know this because I found two or three cunt magazines under his bed. And here was Sheila telling me she wasn't dependent on me any more either. We'd had a blue-blazing row. And then this episode with Phil. Why did he get punched in the mouth?

Because of the cunt books, probably.

Not because I'm a prude. It's only pictures. And what are pictures? And what if pages were wings? No, not because I disapproved, but because I hated their youth. Hated it. Because their youth meant that it was flowing away from me. All going. My little tribe. My tin-pot empire. Flowing away.

Oh Phil, I'm sorry for that wild punch. It swings back at me every day. How could you know what a child your father was?

And by Christ, Khiem's tattoo did sting.

During the application of the tattoo, Phoo chatted away quite happily, and we learned some interesting things about both Jack and the dead man. 'Tomorrow night Jack go cross mountain. Jack-nephew go missing. Big problem Jack wife-brother. Tee-hee-hee. Jack-nephew smoke much pipe. His fadder say oooooo! Jack, please take stupid boy, you can please knock him head, oooooh please! So Jack knock him head for brudder-law, oooh, don't do that! Tee-hee-hee. So him nephew make own gang once say Jack.'

'With Khao?' I asked as Khiem scraped the incisor down my arm. 'He was making a new gang with Khao?'

'Shhhhhh!' Phoo didn't like Khao's name to be mentioned. 'Maybe nephew go now Jack-brudder. Make new opium-plan. Jack no like this. Ooooooh! Him go cross hills, tomorrow, gone for two day, maybe three day. Maybe make peace, maybe make war.' I winced and Phoo went, 'Tee-hee-hee! Fuck-hurt eh? Tee-hee!'

'You catching this?' I said to Mick.

'Oh yes,' Mick said thoughtfully. 'I'm catching it.'

When it was over, Khiem began putting his tools into his embroidered bag, but Mick rolled the sleeve of his T-shirt, offering his own arm. Khiem looked thoughtful and said something to Phoo.

'You no daddy,' Phoo laughed. 'You no carry spirit for she!'

Mick didn't move, still presenting his mighty arm for Khiem, staring him down.

'I afraid for you!' said Phoo. 'You want hep you fren but spirit too heavy for you carry!'

Khiem seemed reluctant. He muttered a few sharp words to Phoo, who said, 'You no have same daddy blood for she. Spirit make 'tack on you for you hep fren!'

Mick pointed theatrically at his arm. 'I came this far, didn't I?'

Khiem shrugged, unrolled his bag of equipment and set about Mick's arm. He had to go to the inner biceps to find a clear space. If I thought Mick was taking it too lightly, I said nothing. In one sense he wanted a little souvenir to show the folks back home, yet it was also his way of displaying full support.

So Charlie, Mick and I all had the same mark. Some kind of ideogram, I suppose. Not Chinese lettering but something quite like it; and with horns uppermost there was the crescent moon, presumably the slice that Charlie had stolen.

Later, when the two of us had a quiet moment to ourselves, Charlie said, 'He'll do anything for you, won't he?'

'Who?'

'Who?' she mocked. 'Who might I mean?'

'You mean Mick?'

'Yes. Mick. He'll do anything for you.'

I think I shrugged.

'Must be incredible to have a friend like that,' she went on. 'Wonderful. To follow you into the jungle like this. Without question.'

'It's *you* he's come to help.'

'That's crap, Dad. He's here for you. To help me, yes, but for you. You told me he even put his savings at your disposal. He'll fight your battles for you. He'll even take that tattoo for you.'

I instinctively fingered the fresh scar on my arm. 'So?'

She twisted her lips, and supposedly in imitation of my gruff tones said, 'So? Is that all you can say: so?'

'What do you want me to do? Jump up and down?'

'You might recognise what you've got for a start.'

I didn't like where this was steering. 'What's your point?'

'I don't have a point, Dad! I'm just saying how obvious it is!'

'Obvious? What's obvious?'

'Mick. He'll go with you anywhere. He loves you.'

I shot out a dismissive, barking kind of laugh at this.

'You're so blind, Dad. So blind.'

'What are you saying?' I cackled. 'That Mick wants to get up my arse?'

Charlie was furious. 'How can you reduce it like that? Even if it were so, how dare you sit there and *reduce* it so? How can you do that?'

This angry talk, or the tattooing, or both, had made me feel distinctly queasy, so I went outside. Plus the heavy incense smoke was beginning to get to me, and I needed to know what Phil was doing in the poppy fields. Mick wasn't far from the hut. He stayed behind – we'd agreed not to leave Charlie unprotected after recent events.

Up on the hillsides I could see that the glory days of the poppy were beginning to thin out. I was losing track of time, and I had to count the days to find out how long we had been in the village. Incredibly, we had been there for only six days, and yet it seemed like a season.

It was the middle of the afternoon: the fields were empty and the harvesters had returned to the village. Many of the poppy pods had shed their petals and were incised and harvested. I guessed the short season helped Jack and the villagers: they could harvest quickly and shift the stuff rapidly. Jack had already told me that this village would then not be used for a season. He kept his men moving. It was guerrilla farming.

At first I couldn't see Phil anywhere. He'd taken more and more to wandering the upper slopes of the poppy fields, so he could be closer to God I suppose. The thought of him going to and fro amid the poppies, talking aloud, wrestling with his conscience and looking for divine guidance was shredding my nerves. He was a ticking bomb. I knew I was going to have to do something extreme to get us all out of there, but what?

Some of the poppy pods still had traces of the brown juice

where the pod had continued to sweat after the harvesters had passed by with their garnering tools. I broke a waxy crystal from one pod to examine it. Treacle-coloured sunlight fizzed at its surface. I sniffed at it and tried it on my tongue, but it didn't taste of anything. I flicked the tiny nugget from my fingers.

As for Charlie, I was out of ideas about getting her to leave the hut. I'd pleaded with her. I'd talked to her about home until even I started to despise the phoney haven I was trying to make of it. I had no talk left. I just couldn't reach her.

I heard Phil before spotting him. He was on his knees amid the poppies and praying loudly. Furious, I charged over to him, but something made me pull up short. Phil was almost shouting, over and over, the first line of the Lord's Prayer, barely drawing breath. *'Our father which art in heaven our father which art in heaven our father which art in . . .'* But his face and clasped hands were smeared red.

I cried out, thinking he'd hacked himself. It was a yelp of horror.

When I knelt before him he barely even seemed to see me. He was shivering and his eyelids fluttered as he prayed wildly. I looked for the source of the blood but couldn't detect an incision anywhere. Not until I put my fingers to his cheek did I realise the red substance staining his face and hands was not blood at all, but betel juice. He'd smeared himself with the stuff.

I pressed my hand over his mouth. 'Phil. Phil. You'll give us away, son. You'll give us away.'

'You can't help me,' he said, his voice flat.

I spat on to my hand, trying to rub the red dye from his face. He shrank away from me but I pushed him down in the dirt. I had to kneel on his chest to hold him down. I didn't have enough spit. He struggled underneath me. I spat and rubbed at his cheeks, desperately trying to clean him. Tears squeezed from his eyes, mixing with the spittle from my fingers. I could taste the salt of his tears as I tried to lick the stains from his face, frantic to get him clean. I pinned him down and licked his cheeks again, using my T-shirt to rub his face.

He seemed to come round. 'I'm all right,' he said.

I was panting heavily, where he seemed suddenly calm. 'You can't let anyone see this, Phil.'

'I'm all right. I won't give you away, Dad.'

He wanted to stand but I didn't want to let him go. Finally he pushed me off roughly and scrambled to his feet. 'Let's go back to the hut,' I said.

'Leave me. I'm all right. I'll get cleaned up. I'm sorry.'

He didn't want me. He jogged away in the direction of the village.

I stood quite still amongst the tall poppies. I couldn't see any way out of this. Events were getting worse, not better, and I had no resources and no ideas. It was while I stood there despairing that one of the plants suddenly shed all its luxurious red petals. I don't know why, but it made my skin flush. Then it happened to another, nearer this time, the petals falling to the earth with a dry whisper. Finally a third let go its white flower, very close to me. A kind of static parted the hairs on my forearms.

I had the bizarre and quite ridiculous notion that the poppies were communicating with me; or that some invisible being, some unseen presence, was drifting towards me through the crop, tentatively, a few paces at a time, in order to stand next to me, dislodging the petals as it passed. I felt a lick of fear. Then instantly I relaxed.

This presence I recognised.

Amid the splendid, tall poppies, under the hazy sky and the diffuse yellow sun, I had the clearest of insights. I knew exactly what I had to do. I had to go to the realm where Charlie was, to stand next to her.

I had an appointment with the Dark Interpreter.

35

'Complete and utter madness,' Phil seethed from his corner of the hut. 'This is insanity! This is *exactly* how it starts.' He seemed to have recovered from his seizure in the poppy fields. He'd washed the smeared juice from his face and hands at least.

'I hope you know what you're doing, that's all,' Mick said.

I shot him a look intended to say *of course I don't know what I'm doing but what other action is there?* Mick's objections were of a different character to Phil's: he was uneasy about being marginalised by my actions. Banished to the role of onlooker, he didn't like it. If I'd asked him, he would have joined me – no question – but what would have been the point of that? Anyway, I needed him straight.

Nabao had been recruited to administer the thing. She arrived with her gear and, obscurely, a pile of banana leaves. I'd tried to make her understand what I intended to do. She looked solemn, seeming to intuit what was necessary. Anyway, I gave her a pile of Thai bhat and she wasn't going to object.

Out of all of them, the one most unnerved was Charlie, exactly as I'd anticipated. 'Trying to prove some kind of a point?' she said scathingly as she watched Nabao lay out her gear. Charlie wrung her hands, massaging her fingers as if trying to peel off a layer of skin. 'Is this your big statement?'

'Think of it as me coming to join you, Charlie.'

'Don't. Not on my account.'

Khiem's rituals had been faithfully repeated at intervals. Candles flickering out in the hut had been renewed, as had the smoking bowls of incense. Meanwhile Nabao rolled a piece of opium between her fingers before impaling it on a pin. She lit a spill with a plastic cigarette lighter and flamed the ball of opium.

'You've beaten us, Charlie. We're stuck. So if I have to stay here, I'm going to be with you in spirit as well as in body.'

'Lovely. But it won't make me change my mind.'

'I don't expect it to. I just have to see things from where you stand.'

'You're about to make a big fool of yourself.'

'Can't improve on nature, Charlie. How many pipes do I have to smoke before I could call myself an addict?'

'Dad, you are so fucking ignorant. It doesn't work like that. It takes a while to get addicted.' She cracked her knuckles, and added cynically, 'You have to work at it.'

'How many pipes could you go in one session?' I asked her. 'Ten? Fifteen? Twenty-five?'

'Twenty-five pipes would kill an elephant,' she said. 'Why don't you stop playing games? This does nothing to my head. You'll only end up hurting yourself.'

Phil suddenly exploded. His face was distended and almost purple with anger. It made me think of the carved face of a Thai puppet. 'I refuse to have anything to do with this!' he said, thumping a fist into the open palm of his other hand. 'I won't take any responsibility for what happens from now on!'

His impotent rage was actually quite funny. 'What are you shouting about?' I said. 'Sit down and put your head in a prayer book.'

Further provoked he said, 'Mick, do you know why he's doing this? Jealousy. Did you know that, Mick? He's always been jealous: jealous of our opportunities; jealous of our education; jealous of our independence from him.'

'Rot,' I said.

Phil hadn't finished. 'When I went to university he was jealous, but he couldn't say so. Then when Charlie went to Oxford he was even more upset, because Charlie was his little girl, and she was outstripping him, cleverer than all of us. The only way he could speak to us was by mocking us. Mocking Charlie's boyfriends, mocking my lifestyle. Endlessly mocking. He's spent the last half of his life in a jealous rage. You see what he's doing here, now? He's *competing* with Charlie.'

I'd had enough of his woe, and of his spirit-depleting manufactured suffering. 'You know what, Phil? I'm sick of your misery. I'm sick of your whining. In fact I'm sick of your face—'

'Shut it, Danny!' Mick said with surprising force. 'Leave Phil alone.'

'Look, if I want to say—' I tried.

'You hear me? Just get off Phil's case. Leave him alone and get on with what you're going to do.'

The sharp note in Mick's voice warned me to let the matter drop. I looked to Charlie for support. She folded her arms. 'Phil's right, Dad. Why do you always think we're in some kind of competition?'

By now Nabao had the first pipe heated and smoking, but as she passed it to me Phil intercepted it. 'Here, I'll do it for you, shall I?' He took a deep tug on the pipe. His eyes watered but he held back the smoke without coughing. I shrugged. If Phil wanted to join me I wasn't going to argue. In the event, Mick stepped forward and gently took the smoking pipe from Phil and gave it to me.

Phil collapsed on to a mat in the corner of the hut, head in his hands, defeated.

Though the mood had soured I wasn't going to let it stop me. I stretched out on my sleeping bag and got comfortable. I took a deep draught on the pipe and held the smoke in my lungs. Nabao plucked a banana leaf and tore a strip from it. This strip she placed beside her, and proceeded to prepare a second pipe.

I puffed away at the pipe until I realised that the thing had gone out. There was a tiny twist of ash in the brass bowl. Nothing was happening yet, though I was aware of how seriously I had become the object of everyone's attention. Mick sat back quietly, puffing instead on a Marlboro. Charlie regarded me with her lip curled. Nabao, intent on preparing the pipe, flickered glances at me from time to time. I noticed Nabao had refused to make any eye contact with Charlie.

'Satisfied?' Charlie said. 'Not much to it, is there? Made your statement? Anywhere I can go you can go better.' I'd stolen from her the armour of defiance, of youth, and I'd reversed the roles. She didn't like it.

Nabao passed me the second pipe. Again I pulled the smoke deep into my lungs and held it. Nabao tore another strip of banana leaf and placed it on top of the first.

After the third pipe Charlie said to Mick, 'Are you going to stop him?'

'I don't see what I can do. I can't stop him,' Mick said pointedly, 'any more than *he* can stop *you*.'

Phil still held his head in despair. I suppressed a snigger.

Charlie stood up. 'I'm not going to stay here and watch him get wrecked just to prove a point.'

'Fine,' Mick said. 'Where, exactly, are you going to go?'

It was a good question. I puffed my pipe and looked at Charlie. Our eyes locked. I chose to say nothing. Charlie shook her head slowly. 'I never really knew how bad it was in him,' she said, 'until the day he waved me away to university. If he could have done, he'd have packed his bag and come with me and sat in on my lectures. Just so that I wouldn't know more than he does. He can't stand it.'

Mick scratched his head. 'Yes, he is a bit of a pain like that.'

'I'm surprised he has any friends,' Charlie said. 'He's so mean-spirited. The moment anyone wants to do anything outside his control, he stops *giving*. He doesn't even give you an argument. He shuts down. That's what he did with me when I got old enough to want to do things my own way. Stopped hugging. Stopped being kind. Stopped being interested. It was like I was overdrawn at the bank one day.'

I sniggered, because I didn't take seriously these emotional attacks. It was as if they were talking about a cartoon version of me.

'I have noticed,' Mick put in, 'that he's a bit tight with information.'

'He's an emotional miser,' said Charlie. 'A skinflint with his affections.'

'Probably why Mum left him,' Phil added.

'What?' Charlie said. This was news to her.

'Oh yes. Or put another way, he drove her to another man.'

I snorted derisively at this, too. Well it was all hurtful sure enough, but it didn't seem to upset me, because once again it didn't exactly seem to be *about* me. I would have said the opium was making me apathetic, except that I couldn't feel any effects. Every time Nabao gave me a pipe she tore another banana leaf. I was on to my fifth pipe when I began to suspect that she wasn't actually putting any opium in the bowl, or that I was smoking some placebo, or that she was setting me up with tiny doses. I thought this because nothing seemed to be happening.

I'd smoked all five pipes of opium and I felt absolutely nothing. Except that my tattoo wasn't stinging anymore.

Charlie listened in dismay as Phil got her up to speed on me and Sheila, and I was enormously amused by the expression on each of their faces. Charlie, arms folded stiffly, gazed down at me with her features moulded into those of a mother who, intensely annoyed by the antics of her child, is powerless to act. I'd seen that facial cast on Sheila many times when Charlie was a child herself. I'd probably worn the same expression myself once or twice over the years. Phil meanwhile had taken out his pocket Bible to wave under my nose as he spoke, sermonising like a street-corner preacher but about *my* life. It made me snort again. Finally I looked over to Mick, perhaps to see if he too thought it funny, but he only regarded me lugubriously. With his perspiring face darkened by shadows and with his poached-egg eyes, he too looked faintly ridiculous and I laughed. The fact that none of them seemed to find the situation amusing made me cackle with laughter.

'It's not this dope that's making me laugh,' I tried to explain to Mick. 'Really it's not. It's the expression on everyone's face.'

His dumb response only made me laugh more.

'You're going to overdose if you keep smoking it at this pace,' Charlie said.

'That's the idea,' I said, and this banal phrase seemed so witty that I found myself giggling again. Charlie shook her head.

What happened over the next couple of hours is not easy to recall. I lost track of how many pipes I had. I got fixated on the swish of Nabao's banana leaves, so much that I found I could replay it in my mind – the turn of the leaf as it was placed upon the pile, swish, leaf, swish, leaf, until I wasn't certain whether I had merely replayed the image in my mind or whether Nabao's sinewy hand had actually turned a new banana leaf. The thing which surprised me most was not that I went into any kind of trance – which was what I'd expected – but that the procession of my thoughts actually came to seem like real events in front of me. That is, the interior world became exterior, and vice-versa.

And the world was not transported into a beautiful place, as I'd expected. The phrase 'the milk of paradise' which was buzzing around my head like a fat bee seemed inappropriate. A swattable phrase. Rather the world had muddied its colour palette, so that I was in a tea-brown or dirty orange universe, almost identical to this one, but seeming to intersect this world at a very slight tangent. A double vision.

'Perhaps it's the light,' I said aloud, commenting on this, meaning that the orange glow of candlelight was playing with my senses. Mick answered, but frankly I didn't care to pay any attention to what he was saying. I kept thinking what an *old* world was this one that I was seeing, unspeakably old, and spent, and over-evolved. That sounds as if I became unnerved by it, but that was not the case. I felt totally neutral, and not at all anxious.

Actually it's not true to say that I felt neutral. There was something else going on, beneath my perceptions about the ancient character of this opium world. Whatever it was, I liked it. It took me a time to appreciate that what it was was a scent in my nostrils. When the certainty clicked in me, I remember going *ha!* It was that new-born baby smell. The fontanelle. The original, pungent love amalgam, but to the power of nine.

Of course there was no baby anywhere near, and I knew the *earth* had opened up its fontanelle to me.

Physically I felt so comfortable that I didn't want to move. The blood in my veins had been replaced by silk. But intellectually I felt very stimulated, and fascinated by this strange world. I got up and walked out of the hut.

That is, I *believe* I got up and walked out of the hut. I clearly remember taking a walk out to the poppy fields, but Mick afterwards told me I'd only been gone a few minutes before coming back and smoking another pipe; but that would not have been enough time for all the things to have gone through my mind.

Swish, the hand turned the leaf.

Perhaps I only thought it, and my thoughts deceived me, but

I remember walking to the opium fields and standing amidst the poppies. The villagers had gone, having completed the day's harvesting. My legs felt like rubber and my muscles had turned to a kind of slush. Progress was difficult, and when I got there I sat on the red earth looking up at the incised pods. I was struck by the number of poppy heads weeping. Not just seeping opium, but suffering with it, and yielding.

Then back in the hut. Charlie, crying now. And Phil, kneeling by my side, hands clasped around his pocket Bible, whispering unwanted prayers in my ears, a whisper like a dry banana leaf turning.

I saw very clearly how we are all of us incised by the experiences of life. We are pricked, we weep, we yield. And the substances we weep and we bleed harden in the cold of the night, under the moon. I had very fanciful notions about where this stuff went; about the varying quality of this stuff; about who was collecting it and why. It seemed to me that our first breath as a newborn baby comes to us sharp as a blade, as an incision. We take it in. We give it out in our first howl, a hymn to life.

Let it in. Give it out.

Swish. The leathery hand turned the leaf.

Who was harvesting this human stuff? Was there a place where they could sell the love amalgam, a city where the rats run free? I had a smuggling plan. Get everyone hooked on this. Weeping. Bleeding. Hardening overnight on the bed pillows. Fairy bandits decked in poppy hoods scraping it from the sheets. Get the Western world on this stuff. Give it a name.

Love. I loved Sheila. Charlie. Phil. *Let it in.* You experience it. You cry. You laugh. *Give it out.* You take it in, you give it out. Drugs. Alcohol. Religion. Sex. When you get older you don't cry quite so much. All music, all singing is a kind of weeping. Orgasm too, a kind of crying. Spilling, splitting, seeping, oozing seed, giving. Love lies weeping.

'Don't cry Dad, don't cry!' It was Charlie. She was unlocking my fingers from around a pipe. A leaf turned somewhere. Swish. 'Please don't cry! I can't stand to see you cry!'

'Am I crying?' I didn't think I was. I certainly didn't feel sad. Not at all. The fact is, I didn't care about any of this. I saw it all, flowing like a pearl-green river under an indifferent diffuse yellow sun, and I didn't care. If I had to cry it was only like the poppy, because I was incised, and I was yielding. It was my time.

I remembered when Charlie was a little girl, and when she used to cry about small things, as children do, and sometimes I would respond by teasing her with a terrible affected boo-hooing of my own. Perhaps not a very effective way of responding, but this would often bring her round. The spectacle of her father pretending to blub was usually worse than whatever had prompted her own bout of sobbing. I suspected that what I was doing now was something of the same pattern. And yet somehow I'd moved beyond being troubled by either Charlie's or my own distress.

The truth is I'd even allowed to get myself side-tracked. I didn't care any more about why I was smoking these hilarious opium pipes. I mean, I knew it had to do with Charlie and what I was after, but that all got pushed aside. What's more there were other people in the hut, lots of people, and I didn't like the look of all of them. Some of these people were half centipede. One was feeding from Charlie's foot. I smote it with a thought. I was able to chop the centipede in half simply by the power of thought. It shrieked and it bled and it withered, and I giggled, and the giggle made me cough.

Mick was patting my back, until the coughing fit subsided. 'Enough,' he whispered. 'That's enough.'

I wasn't having that. I reached for another pipe. Nabao's eyes were sugary black reservoirs.

Her hand turned another leaf.

Charlie was speaking to me but instead of hearing her I could actually see the words pouring out of her mouth, densely scripted, spiralling in the air. I tried to read these airborne, winging words but I couldn't get them to add up: 'Porlock's poorlot postmen pertaining principally prior to poppy poppa pappa pipped piqued punishing paternally pisstaking and puppeteering podsqueezing papaver . . .'

Phil too was at it. His words came thrumming out in gothic script, like a cloud of insects swarming the hut, and making no more sense than Charlie's. 'Thou shalt therefore being of the

Father that thou shalt with His only son and thou shalt get thee into the land of Moriah and God will Himself provide a lamb and behold thou hast not withheld thine only son...'

The sultry, sticky, smoky air became a dense, burning thicket of words, consuming itself.

The hand turned the leaf.

I asked if anyone was counting. I was back in the poppy field, and the Lord of the Poppy said to me, 'Oh, we never stop counting.'

He looked only a little like Khiem, although he was sensationally tall and thin, maybe eight feet tall, and he was dressed in a tunic and a cape stitched with massive red, mauve and white poppy flowers tough as canvas. His treacle-brown pod of a face was a mass of warts. The reek of opium overwhelmed me. He seemed to have dozens of toes on each foot, all of which were half buried in the cracked, dry earth.

I was distracted by a movement at the top of the hill. It was Phil. He was running, running through the poppies, roaring, tearing off his shirt as he ran. I seemed to see this in slow motion as he went by. Then he disappeared over the other side of the hill.

I felt embarrassed by my son's behaviour. The Lord of the Poppy looked at me as if I should say something. I didn't know what to say so I asked, 'Have you had a good year?' It felt a bit stupid, but it was all I could think of.

This made him laugh. 'The idea!' he said. It made me laugh too. We chuckled long and loud at that, the Lord of the Poppy and I.

My new tattoo seemed to pulse and glow. I felt quite proud of it.

'Can I have her back?' I asked him. 'You know, I love her very much.'

'Sometimes that helps and sometimes it doesn't. But I will ask my sister.'

'Your sister?'

He floated a warty, pod-like finger at the sky. 'The moon.'

'Of course. Take me in return for Charlie,' I suggested cordially.

'Sorry.' He turned to me and I noticed that his eyes were mirror-bright milky cascades. 'You're not quite up to the mark.' It was then that I noticed he was weeping. Tears of milky but resinous sap tracked his leathery face. It was a shocking sight, this weeping of the guilty poppy. I sensed he was embarrassed by my seeing him this way. I was about to ask what he meant by saying that I wasn't up to the mark: perhaps he was suggesting that somehow I was responsible for keeping Charlie here.

Not giving enough, in the way Charlie and Phil said I was not giving enough? Is that what he meant? I thought I'd been giving all my life. Fatherhood was like being the incised poppy. I took the incision every day like a man, and at first I was the dark loving juice to which they all returned. And then I was so afraid they might not return that I stopped the flow.

It's hard, I wanted to explain to the Lord of the Poppy. So hard. They tumble into your hands, pink, wrinkled and vulnerable; like tiny shellfish from out of the roaring and infinite black sea, minute in your leathery grasp. And then before you can even smoke a pipe-length of life's experiences they've outgrown you and climbed over your head; before you've even had time to explain to them the half of it.

And I wanted to explain the half of it, because I need to be needed.

But I never had the chance to put this important point to the Lord of the Poppy, for I was back in the hut. Phil in the corner on his knees, bare-chested now, praying. Mick surveying me with a baleful eye. And then Charlie was screaming and raining blows on my chest, blows to which I was almost oblivious. It seemed to happen at a distance, almost to someone else. Mick and Nabao pulled her away from me, yet all through this attack I remember talking, brightly and perceptively.

You see, I wanted to comfort her and tell her that just as we take the incision, so must we give out, and that she'd been right and I'd been stupid. There had been a day, oh, long before her departure for university, when I'd realised my children were beyond me, and I had indeed foreclosed on them. It was self-protection. I thought I couldn't go on bleeding like that for my children. I wanted to explain to her that I thought I'd found a way to hover serenely above the uproar of life. I'd thought to control my love by withholding it and rationing it.

But now everything's in order, I wanted to explain to her. Now I understand. We take it in, we give it out. I'd had to come all the way out here to be incised all over again. But I couldn't get through to her; my lips mashed on the words and I couldn't communicate the richness of this thought. I watched her hysterical sobbing as if she were a child crying over something quite unimportant, and I accepted another pipe.

Swish.

The leathery hand turned the leaf.

36

I slept after my opium marathon; or to be more accurate my opium session concluded with a sleep. I woke up the following morning with Charlie exercising a damp cloth around my face and neck. I was sticky with perspiration. I blinked at her. Though my head was something like straight again, my field of vision was still rich with residual opium disturbance. Soft contours were bleeding colour; sharp edges cast shadows. Charlie clamped her lips hard and refused to meet my eyes. That crease above the ridge of her nose was getting deeper.

'The bastard's awake,' she called.

Mick was just outside the hut. He came in. 'Back in the land of the living,' he said. It was the sort of remark I'd expect him to make if we'd had eight or nine pints of Jubilee Ale down at the Clipper.

Other than the visual strangeness I had no hangover to speak of, at least not as with alcohol; though I did feel as though my insides had been pulled about a bit and, as I say, my eyes were still trailing something of the opium in me. My throat was very sore. 'Water, please.'

Charlie folded her arms as if to say get it yourself, but Mick brought me some water. I sipped it and then I had to get up because my bladder was bursting. Before I went out Charlie said, 'Well, did that change a single damned thing for anyone?'

I stopped. 'Yes. It changed quite a lot, actually.'

Charlie and Phil glowered, waiting for more. I gestured to Mick that he should come outside.

He followed me into the out-house. 'I don't know what you were trying to prove, Danny,' he said as I relieved myself. 'But we're no further on.'

'No, we're a lot further on.' I could recall most of what transpired with absolute clarity, except that I was confused about

249

what was actually event and what was opium-induced imagination which only *felt like* event. 'Mick, tell me what you saw.'

He scratched his head. 'You were babbling. Charlie couldn't stand to see you getting further and further out of your head. I watched her. At first she made out she didn't care, but it was eating her up. Phil, too; he was off his head just watching you. He followed you outside. I went to the poppy fields to get you but I ended up bringing him back instead. Then Nabao started to get agitated, thought you'd had enough. Looking at me, like. You wanted another pipe but I told Nabao to take it away. You were vomiting. You were hell-bent, Danny. Hell-bent.'

Vomiting? I didn't remember that. I had a sudden flash of Phil running through the poppy field, dragging off his shirt.

'How many pipes did I have?'

'Look for yourself.'

Back inside, Nabao's banana leaf strips were lying on the mat. I counted them. Fifteen pipes of opium.

'You could have killed yourself,' Charlie said.

'I quite liked it. Might do it again, tonight.'

'Ha!' went Phil.

'No, Phil,' Charlie said. 'It doesn't happen that quickly. He's learned nothing from this.'

Her superiority riled me. 'Oh I've learned plenty,' I raged. 'Plenty. Shall I tell you – you and Phil – shall I tell you what it is a father wants? To love his children without conditions and to be loved in return without conditions. But it seems that's too much. So what he hopes for is that his children will grow up to do the things he likes doing and to like the things he likes. But why should they? So he can't have that either. Also too much to ask for. So what he then hopes is that his children will at least grow up to speak in the same voice as his, so that they might talk together and not be divided in his own hearth.'

I could hear myself ranting, but I couldn't stop. I wasn't speaking the words; the words were somehow speaking me. They ripped from my mouth with an ugly sound, like the tearing of cloth. Something was breaking up inside me. 'But why is it I can't even have that? Why is it my children talk in voices I don't understand? Where are my children behind these strange languages? Who gave them these shrill, incomprehensible accents?'

Something in me had hardened, crystallised, and not against Charlie, but against her position. As for the opium, I'd seen how good it was, how damnably selfishly good. I liked it. It was all about me and nobody else. It was about my insignificant little cry, my pathetic bleat against the uproar of life, and my little bleat, so it seemed to me, was as important as hers or anyone else's. I could see how luxurious it was to sink into a magnificent selfishness like that, one which had no bottom, and through which you could go on falling and falling and falling. You could be asked to undertake the rewiring of hell and it would seem like nice work.

'Yes, all along, it was me. I somehow terrorised my own son and daughter into putting on masks and affecting voices so that they wouldn't have to talk to me. And you know something? I don't even know how I did it.'

'Stop it, Dad,' Charlie said.

'Why, Charlie? For two years you haven't had the basic courtesy to phone us at home, if only to say you were all right!'

'That's not true. I spoke with Mum regularly before I came out here.'

'What?'

'Yes. You just didn't know about it.'

'What?' I was stunned.

'I told her I'd stop calling her if she told you. It seems hateful now. But I was so angry with you.'

This piece of information tilted the world ninety degrees. I had absolutely nothing to say. It meant that Charlie and Sheila had made a pact to keep in contact but to exclude me. To keep me in darkness for nearly two years. I looked at Phil, and I heard my voice fracturing as I said, 'Did you know about this?'

I saw him swallow. He nodded. He tapped his fingertips together, trying to frame a response. It was Charlie who reached out a hand to my shoulder. 'Don't! Don't touch me!' I said. 'I don't want you to touch me!'

Coconut's machete protruded from under my sleeping bag. I picked it up. 'You know what it feels like to hear this? I'll tell you. It feels like this.' I closed my left hand over the blade and dragged the razor-edged knife sharply downwards. The palm of my hand opened up in a grisly, bubbling incision. Then I ran from the hut before they could see my face, in which loss, in which perdition was complete.

'Dad!' Charlie shouted.

I ignored her. She came after me.

'Dad! Come back!'

I turned. She stood on the porch, pointing at me.

'Dad. Please.'

The pain in my hand seared. I had to close my fist to stop the blood flowing on to the red earth. But as I stood there, bleeding, I realised something that instantly took away the pain. 'Charlie. You've stepped over the threshold.'

She hugged herself, and looked up at the sky in dread. Then she looked back at me. Her mouth formed an O. 'Yes.'

We just looked, giving each other galaxies of space, and when she finally stepped back inside, I followed her. There she instantly took my hand, putting the wound to her mouth. 'Charlie,' I said. 'You broke through.'

'I'll do it, Dad.' she said. 'Tonight. I'll do it for you.'

'Charlie. Come here. My heart.' I held her. 'And you, Phil.' He came to me, and I put my bloody hand on his shoulder. I was bleeding all over them. The three of us leaned together in an embrace of utter depletion, and my hand pumped with pain.

I heard Mick suck his teeth.

Later, with a bandaged hand, I walked up to the poppy fields. Some of the villagers stopped work to regard me strangely. I was trying to get things straight in my mind. I couldn't determine whether I'd actually gone there in my drug-induced condition or whether I'd pipe dreamed the whole thing. I looked for a likely spot where I might have sat down with the Lord of the Poppy, casting about in the red dirt for scientific evidence of that absurd encounter. What's more, the memory of it was like a mosaic with stones missing or crumbling even as I tried to piece it together.

On my return I found Mick standing by the radio in the

centre of the village, and in earnest conversation with Phoo. Mick beckoned me over. Jack's henchman looked shifty, nervous. 'Tonight,' Mick said, 'Charlie is going to make that walk.'

'Oh yes?' I doubted it, somehow.

'Too right she is. And during the commotion this boy is going to get us back on the road to Chiang Mai. Isn't that right, Phoo? Chiang Mai?' Mick flashed his wallet.

Phoo didn't seem persuaded. 'I no so sure.'

'Let's step in the hut,' I suggested.

The three of us went inside the generator hut, where the useless Calpol was still piled high in cartons. We squatted. Mick took a huge wad of dollars from his moneybelt and unrolled it. 'This *now*,' he said, peeling off a few banknotes. 'And *all this* later.'

'Oooooooh. Oooooooooooh.' Phoo shook his head. 'No so sure. Jack find out, he kill me for sure.'

Mick fanned the rest of the banknotes for him so he could see how much was there.

'Ooooooooh!'

Mick turned to me. 'Phoo says after Charlie walks there will be dancing, bonfires, festivities. Full-moon party. It's absolutely the moment for us to slip away. We won't get a better time. No one will notice us. And Jack is away. Phoo here will take us to the river, and on a raft.'

I suspected a trap. I had a feeling Jack had a good idea what had happened to his nephew. It would suit his purposes to get us out into the jungle, away from the villagers who themselves bore us no ill-will.

'What the hell is the matter with you?' Mick hissed. 'This is it, Danny! This is *fucking well it*! We've got to go while Jack and his men are away! You want to stay here until they turn something up? We go by raft, and Phoo will have a man waiting by the road with a truck.'

'How the hell is he going to arrange that?' I protested.

Phoo unbuttoned his breast pocket and took out a slim black object. 'Cellphone!' he said eagerly.

'What's more while you were away, something good happened,' Mick said brightly. He held out his amulet for me to see. 'I found it outside the hut.'

'Well,' I said, 'that improves our position enormously.'

I didn't like it, but Mick was right. I smelled Jack's rancid finger in all of it. But it was a chance we had to take. 'So you'll do it then?' I said to Phoo. 'Yes or no?'

Phoo rubbed his chin in agitation and looked at the wad of notes in Mick's fist. 'Oooooooh!'

We spent a hideous afternoon. Charlie was in a dreadful state, sleeping in fits, crying through her nightmares, thrashing her arms, soaking her bed with sweat. I cradled her as much as I could; I found myself holding her foot again. I had no idea what she would do, come the hour. We briefed Phil on the plan, and he spent the time wrestling with his own demons.

It had to work. We couldn't wait around any longer for that body to be turned up. I tried talking to Charlie even though she was sleeping. I tried telling her that this had to be the moment.

Khiem appeared late in the day, relighting the incense, performing his inscrutable rituals around the hut, singing songs of a repetitive rhythm. 'Moon!' he said to me. 'Moon!' He wanted me to be ready. He also asked, by means of gestures and pointing, for some personal things of Charlie's, which I gave him.

Just before twilight Nabao brought us one of her noodle soups, but I had no stomach for it, and neither did Charlie. Her guts were rioting as the hour approached and we had to keep leaving the hut for the sake of her modesty. Even Mick, though he ate, had gone quiet. In fact he was in a decidedly strange mood. He kept fingering his amulet.

'What is it, pal?'

He let out a big sigh. 'Remember that Buddhist monk in Chiang Mai? The one having a ciggie under the bo tree?'

'What of it?'

'I keep thinking about something he said. He told me that the pot had to break and become the clay and that broken things are made whole again. Odd, isn't it? Charlie here thinks she's been punished for stealing a piece of the moon. And I show up with a quarter-moon amulet. And if that's not enough, then I lose it and find it today, on the evening of the full moon. It's all got to snap together, hasn't it?'

'What are you driving at?'

I noticed Phil listening intently to this. 'Mick's saying it's a sign. It's like we were meant to be here, at this very moment.'

I looked hard at him. 'Mick, you've got to keep your head together.'

He stared meaningfully at my bandaged hand. Then he turned to Phil and arched a single eyebrow.

Dusk fell and the temperature began to plummet. I knew something was about to happen because the radio was suddenly silenced, and this time I knew it wasn't a fault with the generator. Then, as darkness descended on the village, I heard movement outside the hut. I went to the porch. Villagers were gathering from all directions, men, women, children, even some very old people I hadn't seen before came hobbling to join the assembly. Two or three of the men held burning flares aloft, but the others, including even the smallest child, carried metal pans, mostly aluminium saucepans or stainless steel dishes. The villagers lined up on two sides, forming a path. At the far end of the path stood Khiem.

Khiem gave a cry, half shout, half ululation. When he stopped, the villagers began banging their pots and pans very quickly with sticks or spoons. I looked up at the moon. It was full, like a plump silver gourd hanging incredibly low in the sky, waxy and benign.

I went into the hut. 'This is it,' I said. I didn't know what was going to happen next. It was down to Charlie. Then there was a rustling sound by the door.

It was the sound of a single bamboo strip torn away from the hut, next to the door. On the other side of the door another strip whistled as it was plucked away from outside. I saw what was happening. The villagers were widening the door for us to come out. They were going to dismantle the hut stick by stick.

'Oh no,' Charlie said. 'Oh no.'

Nabao was inside, stroking Charlie's hand. The old woman looked up at me with infinite pity. She knew this had to be the moment. She'd prepared a pipe of opium, and gestured towards Charlie.

'Yes, give it her. She's going to need it.'

While Charlie smoked her pipe more strips of bamboo were plucked out of the wall. I unpacked something from my bag. I'd been saving it for this moment. It was my own bit of dark magic. 'Something was taken away from you Charlie while you lay in this hut. I got it back.'

It was the passport Brazier-Armstrong had returned to me in Chiang Mai. I held it open at her photograph. It occurred to me that if the villagers believed in photographic magic, then perhaps Charlie could have her soul returned in the same way. She took the passport from me with a trembling hand.

In the passport photograph a sweet young girl smiled at the camera. The photographer had caught her about to burst into a laugh. It had been taken two weeks before her eighteenth birthday. 'Look at that,' I said. 'It's my girl. When she was little.'

I guess I'd meant that it was my girl when I was still in control of her life, in a way that I had never been after that photograph was taken. Charlie looked at me and said, 'Is it going to be all right, Dad? Is it?'

'Of course it is. That's why I came for you.' I had a leather wallet with a neck strap. I took the passport from her, slipped it in the wallet and hung it around her neck. 'But it's not just a photograph, is it? It's love all the way, Charlie. Me and Phil and Mick. Our love is going to carry you out of this place. Isn't that right, Phil?'

'That's right, Charlie,' said Phil.

'That's the one, Charlie,' said Mick. 'That's the one.'

Outside the din of battering metal grew louder and more impatient. More strips of bamboo were torn out of the walls, now on all four sides. Mick stepped forward. 'Here,' he said, hanging his amulet around Charlie's neck.

'Oh God!' Charlie was trembling and crying now. 'Oh God!'

'Will you take this?' Phil said. He wanted her to have his

256

pocket Bible. Charlie closed her fingers around it, grateful for magic of any colour. Phil seemed mightily relieved.

'This is it, Charlie,' I said. 'I'm so proud of you but I need you to do this one thing.' Her eyes were closed but she was nodding at me. I actually started to think she might come through. 'I also think I could do with a tug on that pipe,' I added.

I took a draught of the opium. Charlie giggled, but it was an hysterical giggle, almost a shudder. 'I might need you to carry me,' she said faintly.

'We can do that,' Mick said. 'Easily. This time with your permission, eh?'

She shivered uncontrollably. One of her hands clasped the passport wallet and the amulet, the other Phil's Bible. Mick and I linked arms and made a chair for her to ride and we carried her to the threshold. Phil fell in line behind us, breathing steady encouragement down the back of our necks as we stepped towards the door. When the villagers saw us appear at the threshold the racket and their excitement soared. In the din I could barely hear myself think. Charlie flung her arms around my neck, burying her head in my breast. 'It's all right,' I said to Mick. 'I can take her. She's my baby.' The pain in my hand seared as I carried her. But I wanted it. Wanted the pain of carrying her.

'We're right behind you,' Mick said. 'All the way. Right, Phil?'

'All the way, Dad,' said Phil.

Charlie convulsed hideously as we passed outside. I feared she'd gone into a fit. The tumult in our ears augmented, and the huge moon seemed to crash on our heads like a cymbal. Khiem stood before us, fantastically attired, a terrifying apparition in the silver moonlight. He wore a felt cap sewn with poppy petals, and a long tunic. The belt round his waist jingled with silver discs sewn together like the scales of a fish. Draped from his neck were a great number of larger, circular, silver amulets, and in his hands he carried a wooden staff and a silver disc. He approached Charlie and touched her chin gently, so that she might look him in the eye. As she opened her eyes she was caught by his gaze, and for two or three seconds it was like watching someone draw a sting. Something passed between them in that moment, and I felt her relax marginally, surrendering a little in my arms. She gasped at his wild appearance, not least because also hanging from his neck was a familiar looking animal.

'He's got Rupert Bear,' Charlie breathed.

'That's right, Charlie.'

I'm not sure if she fainted or merely gave herself over to us, but Khiem beckoned us on, turned, and led us slowly through the clanging, banging, clattering tumult of villagers. I saw Phoo in the small crowd. He looked anxious.

Behind us our hut was being emptied of our backpacks and other belongings. Khiem proceeded at a painfully slow pace, and as we passed the villagers peeled away and ran on up ahead, rebuilding the path in front of us, still thrashing their pots. I felt lost and bewildered in the cacophony of sound, though in a strange way protected by it. It was an island of noise in the sea of the night. 'Are you there, Mick?' I heard a slight panic in my voice.

'Right behind you, brother!'

We shuffled on, this bizarre procession illumined by the massive, pendulous moon. Perhaps it was the blast of opium I'd taken before coming out of the hut, but I saw the event as if from above, singular and inexplicable, Khiem leading us with an outlandish gait that was almost a dance, me following with Charlie in my arms, Mick keeping step behind and Phil bringing up the rear, intoning psalms. And at the periphery of the crowd I saw other figures assembling, behind the villagers as it were, as we approached the spirit gate. Hordes of figures in shadow, or in silhouette, pressing in behind the villagers. I blinked them away.

On either side of the spirit gate lighted torches were burning, throwing off a waxy, syrupy smoke, and as we approached, I saw that the moon had settled exactly behind the arch of the gate. We inched towards it as if towards a prize. It seemed to occupy the entire sky. I wanted Charlie to see it. 'Look at it, Charlie! Look at the moon!'

She opened her eyes, encouraged by the spectacular formation. Moonlight drenched everything. It flooded over us, milky
light. I could even smell it. The villagers spurred us on with
renewed urgency, clanging pots and pans dangerously close to
our ears.

Charlie started to feel even heavier as we approached the
spirit gate. My lacerated hand burned. Sweat was streaming into
my eyes, but I dared not put her down. The smoke from the
flares thickened near the gate, and in the haze and in the din I
again began to have the strange sensation of crowds of figures
congregating behind the villagers, pressing in on us. Moreover I
saw complex structures assembled behind them, platforms and
piers and landings, and ladders of bamboo and stairways, all
with people coming and going and climbing or descending.
Some of these figures were paying us no attention; others were
interested in the proceedings; one of the grey shapes formed his
mouth into a trumpet and leaned through the villagers to blast it
in my ear; others again reached their arms through the villagers
and tried to press down on Charlie, making her weight
unbearable. Still others appeared to want to help, and were
making noises of encouragement, blowing cool air on my
burning hand, assembling in greater number as we approached
the spirit gate.

These tortured visions lasted for only fleeting seconds, and
would have stopped me in my tracks were it not for Khiem and
the villagers who came back to urge me on. The din from the
thrashing of the metal pots kept the spirit multitude at bay,
allowing us to make progress. The visions cleared from my
mind as at last we staggered through the gate, to the cheers and
ecstasy of the villagers, who threw down their pots and
applauded wildly, whistling and shrieking. Then they began
singing.

'Are you all right?' I asked Charlie. She was still shivering.
'I'm just cold, Dad.'

I wanted my heart to break. I let her slide to the floor.
Someone placed a blanket round her shoulders, another pair of
hands gave her a bowl of some evil-looking concoction, which
she sipped but which made her cough. I looked up, and the disc

of the moon was stupendously low in the sky, moist, dripping with a silvery vernix like that covering a new-born baby. My relief was that which follows the safe delivery of an infant. As I cradled Charlie to me I saw flames leaping in the air from somewhere behind us. It was our hut. The villagers had torched it.

There was no going back.

The villagers lit new fires, and began to dance, forming a horseshoe around us, clasping each other at the shoulders, singing loudly, swaying rhythmically.

It was a party, and it was for us.

Khiem entered the horseshoe. He was beaming happily, still presiding over events, evidently very satisfied with the way things had gone. He took Rupert Bear from his neck and pressed it into Charlie's hands. Perhaps the Lord of the Moon had decided to make Charlie whole again.

Mick produced what was left of the whisky Jack had given us and I took a good hard swallow. It warmed as it went down. If there were demons in the air, they were dispelled after a glug of Scotch whisky. I even poured some on my bloody hand

'Give me some of that,' Phil said, grabbing the bottle from my grasp and taking a deep swig.

Some children stepped forward and placed garlands round Charlie's neck and then round mine, Mick's and Phil's. The singing went on. Some of the men queued up for a tug on the whisky. I was happy for the festivities to continue through the night: Charlie was out of her cage. I squeezed her. 'Are you all right, Charlie? Really?'

'I'm all right. It's gone. Whatever it was, it's gone.'

I looked at the villagers, their faces softly lit by the fires and the burning brands as they danced. I loved the excitement of the children, who were not excluded from any of this strange ritual. I loved the fragrant, syrupy smell of the air streaming from the poppy crops and from the jungle. I looked up at the moon, and felt a moment of delirious happiness. I may have let a pagan prayer of thanks pass my lips. Even in this exotic and alien place, the world was returning to order.

I took another gulp of whisky, and looked about me. 'Where's Mick?' I said to Phil. 'Have you seen Mick?'

'No,' Phil said.

I scrambled to my feet. Mick was nowhere to be seen in the mêlée. Neither could I see Phoo. The pair of them had vanished.

37

The villagers danced in circles around their fires, stamping the red earth. They sang loud and their voices soared in the chilly air of the evening. Some of the men produced bottles of moonshine and proceeded to get very drunk. They made free with the moonshine and though I pretended to take deep swigs from the bottle I needed to keep my head. It was almost an hour before Mick and Phoo turned up again.

Mick was perspiring heavily. His face was streaked with red dirt. 'Time to go,' he said.

I had a nagging doubt about Phoo. I was still afraid he would betray us, and I was waiting for Jack to appear, smiling psychotically. But we had to go. Mick suggested we slip away one by one to assemble on the jungle path at the edge of the village. Then Charlie wanted to say goodbye to Nabao.

'Not a chance,' I hissed. 'She can't know that we're going.'

'I have to do it,' Charlie said. 'I can't just vanish on her.'

Charlie pleaded. Nabao had nursed her through the last few months. In any event we couldn't all leave together. 'We'll be two minutes,' I said to the others. 'We'll see you on the path.'

Charlie and I found Nabao sitting on the threshold of her hut, smoking her huge tobacco drainpipe. She hadn't joined in the festivities. On seeing us she put aside her pipe, stood up, and held out her arms to Charlie. She knew exactly what was happening. The thought didn't comfort me, serving only to make me more paranoid, but I guessed the old woman had intuited what we would do. Charlie embraced her and I saw Nabao's sugary eyes film over. When they'd finished hugging, Nabao dashed inside her hut to retrieve something, emerging with the Fred Flintstone clock sleeved in its plastic wrapping. She spoke rapidly and tried to push the clock into Charlie's hands: a parting gift, and probably the most valuable thing she owned.

Charlie refused the clock. She said a few words, and Nabao seemed satisfied. 'Give me your watch, Dad. I told her that at midday every day I would look at the time and think of her.' I handed over my wristwatch and Charlie strapped it on. My daughter's eyes were wet. Nabao smiled. For myself I grabbed Nabao's hand and I kissed it. Her own face was utterly expressionless.

'Come on, Charlie,' I said, and we slipped away into the darkness.

Mick and Phoo were waiting for us on the path. The villagers had removed our belongings from the hut before torching it, and Phoo had already assembled our backpacks for us. 'Where's Phil?' I wanted to know.

'We're waiting for him,' Mick said.

'Christ!'

Almost frantic, I jogged back towards the village and there I saw Phil sitting down, calmly watching the festivities. 'Today would be good,' I said.

'Not coming with you,' Phil said.

'What?'

'Not coming. Can't come.'

This was exactly what I needed. I squatted before him and took his face in my hands. 'Phil, I apologise for anything I said to hurt you.'

'It's not about anything you said. I have things to put right here.'

'Phil, I'm sorry for anything I've said or done in the past twenty-five years. I'm sorry for being a crap dad. I'm sorry for the time I punched you in the mouth.'

Phil shook his head. 'You're crazy. It's not about those things. It's about me and the Lord. Don't look at me like that! I'm perfectly calm and composed. I've been thinking about whether I could make reparation here. Maybe I could help with the refugee organisation we heard about. Yes. You see, I've got to make reparation.'

'Phil, I don't know what you're talking about, but if you come now I'll go to church with you every Sunday for a year. I can't leave this place without you. I didn't come here to find my daughter just to lose my son.'

I heard Mick thundering up behind us. 'What the fuck is going on?'

'He says he's not coming.'

'What a fucking family!' Mick cried. 'I don't believe you! Any of you! What am I doing here with you? Phil, if you don't come now, how are we going to get Charlie out? Your old man has only got one good hand.'

Phil looked up directly at Mick, brilliant moonlight starbursting in his eyes.

'Phil, I love you dearly,' I said, 'and I can't leave this place if you won't come. I'd have to stay here with you.'

Phil shaped his mouth to say something.

'Right, that does it.' Mick attacked Phil, grabbing him under his arms and hoisting him over his powerful shoulders. I heard Phil splutter as Mick jogged away with him into the bush. I cast about to see if anyone had seen us, but the villagers were intent on getting drunk and whooping it up.

When I joined the rest of them, it seemed the matter had been resolved. Phil was coming.

'Get packs!' Phoo hissed at us, highly agitated.

Charlie wanted to open her pack to stow her Rupert Bear. When she began picking with the strings Phoo went out of his mind. 'No time!' he whined. 'I no fuck go wiv you! No time!'

'Leave it,' I said. 'Pick up your bags. Let's go.'

We hoisted our backpacks and followed Phoo along the moonlit trail, half walking, half jogging. Charlie was too weak to keep up under her own steam, so we made progress with Phil and Mick shouldering her along the path. I brought up the rear.

After a few hundred yards I began to get a bad feeling. There was something distressingly familiar about the trail we were on. At first I kept my thoughts to myself. Mick, struggling with Charlie up ahead, turned and shot me a look. He recognised it, too. I couldn't tell if Phil had guessed because he had his head down. We were on the same trail we'd taken the morning we'd buried the body. I had a bad weight in my stomach.

After a while I halted, and everyone else stopped.

'Why stop?' Phoo hissed. 'Come quick now.'

I couldn't speak. If I disclosed my misgivings I'd be revealing everything to Phoo. On the other hand I suspected this was an elaborate ploy to lure us to the spot where we'd buried Jack's nephew. I imagined four new moonlit graves, freshly dug.

'Come on, Danny,' Mick said gently but firmly.

I tried to make my eyes tell him what I suspected, but he turned away from me, manhandling Charlie from the waist. I followed. It was agonising. I'd taken Charlie and Phil from the safety of the village to the open jungle. I had a sudden insight into what had happened to Ben, Charlie's original travelling companion. We had been duped.

I couldn't think of a way out as Phoo led us to the cadaver. The scene of the scrambled burial loomed closer and closer, and at each step I was ready for Jack and his men to jump out from behind every bush. I saw the flitting shadows of opium bandits behind every tree; I heard them skitter beyond every shrub.

Phil dropped back, leaving Mick to struggle with Charlie. 'Do you see where he's leading us?'

'Yes.'

'I can't do this. Really I can't.'

'Coincidence, Phil. It has to be coincidence. We've got to keep up.'

We reached the burial spot and Phoo seemed to slow and fiddle with his belt. Phil stole a glance at the covered grave, and I did too. Behind the leafy mound a grey figure moved in the moon shadow.

An animal, fleet in the moonlight, nothing more.

We passed the spot without event, and Phoo directed us along a smaller path descending the side of a ravine. We were already breathing heavily, making slow progress down the steep ravine, though the huge moon floodlit the jungle affording good visibility. Even so I slipped from the path, but Phil's sharp reflex action caught me by the shirt and tugged me back.

After almost an hour I heard water rushing from below. We'd arrived at the river.

A bamboo raft awaited us. Identical to the one on which Mick, Phil and I had journeyed with Bhun and Coconut, it was rigged with a stout tripod to keep our packs dry. Phoo immediately busied himself with lashing the packs on to the tripod. I looked around uneasily, certain that Jack and his cohorts were about to spring. The moon made the swift-flowing water ripple like a bolt of silk. Everywhere else the jungle was still.

'So far so good, pal,' Mick said.

'Will that raft take all of us?'

'He seems to think so.'

'Shoes!' Phoo said after fiddling with the packs. We took off our shoes, and he laced them over the packs at the top of the tripod. 'We go!'

There were poles for each of us. Phoo said he wanted Mick to take up the rear position. Charlie slotted in between Phoo and myself, with Phil in front of Mick. We pushed off, gliding sweetly into the middle of the jade-green, moonlit river. The brisk current took us in and we made steady speed. The river was faster here than when we'd come with Coconut and Bhun, but wider, too, and less strewn with obstacles. Phoo made motions to right or left when he wanted us to punt to either side; otherwise he was piloting from the front.

'How long?' I shouted to Phoo once we were properly underway.

'Five, six hours,' he said.

It was a long time to spend on a raft with your feet washed by cold, snake-infested water, but I felt exhilarated to be moving, and overwhelming relief in putting the village behind us. What's more, I'd got a full cargo of passengers, a complete inventory. But I also felt small and vulnerable, a straw riding the flow.

The river continued to move us at a sprightly pace, and though the water lapped across our feet, the bamboo raft gliding just under the surface seemed remarkably easy to control. Phoo twitched his pole against the riverbed to correct the drift, occasionally holding up his arm to indicate for us to help.

Pretty soon Charlie got tired on her feet. There was nothing for it but for her to kneel in the water, gripping the tripod. The green river wound through miles of ghostly verdant jungle and we proceeded in silence. On the steep-sided banks at either side, miraculously spindly trees rose above the upper canopy of the jungle. A midnight mist smoked the leafy canopy itself. We drifted by herds of water buffalo bedded down in the mud for the night. We also passed small settlements where no one stirred; we could have been ghosts in their dreams.

In places we shot through gaps between smooth, white boulders where the water foamed like churning milk, and where the bamboo underside scraped alarmingly. But the raft stayed secure. For two hours we journeyed in an ethereal silence, each of us mesmerised by the alien splendour of the moonlit river, the raft stately in its progress. Then we reached some treacherous rocks. Without warning Phoo leapt into the water, guiding the raft by hand around the rocks. Mick and I had to do the same to help him. Eventually everyone got wet, half floating, half portering the raft across the boulders, until we got beyond the rocks and the white water. It jolted us from the trance of the river. Charlie was with us in flight, battling to do her share. Another herd of water buffalo wallowed and snorted at us from the muddy bank.

We got back on course, drifting a little slower now. I dipped my pole in the water and then heard a tiny sob behind me. I turned to see Phil squatting, and weeping. 'Phil!' I laid down my pole. 'What is it, Phil?'

He shook his head. I glanced at Mick but he didn't want to make eye contact with me either. He pushed hard on his pole, training his eyes on the riverbank. I squatted before Phil and took hold of his hands. He gazed at me, his eyes full of tears. 'I'm in hell, Dad. You can go home but what about me? I've put myself in the darkest quarter of hell. You're clean, but there's blood on my head.'

The truth dawned on me. How could I have missed it? How could I have been so stupid? All that time when Phil was in torment in the poppy fields. I looked up at Mick for confirmation and Mick, seeing what I'd worked out for myself, gave me the briefest of nods.

'Oh God,' I said. 'Phil, oh God. I never knew.'

There was a brief cry of alarm from Phoo at the front of the raft. We were approaching another stretch of white water, and suddenly everyone had stopped punting. I stood, picked up my pole, dipped it in the water and, despite the gash in my hand, pushed hard. We all did. We guided ourselves neatly between the smooth boulders in an S curve, and when I glanced round again Phil was back on his feet, pushing on his pole with a grim determination.

At a later point in the journey we passed another settlement where a dozen rafts were drawn up on the bank and where two natives sat around a small fire. They stared at us in astonishment, but Phoo made no attempt to communicate. 'Hmong,' he whispered as we drifted past the staring men.

I wondered if all the people along this stretch of the river were in Jack's pocket. 'Do they have cellphones?' I asked.

Phoo cackled an answer. 'Oooooooh! No cellphone for Hmong!'

He seemed much more relaxed now. The greater the distance we put between Jack and ourselves the more I felt we might succeed; but relaxed was something I wasn't going to feel until we'd at least reached Chiang Mai. The drifting seemed endless, and the state of our nerves made the operation exhausting. After four or five hours the sky began to whiten, and we found ourselves in the grey light of a false dawn.

We started to pass individual natives up and about their business. Riverside activity increased. Natives smiled or stared at us, or more frequently ignored us. The jungle ahead began to blush pink and then the sun came up, boiling and rosy, flooding the river with red light.

Further downriver we saw more activity. It was a military camp. Thai army. Phoo became very tense. One armed soldier stood on the riverbank, watching us float towards him. He shouted something and his words echoed in the pink dawn mist, skimming across the river like a flat stone.

'Bad!' Phoo steered towards the bank. 'You tell him I tourist guide,' he said over his shoulder.

'Why?'

'He Jack man. Jack pay Thai army here. Army have cellphone.'

We banked the raft, and climbed off, grateful at least for a chance to relieve the punting posture we'd had to endure for the last five hours or so. The soldier seemed puzzled and suspicious. His comrades were busy striking camp some way off, though they appeared less interested in us than he was. He asked Phoo a lot of questions, and Phoo, extremely tense, replied mostly in monosyllables.

The soldier turned to us. 'What you do here?'

'Trekking,' I said jovially. 'Tourists.'

'Trekking? No trek! No trek here!'

'Yes,' I offered with desperate brightness. 'Best trek in Thailand! No tourists! Beautiful.'

The soldier barked at Phoo, who kept his eyes averted. 'No trek!' he said again to me.

Then I remembered I had a receipt in my wallet, written out by Panda Travel after we'd negotiated the services of guides on our way in. I made a big show of taking out the receipt and presenting it to the soldier as if it was a warrant signed by the King of Siam. 'Panda Travel!' I said.

He obviously couldn't read the English, in which the docket was made out, but he pretended he could, squinting at the details and checking the Chiang Mai address, which was at least printed in Thai. 'Chiang Mai!' I added helpfully.

'Chiang Mai?'

'Yes, Chiang Mai. Panda Travel.'

'Panda Travel!'

'Yes,' I said. I wondered how long we could spend repeating each other.

'Ask him,' Mick suggested to Phoo, 'if he can sell us a few cigarettes.'

Phoo did so and the soldier laughed. He produced a packet of local brand and Mick peeled off a banknote from his wad. Charlie, Mick and I each took a snout and we smoked them, theatrically it seemed, as if the soldier had just saved our lives. The soldier laughed again. Mick bought the packet from him, and the large bill was expertly trousered.

But the soldier wasn't entirely satisfied. He smelled a rat, but he couldn't quite figure us out. We certainly had the look of a trekking group: four pink-faced Westerners and a Thai guide. The thing is, I too sensed something wrong, and I couldn't work it out either. The soldier gave me back my Panda Travel docket and stepped over to the raft. He began to fiddle with the straps on our packs. He struggled first with the knots on the shoelaces, but couldn't seem to unpick them. Phoo had made them doubly secure. Then he got bored and turned back to me. I was still smoking luxuriously.

'Panda Travel?'

'Yes, Panda Travel.'

I was making heavy weather of trying to sound casual. As I stood at the river's edge I happened to glance down at the water. The pink morning light made a mirror of the water, and in it I saw a desperate and haggard individual with psychotic, boiling eyes staring back at me. It was an image of a man at the end of his rope.

With a minimal gesture the soldier waved us on. Phoo inched the raft back into the water and we climbed on board. We pushed off with an air of fanatical nonchalance, and the soldier stared after us until we'd drifted around a bend in the river and out of sight. 'Will he contact Jack?' I asked Phoo.

'Maybe yes. Maybe no. Keep going.'

We wouldn't know until we met Phoo's collaborator.

About an hour further downstream and on reaching a small clearing, Phoo deftly guided the raft to the bank. A Thai man, completely expressionless and smoking a cigarette, waited under the trees. I could see a yellow Jeep parked higher up on a red-dirt track. As we put on our shoes the man helped Phoo untie the packs from the tripod and the two of them carried the packs to the Jeep. Then Phoo returned to the raft, gently pushing it into the flow of the river, where it sailed on minus its cargo.

Phoo rode up front with the driver and the packs, while we four sat in the back of the vehicle, avoiding eye contact with each other, hardly daring to believe we'd made it. We sat in silence. I knew why: it would tempt fate to celebrate too early. The Jeep bounced and jolted slowly along the dusty track, and after another hour we came to a proper metalled road. After that the Jeep made good progress.

There was a delay outside Chiang Mai as Phoo negotiated a *songthaew* driver who would take us into town. We were transferred to the back of the *songthaew* truck.

'You pay me now,' Phoo said seriously.

'Sure thing,' said Mick. He pulled the roll of notes from his belt and handed it over to Phoo. With that, Phoo fetched our packs and flung them in with us.

'Ooooooh! Bye so long!' grinned Phoo. He jumped into the yellow Jeep and it roared off the way we had come.

The *songthaew* drove us through the outskirts of Chiang Mai. The great brass, ticking engine of the sun was well up by now, and already we were missing the cool of the jungle. Mick, sitting in the open back of the vehicle, handed cigarettes round and we lit up.

'These packs,' Phil said.

'What about 'em?'

'They're not the same ones we've been carrying for the last six hours.'

We looked at the packs. He was right. We opened them, and though they were stuffed with our clothes and belongings, Phil was correct. These were not the same backpacks we'd carried out of the village.

'I thought mine was a little heavy,' Charlie said.

Mick took a deep drag on his cigarette. He blew a thick plume of blue smoke at a tuk-tuk roaring inches behind the *songthaew*. Then he looked at us.

'We've been shafted,' he said.

38

We had indeed been shafted. Later, we estimated that we'd each carried at least five kilos of jungle morphine into Chiang Mai under the noses of the Thai army. Of course, it might have been Phoo's enterprise, but at the back of it I saw Jack's puppeteering hand. He'd made sure Phoo let us know that he was going to be away, knowing we'd try to bribe someone to take us out as soon as Charlie was ready to go; and he knew that we had every chance of squeezing through the army checkpoint downriver. No doubt if that army soldier had been more persistent and we'd been caught, we would be locked up in Chiang Mai jail with only Brazier-Armstrong to help us, and the story would start all over again. No doubt, too, that Jack's money would have sprung Phoo. The rest of us would have been hung out to dry.

And no one would have believed us.

If I understood Jack correctly, the morphine base we'd brought downriver would be worth more than twenty thousand dollars in Chiang Mai, and would make business worth twenty-five *million* dollars on the streets of London, Paris and New York. It made us complicit in the smuggling of drugs, but there was a far more serious crime that one of us had to carry.

We had to spend a night in Chiang Mai before we could get on a flight to Bangkok. We returned to the River View Lodge to reclaim our stored suitcases and there we took two double rooms. I was never going to be happy until we were on our way to London. I wanted medical attention for Charlie, but it had to wait. Significantly, I chose to room with Phil while Mick agreed to share with and keep a close eye on Charlie, though we spent most of the time together, not wanting to venture out.

I could only guess at what Jack might do if the body surfaced while we were still in Chiang Mai. If Jack had wanted to kill us, he would have done it at the riverside before we'd exchanged the backpacks. But would his attitude change if he knew we'd murdered his nephew? My best hope would be that Jack's guerrilla farming would take him on to another place long before some scavenging animal or hapless villager turned up something nasty.

We had a difficult time organising a flight out. I spent agonising hours on the telephone trying to make reservations. Finally we discarded our original tickets and bought four new one-way flights from Chiang Mai to London Heathrow via Bangkok.

'Are you going to tell me about it?' I said to Phil in a moment when we were alone.

He looked pale. He lowered himself gently on to the edge of his bed, put his hands on his knees, and stared at the wall.

I tried again. 'This notion of release, Phil. Giving it up.'

'Ha!'

'What is it?'

'Hearing you talk like that. It seems odd.'

I knew it wasn't gratitude he wanted from me, but I had to say, 'I suspect I owe you more than I'll ever be able to tell you.'

'It was over in a couple of minutes,' he said. His voice was flat. 'When you went out there that night, we followed, of course. He knocked the knife out of your hand and he kicked you unconscious. You were out. Belly down in the dust. He lifted your head by the hair and took a knife to your throat. I scooped up your machete and I hacked it into his neck before he could cut your throat.

'It was like when you lodge an axe in a tree. I was gripping the handle of the machete and I couldn't pull it out of his neck. I was still trying to dislodge the damned machete when he spun away from me, and he convulsed and smashed his head on the edge of the porch.

'I wish I could say he died quickly. He didn't. He couldn't cry out. The machete was half buried in his neck.

'I was useless. Shivering, still shivering. Mick rolled the body under the hut. He got under there himself and pulled the machete out, and the man bled to death, there, under the hut.

273

Then Mick got me and you inside. He cleaned up before you came round. That's the whole story.'

Although Phil said that was the whole story, it wasn't the case. Now I understood what he'd meant when he'd said he was in hell. He had violated the holy injunction not to kill. He'd broken the sixth commandment to uphold the fifth, to honour his father: not in any intellectual ranking or ordering of these injunctions, but in the imperative of the blood and the moment.

Now I had to stand in awe of him.

But for Phil the entire saga had not after all proved to be a *Pilgrim's Progress*, not the treading of a difficult but steady path to grace or redemption, but a sudden tilting plunge into hell. Back home he was an Elder of his church. Here he was a murderer. How was he going to find a way out of hell? I didn't even know if there was a way out. If I could have exchanged my soul for his, and accepted his penalties in an afterlife, I would have done so without a moment's hesitation.

But I couldn't.

'Is there anything, anything at all, I can do?'

'No, Dad. Nothing.'

I wanted to cry for him. My dumpy little boy, whom I'd also lost. There was no fixing this. I was learning that there are so many things a father cannot fix. I even made a silent appeal to the God in whom I have no belief: you saw what happened, surely you cannot blame this boy? Come the moment, Phil had placed the affiliations of blood even above his deepest religious convictions.

Would not any God, of any stripe, forgive that?

Though exhausted from the flight from the village, we were wired, and a long way from sleep. Charlie, Mick and I drank heavily with no apparent effects. We sat in the hotel room, chain-smoking and sighing. We talked continuously, though not about anything with gravity. Every so often one of the group would look at the locked door of our hotel room.

Until I couldn't stand it any longer, and it was to Phil I turned. 'But why in God's name couldn't you tell me what had

274

happened? Why couldn't you say? Then at least I might have understood what you were going through.'

Mick answered for Phil. 'He was protecting you.'

'Protecting me? It wasn't me who needed protecting! You were going out of your mind up there, Phil! Out of your mind.'

'Danny,' Mick said quietly. 'It's true that Phil had some wobbly moments. But it was *you* who was going out of your mind.'

All three looked at me intently. I thought of the spirits I'd begun to see massing in the village. I thought of the opium, and of the paranoia. 'Me?'

'Yes, you. There was never any danger of Phil letting us down.'

'What was driving Phil crazy,' Charlie added, 'was the prospect of not keeping you together.'

It was later, at Bangkok airport, that Charlie took off Mick's lucky amulet and handed it back to him. 'I really value this,' she said, 'but I'm going to let you keep it.' He offered it to her for a second time.

'Why?'

'I want you to make a promise,' he said, taking a swig from a bottle of Singha beer. 'You'll give it back to me only when you have your next dope.'

Charlie clamped her lips. The crease in her brow writhed momentarily.

'Nothing need be said,' Mick suggested. 'No harsh words. No criticism. We're beyond that now. Only after all that's happened I think you owe it me, to tell me if and when that day comes. Don't take the amulet off me if you can't at least do that.'

'How much of an addict are you?' I said. I had no idea of the implications of her addiction, nor of sudden withdrawal.

Charlie looked at me. She took the amulet and put it round her neck. I could have kissed Mick.

There were other deals going on. Phil turned to me and said, 'You made a promise, there in the jungle.'

'Oh?'

'Yes. You said you'd go to church with me every Sunday. For a year!'

I thought about it. For one disgraceful moment I was about to bring up the fact that Mick had had to put him across his shoulder. 'I'll do it,' I said. Phil pushed out his bottom lip, and then he sniffed with apparent satisfaction. He even took a sip of my airport beer to seal the contract.

He'd been entirely correct about this jealousy thing. I could see that now. And I'd driven them all away with it, Sheila, Phil, Charlie. Phil and Charlie, I now realised, both had to go to places where I wouldn't follow them. Or at least, if I did follow them, then it was to places where they'd each got me on their own terms. And if I could follow my daughter into the jungle, then I could follow my son into his evangelical church. Not to bring him back – that wasn't the point any more. It was just to say: I'm here. With Mick's arm-twisting help, I managed to wring out of Phil a reciprocal promise that he would come over to see us once a week.

From Bangkok airport we telephoned Sheila. Charlie and Phil took turns talking to her, though Sheila appeared to spend most of the time crying. Then I had a few words. We made it sound as though we'd come to the end of a fabulous holiday.

'Are you coming back too?' Sheila said evenly.

'Well, I'm not staying here.'

'Stop it. You know what I mean.'

'Yes, I know what you mean. We've got a lot to talk about, Sheila. All of us.'

In the air somewhere between Bangkok and London, with Charlie sleeping next to me, I fell into a doze. I dreamed I was on the jade-green river on a raft made out of aeroplane parts.

39

It seems only moments ago. A lotus flower unfolding in a single hour of the morning sun. And a lifetime in another incarnation.

Charlie meanwhile, leaning against my shoulder, continues to slumber, hugging her Rupert Bear. Her hair blows minutely in the soft airstream from the overhead vent of the pressurised aircraft cabin. One arm is held down on her lap and the other points up oddly above her head. She has resumed her flying position, the one I would spend hours watching when she was in her infant cot. Mick's amulet hangs from her throat. I think Phil's particular sacrifice will always weigh in her karma, not his.

Karma. Do I sound like a hippy now, or a Buddhist? I'm not even sure what a Buddhist is, but I don't think I'm one. I don't really care for any kind of creed. Religion is like the dope, which is like the whisky, which is like the stupid television. Same fuck of a different colour.

But I do believe in spirits. In ghosts. Only now I know what they are. They are not the dead. They do not come from an afterlife. They move about us. They live on our shoulders, or at our right or left hand, and they are created by our actions. I was followed all the way by one small spirit. It practically had to tug me by the sleeve that day in the poppy field before I would acknowledge it. It was the crying spirit of an absence of core in my life.

Phil is seated in front of me, along with Mick. I intend to keep my promise to Phil and I will attend church every Sunday for a year, no matter how unspeakably awful it is. And it will be unspeakably awful. But every week I will approach this awfulness with a glad heart, because it's a means for me to get back to Phil, and if in some way it begins to unburden him, then I'll do it. I'll even take along my own teabags.

Then there's Mick. What can I say about him? A man who would go into the jungle with you; a man who would put his entire wherewithal at your disposal in a time of need. I'm in awe of him, too. Every step of the way his behaviour was impeccable and ultimately beyond reproach. A giant at my side. But he's changed. I've noticed no fake-*wai*ing and farting on the way home. A superficial difference, which I suspect is only temporary.

I think of what Charlie taught me, and I see how Mick's desire to be needed by me is no different to my own desire to be needed by my children. Only he's better at it than I am. More than anything I know that through his actions he gave me that grace and generosity – so deplorable in its absence up until now – to finally be able to call him my friend.

Next time I have some trouble, I'll tell him about it first.

Because I have come a long way. As far, if not further, than any of them. All this time I have spent thinking of Charlie as a child and never as a woman. And all this time I spent pretending to be the great protector, when it was ultimately Phil who forfeited everything to protect me. It's a shocking and humbling thing to realise how much your children have to teach you.

I've been a selfish child pretending to be a man. I allowed fatherhood to become a creeping cataract, preventing me from seeing the changing needs of those around me. But I didn't know then what I know now. That you have to let them pluck from your heart with bruising fingers great, sparkling, golden, resinous chunks of love, and never ask under what moon they smoke it or where they spill it.

I remember when Phil was born. In those first days when I displayed him proudly and everywhere, and with the oafish grin of the neophyte father indelibly painted on my stupid jaw, a mean-spirited and mealy-mouthed old woman approached me and said, 'Yes, and he'll break your heart one day.'

Break your heart one day? I wish I'd known then what I know now, and I could have gainsaid the old harridan. Your children break your heart *every* day. You only have to look at them and your heart shreds. They lacerate it. Pulverise it. And then they mend it for you, each and every day, with a gesture or a smile or a sly glance, just so that it can be shredded and wrecked all over again. And all over nothing.

That's what it means to be a father. That's my definition: a father is a person with a mashed heart and a wounded hand. And that's perfectly normal.

But you have to be so careful while your heart is being mashed over nothing, that your heart doesn't harden when you can't take any more. Because if that happens you've lost the possibility of salvation that becoming a parent gave you in the first place. Did I let that happen? I won't again. I've stopped despising my children for what they are. My daughter is a drug addict. I'll try to help. My son is a religious fanatic. So what? I've stopped hating them for the things that make them different from me.

The pressure changes in the cabin and I know we will soon be coming in to land. I make my way to the toilet at the front of the cabin, and in there I bolt the door behind me and I let myself cry.

I've got my family back. Not in the way I might have idealised, but they are there. Phil has a long way to go to work out his redemption, but at least now he will allow me to be with him in the enterprise. Charlie too has a lot of work of a different kind, and I have the feeling that she will or will not work out her salvation regardless of what I do. But – and it's an important but – she's still wearing Mick's amulet. Seeing that amulet gives me the optimism I need.

I return to my seat and the safety-belt sign comes on before the plane makes its approach to Heathrow. The cabin lights go down and the air pressure changes again, and the plane begins its descent towards our uncertain future. I gently wake Charlie and get her to put her belt on. It's not until touchdown, with the reverse thrust roaring and the unbuckling of passenger belts clicking over the cabin, that Mick turns to look at me from his seat in front.

He tips me the long, long wink. 'We're home,' he says.